The Devil to Pay

Katie Daysh works in retail but her passions are writing fiction and history, which she has an Open University degree in. She is the author of the Courtenay and Nightingale queer naval adventure series. She lives on the Isle of Wight.

Also by Katie Daysh

Nightingale & Courtney

Leeward
The Devil to Pay

KATIE DAYSH

THE
DEVIL
TO
PAY

CANELO

First published in the United Kingdom in 2024 by

Canelo
Unit 9, 5th Floor
Cargo Works, 1-2 Hatfields
London SE1 9PG
United Kingdom

A CIP catalogue record for this book is available from the British Library.

Print ISBN 978 1 80436 567 0
Ebook ISBN 978 1 80436 569 4

Cover design by Head Design

Cover images © Shutterstock

Look for more great books at www.canelo.co

Printed and bound in Great Britain by Clays Ltd, Elcograf S.p.A.

To my mum, my dad, George and all my other family and friends for their love and support, and for listening to all my doubts and strange naval-based questions.

To Medina Bookshop and Waterstones Isle of Wight for being amazing at uplifting local authors.

To the Flirties and the Rainbows on Discord for giving me such wonderful, supportive communities.

PART I

Chapter One: Fickle Fate

September 1801, the Mona Passage, between Santo Domingo and Puerto Rico

Arthur Courtney, the first lieutenant of HMS *Scylla*, hauled his legs up into the maintop and groped for the cap above his head. Feeling the comforting presence of the backstays, he forced himself to rise to his feet, unsure if the sea was rolling the timber or if his shaking knees were doing that. More than ten years he had been on the sea and he still could not quite abide these heights.

One look to windward softened those fears. HMS *Meridian* sailed within signalling distance of the *Scylla*, close enough that Courtney could see a little blue dot against the expanse of t'gallant canvas. That dot, a *Meridian* man, had climbed far higher than Courtney. Sucking in his breath and willing his palms to stop sweating, Courtney mimicked him, shoving his heels into the mesh of rigging and making the accompanying *Scylla* topman follow.

The world bloomed about him as he stuck his head into the azure sky. Fragile ribbons of clouds echoed the sails, fluttering by, almost within arm's-length. The line of the horizon encircled the *Scylla* and the *Meridian* as though they were two model ships in a miniature globe. The form of Monito Island approached, its high rocky face jarring the expanse of the sea. The *Scylla* was starting to feel the influence of the forceful tidal currents which lashed white-rimmed waves up against its craggy shores.

There was reason for the two ships to brave the hostility of the Mona Passage though.

A distant, tiny voice called from the deck below.

'What do you see, Lieutenant?!' shouted Captain Hugh Robinson through a speaking-trumpet.

The unidentified ship was two points off the starboard bow. She was a frigate, that much was certain — and had been certain over the day that they had been chasing her. This, in the wind blowing one point abaft the beam and favouring the British frigates, was the first time they had approached her so close. Courtney steadied himself on the crosstrees and felt for the spyglass in his belt. He focused it upon the vessel, knowing the *Meridian* officer would be doing the same. Through the lens, he could count fourteen guns on the frigate's starboard side, with twelve on the quarterdeck and forecastle; in all, she would have more armaments than the *Scylla*. He recognised the French design.

Courtney was no stranger to long chases and all of the variables that accompanied them, yet he still felt the impulsive itch of impatience as he saw how they neared the French frigate. An enemy ship could form two paths for a man who had been a dedicated lieutenant for eight years: the potential of scrabbling up the tentative ladder of promotion, or being thrown off it entirely into a bloody death. Courtney had been at those crossroads for too long.

Captain Robinson and Lieutenant Adrian Derby waited for him at the foot of the mainmast. They had served on the *Scylla* for almost a year but seeing them there, amidst the *Scylla*'s familiar cordage and timber, always seemed strange. Robinson, with his grey, plain looks and mundane manners, seemed a man coming to the end of his career – the type of commander to see the unlucky *Scylla* to the breaker's yard. Even more reason to engage this French frigate. There was fight in the *Scylla* yet.

'Forty guns,' Courtney said, jumping to the deck and pulling on his uniform coat. 'Course south-west. With this breeze, we can have her within the hour.'

Robinson nodded. He looked past Courtney's shoulder towards the *Meridian*, perhaps to see what her actions were. Derby glanced at Courtney, an unreadable expression crossing his face. The second lieutenant had arrived on the *Scylla* with the captain after the events of the year before, but sometimes Courtney thought he wished he hadn't. As soon as Courtney met his gaze, he immediately looked away.

When Robinson did not reply, Courtney swallowed his frustration. 'Shall we clear for action, sir?' he prompted. 'She has forty guns, but combined with the *Meridian*, we—'

'Yes, Lieutenant,' Robinson interrupted. 'Clear for action.'

'Clear for action!' Courtney shouted without hesitation. The mid on watch took up the call, then the petty officers, rolling down through the ship with a flurry of drumbeats. Courtney followed the cry, leaving Robinson with Derby. He did not have to supervise the preparations – in truth, he probably should not – but he liked to see the crew and for the crew to see him. Across the turbulence of the last two years, he had been one of the only constants other than the old *Scylla* herself.

Below-deck, the men scurried to work. The seamen who had not been on watch shoved mess tables up into the timbers by their pulleys and broke down the partitions that separated the captain's cabin from the rest of the deck. Each of them gave a respectful nod and salute to Courtney as he passed. He only stopped to help Toby Warren – who had never quite recovered from a severely broken foot – and his gun crew drag their twelve-pounder cannon, *Banshee*, to the gunport. Fire buckets were already being ferried up to each great gun, along with spare flints and casks of water for the suffocating heat that battle would bring.

Henry Smythe, the senior midshipman, passed Courtney on his way aft to direct the dropping of the boats astern. He was strapping and re-strapping his sword-belt around his waist which had stretched, along with the rest of him, in a late adolescent growth spurt. Soon, he would be ducking under the timbers as Courtney did. Courtney grasped his arm before he could scramble up the companion-ladder. 'Cook said that there was a newborn kid this morning from the Matriarch,' he said, referring to the mother goat in the manger. 'Ensure she gets put in the boats. And keep an eye on Jones. If the man has his bloody pipe on him again, confiscate it. I won't deal with another fire again, not in battle.'

'Yes, sir,' Smythe said, and clambered away.

A hundred things filled Courtney's head that he doubted Robinson, or Derby, had thought of. They were fortunate that this crew knew their ship like a second home; for some, it was their only home. And in the way of any household, everything and everyone had their place and their duty.

Marine Lieutenant Ferguson stood by the magazine as the master gunner, Thomason, watched over the powder monkeys running ammunition and powder up to the gundeck. Courtney nodded to the racing boys and ploughed into the lantern-lit gloom of the orlop to ensure the rest of the midshipmen were out and Dr Archer had taken over their berth for his sickbay. The sound of sand being sprinkled over the deck and surgical instruments being laid out confirmed it, although Courtney still stuck his head around the curtain to check that Murray, the youngest and most petulant of the mids, had not stowed himself under the locker, or some trick.

'Lieutenant,' Dr Archer greeted, both he and his loblolly boy nodding at him. 'French?'

'I believe so. The same we've been on the tail of.'

The last place Courtney visited was his own berth, finding his sword and sticking a flintlock pistol into his belt. An open letter lay on his small writing desk from that morning. Courtney looked at it longingly and wondered briefly whether he should add another note to Hiram Nightingale, all the way in England. He pressed the thought down. He did not like to act as if this would be his last battle; thinking it seemed to bring it closer to reality.

The clearing had taken a mere fifteen minutes. By the time Courtney returned to deck, Master Josiah Loom at his side, an arms chest had been laid in preparation for boarding, sharp points of grapnels and axes glinting in the afternoon sun. A rigging, protection from falling spars and boarders, was still being organised, sending criss-crossing shadows over the wood.

Robinson watched him approach. 'Is everything in order, Lieutenant?' he asked.

'Yes, sir. Everything is prepared.'

'Your eagerness for battle always astonishes me, Lieutenant.'

Courtney opened his mouth to respond, then decided it was best not to. Nobody was ever eager for battle, but there was a difference between wearing an air of confidence, and an air that spoke of uncertainty and lack of care.

Aft, the signal midshipman had hoisted the pennant for the *Meridian* to clear for action, but Courtney knew Captain Bryant would have already performed it. Proving him correct, the *Meridian*'s gunports suddenly sprang open, the mouths of the cannons run out to the holes.

Now forward of the starboard beam, the French frigate seemed far closer, no longer a fleck on the horizon but a well-formed, rigged ship where Courtney could count off her sails as they caught the wind. He fetched his spyglass and directed it towards her stern, finding her name beneath the elegant gallery windows. *Cygne*. He spoke it aloud to Robinson, only for Derby to correct his pronunciation. He blushed furiously when Courtney turned to him, as if unbelieving that he had said it beyond his own thoughts.

The *Cygne* led them towards Monito. Since dawn's light, the *Scylla* and the *Meridian* had tacked and beaten through the trade winds; combined with the fierce currents advancing their speed by knots, they had so far fallen well on their seamanship and charts to avoid the dangerous shores. But, even to the naked eye, Courtney could see more of those wicked sandbars stretching around the island, promising fluctuating depths.

Murray was ordered from below to throw the lead-line. He called out the fathoms from the main chains, decreasing the nearer the *Scylla* approached the enemy ship. A patchwork of shades coloured the blue waters. It was not a battleground Courtney liked, nor would have chosen.

But, still, the awaited order came.

'Beat to quarters,' Robinson said, and Courtney again shouted the words down the deck.

The hurried procession of 180 men advancing to their stations was impressively organised, each sailor from the forecastle division to the afterguard knowing precisely where he should be. Marines took their positions in a flurry of red and white, some of them climbing into the tops, some lending a hand on the gun deck. Lieutenant Derby disappeared with them to watch over the gunnery, taking Smythe with him.

With both the *Scylla* and the *Meridian* racing towards her, the *Cygne* no longer attempted to escape. Her bulkier, heavier frame worked against her, allowing the English ships to close on her stern. Within minutes of the French tricolour blooming into sight, her stern chaser flared and sent a ball soaring between the *Scylla* and *Meridian*. The *Meridian* answered first, a bow gun taking chips off her taffrail. Courtney glanced over to the fellow ship and noted Bryant and his lieutenant, Godfrey, upon the quarterdeck, both of them standing calmly. He hoped Robinson and Bryant thought the same thing as he did: it would be most sensible to approach the *Cygne* from both starboard and larboard sides before she had a chance to reach Monito. The threat of two broadsides, and the strain of forcing her to man two sides of the gun deck at once, was a risk but might prompt her to surrender without a boarding.

'Course south-west,' Robinson instructed Barty Abbott at the conn. 'Lay us alongside her.'

The *Scylla*'s course diverged from the *Meridian*, peeling towards the larboard side of the *Cygne*. Ahead, the *Cygne*'s bow began to turn, yards shifting, slowly bringing the waist guns to bear. Courtney glanced again at the *Meridian*, partially relieved to see her sails filled in an attempt to overhaul the *Scylla*. The three sides of this strange triangle shifted; if the *Scylla* did not move fast enough, the *Cygne* could rake her, sending a broadside from stem to stern. Yet if the *Meridian* pushed too quickly with her full canvas still flying, she would run onto the sandbars.

Courtney turned to Robinson, stomach tightening. The *Cygne*'s larboard guns emerged, one by one. They must respond. They must turn.

Robinson gave the order, but Courtney felt the delay: only a few moments, but enough for three twelve-pound balls to reach the *Scylla*'s bows. Two skimmed her timbers. The other took the starboard head out, raining splinters up and over the bowsprit. The deck shivered but Abbott and his mate at the helm held firm. With the increasing wind and sucking tidal currents, the *Scylla* moved easily, almost too easily. The canvas shivered, but it was soon drowned out by the *Scylla* unleashing her gundeck.

Her forward cannons roared and punched two ragged holes above the *Cygne*'s waterline. A porthole lid flew, revealing a huddle of smoke-marred faces through the gloom. With two frigates bearing down upon them, those men would suffer. It would be merciful to fly the white flag. The *Meridian* crept ahead, using her bow chasers to threaten where the *Scylla* could not. Her white canvas still billowed: the dangerous, awful majesty of a frigate in flight, cutting through her stream of gun smoke.

Murray cried out the water depth. Seventy fathoms. Sixty-five fathoms. Robinson directed Abbott at the helm, dragging the *Scylla*'s head further from the island, letting the wind push them from the teeth of danger. For a minute, the *Cygne*'s guns fell silent as they too avoided the labyrinth. The *Meridian* took her chance, emptying shot across the *Cygne*'s quarterdeck. One cracked the mizzenmast, jolting the yards and arresting their ability to keep the *Cygne* on a steady course. Courtney thought she would hit the protruding bar, but with a miraculous weave, the main and fore yards yanked around by their braces, she rounded it.

The *Scylla* ran too quickly. As if in response to the *Cygne*'s driver sail tautening, threatening to loosen, the *Scylla*'s canvas reduced. Only then could she hope to navigate the maze and its outer reaches.

Sixty fathoms. Fifty-five fathoms.

The *Meridian* made no such moves. Hungry with bloodlust for the prey, she drove on.

'She must reef her canvas,' Robinson said. 'The French ship is not worth the risk.'

For once, Courtney agreed. Above, the mainsail slapped in a rising gust and then was laid flat aback. The rest of the canvas followed. Within a moment, they lost their headway – and across the water, the *Meridian* had no chance. A failed tack heaved her head into the veering wind and clapped her in irons. Her sails shivered, the spanker canvas tore straight from the boom, and there resounded a hideous crunch. Without control, she staggered onto the bar. The arching bows were only stopped by the thick sand.

The *Scylla* had no time to react. Robinson ordered for hands to the braces. Before the yards could be braced around, preventing the *Scylla* from careering onto the bars, her stern began to turn towards the *Cygne*. As the helm threatened to spin out of Abbott and his mate's hands, Courtney hurried to them, grabbing on to steady the rudder.

At the same moment, Lieutenant Derby emerged from the hatch. His eyes widened as a shuddering succession of blasts resounded from the *Cygne*. Courtney's legs nearly buckled when the shots impacted. The mizzenmast lurched; chunks of timber exploded; Abbott cried aloud and fell into Courtney, taking them both down onto the deck. Pressed to the timber, Courtney could hear the cries and orders of the mids and gun crew below, preparing to return the shots. Smoke poured out the portholes.

Courtney scrambled to return to his feet, only to find his limbs and palms slipping in a pool of hot liquid. His stomach tightened. Red soaked through his coat and breeches. Frantically, he felt for the injury, mind racing to that letter he had never finished. But he felt no pain or loss.

Abbott. The coxswain was alive too, though sprayed with the same blood and gore which Courtney now felt dripping through his hair and over his skin. He stared aft, pale beneath the crimson.

Captain Robinson's death had been quick, and that was the only mercy. One of the *Cygne*'s shots had taken him through the waist, sundering him almost in two, snuffing out all his years in a single second. Bile rose in Courtney's throat. He desperately swallowed it and rose to trembling legs. For a moment, he had no clue what to do. His life condensed to this one bewildering, awful moment.

Then he saw Derby half-collapsed upon the companion-ladder, looking as though he was nearing hysteria; Abbott and his mate, stricken, upon the deck; the remaining topmen and Murray, in the chains, ashen with shock. Courtney wiped the blood from his cheeks and gripped the sword at his waist. 'Hands to the braces!' he shouted to the tops. 'Ready about! Lieutenant Derby, to the gun deck!'

It was a risk to try and tack in the rising wind, but Courtney trusted this crew and trusted this ship. In the heat of the *Cygne*'s fire, the canvas was shortened, the mainsail hauled and the yards ached about. With what felt like inches to spare, the foremast came around and they soared past the stuck *Meridian*. She signalled for aid, her bows jammed into the protruding sand. Men had already climbed down her sides to assess the damage, which Courtney could see was not serious. They could have her off at the turn of the tide. As long as the *Cygne* did not empty her guns into her vulnerable frame, she would sail for many years to come.

'Seventy fathoms, sir!' Murray cried. The *Scylla* had avoided the worst of the bar and now deeper water awaited her. Safely on the starboard tack, she left the *Meridian*, drawing the *Cygne*'s fire. Her progress was marked by the forward starboard guns blasting across the clear waters as the *Scylla* beat on towards the *Cygne*'s flank. Closer, Courtney noticed the previous damage done to her: a stern chaser off its carriage, rudder chipped, spanker-boom hanging on by its stays. The next shot cracked it entirely. The sail and timber fell with a resounding clatter, nearly crushing the man at the helm.

'A little nearer and she'll be in range of a broadside,' Courtney said.

Though she had just delivered devastating fire across the *Scylla*'s deck, Courtney knew the *Cygne* struggled. Troubled by the harm to her spars and rudder, she already floundered towards the island, trying to cross the *Scylla*'s bows and prevent the might of a thirteen-gun broadside which would cripple her. A minute adjustment to the course had the *Scylla*'s cannons maintain their targets along her hull, but the *Cygne* still turned, closer, ever closer to the rocky shore.

Courtney turned to stare at the unforgiving walls of Monito Island. The ragged cliffs vaulted high above the ships. Courtney would not play the fool and chase the *Cygne* so close. She could maul herself on those rises.

A blast from the *Scylla* brought his attention back to the *Cygne*'s gun deck which had just been lacerated by shot. One of the portholes at the waist ripped wide open and a cannon's muzzle disappeared. Courtney thought it had overturned but then, violently, a hail of timber blasted from the *Cygne*'s flank. The force made him flinch. He ducked on instinct, seeing chunks of heated metal pinwheeling through the air and plummeting into the sea. A gaping hole remained, full of felled men pressed together in a gory mass.

'A cannon!' Courtney gasped to Loom, who stared as aghast as him. 'A cannon has erupted!'

Flames suddenly flickered on the frigate's gun deck. It sputtered out of the void in the hull, before tearing back, igniting the dry wood. The *Cygne*'s other guns fell silent, the absence of sound strange and ominous. Dead bodies, struck down from the explosion, were heaved from the ship as crewmen scrambled to douse the blaze. Fire at sea was a sailor's worst fear; it could destroy a ship in minutes.

That was all it took for the *Cygne*'s waist to turn into a sparking beacon. With men drawn down to deal with the blaze, and the damage eating through the vessel, the frigate kept drifting, sailing towards the island, the wind fanning the danger. Little figures hurried past the shimmering heat, fire buckets at hand. But the deck was a keg, stuffed with gunpowder. Across the waters, Courtney could hear it popping and bursting.

'Good God,' Courtney muttered aloud. 'Mr Abbott, helm amidships. We'll not endanger ourselves. Lieutenant Derby!'

Courtney's shoes slipped in Robinson's blood as he ran to the hatch down to the gun deck. Gunsmoke bled through the dingy space below, making the crew look like ghouls. Derby emerged, wraith-like, fair hair streaming out of its tie and plastered to his forehead. Smythe was not far behind. 'Lieutenant Derby, avast firing.'

'Sir—' But then Derby turned to larboard where the *Cygne* burnt. The sunlight was choked with fire. 'Good God,' he swore. 'Did we do that?'

Within minutes, the conflagration had raced up one of the *Cygne's* companion-ladders, reaching her quarterdeck. The foot of the main-mast became encircled with fire, cutting off the topmen's escape. Grey smoke started to churn, flooding over the sides. Courtney saw shadows falling through it, splashing into the waters.

'They're abandoning her,' he said. 'If that fire reaches the powder store...'

He did not finish. Courtney had seen two ships erupt before: the *Ulysses* and the *Fénix*. He had no desire to witness the deaths again.

With the smell of blazing timber covering his lungs, and the infernal heat swarming across the sea, he knew he had to make a decision. He could not simply stand there and watch the French frigate burn to the waterline.

'Mr Smythe,' Courtney said. 'You and I are going to attempt to rescue any survivors. Assemble a party of thirteen to man three of the launches. Quickly!'

Smythe disappeared without question but Derby's eyes widened, perhaps at the prospect of temporarily captaining the *Scylla* or perhaps at the idea of Courtney saving the crew they had just been trying to kill. He did not have time to question it before Smythe reappeared, accompanied by his men. Courtney was relieved to see Obi, one of their strongest and most dependable. He caught his breath and ordered, 'Pull anyone still alive from the water. Return them to the *Scylla*. If they reach the island, then let them. Do not approach the *Cygne* too closely. She does not have long.'

Courtney knew he should not accompany them – the danger was too great and Lieutenant Derby could not handle the *Scylla* – but he remembered how Nightingale had rescued the survivors from the *Fénix* when a lightning strike had ignited her. It had been the first time the man had inspired him.

With the animals removed from the launches, Courtney, Smythe and the men climbed down into the boats. Courtney perched in the starboard bank of the largest cutter, grasping an oar and ignoring the looks of the crew.

They did not set the cutter's sail, but pulled over the water, the heat growing the closer they approached the doomed *Cygne*. The masts had now turned into pyres, belching smoke and debris. Sails ignited and disintegrated into shreds of white canvas that flew in the wind until coming to smoulder in the sea. Bare heads bobbed above the surface, desperate arms protruding and splashing in an attempt to reach debris. Courtney wanted to call out that they would be rescued, but knew no French. Thankfully, Smythe's voice shouted as he directed his launch towards the sandbars. *Cygne* men began to heave themselves towards them.

'Lay on your oars!' Courtney ordered and the cutter came to an unsteady halt. Men's chilled, wet hands pawed at the hull, slipping on the damp timber and trying to grope for the gunwales. He reached overboard and grabbed hold. With their waterlogged clothes, he had to strain to haul them from the sea which sucked and dragged at them. Courtney helped a young, thin lad crawl into the cutter, followed by a man older than Master Loom. They all rested against the safety of the empty benches, shivering, coughing, some of them vomiting salt water. Courtney could see no officers.

The two other launches were becoming full. Smythe's boat sagged deeper into the sea, water lapping higher and higher. 'To the *Scylla*!' Courtney ordered in a harsh cry. The oarsmen had to labour to manoeuvre the heavy vessel and by the time they reached the *Scylla*, Courtney's arms and shoulders were burnt. But he still grasped the French sailors and helped shove them up the ladder towards the waiting Scyllas on deck. An old seaman's legs trembled so vigorously that Courtney climbed halfway up with him, a hand constantly on his back. To his relief, Lieutenant Derby reached down and helped him up the last steps.

'We can save more men!' Courtney shouted up to him.

'The *Meridian*, sir—' Derby began, but Courtney had already sat back down at the oars.

Fifteen more they heaved from the water. Courtney's back was in agony from leaning over the gunwales, and he was chilled to the bone despite the roaring conflagration. But he refused to let go of a man who flapped and twisted in the water. He shouted something in French, drinking gouts of salt water every time he opened his mouth. Courtney caught him on the back of his shirt and dredged up his dwindling strength to scrape him over the side of the cutter.

'Sir!' Obi, at his side, suddenly shouted. Courtney glanced up, his arms still full of the struggling sailor. The *Cygne*'s mainmast blazed completely now, the yards resembling a forest consumed by a wildfire.

Flames spat out of gunports, untouched by the sea. For a moment, the ship and all her sailors held their breath.

'Down!' Courtney yelled. 'All hands, down!'

In case they did not understand, Courtney grabbed the nearest French crewmen and shoved them into the shell of the cutter. He felt Obi collapse close to him: the last thing he was aware of before the world erupted. The scream nearly obliterated his eardrums, catching him in the chest through the hull of the boat and rippling through his limbs. The shock of the explosion tore the waters asunder, hurling waves over the cutter and soaking their prone bodies. Courtney gripped the men beside him, shielding them from the debris which started to fall, praying nothing would come nearer than the chunk of timber which nearly split their tiller.

Slowly, Courtney raised his head. The *Cygne* had been reduced to nothing but a smouldering hulk, vomiting the last spurts of flame before fizzling into black ash. The bowsprit groaned and tumbled into the sea, taking with it the last of the swan figurehead. All around the cutter, litter bobbed on the waves.

Courtney gradually raised himself to his knees and looked around at the prostrate sailors. 'Is anybody hurt?' he asked, surreptitiously checking himself for injuries and finding none, other than the ringing in his ears and the throb in his head from the noise.

No one replied in the negative, but no one replied in the positive either. Courtney knew half of the men in the cutter had just witnessed their own ship explode; there was now no hope for them other than as prisoners.

And there was nothing more that he could do but return to the *Scylla*.

Chapter Two: The Doldrums

Soaked and trembling with the cold, Courtney waited in the cutter, ensuring all the French sailors and his own men returned to the *Scylla* before him. He knew he had done all he could, but guilt still threatened. Once the numbness wore off, it would crest over him for certain. For now, he wordlessly urged Obi back aboard and then followed him up.

A wide-eyed, pallid Lieutenant Derby met him on deck. Ignoring his surprise, Courtney stripped off his waistcoat and squeezed out a deluge of red-coloured water. Robinson's blood still drenched him.

'Sir,' Derby tried. 'Mr Smythe has a prisoner who you will wish to see.'

'We have many prisoners, Lieutenant. And the *Meridian* is still grounded. I must see Captain Bryant.'

'Sir,' Derby said again, but before he could elaborate, Smythe approached with a man who was, somehow, still wearing a bicorne hat decorated with gold lace. His dark navy uniform was even darker with seawater, bits of his embroidered waistband and golden buttons scuffed with burn marks and his black stock hanging loose, but he walked proudly, tasselled boots resounding on the deck. His green eyes swept over Courtney, lined mouth taut.

'This man claims to be the captain of the *Cygne*, sir,' Smythe said.

'I do not claim,' the captain said in heavily accented, but perfect, English. He remembered his obligations and removed his hat, revealing hair streaked with grey. 'I am Capitaine Bonfils of the *Cygne*. I should like to speak to a senior officer.'

'I am the senior officer, sir,' Courtney replied, knowing he did not particularly resemble one in his shirt and breeches, dripping on the deck like a drowned rat. 'Lieutenant Courtney of the *Scylla*.'

'Where is your captain, Lieutenant?'

Courtney was tempted to gesture to the heavy blood smear over the quarterdeck. 'He is dead,' he replied simply. 'So you shall surrender your sword to me, if you please.'

Bonfils hesitated, fist tightening around the hilt of the sword at his belt. With so many eyes upon them, French and British, Courtney reddened. He had been temporarily in command of this vessel for less than an hour and had already witnessed the destruction of an enemy ship, overseen the rescue of its sailors, and now tried to negotiate the surrender of its captain. If Bonfils refused, Courtney did not know what he would do. But he stayed firm for the sake of the crew until Bonfils took a breath and unclasped his sword-belt. He removed it, turned the handle towards Courtney, and Courtney grasped it, glad for the water hiding the sweat on his palms.

'Thank you, Capitaine,' Courtney said. 'I am sorry for the fate of your ship.'

Now that handover had been completed, a thin, resigned smile crossed Bonfils's mouth. His shoulders loosened. 'Thank you, Lieutenant.'

'My marine lieutenant, Ferguson, shall accompany you to the great cabin and we shall speak. I shall be down shortly.'

Bonfils nodded as Ferguson appeared and led him away. Courtney sighed and turned to the men still gathered on deck. The marines, a comforting red presence, had come to stand by the mass of soaked prisoners. Seeing them together made Courtney realise how few they had truly saved: thirty, perhaps thirty-five, out of a crew as large as the *Scylla*'s. Guilt pulsed again. 'Sergeant,' he said to Vickers of the marines. 'Take them into the hold. Ensure none are armed. And Mr Smythe, tell Cook to light the galley fires. They shall be fed and given water.'

'Lieutenant,' Derby, still hanging at Courtney's side, said. 'What shall happen with Captain Robinson? He is still—'

'He has not been moved?'

'I... Mr Abbott and I propped him against the helm.'

Courtney fought the urge to swear. His mind tangled with the various responsibilities. There was no deeper water he could have been thrown into; not even holding the *Scylla* together during the infestation of yellow fever had given him such a turn. Now, he knew, he was closer to true command, and any misstep would send him plummeting to the seabed. 'Fetch Master Loom and cover the captain with sailcloth,' he decided. 'Take him below and I shall consult Captain Bryant about...'

Captain Bryant. The *Meridian* had been cast to a small corner of Courtney's head. He felt for his spyglass, but could not find it; it must have been lost overboard. Instead, he peered aft and saw the sorry shape of Captain Bryant's frigate still wedged into the sandbar. More of the ground had been revealed by the shifting tide and little silhouettes of men stamped around the uncovered hull. Courtney could make out the lines of anchor cables running through the hawse-holes out into the water. Bryant would hate him for it, but he could not leave the *Scylla*, not with the French prisoners aboard.

'Take the captain below,' Courtney said again. 'And I shall deal with Capitaine Bonfils and then Captain Bryant.'

Which would be the most acrimonious, Courtney was not sure.

–

In the end, Captain Bryant arrived himself as Courtney was finishing with Capitaine Bonfils. It had been a painfully awkward interview. Bonfils answered graciously but shortly, only revealing the bare minimum. Courtney merely discovered that the *Cygne* had been ordered to the waters around Hispaniola – and then the meeting was terminated by Bryant being piped up the side of the *Scylla*.

Despite Courtney's certainty that he had performed well by chasing the French frigate, and then acted honourably by pulling the survivors from the water, he had no doubt that Bryant would find the gap in his armour. That gap was the *Meridian*, still lodged on the sandbar.

The *Meridian* captain knocked on the cabin door once, the marines opened it, and he stood there behind Bonfils. He wore his undress uniform, hat beneath his arm, a man merely a decade older than Courtney but from a different world. They were only united by their dedication to a life on the sea. Before Bryant took in the sight of the great cabin, Courtney caught a glimpse of true emotion upon his face: the rigid tightness of his jaw; the flaming anger in his eyes; the ramrod straightness of his back. Then he noticed Bonfils.

'Lieutenant Courtney,' he said, unable to disguise his shock. 'What in God's name happened?'

Courtney had risen to his feet. Now, Bonfils did so too. Courtney saluted Bryant and realised his arms were still red with blood. 'Captain Robinson is dead, sir,' he said.

Bryant paused. For a moment, sadness minutely softened his harsh expression. 'That is hard news,' he sighed. 'He was a good man. May I have a word with you, Lieutenant?'

'Yes, sir. I do not believe I need anything more from Capitaine Bonfils. Lieutenant Ferguson, if you would accompany him below to steerage.'

Bonfils nodded to Courtney and followed Ferguson from the cabin. With him gone, Courtney wanted to breathe out and resettle his head, but Bryant prevented that. He finally moved from the door, closing it behind him. He glanced at the skylight – the other possible means of eavesdropping – and stepped close to Courtney. Courtney could smell the sweat on him and the salt spray mixed with ash which still floated across the water.

'When did Captain Robinson die?' he asked plainly.

'In the *Cygne*'s first broadside, sir. Shortly after you – after the *Meridian* grounded.'

Bryant looked away. The shade of his true feeling swept over him again and he walked to the desk. 'I signalled to the *Scylla*, requesting aid.'

'The *Meridian* did not seem to be unduly damaged, sir. I thought it my priority to pursue the *Cygne*. We had been following her for almost a day.'

Courtney said it in the most level tone of voice he could muster, thinking that any variation would break Bryant's fragile composure – whilst also convincing himself that he could remain calm.

Still, Bryant shook his head. 'I am the senior officer between these two vessels,' he said. 'When my ship was damaged, I wished for aid but you delivered that aid to our enemy.'

'The *Cygne* was destroyed, sir. I did not want two hundred men to drown.'

'But you did not save the ship.'

Courtney wondered if that was what his anger swelled around. If the *Scylla* or the *Meridian* had captured the *Cygne*, she would fetch a hefty fortune in prize money. Sailing away from an admiral's charge meant that the bulk would come to the officers. Neither the *Scylla* nor the

Meridian – nor any vessel out of the Leeward Islands Station – had fared well these last months with prize ships. Courtney knew who Bryant blamed for that – and who he also blamed for the desperation of gaining prizes. The loss of the *Ulysses* still hung over each man and officer.

'She was ablaze, sir. If I attempted to capture her, the *Scylla* could have been destroyed also.'

'Yes, you have an intimate acquaintance with vessels that come to be ablaze.'

'That is unfair,' Courtney said without thinking, and when Bryant's eyebrows raised, he added a bitter, 'Sir.'

'Unfair or not, Lieutenant, it is true. Where are the *Cygne*'s papers? I presume the muster book and all other documentation were rescued.'

Courtney's silence said it all. He felt a ridiculous spark of guilt, though it had been no fault of his own that the *Cygne*'s officers had not saved their critical cargo. Bryant sighed.

'Well, that is something that shall have to be explained later. I have to think of the *Meridian* now. Once she is re-floated, I expect Capitaine Bonfils to be sent across and I shall deliver him to English Harbour. The *Scylla* shall accompany with the prisoners, and with Captain Robinson's body aboard. Lieutenant Godfrey shall come to you to help keep order.'

'Sending Lieutenant Godfrey across is not necessary, sir,' Courtney pressed, wondering if Bryant was doing this now simply to embarrass him. 'Lieutenant Derby and I can manage. I have handled a ship full of prisoners before.'

Bryant sniffed. 'When the *Scylla* carried the *Ulysses* prisoners, she was aided by Commodore Harrison in the sixty-four-gun *Actium*. I would feel more comfortable with my lieutenant aboard. Now,' he said quickly, as Courtney opened his mouth to utter more, 'with the turning tide, we may have the *Meridian* off the bar within the next two hours. Anchor the *Scylla* and organise men to come across to our aid.'

Courtney knew he did not have a choice. Even though Bryant commanded a separate frigate, he was the senior officer on the two ships, and he had been a post-captain for the entire duration that Courtney had been a lieutenant. The *Scylla* and the *Meridian* had sailed from English Harbour together not two months before in response to the growing Spanish and French presence around Hispaniola; so far, the longest time Courtney had spent in Bryant's vicinity had been at a handful of dinners in the respective great cabins. He had wished to keep it that way.

But, for all his rank and background, Bryant did not have what Courtney had: the knowledge and experience of the *Scylla* and her crew. When Courtney organised the men to go temporarily across to the *Meridian*, he knew they would work well, and almost cruelly, he hoped they would outstrip their fellow sailors on the *Meridian*. It had been a long time since someone other than the *Scylla* officers had believed in her men.

Courtney watched them go and wondered when he had become so spiteful.

–

The bell was sounding for the middle watch by the time Courtney was able to close his cabin door on the day. He wished its events could disappear as easily as the sun which had long vanished beneath the horizon. Instead, they hung around him and inside of him, making his bones ache and his head, which had not stopped ringing since the explosion, throb. As he stripped out of his soaked coat and wrenched the stiff cloth from around his neck, he cursed the string of bad luck which had befouled him and the ship he had always been so fond of. First, the aftermath of the court martial the year before and the way it had hindered any hope of advancement. Second, the months spent in English Harbour, cast on the beach on half-pay and wondering if the *Scylla* would ever be sent out again. Third, the lack of prize money that could help tie up that time relying on Commodore Harrison and Miss Tabitha Sandham's aid. And now, a chance to prove himself as an emergency commander, dashed by Captain Bryant and his pig-headedness.

Courtney was not a man to believe in fortune, or that a dearth of it could be the judgement of an angry god, and he was also not a man to blame himself, but he was starting to think he must have performed some evil deed to be so condemned.

Two comforts awaited him in the small cabin off the gunroom. Away from the deck and the raucous din that had only recently ceased after the turning of the capstan raising the *Scylla*'s anchor, the dimly lit space was quiet and, if he could use the word about a Royal Navy frigate, peaceful. His hammock swung lightly with the newly serene waves and, with only Murray off watch, he did not have to listen to Derby's snoring in the cabin along.

The other comfort lay on his desk, still unfinished from that morning.

But before Courtney could return to his letter, he balanced his miniature shaving mirror against a bulkhead and slumped before it. The teeming rain of the squall had rinsed the worst of Captain Robinson's blood off his face but there were still smears of it gathered in his eye sockets and around his temples. It stained his collar and would be a nightmare to wash out of his cotton shirt. Courtney had not been able to change since returning to the *Scylla* with the prisoners. He had stood multiple watches of four hours without stop and without rest, even whilst Captain Bryant retired on the *Meridian*.

He is content to send Lieutenant Godfrey across to keep an eye on me, Courtney thought, *but will not supervise his own ship when I go across to help strain at his capstan and labour in his hold.* It was pertinent behaviour from a man who had been sent ashore by the demands of the Spithead mutineers four years previously.

Courtney dipped his hands into his bowl and scooped cool water over his face. He rubbed his weary palms across his cheeks, finally realising the extent of his exhaustion. In the lull after the mania of the day, he might have expected his frustration with Bryant – with the *Meridian* – with his entire situation – to simmer, but it boiled as hotly as before. During these low, tired, anxious moments, he despaired of ever gaining a promotion, of ever gaining any recognition for what he had achieved. When Captain Carlisle had died of the fever two years before, Courtney had commanded the *Scylla* even as her crew vomited and fitted and died. He had withstood months of terrified quarantine and then, when Hiram Nightingale had been named as captain, Courtney believed he had behaved well as his subordinate – perhaps not at the beginning, but certainly later, when their enemies' web of deceit had tried to ensnare them.

Then, it had been snatched away, and Courtney, and the *Scylla*, had languished in the doldrums for an eternity.

He sighed and looked into the fatigued green eyes that watched him from the mirror. He was certain his age had caught up with him during that time of confinement ashore. He had never had dark lines ringing his sockets or such pale skin, not in the heat of the Caribbean where he had been stationed for the last years. Not even thirty, he thought, and already speaking of himself like a man of double the time. He had chastised Nightingale for such thoughts over and over again.

Courtney pulled off his shoes, took the letter from the desk and swung himself into his hammock. The tie of his hair jammed into the back of his head so he pulled the ribbon and ruffled barely tamed curls. He knew Nightingale would not mind a jot if his writing was cramped and bordering on illegible so he rested the paper on his thighs and picked up the pen.

...I have just this last half-hour stepped down from a watch which has lasted from late this morning – perhaps yesterday now? – to gone midnight. I started it by climbing to the crosstrees and ended it in the gloom, straining at a capstan. We spied a French forty-gunner almost two days ago and chased her to the conclusion when she was destroyed and Captain Robinson was sadly killed. I did all I could in command yet Captain Bryant found fault. The Meridian became grounded on a sandbar when she was driven too closely into the wind, and we have only recently managed to free her.

Courtney found he wished to write more. He drew up his remaining restraint to filter the words from his mind to the pen nib. He knew Nightingale would burn the letters if they became too incriminating but did not want to put him in an awkward position.

Moreover, some sensible part also knew Nightingale would tell him that he had been difficult at the start of their voyage. Courtney was aware he had been standoffish and cold, angry that he had been passed over for command and frustrated that his new captain had been a seemingly feeble and indecisive man. He had softened when he had discovered the truth about Nightingale.

Such a thing could not happen with Bryant. Courtney saw nothing in that man that he could see in Nightingale.

We shall transport Captain Robinson back to Antigua, Courtney continued. *I do not feel comfortable with his body in the hold, but I would also not feel comfortable burying such an officer at sea. His wife will not know for some time as she is still in Felixstowe. I do hope that he can be brought home but...*

It had been terrible to carry Robinson down into the dim hold. Courtney had taken command of that task, heaving Robinson's bloody, shrouded body with a volunteer, Obi. In the guttering light of a lantern, smelling the bilge water and pall of gun smoke still clinging to the ship, they had sewn him into sailcloth for the three-day journey to Antigua. Dr Archer had treated him in the hopes his body would not be too badly affected.

Despite my frets about him, he was a good man. I worried that he had been put on board to see the Scylla *into her last journey, and I'm still not wholly convinced he was not. I know what you will say. I will begrudge any man who does not meet my expectations of this ship. It is difficult not to feel affection for her after all she has been through. I try and resist doing too much, but I feel as though I know this ship and crew better than any now, aside from Master Loom. Perhaps that is another reason to hope for another command, although I did so wish I could—*

Courtney cut his sentence short again. His eyes were becoming too heavy, his mind too jumbled, making him write nonsense. Nightingale did not want to listen to his self-pitying complaints and his desires for command. He knew all of that already. But the man had become the one person Courtney trusted more than any other, aside from his sister, Jane. She had her own life now in Norfolk and Courtney never liked to trouble her with too many stories of the sea and the *Scylla*, which had caused her so much pain.

One day, Courtney would return to Nightingale and Jane, both. Letters were no substitute for seeing them again.

Yet, if Bryant had his way, he would be stuck out here forever, continually a lieutenant, continually at those crossroads he so hated.

He sighed and set the letter aside. He would finish it in a better time. Dousing the lantern, he bid farewell to a day he would not miss.

Chapter Three: A Different Shore

June 1802, Portsmouth, England

With the piece of paper in his hand, Lieutenant Courtney ducked out of the coach and breathed in the fresh sea air. So many years in the West Indies had trained him not to trust any lungful – miasmas of fatal diseases bloomed and bred in the tropics, and he had been fortunate not to suffer with them. The lack of that fear was one of the many things that would take some accustoming to, now his feet were back on English soil.

With his one piece of luggage under his arm, Courtney paid the coachman the last sixpence in his coin pouch. A whip touched the coach's horses, the wheels rattled on the rough track, and then the vehicle with its curious passengers vanished back down the hill. He was finally left alone with his thoughts and the neatly written note.

The past fortnight had been a rush in which he had barely had time to stop and contemplate. A long-awaited visit to Jane's new home in Great Yarmouth had exhausted him more than the three-week journey across the Atlantic from Antigua. He had been at the mercy of a wave of feminine energy, fussed over by Lieutenant Wainwright's seven sisters and Jane's soon-to-be mother-in-law. Years on a ship populated solely by men had made Courtney forget how to behave around so many women. He had been unprepared for their probing questions and giddy enthusiasm. But he had been glad to see their open affection had brightened Jane's eyes and cheeks. The last time he had seen her, she had been sailing into the Caribbean horizon, wrung dry by the court martial on the *Leviathan*.

That mutiny, and its aftermath, seemed another world amongst the sun-drenched, warm fields along the Norfolk coast where she lived. Jane had started a new life.

Yet beneath Courtney's relief at her safety, a deeper note pulsed. Her rebirth only more sharply illuminated his own uncertainty.

The heathland around Portsmouth sang softly as Courtney made his way off the path and into the countryside. Cattle and the occasional roaming goat replaced the bustle of the town with its residents of listless sailors and tacitly cheerful civilians. The peace had brought a mix of reactions as tangled as the ones now inside of Courtney. After the cautious discussions of the previous year, the treaty at Amiens had not come as an entire surprise – yet the talk of peace and the reality of it were two very different situations. Once the initial celebrations and ringing of bells and illuminations had ended, the harsher practicalities settled: the half-pay, the domestic concerns, the nagging worry of how far Bonaparte would disturb Europe before reactions had to be contemplated again.

Courtney had sworn his life to the service of the King's Navy. Since he had been a boy, he had only known almost continuous war. Peace had a strange hollow quality to it.

Hoping he was not trespassing, Courtney took a route beside a copse of overhanging trees. The uneven ground crunched beneath his feet and he nearly rolled his ankle over more than once. He had not expected the land to be so rugged and unkempt, but he had not helped himself by dressing in his best uniform with its heeled buckled shoes, snug breeches and heavy woollen coat. If he reached Haywood Hall without ripping his stockings or staining the pristine white, he would consider it a miracle – if he reached Haywood Hall at all, that was. All he had to refer to was the address and vague description Nightingale had written, and the directions from the coachman.

Nightingale did not know he planned to visit him; he did not even know Courtney had returned to England. Despite their frequent letters, Courtney could not rid himself of the feeling that Nightingale might not have a place for him here. Every plan Courtney tried to make, every thought of the future, was tempered by the doubt around what they shared. Nightingale had had more than long enough to reconsider and to tease out all his fears of their...? Courtney did not know how to define it.

Yet, as the dense tangle of trees and bushes opened into a wider, rolling field, Courtney could not ignore the thrill of anticipation in his chest. He quickened his steps, climbing the gentle rise of Portsdown

Hill until he spied a glint of man-made material: wrought metal gates in a low brick wall. They were open, fuelling his hope and his nerves. He checked his clothes, relieved to find only a small blemish on his coat which he batted away. The afternoon sun had brought sweat out upon his temple and the heat had strengthened the lavender and citrus fragrance he had stupidly spent his money on at a Portsmouth barber's.

He could delay no more as he stepped through the gates and walked down the long gravel drive. The house which sat at the end of the pathway surprised him. He had known Nightingale was not impoverished but the building was of the kind Courtney had believed were only set pieces as a child: he had not thought anyone could obtain such money to maintain them. Wandering towards it, he felt again that sense of disconnect. There was a whole other world above him and he, without a coin left in his pouch, without a commission or place, could not hope to climb to it.

He grasped the brass knocker on the front door and then stepped back to again admire the spouting fountain, the carefully tended allotments and the many windows peering down at him. When the door opened, the butler stared at him with sharp blue eyes in a face of stone. Courtney knew he must have looked a sight, trussed-up in some semblance of a best uniform, witlessly gazing at the house as if he had never gone beyond his village before.

'May I help you, sir?' the ageing servant said.

'I, uh...' Courtney cleared his throat. 'Is Mr Nightingale at home?'

'He is out, sir. Is he expecting you?'

'No. Perhaps I should have said. Is there any— Do you know when he'll be home?'

The butler's expression did not change. 'He is due to return from Portugal later this afternoon. Perhaps you could return another time, sir?'

'My name is Arthur Courtney,' Courtney blurted. 'I served with Captain Nightingale on the *Scylla*.'

Nothing crossed the butler's face. He remained with those steely eyes and that jutting bottom lip. Then, without another word, he slowly opened the door and swept his arm, prompting Courtney to enter. Courtney removed his hat and with a bobbing nod and smile, hurried inside before the man could change his mind.

He was directed into a parlour busy with decoration and trimmings. Worried about scuffing the carpet, Courtney perched on the edge of a paisley chaise lounge and placed his hat delicately beside him. Looking around the room, Courtney could not see the Nightingale he had known. Perhaps it was his wife's influence in the bird-adorned wallpaper and the china figurines. Idyllic rural paintings furnished the walls, interspersed with watercolour sketches of harbours and calm seas. In the corner, Courtney was surprised to recognise Nightingale's face, painted in dull oils and at least a decade younger. The artist had not captured him truly; he looked too impulsive, too naive. Perhaps once he had been that way.

Without his direction, a maid entered and placed a plate of seed cakes and biscuits on the low table before him. She returned within five minutes with a steaming teapot, pouring it for him when Courtney garbled an embarrassed, 'Yes, thank you.'

As he sipped gingerly at the tea in its pretty cup, he finally absorbed what the butler had said: Nightingale had been in Portugal. The peace most likely made travelling easier to that country which had long been pulled about by France, trying to gain its alliance. More personally, Courtney knew Nightingale had family there: his uncle, and his mother who had been estranged from his father for many years. As much as he wished Nightingale's family well, he also selfishly wanted him here.

Fortunately, he did not have to wait more than an hour – a long, painful hour interrupted by maids and the roaming eye of the butler – before the front door again was opened. Courtney sprang to his feet, brushing at the minute crumbs on his jacket and feeling a sudden tightness in his stomach. A woman's voice greeted the butler and then warm, male tones.

Nightingale appeared in the doorway of the parlour. He looked harried from the journey, eyes ringed with dark shadows and skin paler than when he had captained the *Scylla*. But finally, after the bewilderment of this strange house and the doubts of being so far apart from one another, was the man Courtney knew: unassuming in stature, a kindly air in that green gaze, auburn hair pulled back neatly into a low tie, and well-tailored dark clothing that made him into the most handsome person Courtney could imagine.

'Arthur,' Nightingale said dumbly.

'Hello, Hiram,' Courtney said, running his fingers around the gold lace of his hat which he clutched before him. 'I apologise, I should have… I should have written ahead that I was visiting.'

'No. Not at all.'

Nightingale rounded the chaise lounge and lingered awkwardly in front of him. His hands twitched and Courtney could see him working through this new arrangement: Courtney, not on his ship, but in his private home. Despite their admissions in Trinidad, this suddenly seemed the most intimate thing between them. Finally, he relented and grasped Courtney's hand, shaking it vigorously.

'It is wonderful to see you,' he said, voice thin. 'I did not know you had returned to England.'

'I only arrived a fortnight or so ago. I have been with Jane and Lieutenant Wainwright. I wanted to surprise you. I hope it is – well, I hope it's a pleasant one.'

'Yes, yes, of course.'

Nightingale smiled, eyes shining with what Courtney saw were unshed tears. Blinking them away, Nightingale released Courtney's hand and gestured towards the door. Courtney realised a woman was standing there, astonishingly beautiful even though she wore the simplest of blue day dresses. Her hat framed dark curls that fell around a sharp, inquisitive face. At Nightingale's introduction, she softened a little, mouth rising in a cautious smile.

'This is my wife, Mrs Louisa Nightingale,' Nightingale said. 'Louisa, this is Arthur Courtney, First Lieutenant of HMS *Scylla*.'

'Not anymore,' Courtney said before he could help himself. Nightingale glanced at him. 'It is a pleasure to meet you, Mrs Nightingale,' Courtney continued. 'I have heard much about you.'

'And I, you. From Hiram, and also from my father.' Knowing his and Nightingale's previous experience with Sir William Haywood, he could have said anything about Courtney. 'Shall I call for more tea?' she asked.

'I don't want to encroach on you for too long,' Courtney rushed. 'I only wanted to invite Hiram – Mr Nightingale – and yourself, Mrs Nightingale, to my sister's wedding in November.'

'I thought it was set for next year at the earliest,' Nightingale said.

'It was, but Edward – Lieutenant Wainwright – does not have much hope of the peace lasting too long. He does not want Bonaparte to spoil his wedding day. And, in any case, I wished to give an invitation to Mr Nightingale. I have recently returned to the island – the Isle of Wight, that is – and knowing that you used to visit…' Courtney could not get the words out, worrying what they might insinuate.

'I…' Nightingale glanced back to Louisa. 'I should like to attend the wedding. And it would be pleasant to see the island again. I've not visited for many years. But we have only just returned from Porto. I find I am quite tired from the journey.'

'Of course.' Courtney fought the swell of disappointment. He had been foolish to think that Nightingale would drop everything at the sight of him, and he had also been foolish to suggest such things in front of his wife. Their letters had not been the safest environment to discuss precisely what Louisa Nightingale knew about her husband's friendship with him.

Courtney had obviously not hidden his reaction very well, for Nightingale then said, 'But I will be less weary in a few days. After I have settled a few things here, I would be happy to join you – if you do not object, my dear.'

The last comment was directed at Louisa. The 'my dear' made Courtney's stomach squeeze. Louisa's careful smile turned genuine, touching her blue eyes. 'I have been meaning to visit Robert in Bristol,' she said. 'We shall coincide.'

So it was with a curious mix of trepidation and anticipation that Courtney stood at the port at East Cowes a week later. Nightingale had written to him, giving a precise date and time, even the tide he would be sailing in on, but Courtney could not shed the feeling that he would not see white sails coming in to moor. He had waited in a small tavern during the early afternoon, surrounded by fishermen and dock workers, but the coffee had made him nervous. He had not felt this way aboard the *Scylla* even during the dirtiest of weather or when any order to beat to quarters was given. Then, he knew precisely what to expect: which sails to haul in, which men would be at which station, which tack to pursue an enemy vessel on. Nightingale was no simple equation of canvas and wind and waves.

Courtney knew what Nightingale had been through. His soul-baring confessions had stoked the embers of affection Courtney felt towards him. Yet they also simmered in Courtney's mind now; only Nightingale knew if he could hurdle them in the long-term. They were not in Trinidad any longer, floating on the joy of acquittal and healing wounds. A long time had passed, and England was a different shore.

In his other life, before he had been dismissed from the service, Nightingale had commanded ships of the line. Yet it was a small, two-masted brig that finally appeared against the evening sun. She was as trim and neat as Courtney would expect of Nightingale. As she neared the headland, her fore and mainsails furled to the bare poles, left only with the topsails and trysail to guide to her mooring. The pilot boat ferrying her in peeled away and slowly, her anchor was let go. In time, a launch was lowered and Courtney hurried to the pontoon where it would alight.

'I did not expect you in your merchant vessel,' he said as the boat came alongside and he helped to tie her to the pier. Nightingale, in the stern, delicately stood and climbed up onto dry land. Courtney offered him his elbow and he took it without hesitation.

'My brother-in-law, Robert, and I have chartered her out to her former master. She'll be back to return me home in a week.'

'She is a pretty little thing,' Courtney said, and meant it.

'She is not the *Scylla*,' Nightingale commented. 'But a merchant ship from my brother-in-law's shipyard is almost all I can hope for.'

Courtney was unsure how to respond. As much as he wanted to again reassure Nightingale that was not the case, he feared it was. Even on the island, Captain Hiram Nightingale was known as the man who had burnt a king's ship to the waterline. Both he and Courtney knew why he had done it, ridding the world of a tainted ship and of tainted gold that was to be unlawfully siphoned into the scheming Lord Fairholme's hands. But now Lord Fairholme had been banished to the far corners of the Americas, his lands and title conferred upon his brother, and Fairholme's lackey, Lieutenant Hargreaves, was safely in an asylum, Nightingale remained the major player in the mutiny on HMS *Ulysses*.

He leant on Courtney as they made their way to a coach for Ryde. Courtney wished there were no other passengers. He had much he wanted to say to Nightingale, even if the idea of broaching those topics tied him in knots. Now, he could only help to stow Nightingale's luggage and sit beside him quietly. He uttered a small, 'Have you been well?', and received an equally small, 'Tolerably,' in response.

The journey to Ryde continued in almost absolute silence but for the horse's hooves on the rough road, the creaking wheels and eventually, the cry of nightjars and cows beyond the carriage. The coach finally shed its other passengers into the lowering night and Courtney checked Nightingale had not fallen asleep with the rocking of the vehicle. His head was down, almost against his chest, but with a soft touch on his arm, he sniffed and looked up.

'We are nearly there,' Courtney said. 'I shall explain all when we arrive.'

At last, the setting sun gave way to darkness and the coach rolled to a halt. Through the window, Courtney saw how the trees still hid their destination. He opened the door into the cool night air and hopped out to help the driver with Nightingale's case. Hitching it beneath his arm, he reached back into the carriage to see Nightingale to the uneven ground.

'Come, it's getting cold,' he said. 'Just this way.'

Courtney guided him to a gate which emerged through the tangle of hedgerows. He nudged its creaking hinges back with his foot and, beating back the thorns, he revealed what he suddenly worried Nightingale would compare critically with his own sprawling home.

Lit by the rising moon, the cottage sat in the embrace of overgrown trees. Cracked white paint contrasted with the stark Tudor latticework, perhaps only touched up a handful of times since its construction. Shuttered windows watched over a green maze of a garden and the half-hidden path they now walked. It was one of the only houses they had seen since leaving the little hamlet of Ryde.

Courtney waited for Nightingale's reaction. Near the door, Nightingale finally paused and asked, 'Is this yours?'

'Well… No. I hope in the future it might be, but I'm a lieutenant on half-pay without a commission. My savings are…' Courtney waved his hand into the air where his imaginary money existed.

'Ah,' Nightingale said. 'Then, if it is not yours, who does it belong to?'

'It is a sad story. It belonged to the nephew of a man I know. He had been out in India for the past three years but last December we received confirmation that he'd died of the fever. He never married, never had a family. He and Mr Woods managed the upkeep of this cottage and its fields under the landlord. In the will, it all came to Mr Woods but he's getting on in years now and didn't think he could manage it alone. He'd been struggling since his nephew left.'

Courtney opened the door. The inside swirled with motes of dust but the hallway came to life with an array of candles and lanterns. The warm glow transformed the space, illuminating stonework, walls decorated with pastoral sketches and paintings, a cabinet full of decorative plates and further along the foyer, a silent grandfather clock.

'It has been vacant for some time but fortunately, Mr Woods's nephew sent enough money before he died to cover the costs of rent for a while. When Mr Woods knew I'd be returning, he wrote to the landlord and we organised it so I could move in. It is all very temporary still. I hope one day I can truly pay my way beyond lending a hand with the land and the farming, but...'

Courtney's voice faded as his thoughts wandered. Speaking it aloud had made him realise how little he had truly stepped away from his childhood. He was still living under the charity of Mr and Mrs Woods, unsure where he would be in a month or two. After the debacle with the *Scylla*, his chances of a solid career looked slimmer and slimmer.

Nightingale turned to him from the dark living room he had walked into. 'Mr Woods was...'

'The man who looked after me and Jane when our parents were...absent.'

Courtney had not told Nightingale everything about his past on the island, only that he had run away from home at a young age with Jane, fleeing a drunken father and a melancholic mother. He had also not revealed what had led him to this uncertain ground. Everything that stood before him – this cottage, this peace, Nightingale and their unspoken bond – was a ship with an uneven keel and unfamiliar yards.

'Come,' Courtney said. 'I shall show you to the bedrooms. Watch your footing. The floor is a little uneven.'

Courtney did not say that he had been working like a deckhand this last week, scrubbing and cleaning on his hands and knees and turning out the bedrooms ready for Nightingale. There were no maids or butlers here. He opened the door to the room he had been sleeping in and said, 'This is the master bedroom. And next to it is another. I do not mind which you prefer.'

Nightingale looked tentatively between the two rooms, spending more than enough time contemplating the spaces. He wrung his hands and was quiet for so long that Courtney thought it would be safe to suggest, 'Unless you would prefer to...'

'Yes. I would.'

The decision made, Courtney allowed Nightingale to change out of the clothes he had been wearing through his long journey. It was still strange to see him in civilian dress after the finery of a post-captain's uniform. Courtney undressed quickly, peeling himself out of his frilled shirt and silken stockings – the best he owned – and joined him in the warmth.

The last wall of doubt lingered between them. It wobbled when, without a word, Nightingale sank against him, laying his weary head on Courtney's shoulder. Unable to bear the distance anymore, Courtney pulled him into his arms, breathing in the scent of his unbound auburn hair and remembering it vividly from almost two years before. He rubbed his back and felt the old scars, the ones that made Nightingale tense and shiver.

'How have you truly been?' Courtney whispered.

'Aching and feeling my age,' Nightingale said softly.

'You are not old, Hiram.'

'I think I am, sometimes. Old and without a single clue about where I am heading.'

The relief Courtney felt was perhaps selfish, but to hear Nightingale's thoughts were as muddled as his own was a comfort. 'We all feel that,' Courtney said.

'I visited Michael Hargreaves in the asylum my mother and my uncle patronise. I haven't seen her for years on end, not since she left my father. That was why I was in Porto. Michael is well, he'll most likely go to his parents soon, but it only...brings it all back to me. Not that I can forget, with every look the sailors in Portsmouth give me.'

'You did the right thing.'

'I know. I only wish more people than you and I would see it that way.'

'They do.' But Courtney knew it would take more than an assuring word for Nightingale to drag himself out of the mires he fell into. He hated how powerless he felt to help, certainly as he could not conquer his own doubt. He brushed his fingers through Nightingale's hair and sighed. 'I have not been entirely honest with you, Hiram,' he made himself say.

'How do you mean?'

'Perhaps I should have told you in a letter before I returned. Not long before the peace, I lost my position on the *Scylla*. That is why I said I am not her lieutenant anymore. And, wait—' Nightingale had raised his head, his mouth open to argue or question. 'It was not through a formal court martial. I was simply removed along with the other *Scylla* officers and she was broken up as soon as the peace began.'

Nightingale closed his mouth. A spectrum of emotions crossed his face, ending with him saying, softly, 'The most important thing is that your name was not blackened.'

'I'm not sure. Captain Bryant and I argued over the *Meridian* grounding during the battle with the *Cygne*. I was blamed for not coming to his aid.'

'Officially?'

'Who on earth knows with these men?' Courtney said, perhaps too venomously. 'I'm sorry… It just galled me to see the *Scylla* taken off to the breaker's yard.'

Nightingale nodded. 'I suppose that she was the pivot on which my life turned.'

'Both of our lives.'

It was the closest Courtney had come to defining their attachment. They shared such a past, one fraught with danger and deceit, and now they were both here: without a ship, without a career, rudderless and drifting, victims of the peace and other people's judgement. Silence passed between them again. Courtney lifted a hand and caressed the backs of his fingers against Nightingale's cheek. 'Can I kiss you?' he asked softly.

The first smile touched Nightingale's mouth. He nodded. Courtney did not press him for much, glancing his lips to his and waiting for Nightingale to respond. When Nightingale's hand came to cup his cheek, he kissed him again, deeper, lingering, falling into the rhythm of the last time they had shared a bed.

'I did so miss you,' Courtney sighed when they broke apart.

'Terribly,' Nightingale agreed.

Chapter Four: Peace

Courtney considered himself an adaptable man, but after so long on the sea, the land bizarrely felt less stable than the deck of a war-bound frigate. He knew he was not the only man to think so – there were scores of sailors thrown onto the beach from the lowest berth to the most experienced post-captain – but each passing day made him wonder if he would ever feel those sturdy timbers again.

Whilst Nightingale stayed on the island, Courtney showed him both his past and the present. They walked through the small fishing hamlet of Ryde, down the single track where boys wheeled carts half-full with vegetables and mothers herded their children away from muddy potholes. Courtney painted the harsh picture of his younger years, hardened by the grey weather and the sight of the skiffs in the foamy waves with empty crabbing traps and nets. He led Nightingale to one of the old houses in which Courtney, Jane and their parents had shared rooms with another poor family. The memories still fluttered, formless, around the door hanging off its hinges and the half-boarded windows. Courtney told how he had worked as a fisherman, a messenger boy, a hunter, a blacksmith, a cobbler, anything that had been required of him for a few pennies, before they had had to vacate the rooms when those pennies were not enough.

In the shadow of that house, Courtney still felt as though his parents were in the debtor's cell, drinking the last dregs of their hope. Countless men and women shared the same fates, and countless children would suffer because of it. He and Jane had left as soon as they could, staying with Mr and Mrs Woods and then their mother's sister and her husband until Courtney could join the navy. To this day Courtney did not know what had happened to his mother and father: perhaps dead, perhaps transported.

He wanted to say he did not care, but this life still clung to him like a smell that officers from better breeding could scent out like bloodhounds. He had more in common with lowerberth sailors than the men of the gunroom and wardroom. He had been one of them once, in the dark days on the terrible old *Grampus*.

Perhaps that was another reason for his stagnation: no connections, no helpful hand up the ladder.

Nightingale tried to suggest easing in a good word for him. Courtney could not travel to the Admiralty Office in Whitehall for his fortnightly visits without his insistence. He refused each time, knowing that no words from Hiram Nightingale could gain him a commission. Only the most fortunate of ships and the most fortunate of officers received such a laurel crown, carrying dispatches, guarding merchant convoys, even departing for far-flung colonies.

In the way of a sick man torturing himself by imagining himself well again, Courtney would read the scant entries in the Naval Gazette and follow the world as it still turned in peacetime. On the continent, Bonaparte annexed Elba and far away, in Caribbean waters that Courtney and Nightingale both knew well, French forces amassed around Saint-Domingue, flaring rebellion. The old, comfortable enemy of France seemed to rattle the bars of Amiens. Peace stretched thin and Courtney kept weighing the terrible scale of it against war. Conflict meant the possibility of sudden death by pistol shot or cannon fire; no man should yearn for that. But it also meant stability and livelihood.

The more he dwelt on it, the more Courtney angered himself. In a cycle, he would condemn his self-pity and try to engage his mind and body in the cottage and its land. He worked alongside Mr Woods and his ward, Walter, dealing with the roof which leaked in all weather, clearing the ice-house in the back garden, auctioning some of the furniture and possessions that Mr Woods's nephew would no longer find use of. Whenever Nightingale visited – and it soon became a regular occurrence after his first stay – Courtney found he enjoyed regaling him with updates on the renovations. He would join them in the fields or in the cottage, sorting through artefacts consigned to the attic, until the old gunshot wound on his side became too painful.

Then, at the end of the day, they often dined at the Fisherman's Catch, the inn owned by Mr and Mrs Woods. Only once did Mrs Woods threaten to rock their drifting boat, when she mentioned how Nightingale looked so very different from the Gilray caricature. Courtney had nearly winced at the reminder of the unflattering cartoon of the major players of the *Ulysses* incident: the aghast faces of the Admiralty overseeing Lord Fairholme and Nightingale pulling at the ship's head and stern in a fiery tug-of-war. But the error had soon been forgotten in a host of dinners eaten at the Catch and an entire history of Courtney's life told by Mr and Mrs Woods, the people he still called 'Ma' and 'Pa'.

As much as the future was hazy, Courtney knew he had some semblance of a family on the island. More and more, Nightingale became another unconventional part of a picture already lacking tradition. Courtney eagerly awaited his visits, and he equally enjoyed how the previous bleakness seemed to lift from Nightingale. He would turn to him whilst working in the fields, catch his eye and smile, and feel fortunate that such a man wanted a life like this. Never once did Nightingale refuse his bed or his embrace.

But such fortune always had a note of bitterness. If Nightingale were not a man, Courtney could openly court him. He could not do so, beyond stolen glances in public or the knowledge that only they had. It was private, secret – sometimes so much that Courtney could not find words for it. When in fine weather, they circumnavigated the island on Nightingale's *Larkspur*, Courtney's mind returned to the *Scylla* again, that crucible where they had forged their connection. One day, they would have to talk of intimate feelings and uncertain futures, but now, Courtney simply wished for Nightingale's presence in any definition.

That, at least, was what he told himself as he lay beside him in the sanctity of their bed. With the leak fixed in the roof and the seams in the walls caulked like an old ship, the room was a little more habitable now. Nightingale always insisted he did not care about such luxuries as an intact ceiling – he had served on more porous vessels before – but Courtney desired every reason to make him want to stay. He had a fine house in Portsmouth, complete with his own wing in the manor. He also had a wife whose knowledge of Arthur Courtney, her husband's intimate acquaintance, was very vague.

Courtney barely knew how to broach that subject. He contemplated it whilst looking at Nightingale's sleeping form beside him. Running his fingers up his chest and into his unbound auburn hair, he tried to formulate the questions: *Does your wife know? How will we continue this? Am I enough for you?* Courtney knew they were ridiculous, born from doubt, but his youth kept raising its head, just as it had in front of the old house in Ryde. He could only think of the last time he had revealed his true self to another – a long time ago, before ascending the tenuous ladder of promotion. That time, with scars and bruises still welting on his skin, had almost upset his entire existence.

And from the small amount Nightingale had told him, Courtney knew of his own troubled past. The first man he had been drawn to – Tom, a stable-boy on his father's estate – had been hanged after a sham trial put on by his own father, Admiral Laurence Nightingale. Then, there had been Lieutenant Leroy Sawyer, a man Nightingale had grown up with, served with as a midshipman and then as officer on the *Lion*. He had died at the Nile, and Courtney knew he must still linger in Nightingale's heart. Courtney was not like Lieutenant Sawyer, in any way. The only thing they shared was a Nile medal; Nightingale had had one made for Sawyer, and then given his own to Courtney. It was wrapped, precious and untouchable, in Courtney's sea-chest.

Gently, in the early hours of the summer morning, Nightingale shifted and turned into Courtney's touch. His eyes fluttered and opened, slowly focusing. Groggily, he smiled and whispered, 'Are you well?'

Courtney nodded. 'I didn't mean to wake you,' he said softly. 'I thought I heard the roof leaking again. Go back to sleep.'

'Mm.' Nightingale rolled back over. Courtney settled down behind him and wrapped an affectionate arm about his waist. Close to him, Nightingale drifted away. Courtney held him, selfishly not wanting to let go. Gradually, the first hints of the sun fluttered through the window, where Courtney now noticed a new crack in the casement.

–

With rain and dark skies bringing the August night down early, Courtney and Nightingale ate at the Catch. Nightingale had become such a regular customer that his preferred meal – a cod pie and ale – was already being made, and he was no longer greeted with the wary looks of friends with a stranger in their midst. Courtney felt as relieved as Nightingale that they did not pry anymore: not about the Caribbean, not about the *Ulysses*, not about Nightingale's old life on the sea – and not why the captain and his former lieutenant were still companions.

At their table, nestled in the corner of the inn, Courtney tried to ignore the rest of the world, but truth be told, he still awoke to thoughts of veering winds and chiming watch-bells. He wished he could settle into this new routine, away from the sea, yet with so much uncertainty, he did not feel he belonged in this world from his youth. Much remained to be dealt with.

Across the table and the tankard of ale already placed before them, Nightingale caught his eye. He drew him back to the present with a small, 'You look well, Arthur.'

Courtney gave a thin smile. 'And you,' he replied. With a glance he wished he did not have to make, he reached over, touched Nightingale's wrist, and then took his mug from his hand. He poured him a drink and said, 'I'm glad you had a week spare. I wanted to speak with you.'

'Don't we always speak?' Nightingale accepted his mug back, allowing their fingers to brush again. The little moments of contact fuelled Courtney, though he always wanted more.

'Of course we do. But there is more to talk about than the cottage and the farm. I—' He paused as Walter trudged by with a plate of potatoes. When he was out of hearing distance, Courtney continued. 'This evening, at home, we'll speak. There are some things I want to be clear on.'

'Home?' Nightingale smiled.

'I suppose it is beginning to feel that way, yes. It is better than any other home I've had before. I only hope I can keep it.'

'Of course you will. That is a matter I've been meaning to speak about, anyway.'

Nightingale stopped again as Walter returned, this time setting their plates down before them. 'Free of charge, Artie,' Walter said, not for the first time.

Courtney sighed. 'I can't allow that again, Walter.'

'Ma insisted.' Of course she did. Mrs Woods had too big a heart for her own good.

'I shall pay, Walter,' Nightingale interceded.

'Hiram,' Courtney began, but Nightingale shook his head and handed over his shillings before he could protest anymore. 'I'm not an orphan needing charity,' Courtney said, once Walter was gone. 'Not anymore, anyway.'

'I want to help you, Arthur. With this and the upkeep of the cottage, if times become too hard.'

'I agreed to take it on, Hiram. It is my own issue. Don't trouble yourself about it.'

'I do. And I will.'

Courtney did not respond, unable to deny his embarrassment at Nightingale's outreach. He could never forget the rift between their two stations and backgrounds. One day, he feared, Nightingale might become frustrated with their imbalance.

They ate in silence with the rain strengthening outside, streaming down the window pane and beating upon the roof. Courtney did not look forward to the walk they'd have to make across the fields to get home, nor the leak that would have sprung through the thatch. Once he and Nightingale reached the cottage, it would not be any easier. Having to dictate and assign terms to what they shared was beyond what Courtney believed he could do. Laying it out before them, like a sea chart upon a cabin table, might highlight the dangerous reefs and waters they'd have to navigate. He was unsure if Nightingale would want to bear more terrible weather in an already troubled life.

He was so engrossed in those frets that he did not notice the door open. The only thing he realised was the sudden cold breeze winding into the inn – and then Nightingale was laying down his mug and rising slowly to his feet.

'What is it?' Courtney asked, looking up at his suddenly pale face. He turned to see the cloaked figure standing at the door. The folds of the cape dripped muddy water onto the flagstones, creating a dirty puddle. As if to chastise the stranger, Mr Woods hurried from the kitchen but Nightingale cut him off. The woman – for a woman she was – removed her hood and even then, it took Courtney a few seconds to recognise her.

'Louisa, my dear,' Nightingale rushed. He grasped her hands and she stared past his shoulder without reaction. Her jaw was clenched so tight Courtney thought her teeth might break. For some reason, her eyes found his and Courtney felt ice run down his spine. 'Whatever is it?' Nightingale asked.

All gazes were now on them. Louisa dropped Nightingale's hands and stepped around him. Courtney stood, frozen, as she came close. 'Mr Courtney,' she finally managed, and his skin drew tight. 'My brother and

I knew no one else to suggest. You and Hiram have been summoned to London, to an appointment at the Admiralty Office.'

'Whatever is the matter?' Nightingale pressed, touching her arm. Despite the situation, jealousy simmered in Courtney's chest.

But Louisa did not look at Nightingale, as if by one glance her glassy exterior would shatter and she would weep in front of strangers. She stared at Courtney, who instantly felt formless guilt flood him. Some disaster had occurred and he had been distracting her husband whilst it unfolded.

'It is my father,' she said simply.

Chapter Five: One Misstep

The sun struggled valiantly over the horizon as the carriage reached its final destination. Rain still lashed the coach so when Courtney peered out the window, the outside world was a smear of amorphous forms, melting in the downpour. Anticipation and the need to stretch his legs won over his dismay at the weather. Not waiting for the servant who had arrived with Louisa, he opened the door and ducked into the wet morning.

Before him, the vaulted arches and pillars separating Whitehall from the hallowed courtyard of the Admiralty Office were at once a welcome and a forbidding sight. They were familiar from countless times visiting in fruitless hopes of a commission, but now anxiety churned in his gut, heightened by its emptiness. Twice they had stopped at coach-houses to change horses and it had been four hours since he had eaten a meagre bread roll and ham. Necessity and Louisa's insistence had driven them hard along the road to London.

Helped by her servant, she followed Courtney into the rain. As if fearing the walls of the carriage could hear, she had said nothing beyond her message at the Fisherman's Catch. Now, she clutched her hat in the rising wind and as soon as Nightingale had exited the carriage, strode towards the sentry on duty. The man did not question her presence. They passed unhindered into the courtyard and the old feelings crept over Courtney, that small, prickling sensation of being in the midst of greatness. The Lords of the Admiralty, those imperious figures who had the power to advance or destroy his career without even knowing he existed, loomed large. Every complicated decision in the bureaucratic, tangled web of the naval administration took place here and in Somerset House where the Navy Office resided.

'Are you certain my presence is wished for?' Nightingale suddenly said, voicing the thoughts Courtney had about himself too.

'I would not have brought you here if not,' Louisa retorted, her tone tightened by whatever distress had occurred.

From the entrance, a clerk hurried down the slick steps. 'Mrs Nightingale,' he said as he approached. 'I have been sent to accompany you. Lieutenant Courtney, Mr Nightingale, if you would follow me.'

Instead of crossing the grand column-shrouded threshold, he guided them across the courtyard and through a side door. The carpeted hall was a relief from the rain which became a muted cadence on the stone, but the interior did not match the splendour of the outside. The simple functionality and the lack of decoration told Courtney they were in a secluded wing of the building, perhaps for the servants. This was not a journey designed to impress, as so much of the central heart of London was meant to – and so he knew what awaited at the end would be dirty and unglamorous.

At last, a door opened into a sumptuous hall. Yellow damask lined the walls where monumental naval paintings hung in gilded frames. Courtney feared he was marking the soft carpeted floor with his wet shoes, but he did not have time to worry for long, before the clerk stopped outside one of the many offices. A quick knock and then they were all bid to enter.

Inside, mahogany furnishings and trinkets glittered in the grey light. A middle-aged man sat at his desk, looking harried by the paperwork swamping him. Two other men stood by the large window: one dressed in a simple coat and trousers, one in a post-captain's uniform.

At Courtney, Nightingale and Louisa's entrance, both of them turned. Courtney stopped in his tracks. The frustratingly familiar face of Captain Bryant looked back at him. Bryant's lips tightened into a thin line as he drew himself taller, straightening his epaulette-decorated shoulders.

'Close the door behind you, Mr Jenkins,' the seated man said, drawing Courtney's attention away. 'I will send for you when we are done.'

Jenkins vanished from the room. With the door closed, they were left with the pattering rain and the clock on the mantelpiece mimicking its rhythm. Slowly, deliberately, Bryant moved from the window and came to stand beside Courtney, one step closer to the central desk.

'Lieutenant Courtney, yes?' their host suddenly said. He put down his pen and fixed Courtney with a stern gaze.

'Uh,' Courtney said, then cleared his throat. The reappearance of Captain Bryant had stifled all his words. 'Yes, sir.'

'My name is Sir Rodney. Please, Mrs Nightingale, sit. You must be weary from the journey.'

Louisa obeyed, sinking into the chair opposite Sir Rodney. The man at the window moved to lay a hand on her shoulder which, to Courtney's surprise, she took.

'This is Robert Haywood, owner of the Bristol shipyard,' Sir Rodney introduced. Of course, Louisa's elder brother, and Nightingale's brother-in-law. 'I believe you already know my own brother, Captain Jerome Bryant.'

Courtney's stomach tightened. A tumble of curses raced through his head. He had had no idea that Captain Bryant, a man who he had argued with and implicitly accused of bad seamanship, had a sibling in the Admiralty Office.

'It is good to meet you, Mr Haywood,' Courtney said, awkwardly taking his outstretched hand. Fumbling for words, he managed to continue, 'I hope you are well, Captain Bryant.'

'I have been, Lieutenant,' Bryant replied, curtly not wishing the same upon him.

'I shan't apologise for calling you here, Lieutenant, nor making you travel such a length in this weather,' Sir Rodney said. 'The situation demands it of you.'

'No, sir. I... Yes, sir.'

'Mr Courtney, are you aware of the situation in Malta?'

'I—' Courtney gaped for a few seconds before resolutely shutting his mouth again. He had kept up with the situation in Europe but suddenly, the entire world beyond the room seemed to disappear. *Malta*, he thought, and wished Nightingale would whisper something to him. 'We, uh, Britain... Under the terms of the Treaty of Amiens, Malta was to be a free port for commerce. Britain was to evacuate her troops and the island was to return to the Knights of St John.'

'Your use of "was to" is very telling.' Sir Rodney fell silent again, his dark eyes boring into Courtney. Courtney was unsure whether to risk another word or not. 'Britain has not evacuated her troops and it seems neither will she in the immediate future, not without France making a similar concession. Malta occupies a key strategic position, certainly following Bonaparte's actions in Egypt. And so the question of Malta remains potentially inflammatory.

'Two weeks ago, Sir William Haywood and Hugo Baptiste were due to arrive in Valletta to discuss the situation. Their ship, the *Loyal*, has not been seen from land or sea, and no information from any source has been forthcoming. We fear – we believe – the ship has been lost or captured.'

Courtney remembered Sir William. He had dined with him and a host of Trinidad's officials then, within a space of days, had to defend Nightingale's actions on the *Fénix* to him. He had had a bad impression of the man until he had aided in the *Ulysses* court martial.

Two years on, peace had nominally been written across Europe, but with Bonaparte's movements in Elba and, more recently, in Piedmont, the thinness of the paper was showing. There was a likelihood of the ship being wrecked, perhaps pooped by an Atlantic roller, but there were darker possibilities too. The *Ulysses* affair had taught Courtney that wherever diplomacy and politics stretched, so too did deception.

'You understand that if this loss was to become wider knowledge, it would upset the scales that the treaty rests upon,' Sir Rodney continued. 'One side may blame another, even if both are innocent. Debates in the Lords and the Commons have already been forced because of public criticism towards the peace and its terms. War always threatens to be one misstep away. Do you understand, Mr Courtney?'

'Yes, sir,' he could only think to say.

'As soon as I became aware of this situation, I sent for Mr Haywood. He offered his assistance in planning a voyage to locate their where-abouts. Usually, it would be the responsibility of your captain to inform you of such matters but, with the particular nature of the orders, it was thought best to inform you before the outset.'

Courtney had thought for a brief moment that he was on the verge of being promoted to a commander. It was a short and bewildering second, full of ecstasy, relief that at last his sacrifices had led to more than a distaste of a superior officer, tempered by anxiety of such an important mission. All of those reactions were dashed by Sir Rodney handing a sealed packet to his brother.

'You shall join the *Lysander* at Portsmouth,' Sir Rodney continued. 'She is a vessel of Mr Haywood's to be refitted as a sixth-rate of His Majesty's Navy and entered into the service. Mr Haywood informs us that part of her current crew is formed of Royal Navy men, but she will need to be supplemented further with sailors who can sufficiently hand, reef and steer. He suggested you, Mr Courtney, to act as her lieutenant.'

Bryant would, of course, be the captain. It was not only disappointment at being passed over again that simmered in Courtney's chest, but the prospect of working under the control of Bryant.

'Thank you, Mr Haywood,' Courtney said by rote. 'I would be honoured.'

'We wish to keep the information as quiet as possible,' Sir Rodney insisted. 'I do not have to impress upon you the necessity of discretion, and neither shall I, as I could not impress it upon you firmly enough. On board the *Lysander*, only the officers shall be aware of the truth and of the destination.'

'Yes, sir. Of course, sir.'

Bryant did not say anything. Obviously Sir Rodney had taken him aside beforehand and given him all of the details, then sealed them up prettily in his packet of orders. Courtney glanced to him, unable to deny the pulse of resentment, and then past to Louisa and Mr Haywood. He saw two people whose future peace had been put into their hands. Their future peace, and perhaps all of Europe's too.

'If I may, sir.' Nightingale suddenly stepped forward from where he had been standing silently by the door.

'Speak freely, Mr Nightingale,' Sir Rodney prompted.

'If it is possible, I would like to be entered onto the *Lysander*'s books for the voyage. Sir William Haywood is my father-in-law. He has always been good to me.'

Courtney turned to Nightingale, seeing he was perfectly serious. He did not know if the thought of Nightingale on board balanced his agitation at Bryant or made him more nervous. He felt the weight of Sir Rodney and Bryant's eyes on them and even heard Louisa utter a quiet, 'Hiram...' before Sir Rodney spoke again.

'Mr Nightingale, we brought you here at your brother-in-law and your wife's insistence that you be party to this information. Your service was not in our estimations.'

'I have served in smaller ships, sir, so the cramped space will not bother me. And I shall pay my own way, if that is a concern.'

Sir Rodney looked at his brother. Bryant opened his mouth to speak, but was cut off by Mr Haywood.

'Mr Nightingale has been skippering one of my ships,' he said. 'He is a valuable part of our company and of my family. My father always spoke highly of him.'

'I do not doubt that, Mr Haywood,' Sir Rodney acceded. 'As you say, Mr Nightingale is not in the navy any longer and so we cannot strictly order him on or off the *Lysander*. I shall put the question of a guest to Captain Bryant.'

Bryant was silent for a while. He looked between his brother, Nightingale, and Mr Haywood, weighing his responsibilities and the desire not to offend the man helping to finance and outfit this venture. When he finally spoke, Courtney knew the words coming out of his mouth were not the ones he wished to say. 'As long as Mr Nightingale understands that his wellbeing is my responsibility and thus he will obey my every order, then, yes, he would be welcome.'

'Very well,' Sir Rodney said. 'I believe that is everything that needs to be said. I wish you gentlemen fortune and hope to see you returned with Sir William and Hugo Baptiste in one sound piece.'

Sir Rodney stood and, as if on puppet-strings, so too did Louisa. Mr Haywood took her arm and, tilting his head at Bryant, guided her silently from the room. Courtney followed with Nightingale at his side, suddenly wanting to escape the stifling building. He walked quickly out into the teeming rain until they were finally beyond the walls and ears of the Admiralty. Then he turned to Nightingale and hissed, 'I didn't know he had a brother in the bloody Admiralty Office.'

The look on Nightingale's face immediately told him he should not have said it. Courtney swallowed and attempted to quickly change tack. 'I mean,' he said, 'I am sorry for… For what has happened.'

'You do us a great deed by searching for our father, Lieutenant,' Mr Haywood said. 'I am sorry that you couldn't be the commander.'

'I didn't mean to offend.'

Mr Haywood shook his head.

'Come,' Nightingale said suddenly. 'It has been a wearying night and all of us have barely eaten a morsel or drunk a drop. Let us stop at an inn before thinking of any further travel.'

'I would like to rest,' Louisa remarked. 'Robert, can you accompany me to Cavendish Square where Father…' There passed a small second where her composure wobbled at the mention of Sir William, and then it was gone, wiped away by the rain. 'Where Father has his rooms.'

They had not stopped for hours on end. Courtney's clothes were plastered to him and he felt as miserable as the sun struggling to emerge through the downpour. He knew he should be grateful for a peacetime commission, and that expectation made him even more miserable. Part of him wished to follow Louisa and Mr Haywood and collapse into a bed, resettle his thoughts into a more sensible frame.

'Are you all right?' Nightingale asked after Courtney had stood there mournfully for a minute, feeling sorry for himself.

Courtney nodded numbly. 'I will be.'

'I suppose that was the Captain Bryant you quarrelled with in the Caribbean?'

'Yes.'

'He may not even recall the incident. Times have changed since last year.'

'Before he came to the Caribbean, he was sent ashore by the demands of the Spithead mutineers,' Courtney said. 'They accused him of ill-treatment. I hardly think he's changed his tune.'

Five years previously, in 1797, sailors of the Channel Fleet had demanded better treatment and pay. There had been a handful of struggles and negotiation difficulties, including the banishment of unpopular officers ashore. Captain Jerome Bryant had been one of them. No wonder, Courtney thought, he had been sent to the Caribbean, consigned to the most unfavourable station in the world.

Nightingale did not respond. He took Courtney's elbow and guided him away from the Admiralty. Courtney sighed and leant into him. 'I should be comforting you, not you comforting me,' he said. 'I am sorry for your father-in-law. We'll find him, and I won't let Captain Bryant get in the way of that.'

'Don't... Try not to be so abrasive towards him. You shall both be pursuing the same end.'

Courtney huffed. Where Captain Bryant had received the honour of command due to his brother's influence, Courtney wagered he had only gained the position for the want of secrecy. Bryant must have been chafing at the necessity. And where a man thought he had been wronged, he could act carelessly and bitterly. Courtney knew the sensation well.

He tried to heed Nightingale's neutrality. He knew the older man had mellowed some of his own immaturity in the Caribbean which formed him into a better soul. For the first time, he had felt as though someone understood him, despite their gap in stations and ranks. Continually having to battle against judgements and expectations exhausted Courtney, and he wished he would not take it so much to heart every time.

He hated feeling like the junior officer again, stood before a panel of his social and naval betters, having to convince them of his worth.

Making their way through the miserable weather, Courtney stayed silent, not wanting to drag Nightingale into this doubt, too. It was only when reaching the inn that Courtney remembered the talk he had meant to have with Nightingale at the cottage. The moment had passed now, ducking behind the parapet as it always did. More important matters loomed.

Chapter Six: Good Fortune

With only three days left until the *Lysander* would weigh anchor, Courtney had feared his clothes would not be prepared in time. The tailor in Gosport had evidently become out of practice in working with the dress of the navy, for he had delayed and given excuses every time Courtney had entered his shop. But at last, on the cusp of sailing, Courtney found himself back in a cleaned and pressed version of his undress uniform. With Nightingale sitting by the window and Mr Ramsey, the tailor, directing him like a dance-master, he turned around in front of the mirror, once again seeing himself as Lieutenant Arthur Courtney.

'I had to loosen the trousers a little,' Ramsey was saying, 'and the cloth was as mould-filled as Stilton cheese, but upon the whole, it fits as though it were new.'

It had been almost a year since Courtney had last worn his uniform, and its time in a sea-chest and a leaking attic had made harsh work of it. He admitted Ramsey, as late as he was, had done well with the blue frock coat, white waistcoat and breeches: the same he had worn since he passed his lieutenant's examination.

'Your dress uniform has been adjusted to the same measurements, Lieutenant Courtney,' Ramsay continued. 'As requested, you have two new pairs of shirts, and trousers. I don't believe we have spoken of payment yet.'

'No, we haven't,' Courtney replied.

'It can be charged to my account here,' Nightingale spoke up.

'No, I couldn't ask you to do that,' Courtney said, turning to him. 'You have already purchased another spyglass for me.'

'I want to,' Nightingale insisted, just as he had about the cottage. 'I won't have you refuse.'

With his spare clothes folded in a satchel beneath his arm, Courtney exited the tailor into the dull morning. Rylance, Nightingale's ever faithful steward, waited for them and Courtney took pity on his eagerness to help by giving him his effects. Nightingale had always come alone to the cottage, meaning that Rylance had not been able to perform his zealous duty of serving Nightingale. Rylance had immediately volunteered for the *Lysander*. Courtney liked his presence as a reminder of the *Scylla*.

Outside, a chill had fallen and he felt a stab of sympathy and embarrassment to see an ageing legless man across the street, sitting on the cobbles. He was talking to a lady and her husband who had stopped and Courtney overheard him say he had lost the limb at Copenhagen. He was just one of the many naval veterans littered across Gosport and all the seaside towns and cities of England.

'You shouldn't feel the need to pay for me,' Courtney said in a low voice to Nightingale at his side.

'Nonsense. I said that I wanted to. What was the name of the tavern where the bosun and Mr Pascoe said to meet them?'

'The Bucking Horse. I hope to God they've found some men.' Courtney paused. 'Don't read me wrong, Pascoe's merchant crew will be good for the *Lysander* – they know her, after all – but she's a sixth-rate now, not a merchant ship, so she'll need a crew of at least one hundred and fifty. Even with the reduced numbers the Admiralty have allowed us, we'll need a fair amount.'

In a peacetime vessel, it had not been thought necessary to employ the same amount of men. Perhaps it was for money's sake, perhaps it was under the expectation they would not need gun crews. The presence of fifteen marines assigned to the *Lysander*, under a Sergeant Dawes, struck a strange note beneath that assumption. Marines played a dual role in the naval service; they were deployed during battle on ship and on land, but also formed a barrier between the officers and the men. Trouble could come from within or from without.

Courtney had been aboard the *Lysander* a handful of times, more than once whilst the carpenters and caulkers and shipwrights had been crawling over her. Her main deck now supported twenty-two nine-pounder guns, and on the quarterdeck, four eighteen-pounder carronades from her merchant days. For the sake of privacy and convenience, she had been brought into the Royal Dockyards, away from public eye, but Courtney had no doubt word would spread in these stale times.

He hoped it had spread just enough to entice men into the crew.

The sign for the Bucking Horse squeaked and swayed in the rising wind as Courtney held the door for Nightingale and ushered him in. The interior was dim, lit by a handful of guttering lanterns that didn't quite reach the four walls. Men murmured in dark corners and curious, thin faces turned towards them both as they picked their way through the tables. Courtney peered around for the bosun, Macdonald, in the midst of this grizzled company which stank of ale and pipe smoke. A shout grew in the guts of the building, but no one twitched in response. Neither did Courtney until he heard Macdonald's voice trying to drown it out.

Without thought, he shoved open the door to the card room and strode into a space choked with anger. Macdonald stood by an empty fireplace, arms outstretched towards two clamouring men. Their fellows and a couple of red-jacketed marines had them by the shoulders, holding them apart like two snapping dogs in a pit. When one suddenly broke loose, Courtney threw his satchel to the side and grabbed him by the back of his jacket. The sailor tried to swing around, fist raised.

'Lay a hand on an officer of the Royal Navy and I'll have you flogged until your bones are bare,' Courtney snarled.

The man struggled before his eyes fell on Courtney's uniform. The fight sapped from him, though he still grimaced when Courtney shoved him away. Hand resting upon his sword-belt, Courtney looked about at them all, caught in the frozen positions of their conflict. There were nearly fifty of them packed into the small room, most gathered around the squabbling men to ghoulishly watch, the others dotted around the tables. Enough to bolster the *Lysander*'s books, but their quality was still to be judged.

'I am Lieutenant Courtney of the *Lysander*,' he announced. 'I understand you are here to sign on. I assume Mr Macdonald and Mr Pascoe have spoken to you of your good fortune?'

Blank faces stared back at him.

'Your good fortune,' Courtney repeated. 'The good fortune that has offered you a place on a seabound vessel rather than rotting in the gutters where your only luck would be that one day the pox or the drink might have mercy and end your misery. Tell me how many men here can stand straight.'

No voice replied, but Courtney could see the answer in the half-empty flagons and the bleary eyes.

'There is a man on the street without a leg,' he continued. 'He lost it at Copenhagen, fighting under Nelson. The peace has been a lottery. It easily could have been one of you out there, no doubt on the edge of freezing to death come winter. And yet you are in here squabbling like cats and drinking away the little pay in your pocket. Mr Macdonald, what was the reason of this argument?'

Christian Macdonald, their bosun, turned to him, surprise in his eyes. He was an older man, nearing sixty at least, and Courtney wondered if he'd ever seen an officer act like this. Courtney barely recognised himself; this was not a side he had dredged up for years, since before he had to preen himself in those rigid appearances.

'A family feud, I believe, sir,' Macdonald said. 'Mr Paterson took issue with Mr Arnold.'

'Mr Paterson, Mr Arnold,' Courtney said, and they came forward. Paterson had been the one he had grabbed, evidently a former seaman with a long, tied pigtail and a tattoo of a bird emerging from the collar that had been ripped. Curiously, Courtney could see Arnold had the same on his forearm. 'You shall sign on under my division. As soon as the *Lysander* sails, you shall have head duties until we lose sight of England.'

Neither of them said a word. Courtney could have easily enough turned them loose but he had a point to prove, and the *Lysander* needed seafaring experience.

'Mr Pascoe,' he said again, now the frothing foam of the argument had begun to disperse. 'I assume you have the rolls for the *Lysander*. I shall oversee the men making their mark, if they wish to still serve.'

Gregory Pascoe, the *Lysander*'s former skipper, turned to him and nodded. He had been standing on the fringes of the clamour, a barely concealed scowl on his face. It did not fade even now as he gave the papers to Courtney. He had generously offered his services to the navy as the *Lysander*'s master, being so intimate with her, but Courtney knew that this simple handing over of documents represented the loss of his full authority. Courtney chose not to say any more to him, not yet.

He also did not want to put too much weight on his impromptu speech having any effect on the men, but he sat and watched as each of them approached the muster rolls. Paterson and Arnold joined, along with the fellows who had tried to split them apart. One of them, a sheepish young lad named Mr Lynde, even tried to apologise for them, knuckles to his forehead in a salute. Courtney waved him off.

More crosses and shaky signatures were added beside the men's names and Courtney counted them in his head. Forty-seven able-bodied men joined the *Lysander*, and, with some hope, there would be more over the next few days. Many of them professed previous years spent on the sea, as merchant sailors or Royal Navy men. It was a better effort than a press-gang could have achieved, dragging unwilling folk from their homes and their workplaces and merchant ships to populate the fleet. It was a wretched reality which Courtney had witnessed, and taken part in, many a time.

But, as they looked at him and called him 'sir', Courtney wondered if they realised that. He had not spoken hypothetically to them; poverty and hardship were not imaginary devils to him, as they weren't for so many of these men. He wondered if they saw him as another lieutenant on a pedestal, untouchable by reality, and not the tarpaulin officer he was. Turn the cycle of the world again, and he might be the one brawling in an alehouse.

He was pulled away from his thoughts by the next men approaching the table. Courtney sat up straighter, frowning. Nightingale appeared at his side from where he had been sitting quietly by the fire. 'Mr Smythe, Obi,' Courtney said. 'What the devil are you doing here?'

The two made a strange pair. Smythe, the seventeen-year-old midshipman of the *Scylla*, pale-cheeked and fair-haired, beside the man everyone had always only known as 'Obi', considering he had dropped his former master's surname after fleeing an Antigua plantation. There was no greater representation of the navy's medley of sailors. Many Jacks did not care where their shipmates hailed from, as long as they could be relied upon to work the ship and act as good company. Courtney had served alongside, and commanded, many colours, ages and backgrounds.

It was an equality which did not necessarily extend beyond the berth deck.

Before him, Smythe smiled sheepishly, running his fingers around the rim of his hat. He still wore his midshipman's uniform. 'Hello, Lieutenant Courtney, sir. Captain... Mr Nightingale, sir. Sorry, sir, I know it isn't proper. But I heard about the *Lysander* and that Captain Bryant was commanding her. I wondered if there might be a place for me.'

'The *Lysander* is not carrying any midshipmen, Mr Smythe.'

'I have a letter of service detailing my experience on the *Scylla*, sir, and my father has written to...'

'I am not the person to speak to about that. You shall have to speak with Captain Bryant.'

'Could you put in a word for me, sir?'

Courtney nearly laughed. 'I don't think my word will mean much to Captain Bryant, but I shall try when I see him this evening.'

Smythe's face brightened. 'Thank you, sir. I am so near to my lieutenant's examination, you see, sir, and I thought that... Thank you, sir.'

'And you, Obi?' Courtney asked.

'I wish to sign on too, sir.'

'When the treaty at Amiens was signed, Obi came back to England on the *Lily* with me, Lieutenant Courtney, sir,' Smythe interjected. 'I promised to help him, seeing as he'd never set foot in England before. I hated the thought of him being shipped off to the Caribbean again. I kept my eyes open for any packet ships or naval vessels that were due to sail, and listened in on my father's talks every now and then. Obi was the one who heard about the *Lysander*, here in Portsmouth.'

Despite having served in the height of battle and suffered under the awful pall of yellow fever, Smythe remained remarkably innocent of the world's troubles. Courtney imagined that supporting a former slave had not won him many friends, unless Smythe's father was, like Sir William Haywood, a staunch abolitionist.

'You'll be a great aid to the *Lysander*, Obi,' Courtney said, turning back to the man after Smythe's enthusiastic chatter. 'We need as many able hands as we can muster.'

Courtney had been the one to add Obi to the *Scylla*'s rolls in the Caribbean. He did so again now, for a different ship, a different crew, a different journey. Smythe dropped his letter of recommendation into Courtney's hand and then hurried out with Obi before Courtney could possibly change his mind. Courtney turned to Nightingale when he was gone and raised his eyebrows.

'Mr Smythe's father is a post-captain,' Nightingale said. 'Perhaps he knows Captain Bryant.'

'Everyone seems to know Captain Bryant, or have connections somewhere.'

'Henry Smythe is a good lad, Arthur, you know that. We served with him.'

'I'm not denying that. He's a talented young man, but I don't know what Captain Bryant will say – about him or Obi.'

At last, the final man made his mark and in their absence, Courtney allowed himself to relax, though his mind already assigned men to stations and messes. He made an internal note to keep Obi close to Paterson and Arnold, perhaps a firm, guiding hand for them.

Nightingale brought himself and Courtney a steaming mug of tea and joined him again. Courtney sipped the drink, grateful that his first act as a lieutenant again was over. Quite what impression he had made on the men he was not sure. On the *Scylla*, the crew had known him well. These were new sailors who did not know him at all.

As if reading his mind, Nightingale smiled and said, 'I remember when I first met you, Arthur. You had a great black bruise around your eye from breaking up a fight. I wondered what a brute I had as my first lieutenant.'

Courtney huffed. 'They probably wonder the same thing.'

'None of them left the opportunity to join the *Lysander*.'

'If they stay in line, they'll be a great help.'

Courtney thought back to how he had joined the navy. As a child, he had fled from the Isle of Wight with Jane, tired of their parents' meddling even with Mr and Mrs Woods. One of his first acts of freedom had, ironically, been to join HMS *Grampus*, a squat and lumbering sixty-four-gunner. In that lowly position before the mast he had stayed, on various vessels, until a fleeting position as a midshipman. He had nearly condemned himself to the lower berth forever because of Mr Midshipman Montgomery Lowe and Garrick Walker.

Courtney had not been entirely honest with Nightingale about those years – or to the panel who had tested him for his advancement to lieutenant.

He would not dredge that up now. Instead, he concentrated on the one idea he had suddenly become certain of. 'Well,' he said, 'something has come of all this.'

'What is that?' Nightingale asked.

'I think I have just convinced myself of the fortune of this voyage too.'

–

Inside the walls of the Grampus, *more than five hundred men lived, worked and slept. When Courtney had seen her in the harbour at Portsmouth, surrounded by smaller vessels, she had resembled a manor that had been turned on its side and floated. Two decks packed with guns made her appear dangerous and intrepid, a symbol of the Royal Navy that Courtney had heard so many stories of along the shore at Ryde. Officers in gold brocade and gleaming blue coats had signed his name onto the muster rolls, noting down his age (thirteen, he thought, but he had said fourteen, considering his birthday approached), lanky height, thin chest and strong arms. He knew he did not look like them – but he was there to be a sailor, not a man decorated with awards.*

They had assigned him to the forecastle division, with no description of what was expected of him. But Courtney was accustomed to finding work for himself and dealing with all types of men. At his mess, boys of twelve mixed with grizzled sailors who had spent decades on the sea, alongside folks from as far away as the Americas and the corners of Europe. Courtney strung his hammock beside a Pole and an Orkneyman. He soon came to realise that language mattered naught; as long as a man knew the words for the masts and the sails and the Articles of War, that would be their common tongue.

And that common tongue could be sharp. During his first few days, Courtney had fumbled a brace during tacking and knocked into his fellow men, hauling on the line. The scolding he had received from the mid on watch, Lowe, had been nothing compared to the lashing of the other seamen in his division. Never again had he made the same mistake.

That was how he coped as the weeks passed, accompanying a convoy of merchant vessels south. Courtney barely knew their destination or their purpose. He had simply known, when standing at the Portsmouth docks, that he had to set foot upon a naval ship's decks. No more could he stand the looming shadows of his mother and father or the pall of misery and violence they dragged with them. It had been freeing to leave the shores of England; his one regret had been leaving Jane behind, but he had vowed to send money back to her and to their aunt and uncle, with whom she now resided.

'One day,' she had said before he had departed, 'I shall follow you also.'

Back there, it had been nothing but survival, day by day not knowing whether they would see the next morning. Their conditions had improved since running from home, but that action had embroiled in Courtney the need to keep going – and so he had, into the crowded belly of the Grampus.

Onboard her, he had found a place, and an identity beyond the shame of his parents. For the first time, he had seen a future where he was not dying on the streets. He did not care that he was still running from his life in England.

And then he had met Garrick Walker.

On the Grampus, there were more barriers beyond the division of captain's cabin, wardroom, gunroom and berth deck. The men in each mess watched their fellows' backs and often, competition grew amidst the forecastle sailors and the afterguard and those who manned the tops. The waisters were the least skilled of all the men aboard and often performed the drudging, menial labour.

That was how Courtney crossed Walker's path. After gunnery drill one day, with the metal of the sixty-four cannons still warm to the touch, the boy had been cleaning. A group of his fellows had been with him and at first, Courtney had ignored them. They had jested and jibed amongst themselves and he had tried to find a quiet spot to practise his next letter home to Jane. After only a few years of writing, his hand was still cramped and scrawled. Under the glow of a dim lantern, he attempted again to tell her of his journey so far: two months at sea in what felt like a floating city, full of all the men of the world.

He had barely written a paragraph when a dirty rag fell onto the scrap of paper. Courtney frowned and lifted the fabric with the end of his pencil. The larboard waisters turned away with a snicker, but the boy to starboard looked down in shame. Courtney sighed. He told himself not to get involved – he had learnt young not to poke his nose into other people's business if he did not want it to be broken off – but, despairing of ever finishing his letter, he walked over to the tall boy with the rag still outstretched.

'This yours?' he asked.

The boy gave a small nod and took his cleaning cloth back. Courtney should have left it as that. Something made him stay. Perhaps he thought of the lad from Ryde who had always been berated by his parents and talked to with no more respect than the dirt they came from. Just like Jane, not everyone had the mind or capability to speak for themselves.

'Can you read and write?' he found himself asking.

The boy's eyes flashed in surprise. His hand ceased its movements on the cannon's marked crest of King George.

'Your alphabet,' Courtney continued as if he was dim-witted. 'Reading and writing. Can you?'

'I...' The boy cleared his throat. 'Yes, I can write.'

'When you're done with Fury, could you see if this is right?'

'Fury?'

'Fury,' Courtney said, indicating the great gun. 'Her name. It's on her carriage.'

The boy looked down and seemed, for the first time, to notice the chalked letters beside the cannon's wheel. He looked at it for a long while and Courtney wondered if he had lied about being able to read. But then, a small smile touched his mouth and he said, 'Goddesses of vengeance. In the Greek myths.'

'Pardon?' Courtney asked with a frown.

'The Furies. That's what the gun is named after, yes?'

'I don't think the men know that much, nipper.'

The boy's smile grew and for some reason, Courtney echoed it. From a distance, the lad had not looked like much, just another of the ungainly and anonymous landsmen in the waist, but now that he smiled, Courtney saw that he had well-kept teeth and unblemished skin. His red hair was perfectly pulled back into a short tie and his shirt, though stained from his dirty work, was embroidered elaborately about the collar.

Across from them, the other waisters snickered again and Courtney shot them a harsh look. 'Don't mind them,' he said to the boy. 'What's your name?'

'Walker,' he replied. 'Garrick Walker.'

Walker held out a hand. Courtney looked at it; he had never shaken hands with someone else before. Smiling, he took it and said, 'I'm Artie. Artie Courtney.'

'Pleased to meet you, Artie.'

He had sat with Walker as he finished cleaning Fury, and then, in the time before Courtney's watch began again, they went through Courtney's short letter. Walker pointed out words he had misspelt and suggested sentences that were far more verbose than Courtney's had been. Courtney knew that Jane would wonder what the devil had come over him, but he enjoyed Walker's enthusiasm and the personality that appeared away from the laughter of the other boys and men.

When he returned to deck for the first dog watch, he wondered if he would ever interact with Walker again. He did not need to; he had his own fellows in his mess and his division. But he did not like to think of the boy being hounded by abusers. More for Walker's sake, he hoped they would see each other again amidst the crowd of five hundred men.

Chapter Seven: Overboard

31 August 1802

For the third time, Courtney leant across the small table and rolled the edges of the chart back. The cabin was barely moving in the smooth waters south of St Catherine's Point but these papers had not been consulted for some time and kept trying to fold closed. Under his hand lay the inked swathes of the English Channel beside the wide expanse of the northern Atlantic and the distant innards of the Mediterranean Sea. Seeing the journey mapped out before him did not make it look any easier.

'What I am about to tell you,' Captain Bryant said to his assembled officers, 'must not leave this cabin. No doubt you are wondering why we have been sent out during peacetime in a ship of war. I have been given permission to tell you, although with the condition it is not spread.'

Courtney did not know why he was making such a drama of it. Only three men in the cabin were unaware of the orders: Mr Pascoe; Henry Smythe, successfully onboard through his letters of recommendation; and Second Lieutenant Ralph Godfrey, previously of Bryant's *Meridian*, a younger man than Courtney. The others – himself, Nightingale and Bryant – knew the details of their journey.

'His Majesty's Ship *Loyal* has not arrived at her destination in Valletta,' Bryant continued, 'and there have been no sightings of her since the beginning of August. Many vessels are accepted as missing for many reasons, but the *Loyal* would be a significant loss. She carried Sir William Haywood and Hugo Baptiste.'

Smythe drew a breath and looked across at Courtney and Nightingale. He had served on the *Scylla* during her infamous time in Trinidad and had met Sir William. Pascoe, meanwhile, stared blankly at Bryant.

'Who are these men?' he asked.

'I am not finished, Mr Pascoe,' Bryant said shortly. 'Sir William and Monsieur Baptiste were due to discuss the troubles in Malta that have ensued from the Amiens treaty. For them to go missing could result in a diplomatic crisis.'

The silence that followed was only broken by the creaking of the *Lysander*'s timbers and the waves outside the cabin. Courtney glanced at Pascoe and watched his expression of irritation at being shushed by Bryant turn into reflection. Smythe shifted awkwardly and Courtney wondered if he regretted asking to come aboard.

'A diplomatic crisis,' Pascoe eventually said. 'If both an English and a French diplomat are missing, why would one side blame the other?'

It was a pertinent question, although perhaps not one which should have come from a warrant officer. Pascoe was not a navy man used to the rigid hierarchy which could sometimes be even more rigid with a strict captain such as Bryant. Courtney watched Bryant seemingly decide whether to inform him of this or not, tightening his jaw and giving a strained nod.

'That is not for us to question, Mr Pascoe,' Bryant replied. 'And so far, neither side is blaming the other. Word has not spread. We have been tasked with finding what the fate of the *Loyal* is. It may be innocent, it may not. Hence the reason for our secrecy.'

Secrecy which now involved an ever broadening circle of men. In a flash of spite, Courtney thought it would have been easier, quieter, if he had gained the command.

'Our journey,' Bryant continued, reaching over to smooth the corners of the map back again, 'is towards Malta. The *Lysander* shall pass Le Havre and Brest, then through the Bay of Biscay to round Portugal and enter the Mediterranean through the Strait of Gibraltar. Mr Pascoe has already informed me that the *Lysander* is a weatherly brig, one who can sail closely into the eye of the wind. Her relatively shallow draught means that we shall be able to pass near the shoreline.'

'Do you think she has grounded, sir?' Courtney asked. He was unable to forget the hours he had slaved over the capstan when Bryant had marooned the *Meridian* on that sandbar. 'No one has reported a damaged vessel.'

Bryant glanced at Courtney as he had done to Pascoe. 'I believe it would be wise, Mr Courtney, to keep our minds open. Now, it still feels strange to say so, but France is no longer Britain's enemy. Upon encountering French vessels, there shall be no harsh words. If necessary, we shall salute any ships.'

Courtney knew that would be easier to say than to enact. France and Britain would always be like reunited brothers who had fought on opposite sides; the soreness of conflict would never be healed. It was another doubt hanging over this voyage. Only time would tell if this crew and her officers could act well in peace and diplomacy.

'Gunnery drill shall be held without ammunition,' Bryant said. 'What is paramount is that the men know the *Lysander* from her bilge to her skyscraper. From tack to tack and wearing ship needs to be as smooth as walking in a straight line. I want it to be done in any weather, well enough that the men can close their eyes and feel for the right brace or bowline. Lieutenant Courtney—'

'Yes, sir.'

'You shall supervise each of the drills with Lieutenant Godfrey. This may be a ship in peacetime but I do not want any idling or inactivity.'

'Yes, sir,' Courtney said.

'Mr Smythe,' Bryant continued, and Smythe eagerly looked up from the charts. 'I shall require you to do the same should the need arise. You will continue with your work on navigation, signal flags and daily observations. I shall be perusing your logs and journals, and your father expects frequent correspondence, as much as can be expected.'

'Yes, sir,' Smythe echoed Courtney.

'Finally, Mr Nightingale,' Bryant said, 'I want you to keep below while we are conducting drills. I shan't have the men distracted from their work. You have your place in the gunroom, thanks to the generosity of Lieutenant Courtney, but I would prefer that you stay there.'

Nightingale nodded. Courtney caught himself on the verge of saying that Nightingale could not be confined like a prisoner; he was a guest on the *Lysander* in her hunt for the *Loyal*. He shut his mouth at the last moment, but did not miss the look Bryant again gave him. Just as Bryant laid the *Lysander*'s course upon the charts, he also set his officers into their positions.

Courtney still did not know how Bryant felt about his presence, but he hoped he could at least keep his head responsibly down, away from any sharp blows from the captain. The best way to do so was to follow his orders and to show him how a taut ship and a taut crew behaved. There was precious little else that could illustrate the lay of a sea journey as its first days. The Lysanders had safely seen her out of Portsmouth and into the Channel, but such worries as the Bay of Biscay and the Mediterranean still loomed.

And with the bells ringing out during the afternoon watch, his desire for a taut ship was put to the test. With a steady wind blowing abaft the starboard beam and the northern tip of Cherbourg to leeward, Courtney paced the quarterdeck under Bryant's watchful eye. If it hadn't been for that, he might have enjoyed the fine weather and blue sky; there was no experience similar to standing on a vessel sailing at a comfortable speed under the clear heavens.

As it was, he felt like a Drury Lane actor on a false prop. Both the men below him and the one above would judge him for these next moments. He could not deny the spark of stage-fright.

Behind him, Bryant approached Harris, the helmsman. 'Mr Harris,' he said, 'we shall lay her on the larboard tack. Lieutenant Courtney!' Here was Courtney's cue. 'All hands to station to tack. Ready about.'

'Ready about!' Courtney called and watched as the men instinctively found their positions in the yards of the courses and topsails, and about the stays of the jib. Braces and bowlines and lifts were at hand, ready for the actions that they would need to perfect.

'Helm's a-lee,' Harris said and Courtney felt the movement in the tiller as it turned in the waves. As the spanker-boom came around, hauled against the wind, the *Lysander*'s head eased about.

Bryant remained silent, wordlessly prompting Courtney to take command of this manoeuvre as the first lieutenant. 'Rise tacks and sheets!' Courtney called and the men hauled the clews of the fore, main and mizzen sails up by their lines, shortening the canvas and freeing the upper yards. The wind's angle on the canvas shifted, shifted, the *Lysander*'s head easing into the wind, until Courtney could cry, 'Mainsail haul!'

This was the time when their intimacy with the *Lysander* would be tested: feeling the weather on the ship, hearing the slice of the waves and translating all that through hands and feet on spars and ropes. The men at the lee-braces let them go whilst the weather-braces were pulled taut. With aching, wooden creaks and moans, the main yards swung elegantly, finding the new tack. The wind now buffeted against the foresail's canvas, pushing it aback.

Every ship had a different character in this moment, caught in a delicate balance as the bow turned one way, the stern another.

'Helm, amidships,' Courtney said, hiding the anticipation in his voice. 'Haul taut! Let go and haul!'

The men far down at the bow grasped the running rigging, bringing the *Lysander* directly into the wind. Courtney remembered Bryant's *Meridian*, a year before, trying to tack and missing her stays. She had pitched out of control onto the sandbar, all because of mistiming between the wind, the captain and the speed of the crew. Courtney felt Bryant's eyes burning into him; he could not make the same mistake.

The *Lysander* still turned, guided by her jib and spanker. The next order to brace the foremast around would secure the ability to complete the tack. All had gone smoothly, not a man missing his footing or losing his grip.

No sooner had Courtney thought that, did the canvas suddenly shiver in a way it should not. He felt the wind on his opposite cheek and opened his mouth to shout out, only for the blocks and tackle of the spanker to rattle. With a jerk, the boom lashed around, the momentum throwing Bryant's hat from his head. The rigging flew around and Courtney instinctively grabbed for it, carving an angry burn across his palm. It did not stop the cat's cradle from somehow entangling a sailor and, with the violence of the yawing spar, throwing him over the side.

The resounding splash broke Courtney's haze. In a second, he was at the rails and staring down at the disturbed, frothing water. Bryant appeared next to him, followed by a gang of aghast sailors.

'Man overboard!' Courtney shouted, then, 'Throw a line! Who is it?'

'It's Arnold, sir,' came the voice of Obi, who was hastily running out a line. The crew hurled the rope out into the water towards the two hands groping at the surface. White fingers fumbled for the cord but a wave kept lifting the struggling Arnold up and away from safety.

The man would drown. Without another thought, Courtney shucked off his jacket. He had one foot nearly at the gunwale before a palm grasped his arm. Nightingale had hurried up to the deck. Shocked, Courtney turned to him – enough time to miss Paterson race along the gangway and hurl himself off the *Lysander*.

'Mr Paterson!' Bryant shouted. 'Lieutenant Courtney, control these men!'

Courtney barely heard the reprimand as Paterson resurfaced and swam powerfully through the current. Grabbing the line with the rest of the men, Courtney threw it towards him. Paterson snatched the rope and pulled it towards where Arnold was gargling and bobbing like a cork. To Courtney's relief, he managed to steady Arnold and loop the cord about him. With Arnold in one broad arm, he guided them both to the security of the hull.

Courtney grabbed the back of Arnold's jacket as Paterson pushed him up the ladder. With a rush of strength, he hauled him over onto the deck. The man was pale, eyes closed and mouth agape.

'Step back, all of you,' Courtney ordered, ushering the curious seamen away. 'Hiram, pass the word for Dr Faulkner. Fetch some strong drink.'

'Only his ration, Mr Nightingale,' Bryant said, but Nightingale had already hurried away.

Without waiting for Dr Faulkner, Paterson grasped Arnold and gave him a firm thump on the back. Nothing.

Another crack between the shoulder blades.

Arnold gasped, shuddered, and spluttered. He bent over, vomiting water in great gouts as Paterson soothingly rubbed his spine. By the time Dr Faulkner had dashed up from the orlop deck, Arnold was cocooned in Nightingale's jacket, shaking but alive.

'You did a good deed, Mr Paterson,' Faulkner said, bending down to examine the mute, shocked patient. He peered into his glassy eyes and checked his pulse. 'I shall still need to examine him below. If you would help me, Mr Paterson.'

'You bloody fool,' Paterson suddenly spat, arising to his feet. 'What'd Anne say if she knew you'd nearly drowned? Determined to break her heart, eh?'

'Mr Paterson!' Bryant stepped between Paterson and Arnold. 'I'll have no such talk on this deck! The both of you shall report to my cabin once Dr Faulkner is satisfied you are well.'

'Sir!' Courtney stood. Bryant snapped around to him, eyes wide at the interruption.

'Yes, Lieutenant?' he asked.

A flush rose on Courtney's cheeks. He could sense everyone's stares upon them, including Nightingale's. 'Nothing, sir,' Courtney managed to say.

'That is what I thought, Lieutenant. Dr Faulkner, take these men away. And all else, hands to braces! If anyone would cast an eye on our trim, they'd see we have missed stays.'

Courtney dismally watched Faulkner guide Paterson and Arnold below. In fragmented groups, the other men drifted away. Nightingale lingered, catching Courtney's eye again.

'Mr Nightingale,' Bryant suddenly said. 'I believe I requested that you stay below during drills. Unless you are going to man the ropes, please leave. The men shan't have any other distraction.'

Courtney thought that Bryant glanced to him, but could not swear to it. He walked away to hide his shame and anger, returning to the lee-rail. With Bryant's presence still lingering ominously, he resolved to put the men through their paces again.

–

'You should not have done it,' Nightingale said later in the low light of the gunroom. They sat at the mess table, working by the glow of a lantern to bandage Courtney's damaged hand. Courtney had forgotten he had injured it when grabbing for the blocks and tackles earlier. Only when it came to dinner, lifting a mug of steaming coffee, had the burn throbbed again. Nightingale now gently wrapped the dressings around it, following Dr Faulkner's orders from an examination Courtney had tried to stop.

'I acted on instinct,' Courtney said. 'God knows I couldn't have stopped the spar on my own.'

He didn't admit that Captain Bryant had burrowed into his head. As an officer, that should not matter.

'I was not talking about your hand. You were going to dive into the water after Mr Arnold.'

Courtney gritted his teeth as Nightingale tightened the bandage about his palm. 'Another moment of instinct. I couldn't let the man drown.'

Nightingale did not look up from where he was making a firm knot in the cloth. 'Captain Bryant was not happy with you.'

'Captain Bryant did nothing,' Courtney said without thinking. Nightingale glanced around but they were alone, aside from Smythe in his cabin.

'You should not have started to speak against him.'

'You spoke against many people when you captained the *Scylla*.'

Nightingale said nothing for a moment. He released Courtney's hand and turned on the bench, reaching for his cup. Courtney immediately regretted his words.

'I told you, Arthur, not to follow my example,' Nightingale said. 'You are a lieutenant, still at the start of your career. I was at the end of mine.'

Still at the start of his career. Courtney felt as though he was stalled permanently at the bottom of the ladder. He found it difficult not to follow Nightingale's lead when it was what he had admired the most about him: standing up to the people who had tormented him, doing what was right by the crews of the *Scylla* and *Ulysses*.

'Arnold is well and that is all that matters,' Courtney said, changing the subject. 'What I don't understand is Paterson. They were at each other's throats in Portsmouth and today, Paterson jumped into the sea without hesitation to rescue Arnold. Then he dressed him down again. I don't know who the devil Anne is but...' Courtney sighed. 'Captain Bryant will reprimand them both.'

'Mr Macdonald said it was a family matter. We should leave it at that. Let the two men sort it out amongst themselves.'

'As long as it does not affect their work, which it nearly did today.'

'Then perhaps Captain Bryant should reprimand them.'

Courtney sighed. Nightingale could be frustratingly good at finding the middle ground.

'He is the captain, Arthur. The most important thing is finding my father-in-law and Monsieur Baptiste.'

'Does it not bother you that he chastised you in front of the whole crew? Or ordered you to remain below in the gunroom?'

'He did not chastise me. I came on deck when I shouldn't have.'

'Hiram...' Courtney began, only to be interrupted by movement down the companion-ladder. Lieutenant Godfrey arrived, nodding to the both of them. Courtney withdrew the hand he had been about to place on Nightingale's leg.

'Evening, Lieutenant Courtney, Mr Nightingale, sir,' Godfrey said. 'Captain's asking for you, Lieutenant. He's in his cabin.'

It was not Courtney's watch for another two hours. He had meant to catch a wink of sleep, but Bryant's orders superseded such trivial matters. He sighed and, when Nightingale looked at him like he was a misbehaving child, he crammed his hat back on his head.

'Thank you, Lieutenant. I shall be there directly.'

Godfrey guided him away from the promise of his cot, up through the decks to the great cabin. He only spoke once, to say he was sorry for the trouble of the tacking that afternoon. Courtney was grateful for the sympathy, although embarrassed it had to be said to an officer who had worked a ship in countless conditions and could not now even manage this.

Bryant called him in and he stood by the closed door with his hat beneath his arm. The captain finished annotating his logbook before glancing up. Words came to Courtney's mouth, quickly swallowed down. He knew he was in trouble; he had felt many a similar atmosphere, in ships, on land, always seeming to stir the wrong pot.

'Lieutenant Courtney,' Bryant eventually said. 'You did not inform me that Mr Paterson and Mr Arnold fought in Portsmouth.'

'I thought the situation dealt with, sir. They signed on, I gave them head duties, and thought no more of it.'

'Their little feud almost disrupted the ship today, Lieutenant.'

'With respect, sir, the ship was already disrupted before Mr Paterson jumped into the water.'

Courtney was staring past Bryant at the gallery windows, but he saw the man raise an eyebrow. 'Mr Paterson still spoke very badly on the deck in front of his captain, his officers and fellow men. Do you not agree?'

'No, sir. I mean, yes, sir. He did speak out of turn.'

'They informed me their disagreement was over Mr Paterson's sister. A tawdry business. I told them to leave it on shore. But they also informed me that they are under your division. I expect your men to be more disciplined and smartly behaved, Lieutenant Courtney. We may not be at war but morale and control are still paramount.'

Courtney bit his tongue. 'Yes, sir.'

Bryant paused and leant back in his chair. He folded his hands over his immaculately tailored waistcoat, never letting his blue eyes stray from Courtney's stiff figure. 'I cannot lie to you, Lieutenant,' he said. 'You were not my first choice. I wished for Lieutenant Godfrey to be my first officer, but Mr Haywood informed my brother that you once knew Sir William. Mr Haywood's sister said that you were still friendly with her

69

husband and Sir William's son-in-law, Mr Nightingale. And, unfortunately, you have more years' experience than Lieutenant Godfrey, making it necessary for you to be senior.'

Courtney tried not to let any expression cross his face.

'Know that you are here because of your connection to Sir William, the same as Mr Nightingale. I've read about his exploits with the *Scylla*. And do not think I have forgotten the Caribbean and our…disagreement. I wish to make that very clear, Lieutenant Courtney, before we go further with this voyage.'

The barb towards Nightingale sank beneath Courtney's flesh. He told himself that had been deliberate, that Bryant knew the *Scylla* was a sore point for the two of them. No one, aside from her crew, would ever know what it had been like to be on that ship. He could not have the same argument again, and not with his captain, as Nightingale had insisted.

'You are very clear, Captain,' he said carefully.

'Excellent. You may go, Lieutenant. I expect better of your men. Oh, and one other thing, Lieutenant—'

Courtney paused with his hand almost on the handle of the door.

'I do not know what ship Mr Nightingale ran on the *Scylla*, but you shan't call any men by their Christian name, not even Mr Nightingale, when on deck. I won't have "Hiram" said in front of the men, or they shall come to imagine this vessel as one run on Revolutionary principles.'

It seemed Bryant had not learnt much from his previous experience at Spithead. Courtney was beginning to see why he had been sent ashore.

Courtney returned to the gunroom, anger so heavy that he could feel the heat on his cheeks. Nightingale looked questioningly up at him as he entered but Courtney could only manage to say, 'Well, I know very plainly what my place is,' before retiring to his cabin. He knew he would not sleep, although it was the only thing he wished to do after this rotten day.

Chapter Eight: Brothers in Arms

To Courtney's regret, the following days did not quell the dismal cloud in his head. Outside the walls of the *Lysander*, the weather bloomed fair and blue with a kind, brisk breeze. The wind, billowing from the north-west, ushered the *Lysander* along handsomely without the need to constantly beat towards it. Too far east to face the wildest Atlantic rollers, Courtney attempted to become more familiar with the *Lysander* in the manageable seas. For hours over the next few days, the tide swept them towards Cherbourg and the *Lysander* tried to make the most of it.

She was a sprightly little sixth-rate. Under Haywood and Co., she had sailed the waters of Europe but had previously been a smaller East Indiaman, rigged to weather the wilds of Cape Horn and to support an armament that warded off pirates. Her thirty-two-pound carronades, infamous ship-smashers, were an intimidating force, aside from her additional twenty-two great guns. Though her design was swiftly becoming ancient in the constantly shifting currents of ship-building, she performed her job well: she was quick enough under full sail to overhaul larger vessels and well-balanced to dip and climb over choppier waves. Courtney spent many hours on watch, trialling and testing different trims and rigorously drilling the men at the braces and on the tops. Never again would they fumble such a basic act as tacking.

Over and over, he sent men aloft to lay out on the yards and work the sails. In calm seas, they sent the t'gallant masts up and down, an exercise that had the men fumbling at first then slowly gaining confidence. When they were beat to quarters to practise, the men assembled in their gun crews to perfect the procedures of running out the cannons. They had been provided no extra powder for such a drill and Bryant had not purchased his own, as some captains did, so they acted the manoeuvres, aiming at invisible points amongst the waves.

With the reduced numbers of crew, they could just manage to man each side and have enough to manipulate the sails and braces above.

Courtney had utilised carronades on the *Scylla*, and now he chose a handful of men to operate the vicious guns.

Once he had observed the displays a handful of times, and judged the crew's seamanship, he made small adjustments to their positions amongst the forecastle, afterguard, tops and waist. Courtney scattered trusted hands amongst them all, the most capable in the gunner's crew. To Obi, he gave the position of presiding over the carronades next to himself and the gunner. After years on the *Scylla*, Courtney knew he could depend on him. It had been one of the reasons he had assigned him to Paterson and Arnold's mess, a firm, reliable hand to steer them – not that they had responded so far.

But, even with all the practice, the *Lysander* still felt like the frisky horses Courtney had ridden in his youth. His family could only have dreamt of owning their own steeds, so, as a messenger-boy for any willing patron, he had learnt to deal with all manner of animals. The *Lysander* was a little more tame than unbroken, yet she still kicked at times that Courtney did not expect, or balked when the wind shivered in her canvas in a way she did not like.

And ever since Bryant had dressed the crew down, they worked quietly, not a voice between them – and not in the way that Courtney had sometimes presided over, where he could oversee the men performing in respectful, competent silence. The motions of the naval day ticked like clockwork and they behaved as cogs: watches changed without reaction; the deck was cleaned so morosely that Courtney could only hear the scraping of holystones; even the noon meal was muted. For all the *Lysander*'s liveliness, the men became a dull, functional mass, no rapport between them and the ship.

There was no way for Courtney to admit to them that he knew what they felt: the desperation of work, the unknown of what lay ahead, the distaste of the captain.

Three days into the voyage, Bryant sent word for Courtney and Pascoe to present themselves. It was one of the first times Courtney had crossed the captain again. Bryant preferred to keep below, alighting on deck when required, and he had not yet invited the officers to dine with him. Now, he had Courtney and Pascoe make the observations for the new day's official beginning at noon: headway and speed from Smythe throwing the lead-line; course by the compass; wind direction and strength. In the privacy of the great cabin, Bryant unlocked the drawers containing his own charts.

'Lieutenant Courtney, Master Pascoe,' Bryant said. 'I shall need your secondary confirmation of our location. If you please…'

Using all of the recorded information, Courtney and Pascoe judged the *Lysander*'s exact location: forty-eight degrees north, five degrees west, with Ushant to larboard. Courtney remembered there being a sealed packet amongst Bryant's orders. He wondered if this was the location that meant the seal could be broken.

'Very well,' Bryant acknowledged. 'That will be all for now.'

A mere ten minutes later, Bryant himself appeared on deck. A word to Harris at the helm and the course was adjusted. Courtney tried to envisage the waters before them. South-east brought the *Lysander* tighter to the coast of Brest where the British Channel Fleet had long kept a watchful eye. It was strange to approach it in peacetime, but within the next hour, the squat towers of Fort de Bertheaume appeared through Courtney's spyglass. Through the lens, he could see the battery staring threateningly back at him. Not long before, the sight of a British flag would have ignited the powder in all of those guns.

Beyond the fort, the passage of sea narrowed before widening again into the roadstead of Brest. Courtney angled the glass in that direction.

He knew that the rest of the crew would be as curious as himself about their place here. Captain Bryant, the only man with the answer, remained on deck for once. He stood with his hands behind his back, eyeing the imposing fortress.

Courtney remembered how he had said they should now salute the French, a mark of courtesy in peacetime. But Bryant showed no sign of giving that order. He simply watched the battery and allowed the *Lysander* to creep slowly, almost furtively, beneath her guns. Perhaps, Courtney thought, his sealed orders had given this direction.

The fort approached to larboard. The French tricolour, shades of the Revolution, fluttered in the blue sky. Courtney waited. Not a sound broke the stillness. The *Lysander* strayed further into French waters, only not hostile now because of pen on paper.

'Sir,' Courtney heard himself say. 'Are we to salute?'

Bryant did not reply. Surely if the orders had required him not to salute, he could at least reveal that. Courtney turned away, back to the battery.

He saw the smoke before he heard the report. The noise threw his heart into his mouth. No ball fell, but the meaning was unmistakeable. A warning.

Voices rippled along the deck, not even silenced by Bryant's order for quiet. Courtney whipped around to him. Wars had been started for less than a man's refusal to salute. 'Sir!' he called again. 'Are we to salute?'

Bryant opened his mouth, only for another boom to ripple across the waters. 'Lieutenant—' Courtney heard before hurrying to the hatch to the gundeck.

'Larboard battery!' he cried. 'Seven guns to fire landward! Powder and no shot!'

A naval superstition foretold that even-numbered firing only occurred at funerals. Courtney needed all the luck he could carry as he helped the larboard battery. The men fell back onto their drills, each gun crew acting as quickly as if in battle. Cartridges were rammed home, guns run out and primed, and finally, at Courtney's order, the powder of the nine-pounder cannons ignited in turn as the lanyards were tugged against the locks. For a moment, Courtney thought of how he had not heard the sound for a year. The smell of the gunsmoke and metal brought his career back to him more than any captain's order could.

Then, silence again. The men paused, frozen in their positions around the guns, some of them peering out the ports. Courtney joined them, feeling the heat coming off the cannon's metal. Outside the ship, the *Lysander* drifted through her own haze. High above her, the fort loomed, imposing and quiet on its rocky island. Courtney waited for its reply – or Bryant's disapproval, whichever would come first.

At last, an answer. The noise rolled out across the sea. Courtney released a breath.

Godfrey was beside Bryant when Courtney returned to deck. He gave Courtney a thin smile, but it did not soothe the reproachful look Bryant shot his way. Courtney knew he'd be chastised again later, but for now, he watched the shoreline of Roscanvel near. In short, curt orders, Bryant instructed the *Lysander* to heave-to and after they had succeeded in backing her sails, there was nothing to do but wait.

The *Lysander* remained quiet. Regardless of routine, all on-duty and off gathered to witness the peculiarity of waiting in the bosom of a

French port. Courtney was gaining a sense of what Bryant's secret orders may have been, but he did not want to put words to it. If he was correct, saluting a French fortress would not be the strangest thing they did.

The last time Courtney had approached Brest, he had been on his third ship, the *Pelican*, in Admiral Colpoys's inshore squadron. The blockade of Brest had not been a satisfying period for a precocious and belligerent young man. He had almost looked forward to naval actions then: anything to escape the monotonous duty of waiting, watching for any French vessels attempting to break through the fleet. Yet the short, sharp actions that had occurred taught him how to behave in battle, how to unite as a crew, how to cope when death and injury rained about him.

The sudden cry of the man at the masthead broke his thoughts. 'Sails!' the man shouted. 'One point off the starboard bow!'

Courtney trained his glass again towards the horizon and saw the flutter of white. He turned back to Bryant, but saw he was already speaking with Godfrey.

The unknown ship seemed to move by inches. With little to do, the men on watch stared from the yards at her approach. As one, the crew saw what Courtney did: the thirty-two-gun frigate with her topsails elegantly set, rounding the Pointe des Espagnols with her course towards the *Lysander*. The ensign flying at her stern confirmed Courtney's suspicions.

Smoothly, with far more haste than the *Lysander* had, her gun ports opened and blasted out a clean salute: something Courtney never thought he'd see from a French warship.

'Lieutenant Courtney!' Bryant shouted. 'We shall salute them back, if you please! Promptly, now!'

Courtney gritted his jaw and returned to the gundeck. This time, the men acted quicker and more efficiently. By the time the smoke from their salute had again cleared, the frigate had neared, heaving-to at the *Lysander*'s larboard side. For a moment, both ships eyed the other in heavy silence. They were enemies reunited with only a treaty and a number of signatures preventing them from opening fire.

'*Fantôme!*' Bryant called. 'My name is Captain Jerome Bryant, commander of His Majesty's Ship *Lysander*!'

No reply came. Then a man, evidently the captain in rich deep blue and red, appeared at the rail of the quarterdeck and lifted his hat. Bryant, after a moment of hesitation, did the same.

'Captain Bryant!' the French captain shouted, and Courtney's gut tightened. He knew that voice. 'What an act of providence! The man who I met upon the deck of HMS *Meridian*, once she had been re-floated!'

Courtney shielded his eyes with his hat and squinted against the sun. There was no doubt about the French captain. Defying belief, Capitaine Bonfils, formerly of the wrecked *Cygne*, waved across to them. The three of them – Bonfils, Bryant and Courtney – had last met in a tense exchange after Bryant had made Courtney give up his prisoner from the *Cygne*. Courtney had tried to insist that he could cope with Bonfils and the other captives en route to Antigua, but Bryant had refused. The *Scylla* had slunk behind the *Meridian* all the way to port, as if she had been the ship to beach upon a sandbar and miss out on the battle.

Courtney turned back to Bryant, curious to see his reaction. The man stared in shock. He gave Courtney a cursory glance, mouth working to form words. 'Capitaine Bonfils!' he finally managed, plastering on obviously false delight. 'I give you joy of the peace!'

'Indeed, Captain! Let us put some water between us and the shore, and then dine and speak like civilised men!'

'Of course, Capitaine!'

Bonfils strode his quarterdeck, directing his men. Bryant crammed his hat back on his head and motioned to Courtney. 'We'll make sail, Lieutenant,' he said, seemingly forgetting Courtney's disobedience with the salutes. 'Keep the *Fantôme* to starboard,' and then, pulling Courtney aside, he hissed, 'How the devil did that man get here?'

Courtney swallowed. 'Prisoners were released under the terms of Amiens, sir. He obviously returned to the French Navy.'

'He is to accompany us on the search for the *Loyal*.'

'Then he is our ally now.' Courtney could not believe he was defending the French captain, but that disbelief was only an instinctive reaction. Sailing close to France and encountering her fortress and ship, it had been surprise that they were no longer enemies, a sense of the unreal. He found he felt no distaste for Bonfils or his weatherly frigate, not against Bryant's ire.

'Ally or not…' But Bryant did not finish. He glanced towards the *Fantôme* and shook his head. 'If I am dining with the man, then you must come too. I shall accept no excuse.'

'Yes, sir.'

As Bryant left him, Courtney thought that that order to dinner was the punishment for his insubordination. With Bryant retreating below, Courtney looked across to Godfrey, who swiftly glanced away, evidently not wanting to invite any comment. Courtney sighed. Did he truly think all Courtney wished to do was rage against Bryant? He could not blame the other lieutenant, though. The slightest indecorous implication seemed to stir Bryant.

Courtney would see how the captain would react around Bonfils, the other officer to witness Bryant's disgrace in the Caribbean.

Chapter Nine: Fantôme

With Lieutenant Godfrey in temporary command of the *Lysander*, Courtney followed Bryant up the side of the *Fantôme* to the piping of the bosun's whistle. He could not help comparing the crew that greeted him to the *Lysander*'s men. Dressed in the universal and unofficial sailors' uniform of mismatched shirts and loose trousers, they eyed him and Bryant with curious and bemused expressions. Their ages could have been anything from twenty to fifty; the sea recognised no national flags when hardening flesh and bone. Aside from the tones of the officers' coats and breeches, Courtney could see no outward difference.

But the shock of entering a French vessel, not as a prisoner, robbed any sense of familiarity. Awkwardly, Courtney paused and removed his hat. With it, he saluted the quarterdeck – and then wondered if that was a tradition of the French Navy.

From the gathering, Bonfils stepped forward. He wore an immaculate version of the uniform Courtney had arrested him in. No longer was he the man fighting to maintain his dignity; his golden buttons and embroidered lapels gleamed. Shined boots clicked loudly on the timbers as he walked over, only pausing when he noticed Courtney behind Bryant.

His thick eyebrows knitted together. Courtney waited, holding his breath at this strange reunion. Then, beneath his moustache, Bonfils gave a disarming smile.

'Lieutenant Courtney,' he hailed. 'So many surprises today! I greet you as a brother.'

Bonfils extended a white-gloved hand. Courtney looked at it for a moment. Under Bryant's intense gaze, he grasped it.

'Apologies, Captain Bryant,' Bonfils said. 'I did not expect to again come face to face with the man who took me prisoner in the Caribbean.'

Bryant tilted his head. 'I did not expect to again come face to face with my – our – prisoner.'

Bonfils laughed. 'Come,' he continued, barely touched by what could have been an insult. 'My cook is waiting.'

Following Bryant and Bonfils, Courtney glanced quickly across to the *Lysander*. Taking advantage of Bryant's absence, Nightingale waited at the taffrail. Courtney wished he could have joined them, but Bryant had refused. He had given the excuse of not knowing accepted protocols for a French ship of war.

Ferried along by Bonfils's entourage of officers, Courtney descended into a richly furnished, almost lurid captain's cabin. Red curtains hung about the gallery windows, deeply coloured cloth encased the chairs and the benches, and candles had been lit in candelabras, throwing strange, guttering illuminations about the walls. A drawing of a château surrounded by idyllic fields sat proudly upon the bulkhead.

Courtney hesitated beside the table. Food already swamped it. A rich rack of beef dominated the centre, swathed in gravy and steamed vegetables. Little assortments of pies and pastries and broths and stews encircled it, each in remarkably pretty china dishes. Glasses, polished to mirror-like quality, dotted each place setting alongside cutlery positioned with fastidious accuracy. Courtney barely wanted to move and disturb it all.

'Sit, please,' Bonfils urged. 'Captain Bryant, here, beside me, and Lieutenant Courtney, next to my own lieutenant, Auclair.'

Auclair looked to the English officers with a polite nod. He was a handsome man, perhaps a few years older than Courtney, with curled dark hair and freckles decorating his tanned skin. Courtney smiled thinly and returned the nod. He eased into a chair and cast a quick glance around at the other guests before Bonfils introduced them.

'My sub-lieutenant, Maistral.' A red-haired man whose round face remained impassive even as he smiled. 'Maître Carré.' A round-bellied man, cheeks dotted with pockmarks but a friendly, gap-toothed smile. 'And finally, one of my aspirants, Proulx.' A boy who must have been the French equivalent of a midshipman, younger than even Smythe, vivid blonde hair slicked into a prim tail.

Courtney acknowledged each of them silently, following Bryant's lead. None of them spoke a word in return, although perhaps the language barrier was greater than it evidently was for Bonfils.

The cabin door eased open and an old man, dressed in a pristine apron and carrying two bottles of wine, appeared. At Bonfils's direction, he poured the deep red liquid into the waiting glasses. Courtney could not tell one wine from another, but even he could see the finery of this one in its rich colour and fruity aroma.

'A Bordeaux vintage,' Bonfils said. 'When we raided the cellars of my former landlord, we found wine from the days of *le Roi Soleil*. They have furnished the stores of my ships for many voyages. What year have we reached, Gabriel?'

'It's 1701, Capitaine,' said the cook.

'Try a sip, Captain Bryant,' Bonfils pressed.

Bryant, whose eyebrows had risen at the fine wine's violent origin, looked at his glass. Slowly he tasted it, and Courtney could see his mind working, deciding whether to remain true to his English prejudice and risk insulting Bonfils, or to compliment the French captain. 'Very...strong, Capitaine,' he trialled.

'And you, Lieutenant Courtney?' Bonfils asked.

The scent was overwhelmingly sweet but when he tasted it, he did not agree with Bryant. It was not as potent as the gin his father and his mother had lived off. 'I am not very talented at telling the differences between good and bad wine, Capitaine.'

Bonfils laughed. 'Nor I. But there once would have been a time when this wine was worth more than the lives of myself and my family. So I know that it is good wine because now, my family live well, and its former owner... Not so well.'

Bryant shifted. Courtney remained quiet, considering what Bonfils had said as Auclair carved the beef and doled it out onto the fine plates. After watching the other men help themselves to pies and sweetmeats, Courtney did the same. He wondered if this impressive selection was for show or if it was Bonfils's standard fare. The France he had read of in the newspapers could not afford such luxury. Common folk had rioted over lack of simple bread and intolerable harvests.

With idle chatter rising around him, Courtney glanced over at Bryant. He ate as though it was his last supper, barely moving apart from his chewing jaw. He looked at no one. Courtney had not felt this awkward in a long time, not even at the dinner in Trinidad with Governor Picton, Sir William and Commodore Harrison. He would have taken Picton as his eating companion rather than the silent, passive Bryant.

'The château in the picture,' Courtney said when he could stand no more. 'Is that your former landlord's, Capitaine?'

'It is,' Bonfils replied. 'In what was Gascony and is now Gironde. I worked his land until the Revolution came and he lost his head in the Place Nationale in Bordeaux. His wine, many of his stores and his chef, Gabriel, are now mine.'

'I see,' Courtney managed. 'It is a…nice picture.'

It sounded pathetic. Courtney did not know what else to say. He should have expected such a response but it still felt bizarre to be eating with one of the Revolutionaries he had heard such brutal things of.

'It is symbolic of my rise and the opportunities I seized. I could not enter the navy in the days of the *ancien régime*,' Bonfils continued. 'I did not have the pedigree that was required of officers. The Gardes-Marine were young gentlemen and to be considered, a piece of paper must prove your genealogy. That is a relic of the past now. Young Proulx is an aspirant. He needs no piece of paper. Men of talent populate our navy, not noblemen, since the Revolution and its reforms.'

'I have heard that many of those noble officers fled or were executed. We English have thought that the French Navy was in chaos after the Revolution.'

'It is true that many noble officers were killed. But chaos? It was a chaos that allowed me, and many others, to rise. Chaos is not always evil.'

Courtney chewed on a cut of beef, unable to deny it was the best he had ever tasted. Weeks at sea often interestingly coloured meat and as a child, he had been lucky to receive the dregs of the fish brought in at Ryde.

Reading his silence, Bonfils waved a fork at him and said, 'How about you, Lieutenant Courtney? Where do you come from?'

'I am from a little hamlet, Ryde, on the Isle of Wight.'

'I know it!' Bonfils said unexpectedly. 'When the English took me prisoner after you handed me to them, I was sent across the Atlantic to a prison hulk on the Solent. HMS *Crown*. At times, when the weather was bright and we were allowed on deck to exercise, I could see the island.'

'I did not realise officers were sent to the hulks.' Courtney had seen the dismasted vessels in his youth when they had been first instituted. He had read of their expansion during his time in the Caribbean until now, they dotted the harbours of England like great, stinking sores.

'I was not a prisoner long enough to be granted any parole. The peace saved any further deliberation over my case. I was released alongside many others, I am glad to say. They were dark, wretched things.'

'Many gaols in England are,' Courtney said without thinking.

Bonfils chuckled. 'You say it as though you speak from experience.'

It was Courtney's turn to shuffle uncomfortably. Bryant finally looked up from his food, eyeing Courtney.

'I do,' Courtney admitted.

'You have been imprisoned?' Bryant asked before Bonfils could.

Courtney reddened, again finding himself on the verge of becoming defensive. He had not revealed much of that life to many people. He had even hidden some of the truth from Nightingale – not for embarrassment that it had occurred, but for concern that Nightingale would judge him, even if he did not realise it. They were from two very different worlds. Perhaps Courtney needed to be honest; the two of them shared harsh memories, regardless of their background. Nightingale had once told him what mattered was what they did with such things.

'My family often followed my father into the debtors' cells,' Courtney said shortly.

'Now that is something I would expect from a man like myself,' Bonfils commented. 'Not an officer of the King's Royal Navy. We hear the lower decks are full of brutes, but not the upper.'

'I admit, I share their background,' Courtney said, suddenly losing his appetite. Unbidden, he thought of the *Grampus* and the long time he had been a regular hand, at the mercy of cruel officers and the unhappiness of that ship. He shoved the memories away and said, 'But the King's Navy is populated by men of talent.'

The statement sounded hollow, unlike when Bonfils had uttered it.

The dinner fell once again into awkward silence, aside from the French conversations at the other end of the table. Courtney found he was glad they had not been able to understand his confession. He sometimes thought he wore it too much like a threadbare coat, constantly aware of it, constantly ashamed of it. No captain or admiral in shining gold wanted a lieutenant who did not scrub up to standard, no matter how often they spoke about the equality of the sea. Even successful officers of modest means had connections, men who could turn the right ear.

Courtney had no one. The more he thought of it, the more he realised he had been lucky to advance this far at all, certainly after what he had experienced as a young sailor.

Bryant had told him that he was only here because of Sir William. But what connection was that? He was Nightingale's father-in-law. To Courtney, he was nothing.

When the beef had been finished almost to the bone, Gabriel returned with servants to clear away the dishes. Courtney was unsure if he wanted any of the fruit tarts and marzipan that appeared with more wine, but he ate as Bryant did. It was a relief when finally, Bonfils dismissed the other guests. He wondered if he and Bryant could now return to the *Lysander* but Bonfils made no move to walk out with them. Instead, he beckoned Gabriel over. The cook carried cigars which he offered to Bryant and Courtney. Both declined.

'Captain Bryant, Lieutenant Courtney,' he said once Gabriel had left. 'I assume that you are both aware of the nature of our voyage?'

Bryant nodded. 'We were both informed, yes.'

'My government are as eager to find the *Loyal* as yours surely are. The last sighting of her was in the Strait of Gibraltar.'

Bryant sat up straighter. Courtney opened his mouth but was cut off by Bryant saying, 'We were not aware she had a final sighting.'

'Yes. She was following her assigned course, but between the Strait of Gibraltar and Malta, she became lost.'

'Why were we not informed of this?' Bryant asked accusingly.

Bonfils spread his hands. 'I do not know. The information is new.'

'We should have been informed,' Bryant insisted.

'I am informing you now, Captain. It is what I know. The *Loyal* was last seen at the start of August off Gibraltar. So I suggest that we keep a close eye after we pass the strait. Gibraltar is a prime English port, yes?'

'Yes,' Bryant replied curtly.

'Then you shall easily be able to ask some subtle questions.'

It sounded exactly like what had happened in Salvador two years before. Lieutenant Hargreaves had probed a contact of Lord Fairholme's, and uncovered the *Ulysses* mutineer Ransome's dead, shark-eaten body. Courtney hated deception and espionage. He was starting to make a habit of these dirty cases.

'You do not believe, then, that the French are behind this disappearance?' Bryant asked, and Courtney gritted his teeth. Even he, without his airs and graces, would not have asked such an impertinent question.

Bonfils, however, seemed impervious to offence. 'If I did, I would not be offering my services. No, I would not have been asked to accompany you, even. You do not believe that the English are behind the disappearance?'

Bryant's lips thinned into a white line. He did not need to answer.

With the formalities over, Bonfils finally stretched, blew a long stream of pungent cigar smoke into the air, and slapped a hand down onto the fine tablecloth. 'Well, gentlemen, thank you for joining my Fantômes for dinner. I hope to see the *Lysander* one evening. Please, Captain Bryant, Lieutenant Courtney, I shall accompany you on deck.'

Not needing any more permission, Bryant rose, curtly brushing crumbs of pie and tart from his dress coat. Courtney went to follow, finding his legs a little unsteady from the wine and realising it had been stronger than he had thought. Before he could go much further, Bonfils suddenly put a hand upon his arm. Courtney stopped.

'Lieutenant,' he said. 'Correct me if I am wrong, but was that Hiram Nightingale I saw on the deck of the *Lysander*?'

By the door, Bryant also froze. Courtney felt a chill in his stomach. Any mention of Nightingale now brought up a swathe of emotion. If Courtney was adamant about defending himself, he was ten times more passionate about defending Nightingale and his actions.

'It is, sir,' he said, the temptation to deny it not making it to his lips. 'He is Sir William Haywood's son-in-law.'

'Ah.'

'Do you know him?'

'No, no. Not personally. But I have heard of his exploits. One of Nelson's Band of Brothers, yes? And so recently dismissed from the navy after the *Ulysses* affair. I believe you were a part of that too, Lieutenant Courtney?'

Courtney swallowed. 'I was.'

'The *Ulysses* incident was summarily finalised at the court martial, Capitaine,' Bryant suddenly said. 'Do not mistake Hiram Nightingale's presence onboard the *Lysander* as anything more than…'

'I meant nothing by it, Captain,' Bonfils soothed, shaking his head. 'Former Captain Nightingale has a somewhat impressive reputation in the French Navy. He succeeded in what some captains still have not. Destroying an English frigate!'

Courtney stepped away from Bonfils. He decided not to reply, letting Bryant say, 'Quite,' as a sign that their conversation was over.

Darkness had fallen when they returned to the deck. The breath of a breeze made the *Fantôme*'s topsails flutter elegantly, helping her along in a smooth ebony sea. Courtney looked to starboard, relieved to see that the *Lysander* was but a short distance away. Her British ensign drooped at the stern, a strange companion to the French tricolour. He still could not make his mind up about Capitaine Bonfils or this graceful frigate. Some of Bonfils's words had struck a place he did not expect to be hit in, but others... He was as adrift as the *Fantôme* crew had seemed, judging by the looks they had given him.

As Courtney's attention returned to the *Fantôme*, he caught glimpse of a sight he did not believe. Only when Bryant paused beside him did he know it was real. Arising from a hatchway, holding her white muslin skirts away from her feet, was a woman. Her tall form quivered a little, even on the calm deck, but she did not hesitate to gaze at the two English officers. Bonfils approached her, taking an arm clad in long cotton gloves. Courtney broke through his shock to remove his bicorne hat, as Bryant did.

'Captain Bryant, Lieutenant Courtney,' Bonfils said. 'May I introduce Madame Geneviève Baptiste.'

'Your servant, ma'am,' Bryant stammered.

'I am pleased to meet you, gentlemen,' she replied in perfect English. 'I intended to join you for dinner but I have been feeling unwell. I am not a good sailor.'

Now she was near, Courtney could see a hint of greenness around her blue eyes. But she still smiled and tilted her head to them, red curls bouncing beneath her elaborate hat of bows and feathers and cloth.

'We are honoured that you braved the deck for us, ma'am,' Bryant continued. 'I am sorry we have to return to my *Lysander*.'

'I shall not keep you, sirs.'

Courtney could not help glancing behind him as he and Bryant descended into the waiting cutter. Geneviève remained at Bonfils's side, watching them even as the captain spoke to her. Courtney did not know whether to acknowledge her gaze. He decided not to, although it did not stop Bryant commenting, 'Keep your eyes upon our English vessel, Lieutenant Courtney.'

'I was not...'

'A woman aboard. And a man who puffs his chest out over chopping his landlord's head off. These are our allies.'

'Yes, sir.'

Exhaustion prevented Courtney from wanting to argue more. Fortunately, Bryant kept the rest of his frustration inside, returning to his cabin as soon as they alighted onto the *Lysander*. With Smythe on duty at this hour approaching eight bells in the last dog watch, Courtney went below too. Nightingale waited. No one else disturbed the gunroom so Courtney sat and put a hand upon Nightingale's leg. He wanted to sink against him as well, feel the comfort of lying beside him, but that could not be, not here.

'No more information?' Nightingale asked, giving his hand a squeeze.

'The last the *Loyal* was seen was off Gibraltar. Monsieur Baptiste's wife has come along too.'

'His wife? That is a surprise.'

'Mmm.'

Courtney decided not to mention Bonfils's question about Nightingale. He did not like to bring up Nightingale's former career, if he could help it, but whether they acknowledged it or not, it still followed Nightingale like a shadow. He had been Captain Hiram Nightingale, RN, for far longer than he had been Mr Hiram Nightingale, civilian.

'They were all...pleasant enough as men – and women,' Courtney added instead. 'And I had more in common with Capitaine Bonfils than I thought I would.'

'How so?'

'We both came from a destitute childhood. He had a painting in his great cabin of his former landlord's château and said it was representative of his success and the opportunities not previously open to him.'

'Don't tell me you had sympathy for a Revolutionary.'

'No, no. I hate the bloodshed they have caused as much as any man. But I can't deny that we have faced similar struggles in our careers. It's not so long ago I was an able seaman on the *Grampus*.'

Nightingale tilted his head. 'I don't know much about the *Grampus*,' he said.

Courtney shrugged. He would not go into the grisly details with Nightingale, not now when he was tired and still smarting from Bryant's sniping. The *Grampus* was not the right subject when he was already irritable. Instead, he said, 'I'm stuffed with Capitaine Bonfils's supper. Mr Smythe has the watch so I'm retiring for the night.'

'Sleep well.'

At the cottage, Courtney had fallen into the habit of placing a kiss on Nightingale's cheek before turning in. Here, in the gunroom, he simply squeezed his shoulder and disappeared into his cabin. With precious little space on the sixth-rate *Lysander*, Nightingale had been given the choice of bunking with the officers. Bryant had not offered any part of his cabin, as he might have another guest. Courtney had gladly offered, preferring to sleep in a hammock whilst Nightingale occupied the cot. The acceptable intimacy was nothing like lying in each other's arms in the cottage's bed, but Courtney was still glad for it.

Now, full of food and wine, it did not take long for him to drift asleep. The last thing he wondered was if Captain Bryant would ever repay the visit to Capitaine Bonfils, or if old rivalries would remain too insurmountable.

–

The winter came harshly to the Grampus. *Despite the presence of five hundred heated bodies occupying her decks, the biting chill still ate through the hull, creeping in by the gunports, the hatches and the gaps in her seams. Courtney spent much of his time bundled in his heavy-weather wear, even tempted to wrap it about himself when in his hammock. Working the ship became an even greater hazard than usual. The ropes, lashed with ice and snow, burnt his palm with cold pain. Even after months of tasting it, he came to appreciate the burgoo, pease pudding and the regular pounds of meat, certainly with the beer that warmed his stomach.*

Since their first meeting, he had spoken with Garrick Walker a handful of times. Though their conversations had been brief and mundane, Courtney found his thoughts lingering on the other boy. He wondered if he was well amongst the people who singled him out for attack, wondered if he had spoken up for himself. He knew he should not fret; there was enough to keep his mind busy as the convoy sailed the Atlantic, heading for the wild Cape of Storms. Yet he became a welcome distraction from the worsening weather and freezing nights.

On deck one cold morning, with the sun low in the hard blue sky, Courtney wished for all the distraction he could muster as he and his fellows holy-stoned the timbers. Frost encrusted the seams and the caulking, and he could feel the kiss of it through his trousers where he knelt. His fingers cramped around the little prayer book, as the sailors nicknamed the stones they used to scrape the deck. He had to keep smacking his hand against his side to return the feeling to it, something which had already earned him a reprimand from Midshipman Lowe on duty.

At the gunwales of the Grampus, ice had started to encase the rails. Men risked the slippery deck to clear it away. Amongst them, Courtney recognised Walker's tall form. He was wrapped in more sensible wear than Courtney had, including a warm-looking scarf and gloves. A woollen hat was currently pulled tightly down about his ears. Risking Lowe's wrath, Courtney kept glancing up, hoping to catch his eye. He did not know why he wished to, but sometimes, he told himself, an ally in the harsh world was what was needed. He wanted Walker to know he would be that ally.

When the boy finally noticed him, a warm spark flickered in Courtney's chest. He gave a short smile and was thrilled to see Walker return it. Then Walker was gone, ducking his head and disappearing past Lowe with a tug of his hat in salute.

Courtney returned to the holy-stoning. Above him, he heard Lowe talking to his companion, a fellow mid of a younger age than even Lowe's adolescence.

'These men must be kept active and disciplined,' Lowe said. 'That is what my father says. No matter where they are from, they must be kept in line.'

Courtney was used to hearing such talk about men and boys of his station; those above him often enjoyed thinking they had the rest of the world under their boots and canes. They liked to imagine they needed whipping into shape, and they were the patronising force to do so.

'I know some of their faces,' Lowe continued. 'One cannot move in Plymouth without seeing sailors and miners. Though I did not expect to see some of them here.'

He knew he shouldn't have but Courtney glanced up, as if he expected to suddenly see Lowe differently and recognise him from some event in his past. He didn't, of course, though perhaps Lowe knew him. The boy's sharp eyes immediately located him in the grouping of cleaning men and the little cane he carried rapped against the gunwale. Courtney ducked his head again at a sharp lashing of the boy's tongue.

He decided to close his ears as well. There was nothing to be gained by listening to the rants of a boy who doubtless shared the same opinions as much of the rest of his social set. Courtney could not change those thoughts. The best that he could muster now was to let the veiled insults slide off him and continue to keep his eyes lowered.

The sharp cold soon distracted him, anyway. By the time the bell rang for the meal time at noon, Lowe was gone from the deck and Courtney's mind had turned again to Walker. He noticed him across the deck, aiding the cook with doling out the hot burgoo, and gave a small nod in greeting. He expected nothing more but after the short meal had concluded, Walker found him whilst returning from the head. The other boy swiftly stuffed a small bundle of fabric into his hand.

'What's this?' Courtney asked.

'I had a spare pair. From home,' Walker garbled. 'The weather will only become colder.'

Courtney unfolded the bundle and found it was a pair of woollen gloves. He felt his cheeks warm. 'You're a fool, nipper,' he said affectionately. 'I can't accept these.'

'Yes, you can. I saw how frozen your hands looked on deck today.'

That was all that Walker said before he scurried away. Courtney did not have a chance to argue. And, truly, as he slipped the gloves onto his hands, he did not want to. The soft, warm fabric made his cramping fingers feel more tolerable. But more than that, the gift from Walker touched his heart. He had helped the boy before, and now the boy had helped him.

That, amidst the cold and Lowe's insults, was what he had to concentrate upon.

Chapter Ten: Wooden Walls

The days passed with the western coast of France to larboard and the northern reach of Spain approaching. Now they had had confirmation that the *Loyal* had at least passed the Strait of Gibraltar, Courtney did not feel such an obsession with watching for unfamiliar sails. Yet, even with peace signed and a French vessel at their side, he could not quite settle with the absence of conflict. The sea separated them from immediate contact. With each hour, the cliff-edge of war could have been tilted over. They would not know anything until it found them.

Every time Courtney's watch came around again, he glanced at the *Fantôme*. She often sailed within hailing distance, only departing from view when weather influenced her. They shared the wind's benevolence: sometimes the *Lysander* sailed to lee, sometimes the *Fantôme*. Courtney could not help judging such manoeuvres like in battle. Whichever vessel occupied the weather gage had the advantage, able to move as she pleased against the enemy. If war returned, he wondered, how strange would it be to turn the guns on the *Fantôme*? She was larger, more strongly armed than the *Lysander*, and with a crew who never faltered, no matter the conditions.

The *Lysander*'s crew, meanwhile, slowly became familiar with her quirks. Before diving into the turbulent heart of the Bay of Biscay, Courtney had drilled them more thoroughly on the tacking manoeuvre. This time, as the headyards were hauled, the men kept the *Lysander* from missing stays and a steady handle was maintained. As a means of keeping them sharp, he experimented with putting them through their paces of wearing the *Lysander* also. Godfrey followed his example, capably directing the men. Though he had been Bryant's hand-picked choice, he bore none of the captain's sullenness; in fact, he almost appeared overly pleasant to Courtney, as if making up for his patron. In good weather, Courtney observed him preside over the swinging up of the t'gallant masts without a garbled order or a man fumbling.

Amongst the hands, an unspoken competition began to rise between the former merchant sailors and the Royal Navy men. Courtney had seen much the same friendly feuds between the marines and the regular seamen in the *Scylla*. A seaman, no matter if he was able or ordinary or even a landlubber, wanted to prove himself. After the disastrous start, they had even more motivation to do so – and no one wished to be thought of as less skilled than the French.

One afternoon, as four bells rang out, Courtney occupied the deck with Smythe. He had been the one to aid Smythe with his noon readings, patiently helping him again with his celestial navigation and spending time teaching him the different signals. Captain Bryant had not glanced more than cursorily at Smythe's work.

'I'm so close to entering my lieutenant's examination,' Smythe said as they had manipulated the sextants. 'If war breaks again, I want to sign on as a proper officer, not a mid.'

Smythe was not quite the required age, even though Courtney knew some captains on the examination panel only wanted a boy to 'appear to be eighteen'. He certainly had stretched the truth a little at his own.

'I am sure you shall be very successful, Mr Smythe,' Courtney said. 'You have good experience from the *Scylla* and if Captain Bryant writes positively of you, this shall be another good voyage to add to your record of service.'

'The *Scylla* was a capital ship,' Smythe continued ebulliently. 'I was sad when she was broken up.'

'Yes, well...' Courtney did not want to dwell on the *Scylla*, not when he was still finding his feet on this new ship. She felt so very far away now, a different world and a different part of his career. For all his dedication, his association with her had not pushed his head any further up the ladder of promotion. He wondered how Smythe could remain so hopeful – then reminded himself of Smythe's family connections. 'The *Scylla* was a vessel we all knew well. This one shall be too.'

'Indeed, sir,' Smythe said. 'I did not mean to disparage the *Lysander* or...'

'She is as good as any Royal Navy frigate, Mr Midshipman,' intoned a voice nearby, and Courtney turned to see Pascoe at the ladder to the raised poop deck. He had his own navigational instruments beneath his arm, ready to verify Smythe's calculations. Smythe blushed.

'I am sure she is, Mr Pascoe,' Courtney said, bristling at the man's audacity to speak to Smythe in that way, especially on deck. 'Come, Mr Smythe, we shall allow Mr Pascoe to work. Your eye is required on our trim.'

In the face of Pascoe's bitterness, Courtney felt a tad remorseful for thinking badly of Smythe's privileged background. After all, it was similar to the one Nightingale came from – and Courtney knew such a polished façade hid a mire of troubles. Courtney had had bad experiences with one midshipman as a youth, but Smythe continued to prove he was nothing like Lowe, or other fortunate sons. Courtney tried to refuse to allow his past to affect his present, though such a denial kept revoking itself.

Half to prove to himself that he was not prejudiced, Courtney allowed Smythe to give the orders as they shared the watch. He needed the experience more than Courtney did. Courtney was beginning to wonder if this venture would bear any fruit at all for him.

Across the narrow water, the *Fantôme* sailed under topsails and courses. With the wind freshening, they could easily shake out their t'gallants. Courtney smiled, enjoying being able to judge their own progress against a working, sailing model. He went to suggest it to Smythe, but the boy had already reached the conclusion.

To the sound of bosun's trill and Smythe's orders to lay aloft, men climbed. They clambered over the shrouds and past the topsail yards to the t'gallant masts. As the topmen leant on their footropes and unravelled the t'gallants' gaskets, Courtney glanced across to the *Fantôme*. Her own men ascended the masts, French orders following them. Courtney felt the thrill of the competition, crying, 'Lay down from aloft! Sheet home!'

The sheets at each clew were hauled and on the deck, the braces let go. White canvas flowed free, draping down from the yard.

Minutes after he had spoken them, the same orders echoed from the *Fantôme*. Courtney cast an amused eye at Smythe at the fact the words were in English, then repeated in French. Capitaine Bonfils stood at the weather-rail and he raised his hat at Courtney. Courtney smiled.

That grin faded as steps resounded on the deck and he turned to face Captain Bryant. 'Sir,' Courtney said, noting Smythe stepping towards the lee-side of the quarterdeck.

Bryant held his hat on his head as he gazed up at the t'gallants. 'T'gallants, I see,' he said. 'Did no one consider informing me, or asking for the captain's permission?'

Smythe halted. He opened his mouth, but Courtney interrupted, 'I gave the order, sir. The wind is…'

'Yes, Lieutenant. I have made my own observations. Very well. I shall allow it. But I expect to be duly notified about any major developments on deck or in the tops, certainly as we enter the Bay of Biscay. Mr Smythe, come, let me see your noon readings.'

Smythe looked between Courtney and Bryant. A blush had risen on his cheeks. Bryant had barely given mind to his workings before. Courtney was left in no doubt that he had now done so deliberately, just as he insisted on direct notification. He had expressed nothing in his standing orders regarding the ship, though Courtney knew some captains were more obsessive about information than others. Captain Robinson, his most recent captain, and Nightingale, had given him some leeway as their first officer. And Bryant had barely batted an eyelid when Lieutenant Godfrey had requested the t'gallant masts being swung up.

He watched Bryant and Smythe descend below, swallowing his anger and embarrassment. The Lysanders had performed well, challenging even the Fantômes, but that did not matter. Not if such a thing had happened under Courtney's watch.

That evening, Smythe sheepishly approached Courtney in the gunroom and said, 'You did not have to take the blame for me, sir. I was the one to give the order.'

Courtney smiled thinly. 'I did not countermand it,' he said. 'It is true Captain Bryant should have been informed.'

Smythe seemed to want to say more, but he nodded and scurried into his cabin, leaving Courtney alone with Nightingale. Seeing Nightingale's expression, Courtney knew he would not hear the last of today's events.

'I did not do it deliberately,' Courtney insisted. 'The Fantômes were loosing their t'gallants… You know how prideful sailors can be, especially in competition. Lieutenant Godfrey did not receive any disagreement when the t'gallant masts were swung up.'

'You remember that you and I did not always see eye to eye,' Nightingale said. 'You were difficult to begin with.'

'The *Scylla* was my home. I knew her men better than anyone else. That is not arrogance. I did.'

'Sometimes, an officer must choose between his men and his captain. It is not always easy.'

'You chose the men.'

'I was the captain.'

Courtney resisted the urge to sigh. Nightingale could easily avoid Captain Bryant. He did not even have to interact with him, at least until they neared the region where Sir William had gone missing. But this was the man who had vanquished Lord Fairholme, Admiral Nightingale, and all of the forces of the Admiralty, to do what was correct for himself, the Scyllas and the *Ulysses* men.

Courtney had not found that balance yet. Always he would sacrifice one side of this uneven triangle – himself, the men and Bryant – for another.

In any case, within a day, Bryant's t'gallant masts were struck before the tempestuous nature of the Bay of Biscay harassed the two ships. Enough warning had been given by the *Lysander* topmen and the accompanying *Fantôme*'s to prepare for the incoming squall, fastening the guns and the carronades, throwing canvas over the *Lysander*'s boats and upper deck, preventer braces rigged, and anchors secured. Despite the potential for scudding before it, Bryant made the decision to lie-to rather than test the crew which Courtney thought needed the practical experience of heavy weather. Even the merchantmen had not sailed the *Lysander* under this naval rig.

Yet, with Bryant's reprimands still in his head, he obeyed and watched the *Fantôme* diligently do the same. Fortunately, the dirtiness passed within a few hours, allowing the *Lysander* to continue. The only damage done was to the mizzen cap as the yards overstrained the lifts against it.

Once the skies had completely cleared, the first sail other than the *Fantôme* was spotted from the masthead. The fleeting hope of the *Loyal* was dashed by the identification of the other vessel as a sloop, but she carried post, always a reliever to sailors. With not even a fortnight having passed since leaving England, Courtney did not expect a letter for him to be dropped on the gunroom table. He took the first moment off duty to lift the seal. He had already noted the initials: EW. Edward Wainwright.

But inside, he immediately recognised Jane's own handwriting, the spidery, cramped mass of it, interspersed with crossed spelling errors. Neither of them had learnt to write until the Woods family had taken them in.

She began,

> *My dear Arthur*
>
> *I do not know where you are, but I hope that this letter finds you safe. I am sitting in the kitchen of Eddie's cottage for a moment's respite from his sisters. I love them dearly but you saw how eager they are, especially little Alice. They and Eddie's mother have formed a press-gang, coercing me into the service of choosing flowers and ribbons and gowns for the coming wedding.*

Courtney smiled. Just two years ago, he had watched Jane stand before a court martial on the charges of piracy and murder. Now, the most frightening thing in her life was a gaggle of excited in-laws. He did not go a day without feeling relief for Jane's continual recovery.

> *Eddie has been a gallant rescuer, she continued. He often accompanies me a-walking on the Broads, and sometimes we take a boat on the Yare. I feel I do not have to lie or wear a mask around him, as sometimes I do when we meet with strangers. He understands what is in my mind. We shared the wooden walls of the Ulysses and together, we shall move away from those horrible times.*
>
> *That is why I can hardly wait to wear his ring. And that is also why I wanted to write to you. We agreed, before you sailed, that the date of our wedding would be set for November. I do not know when you shall be home. Eddie and I have decided to move the date to December, in the hopes you shall be there, but he has business to attend to soon after around his late father's will which he wants to involve me in. You and I come from so little, and I cannot disappoint him.*
>
> *Arthur, I pray that you shall be home then, and if you are not, you will understand. We would not have planned it this way*

if we knew you would be sent away so suddenly. Eddie blames
himself as a naval officer; he knows the fickleness of it all. I do so
hope that you are here to hold my arm as I walk down the church
aisle. Bill would have wanted it this way.

   Please, stay safe and well,
   Your loving sister,

Jane

Courtney sighed and closed his eyes. Tangled feelings churned in his chest. All his life, he had desired the best for Jane. He had run from home with her. He had sailed to the Caribbean with her. He had joined her hand with Bill Howard, the master of the *Nereid* and then the *Ulysses*. For many years, she had been his only love, the one thing he clung to and cherished. He could not ever begrudge her happiness, and he would never take that from her.

But he longed to be there to witness her marriage, the step from her tormented past to a better future. In the mania of the past weeks, he had pushed it to the back of his mind, not daring to think he might not be home for it. Now, with Jane's worries laid out before him, he could ignore it no longer. She might have to enter the church without him, and he might have to dive into the dirty work of intrigue, wondering if she was truly happy with his absence.

The dismal mood hung over him as he returned to deck that afternoon. Godfrey glanced at him curiously when he relieved him, but fortunately naval strictness stopped his mouth. Courtney was left with the calm sea and the steady breeze glancing through the canvas. He kept his mind on the *Lysander*'s trim, but had not distracted himself for too long when he noticed a cutter being lowered from the *Fantôme*. Angling his spyglass towards the vessel, he first noticed the post-captain's uniform and its gold braid sparkling in the sun. Bryant. He had not known the captain was off the ship.

Courtney frowned, sweeping the glass along. When he spotted Bryant's companion amongst the boatsmen, he blinked, wondering if the low October sun had confused him. He lowered the instrument and peered with his own eyes across the water.

The trilling of the bosun's pipe wailed in Courtney's ear as Bryant climbed back onto the quarterdeck. Under Courtney's observation, the marines saluted him with a clash of weaponry. Perhaps Bryant had ordered no such formal welcome, but Courtney did not want to test those waters.

And his companion should be shown the pomp and ceremony of an English vessel.

Geneviève followed Bryant, holding his offered arm. She wore a light blue gown instead of the white of their previous meeting, and she kept her other hand on her silken shawl to stop it billowing away. It also hid her bare neck and collarbones from the gawping *Lysander* sailors. More for her than Bryant, they swept off their hats, holding them before themselves like peasants in the presence of nobility. Knowing recent French history, there was an irony in that, Courtney supposed.

'Thank you, Lieutenant Courtney,' Bryant said, a rare smile on his pinched face. 'Madame Baptiste requested to join us for dinner this evening. As we did not have the pleasure of her company on the *Fantôme*, I was very happy to agree.'

'Yes, sir,' Courtney replied, in no confusion as to why Bryant had truly agreed. The captain's thoughts were the same as his men's: Geneviève Baptiste was very beautiful, and even if she had not been, she was still the only woman for many miles around. Countless things separated officers and regular seamen, but a charming lady could lay them lower than any enemy. He felt a stab of sympathy for Geneviève.

'I shall accompany Madame Baptiste below. I have an extensive collection of books she may find engaging.'

Courtney resisted the urge to frown, having seen no books in the great cabin.

'If it is well with you, Captain,' Geneviève said before Bryant could lead her away, 'I should like to observe the deck for a moment. My husband's family have been involved in shipping for many years, and I would enjoy seeing an English ship.'

'Are you certain, Madame?' Bryant asked, but he could not refuse a lady. 'Very well. Lieutenant Courtney, keep your eyes on those men. I don't like the way they stare.'

If it was an attempt to frighten Geneviève into changing her mind, it did not work. She only glanced at the assembled crew and lowered her head. Courtney snapped around as he heard the first signs of an inappropriate whistle. 'Back to your stations!' he ordered. 'We are only a week out of England, you shrews!'

With sullen looks, the men dispersed. As Godfrey took over the watch, Courtney was left alone with Geneviève – or at least it felt that way, as much as possible on a sixth-rate. Since meeting Nightingale, no woman or man had stirred Courtney, but he still lingered awkwardly, twisting his hands behind his back. She looked at him expectantly with sharp and intelligent eyes. 'What would you like to see, Madame?' he eventually asked. 'I'm afraid there are no excitements today.'

'This is an excitement for me,' she said. 'To set foot on an English ship. Capitaine Bonfils says she is a frigate.'

'Well. Yes. She is by term a frigate, but a very small one. She is the lowest rank of our rated ships.'

'How is that determined?'

'Well,' Courtney repeated, walking towards the mainmast. Caught in a subject he was familiar with, his found his tongue. Geneviève followed, crossing beneath the shadows of rigging and sails. 'We define a ship as a vessel with three masts, mizzen, main and fore. With two masts, she is a brig or a sloop. A sloop is below our rating system, and can only be commanded by a lieutenant, sometimes a midshipman. This is a sixth-rate, which means she has to be commanded by a post-captain.'

'A post-captain?'

'A man like Captain Bryant, who has had his name posted in the Naval Gazette. That is a full captain, rather than a captain without a ship or a commander who is called "captain" by courtesy.'

Courtney had hoped he could have gained such a title, even if it had only been for show. Geneviève nodded. 'That sounds as though it could become confusing.'

'Some men stay commanders for years, while some do not even see that rank. Even fewer post-captains become admirals. Our navy is a pyramid with a wide base and a small top.'

Courtney wandered forward with Geneviève beside him. Men at the braces and the belaying pins stepped aside for them, doffing their hats again. 'I suppose that a ship is the same,' Geneviève commented. 'Very many men and few officers.'

'All the world is the same,' Courtney replied with a wry smile. 'Ships are a small parcel of England. There are more than just bulkheads and duties between captains and lieutenants and men. I can show you how we divide our men if you would like. Their evening meal is not due to be served for another two hours, so we will not be run down by them.'

'Yes, I am interested in all varieties of men. Our French pyramid is perhaps turned on its head at the moment.'

Courtney positioned himself to walk down the ladder backwards, keeping his eye on Geneviève. He was accustomed to the pitch and roll, which occurred even in these small seas, but somehow, she managed to jerk and smack her forehead on a low beam. She lost her footing and tumbled into Courtney, who caught her inelegantly.

'Madame!' he cried, hearing running footsteps approach. Paterson, who always seemed to be in trouble's vicinity, helped Courtney move her from the ladder's rungs. 'Madame, are you all right?'

Her eyes fluttered in a daze. A bright red mark bloomed on her pale skin, and to Courtney's fright, he saw blood well in her hairline. 'Fetch Dr Faulkner,' Courtney said to Paterson. 'I shall move her someplace quiet.'

Geneviève's awareness had fractionally returned by the time Courtney reached the gunroom. Nightingale, who had been sitting at the mess table, sprang to his feet. 'Arthur, who...' he began. 'What happened?'

'This is Madame Baptiste,' Courtney replied, delicately sitting her on the bench. 'She took a tumble off the companion-ladder. I've passed the word for Dr Faulkner.'

'I am quite well, Lieutenant,' Geneviève suddenly croaked. She blinked and raised a gloved hand to her head, screwing up her nose when her finger came away red. 'Have I stained my hat?'

'No, Madame. But you should take care. You nearly fell.'

Geneviève tutted and undid the ribbons from around her chin, loosening her hat. Her hair was neatly pinned beneath, with auburn ringlets framing her face. She pulled off her glove but Nightingale offered her his handkerchief and she gently dabbed the drops of blood.

Dr Faulkner took the moment to stagger into the room, followed by Paterson carrying his satchel. 'I was told that...' he began, and stopped at the sight of Geneviève. 'I apologise, Madame Baptiste, I thought that Mr Paterson was taking me for a fool. There are no women on this ship, says I, but he insisted.'

'I am sorry, Doctor,' Geneviève replied. 'I have been the fool.'

'Do not fret, Madame. The first time aboard a vessel wobbles any legs.'

Paterson laid Faulkner's bag atop the mess table and opened the pouch to reveal an array of surgical instruments. On a ship away from hospitals, the doctor had to fill every role from teeth-puller to druggist to surgeon. Courtney looked warily at his sharp tools and medicine bottles, wondering what disaster Paterson had indicated. Faulkner seemed to have been wrenched away from a baser calling, bleary-eyed and with the smell of spirits on his breath.

'May I take a look at your wound, Madame?' Faulkner asked.

'I am quite fine, Doctor.'

'Allow him, Madame,' Nightingale suggested, despite Faulkner's state. 'I too insisted I was fine with every wound, and it did me great damage.'

'I...' Geneviève began, but then relented. 'If you must.'

Faulkner reached to touch her pale skin. He eased back her curls and examined the mark, which was quickly becoming a bruise. He spent only a moment looking at it, eyes a little crossed as he concentrated. 'As I thought, Madame,' he sighed. 'You shall have to come to my sickbay for surgery immediately. Your looks shall be marred for months to come.'

Geneviève's eyes widened. Courtney shook his head.

'Don't be frightened by his English humour, Madame,' he said. 'The doctor is teasing you.'

'*Monstre*,' Geneviève jeered.

'My apologies, Madame. I cannot help myself. The French always seem to lack any joviality. You shall fare well, other than an explanation to your husband of why you are so bruised.'

The fleeting smile fell from Geneviève's face. '*Oui*. If we find my husband, Doctor.'

'Well,' Faulkner said, oblivious to any tension he had caused. 'Now this crisis has been suitably averted, I shall take my leave. Mr Paterson, fetch my bag, would you?'

Paterson did as bid and followed the merry doctor from the gunroom. Courtney glanced to Nightingale and shook his head.

'Are all English doctors like this?' Geneviève asked. 'On the *Fantôme*, he would not have rolled out of his berth for a bump to the head. But neither would he have been so...'

'Not all are like Dr Faulkner, Madame,' Nightingale said.

'Can I check your wound just in case he missed anything with his crossing eyes?' Courtney tried, but Geneviève shook her head.

'I am feeling healthy, Lieutenant,' Geneviève insisted. 'Thank you for your care. And you, Monsieur—'

'Nightingale. Hiram Nightingale.'

'Ah. You are Hiram Nightingale? We have heard of you in France.'

Nightingale smiled thinly. 'Many people know me now, Madame Baptiste. I fought against your country for many, many years.'

'You no longer serve your king in the Royal Navy?'

'No. No longer.'

The old sadness still lurked in Nightingale's words, and the familiar dread of having to explain his situation again. Courtney interrupted before Geneviève could have the chance to press for more. 'Shall I accompany you to Captain Bryant's cabin, Madame? He mentioned something about his books.'

'If it is quite all right, Lieutenant, I should like to continue our tour. I shall watch my feet more carefully.'

'Oh, I...' But Courtney did not begrudge Geneviève her desire to not join Bryant yet. 'Very well.'

'I should like to join you,' Nightingale said. 'If that is all well with you, ma'am.'

'Of course,' Geneviève replied with a smile.

Within the next hour, Courtney had seen more of the *Lysander* than he thought he had in all the time before. With the starboard watch off-duty, the men gathered at their messes, stitching up shirts and trousers, speaking amongst their tightly knit groups, or idling amongst themselves. The literate about them scribbled off notes to home which the next packet ship might pick up. One of the men, who Courtney knew from the forecastle division, strummed a guitar, singing a bawdy version of 'Henry the Poacher'. His words slowly trailed off as Geneviève approached, but Courtney knew she would have heard the lyrics.

Around the men off watch, the larboard waisters flitted up and down to the gun deck, performing the menial duties of cleaning the guns and weaponry or ferrying supplies back and forth to the watch above. Courtney explained how the crew were separated into their stations: forecastle, in the bows and foremast of the *Lysander*; topmen, the most able seamen who handled the sails above the lower yards; afterguard, working on the quarterdeck; and waist, the landsmen and less skilled sailors. Courtney had been the one to position these men after enrolling them, and he vowed to try and learn their names and rankings. He had been adept at it on the *Scylla*, years of suffering and triumph ingraining the crew's identities in his head.

For all he tried to move on from her, remnants of the *Scylla* remained in Smythe, who bowed and blushed just as deeply at the sight of Geneviève, and Obi, who Courtney invited to describe the nine-pounder guns and the carronades.

'Where does he come from?' she asked as they departed for the galley area. Courtney had expected such a question. Although France had nominally tried to abolish slavery, Courtney knew that the situation in the Caribbean had been especially fraught. And only that year, there had been talk of Bonaparte instituting slavery again in certain islands.

'He escaped from a plantation in Antigua,' Courtney replied. 'The *Scylla*, our old ship, had been docked in English Harbour and he stowed away onboard. When I became aware of his presence, I signed him on. Captain Carlisle was willing also. Fortunately, no one ever came looking for him.'

'Are there many men from different nations onboard your ships?'

'Oh, many, many.'

'Does it not disquiet the Englishmen?'

Courtney smiled. 'Some of them, yes. But some of them, no.'

He was unsure what else to say. Each man held different beliefs; Courtney had experienced all opinions of the world and its ways. If Obi had come aboard a different ship, perhaps he would have been turned loose and enchained again. The Royal Navy did not follow the creeds of people like Sir William Haywood, who wished for all slaves to be freed.

Speaking to Geneviève, Courtney realised he still did not know much about Obi himself. Not only as an officer talking to a regular hand, he had been reluctant to broach any such subjects, in the way of Nightingale only tentatively revealing his past. Trauma followed Obi's history. It was a story only he himself could tell.

In the galley area, Rylance, Andrews, the ship's cook, and Bryant's steward, Parker, were chewing tobacco. All three men leapt to their feet as Courtney and Geneviève entered, Andrews tottering on his one leg. The great iron stove was not alight, but the copper bowls still smelt of the salted pork and pease soup they had brewed for the noon meal. Bits of the slush and gristle clung to the rim. No matter how long he had been an officer, Courtney still remembered the trials of picking that out of his teeth for weeks to come.

'Don't fret, men, I'm not here to inspect,' Courtney said. 'Madame Baptiste wished to sample some English food.'

Geneviève looked disgusted. Between the rock-hard biscuit and the thick soup, Courtney did not blame her. But she chewed diligently on a piece of hardtack and kindly complimented Andrews who, by the look on his face, had never heard such a thing before. She continued to surprise Courtney as they walked the decks, interested in the ship, his life and career. Courtney veiled the harshest stages of his past, but spoke of his climb from the lower berth into the officers' mess.

'A ship represents everything to a sailor,' he said. 'She is his home, his school, his court of justice, his prison, his shelter… These wooden walls house all the ratings and colours and backgrounds of this world, all together with the one thing that makes every man equal.'

'What is that?' Geneviève asked.

'The sea.' Courtney smiled. 'Of course, I do not believe all men here could ever be truly alike. As you say, this ship, like the world beyond, is a pyramid. I do not think England's pyramid would so easily be turned on its head.' He was not sure why he said it or why it sounded so bitter; Courtney was not a man to philosophise. Nightingale gazed at him in surprise. Even if men thought such things, they rarely voiced it. There were other, stronger affectations Courtney could have spoken of about the ways of the world, but he stopped, and instead continued, 'But, from my days in my first ship, the *Grampus*, to now, I have always learnt something new about men and how they work.'

'The *Grampus* is a sinister name for a ship,' Geneviève said. 'What did you learn aboard her?'

In a flash, Courtney regretted those words too. He bristled, gave a thin smile, and said, 'Nothing that bears repeating.'

Nightingale's eyes lingered on him. Courtney did not look over, but guided Geneviève back towards the ladder they had descended, distracting her with other practical talk. He knew he stood on more stable ground there. It was far easier to define the wooden walls with their names and sailor's terms, rather than delve into the issues that still plagued him.

Perhaps, therein, by not addressing such things, lay the problem.

Chapter Eleven: In Irons

'She reminds me a little of Jane,' Courtney said to Nightingale that evening. Now dinner was concluded, Geneviève had been safely returned to the *Fantôme*, and Bryant was sleeping off the wine Bonfils had sent over, he finally felt he could breathe. It had been a curious day and had served to briefly take his mind off his sister's wedding. But with those words, it came rushing back. 'Jane would've done the same thing – asked to be shown around a warship. She did, in fact, when she first met Bill.'

'Madame Baptiste is brave to join a ship full of strangers to find her husband,' Nightingale commented. 'Although I think that Louisa might do the same for me, if that doesn't sound too much like flattering myself.'

'I would search the seas if you went missing.'

Nightingale smiled, allowing the implications of that to linger. Courtney still had not broached the subject of their relations, but it was impossible to do so now in such confined quarters.

'Jane sent me a letter,' Courtney continued instead, returning to the coat he was brushing down. 'She and Edward are moving the wedding to December, but she says they have to hold it then because of…some arrangement of Edward's father's will that he has to deal with. I promised her I would be there.'

'You shall. We both shall.'

'I hope so.' Courtney sighed. 'It's stupid of me to worry about that when we still have to find the *Loyal*. War won't threaten if I don't see Jane married.'

'She deserves a celebration and a good marriage. There's no shame in fretting about it.'

Jane not only deserved a healthy and robust marriage because of what had happened to Bill but because of her past. She had followed

Courtney wherever when they had been children, refusing to stay in the drunken misery that surrounded their mother and father. She had sat in the bottom of fishing skiffs, clung on to the back of horses, hurried with him through the fields to deliver messages. Before they had escaped the island, Courtney feared she would end her days in the clutches of drink or in a bordello. She did not have the option he had to run away to sea or to join the ranks.

But then she had followed him one journey further – out to the Caribbean, where she had worked as a seamstress for the English women who had accompanied their husbands west. Bill had looked after her, a pairing of friendship if not desire, until he had been struck down in the *Ulysses* mutiny. Courtney knew, more than ever now, that Jane could care for herself, but he would be forever content knowing she had further loving hands and hearts around her, a new family in the safety of England.

'I told you that I nearly married a girl before,' Courtney continued. 'She was in Gibraltar. Sara Foster. She had a wicked bastard of a brother. I don't know what happened to either of them.'

'Perhaps we shall find out when we dock in Gibraltar.'

'Perhaps.'

She had not been the first passion of Courtney's life. For that initial ardour, he had paid dearly.

'I did not know some of those things about your life that you mentioned to Madame Baptiste,' Nightingale said, as if reading his mind.

'You know a lot about my life.'

'Yes, but not about the *Grampus*. The way you spoke of these wooden walls and what they mean was quite lovely.'

'The *Grampus* was not lovely.'

Nightingale paused. Courtney could imagine him turning his words over in his head, dissecting them. 'What happened onboard her?' he finally asked.

Courtney looked away. He paused in the cleaning of his coat, and tried to form a response. He was saved from it by the sound of lumbering footsteps approaching the gunroom. Dr Faulkner entered, face pinched as if he smelt something evil. Whiteness framed his eyes, no doubt the aftereffects of his drunkenness mixed with dinner. 'Ah, good, Lieutenant Courtney,' he said through clenched teeth.

'Are you well, Doctor?' Courtney asked.

'Yes, yes. A brief illness, that's all. But I... I wanted to speak with you.'

'I'll come along with you.'

'No, no. Mr Nightingale can hear too. He was also present. I...' He swallowed and seemed to be finding his words through the nausea. 'I may have been out of sorts earlier when I treated Madame Baptiste. Mr Paterson was kind enough to aid me. But I did not misplace a scalpel, did I?'

Courtney frowned. 'No one has reported one found. Are you certain it isn't in your medical chest?'

'No. I have searched and searched. It has kept me from my sleep.'

'Why are you telling me?'

Nightingale turned to Courtney. 'He is asking if you saw Mr Paterson take it,' he said quietly.

'Thank you, sir,' Faulkner managed with a nod. 'I did not want to say it directly.'

'Stealing from the ship's stores or the medicine chest is a serious accusation,' Courtney said, then realised why Faulkner had been so hesitant. Drunken sod or not, he cared for the men, and such an allegation could get them flogged or worse. 'I did not see anything. But then I was concentrating on Madame Baptiste and her injury.'

'As was I. Perhaps that is what Mr Paterson was relying on.'

'Why would Mr Paterson want to steal a scalpel?' Courtney asked. 'He has already been in trouble twice.'

'Indeed.' Another voice surprised Courtney. Pascoe stepped into the room beside Faulkner, looking at him sidelong when he smelt his spirit-clad breath. 'Mr Paterson is a wrong 'un, if you ask me, sir.'

'Thank you for your opinion, Mr Pascoe, I...'

'If you want my say, Lieutenant, him and Mr Arnold ain't acting well in the same division and in such close quarters. Bad blood. Ain't just an issue on the ship.'

Courtney tried to ignore Pascoe's questioning of his decision. He had been the one to assign Paterson and Arnold to the same watch and forecastle division. A mere few weeks ago, Pascoe, as skipper of the merchant *Lysander*, would have been responsible for assigning duties to his crew. He still did not quite fit within the naval hierarchy. 'Their behaviour will be dealt with, Mr Pascoe,' Courtney said. 'I will make sure of it.'

'Would you like me to inform the captain, Lieutenant? He should know.'

The idea of Bryant wading into such a delicate matter did not fill Courtney with confidence – worse, it could threaten to unsettle the ship even more. But, damn it, Pascoe was right. If Bryant discovered they had kept such a thing from him, there would be the devil to pay.

'No. I shall tell him,' he relented.

'I will join you, Lieutenant.'

Parker, Bryant's steward, was returning from the great cabin as Courtney and Pascoe arrived at it. He ducked his head to avoid Courtney's gaze but Courtney could see an embarrassed blush on his face. 'Is the captain awake, Parker?' he asked.

'Um... Yes, sir. But he is... He isn't happy, sir. A, um, pain in his head.'

Two drunkards in one ship, Courtney thought. Courtney knew how to deal with drunkards, better than he knew how to deal with officious captains. 'Thank you, Parker.'

The steward scurried away from the scene. Courtney knocked on the door, wondered if perhaps Pascoe should announce their arrival, but decided to risk Bryant's wrath. 'Captain, Lieutenant Courtney and Master Pascoe. We ask leave to report something...' *Improper?* '...important.'

Bryant grumbled from behind the door but eventually beckoned them inside. He was sitting in his nightshirt with a paisley gown pulled around his shoulders, nursing a wet towel upon his forehead. Courtney looked at him, unsure what to say. He doubted Bryant wanted his sympathy.

'Has someone cut off your tongue, Lieutenant?' Bryant snapped. 'I wager you've seen worse states than this.'

Courtney ignored the comment. 'Dr Faulkner has reported an item of his missing, Captain. He is concerned it has been taken.'

'He was with Mr Paterson earlier this afternoon, sir,' Pascoe interceded. 'The man was entrusted with the doctor's belongings for a brief time.'

Bryant's face curled. He released a long sigh and pressed his fingers to his eyes, massaging the bridge of his nose. 'I have never known such a quick succession of offences. Was the man's background not inquired of when he made his mark?'

'The men have many backgrounds, sir,' Courtney said. 'They have many reasons for signing on. What matters is how they behave on the ship.'

'And such is his behaviour.'

'We do not know that Mr Paterson had a hand in this.'

'I beg to differ, Lieutenant.' Bryant removed the towel from his head as if it had suddenly offended him. He winced at the increase in light, if only from the lantern. 'The man's pilfering hands are spread over this case. But I cannot accuse outright. We shall have an investigation. This Sunday, during the inspection of all of the men and stores, I shall cast a closer eye over Mr Paterson. Lieutenant Courtney, you shall accompany me. He is your man.'

'Yes, sir.'

'Thank you, Mr Pascoe, Lieutenant, you may go. When Dr Faulkner is free, please send him to me.'

Courtney wondered if Bryant wanted him for questioning or for his head. He returned to the gunroom with his own heart heavy. He hoped that Paterson had not been the thief. The man had had the opportunity, but Courtney could not believe he would be so brazen or so stupid. Why he would want a scalpel worried him equally as much. The ongoing dispute between Paterson and Arnold threatened to spill over the rest of the crew. Such a small upset could disturb all of the men. He knew exactly what it was like.

–

Sunday arrived, a day on which kind or religious captains could allow their men respite. Captain Bryant was not the first and instead of a church service, he read the Articles of War. Such a decision was not unusual for warships, but as he narrated the sacred naval laws, his words rang deeply about the deck. He pronounced Article Thirty, regarding robbery, with particular vehemence, and if Courtney was not mistaken, Article Thirty-Three about behaviour unbecoming an officer.

Following the service, instead of dismissing the men by their divisions, each was instructed to stand by his hammock below. Bryant had performed inspections beforehand but only with the standards of a regular captain's eye. Now the man was on the warpath, suspicious and resolute.

Courtney joined him aft. Sergeant Dawes, bowed in the low head-space, and one of his marines flanked Bryant, cross-belts polished and muskets at hand. They began in the cockpit, where Faulkner awaited with his medical chest open and his surgical tools laid out. Not expecting to see a battle, the area had not yet been turned out as a sickbay of the kind Courtney was accustomed to during war. Faulkner had no assistant so he answered Bryant's questions about his instruments – with the notable exception of the missing scalpel.

The gunroom came next. Smythe, Pascoe, Godfrey and Nightingale stood outside their respective cabins as Bryant gave cursory glimpses into them. He spent more time in Courtney's cabin, but Courtney had recruited Rylance to neaten any imperfections and Bryant found nothing to comment on. He only nodded and stalked out of the little space, leaving the officers to finally breathe.

The true test awaited them on the gundeck. Here, every man stood beside their living quarters, comprising their hammocks with a width of barely fourteen inches. These hammocks were stored away but each sailor knew his berth by sight, helped by the numbers on the beams. For the inspection, they had gathered their modest belongings, laying them atop their sea-chests. Courtney enjoyed seeing the humble things that gave each of them an identity. Some carved scrimshaws, some decorated their spare clothes with skilful details around the cuffs or collars, some brought memories of home in drawings and trinkets. For the Sunday service, they had scrubbed themselves clean and for an allotted time before, they had laundered their additional shirts on deck.

Courtney performed the delicate work of looking through their possessions whilst Bryant observed them all distantly, only making a handful of remarks. He unfailingly asked Courtney for the man's name.

Courtney felt a beat of satisfaction that he had already memorised many of the divisions.

At last, they reached Paterson. Courtney found himself holding his breath, hand upon his ceremonial sword-belt. Bryant drew to a halt and, in the way of any obedient subordinate, Paterson did not look him directly in the eye.

'I hope that you have recovered from any effects of jumping over-board, Mr Paterson,' Bryant said.

'Yes, sir. Thank you, sir.'

'Lieutenant Courtney, if you will...'

Courtney bent down and gently moved Paterson's clothes from atop his small trunk. The same image as his tattoo – a bird in flight – adorned the lid. He lifted it gently, knowing how rotten and unsturdy sailors' chests could become. To his surprise, more linen sat inside. Bryant had requested all of it to be in sight. Trying not to suspect anything, Courtney picked up the handkerchiefs and loose pantaloons.

'Sir,' Paterson suddenly said. Courtney looked up and saw that the man was grinding his jaw. The word seemed to have burst from him involuntarily.

'Is there something you wish to say, Mr Paterson?' Bryant asked.

At the captain's side, Courtney noticed Sergeant Dawes stand a little straighter. His fingers tightened about his weapon. Paterson's eyes flicked to the tall man.

'No. I...' Paterson swallowed, obviously trying to find his sentences. 'The items in there are...personal.'

'There is little private about a frigate of war, Mr Paterson. Search through them, Lieutenant Courtney.'

Courtney did not want to obey, not only for fear of what he'd find but for knowing the humiliation of personal matters being aired. He reluctantly returned to the clothing, only for Paterson to jerk into movement. The able seaman did not have to shift far before Bryant was looming over him like a furious father. Dawes crowded forward, blocking Paterson.

'Lieutenant, please,' Paterson begged.

'Enough of this insolence, Paterson!' Bryant barked. 'Courtney—'

Paterson tried to step around Dawes. It was enough cause for the sergeant to grasp his striped shirt. Even that did not seem to stop him. To the aghast looks of his fellow men, he tried to approach Courtney, who had made no further movement. He could only watch as Dawes and a fellow marine manhandled Paterson, each of them snatching an arm.

'Sergeant Dawes, arrest this man!' Bryant ordered.

From the gunroom, Godfrey and Pascoe had emerged. The master came running, seemingly on the verge of joining in the ruckus. He stopped at a stern glance from Bryant. Courtney felt helpless, even as

Paterson stared up at him as if he was supposed to understand something.

'Clap him in irons!' Bryant continued. 'I shall not tolerate such brazen disregard for the Articles of War and disrespect for his officers.'

Paterson still struggled as the marines forced him away. None of the other men had moved an inch. Paterson's messmates, including Obi, stood particularly rigid, as if their fellow's actions would condemn them too. Everybody stared whilst Paterson was half-dragged across the deck and down the hatches to the dismal hold. For a long while, awful silence reigned through the ship. Courtney knew words would be whispered over grog and supper, but for now, the men could say, and do, nothing. Without precisely knowing why, he looked towards Arnold, and saw the man had turned pale, perhaps afraid of being thrown to the lions with his friend.

'Blackguard,' a voice suddenly said beside Courtney. He did not realise it was Pascoe until Bryant snapped at him.

'I'll have you return to the gunroom, please, Mr Pascoe. No further talk!'

Pascoe did not respond, only slunk back to his berth with a barely withheld scowl. As soon as he had left, Dawes and his marine returned from the hold.

'Is he sufficiently bound?' Bryant asked, loud enough for all to hear.

'Yes, sir,' Dawes said.

'Then Lieutenant Courtney, search the remainder of his possessions. Such behaviour is enough to blight his name.'

'Yes, sir,' Courtney responded, though he wished he did not have to. Kneeling again, he continued to rifle through Paterson's chest. With every movement of linen, he expected to see the bright glint of the scalpel. But he searched and searched and found nothing, only a collection of letters and notes: the personal effects Paterson had seemingly been so worried over.

'There is nothing, sir,' Courtney said, rising, and relieved for it.

'Are you certain? Lieutenant Godfrey,' for the man still lingered, 'please search.'

Courtney tried to keep his anger from reaching his expression as Godfrey took his place. The second lieutenant also hunted through the trunk and found nothing. Unsatisfied, Bryant leant down himself, casting the clothes and letters aside carelessly. Courtney gritted his teeth.

'Very well,' Bryant huffed. 'I shall speak to Mr Paterson myself about his behaviour. But we shall continue our inspection, Lieutenant Courtney. Onwards, please.'

Now the dramatics were over, the men endured the rest of the inspection in silence. Courtney felt Bryant's curious eyes as he looked through Arnold's belongings, but again, there was naught. Other than Paterson, all of the crew were clean and organised and without a hair out of place. It did not appease Bryant. He returned to his cabin immediately, leaving Courtney to deal with the astonished men. In the midst of them all, with the other officers' eyes also on him, Courtney flushed.

'As you were, men,' he finally managed to say. 'Back to your duties. Starboard watch, on deck. I shall instruct Cook to light the galley fires.'

Bryant had made no stipulations for stopping their food or grog, and Courtney would not punish them all for one man's misfortune. Returning to the gunroom, Nightingale approached him. He reached out a hand then stopped at the last moment before he could place it on his arm.

'What the devil was that about?' Nightingale asked.

'I don't know. Something is wrong.'

'Something is terribly wrong,' Pascoe spoke. Courtney had not looked at him when entering, and neither did he now. He entered his cabin, changed from his best uniform, and returned to the deck where a curious pall hung over the men as they worked.

Something was certainly wrong, he thought again.

But what exactly, he could not tell.

Chapter Twelve: Unyielding

For the next three days after Paterson's arrest, Courtney considered and reconsidered the idea of visiting him in his chains. He had seen men imprisoned on ships and off of them, for crimes they should have been punished for, and misdemeanours they should not have been – had even felt the effects himself.

If found guilty of theft, the merciful punishment for Paterson would be a flogging or a court martial. The ultimate sentence was death, as it so often was in the Articles.

Courtney now wondered if he should test his fortune with Paterson. A surreptitious visit to the hold did not sound so flagrant but he knew Bryant would not look kindly on it – and the captain did not cease pressing Courtney to labour on the *Lysander*, even when it was not his watch. He placed Courtney in the authority of teaching Smythe and assessing his journals; inspecting the *Lysander* with Brooks, the carpenter; and constantly picked up on minor blemishes on his uniform, even whilst knowing that Courtney did not possess the funds to clean it so regularly. When nothing could be found on the *Lysander*, he even directed Courtney across to the *Fantôme* to convene with Capitaine Bonfils. On one occasion, Geneviève Baptiste insisted on guiding him around the French frigate in repayment to his previous tour of the *Lysander*.

Upon returning to his own ship, Bryant promptly reprimanded him for spending too long away.

Courtney felt stretched to breaking point between the two ships, the men and the other officers.

When he confided his idea to Nightingale one evening in a spare breath, Nightingale volunteered to speak with Paterson. Courtney agreed, though urged him to avoid Bryant on his way there and back.

Over pease pudding the next afternoon, Nightingale said, 'He is troubled by what may come but he is physically well.'

Courtney tilted his head. 'You have already visited Mr Paterson?'

'Yes. I have little else to do onboard. I feel so useless sometimes.'

Courtney felt a spike of guilt, but he was unsure why. He had not been the one to order Nightingale to stay below and keep out of his path. 'Thank you. What did you speak to him about?'

'Not much. Even without an official role on this ship, it would be strange to fraternise with the hands. I simply asked him how he was keeping. Dr Faulkner was just leaving him as I went down.'

'Did Faulkner say anything?'

Nightingale shook his head. 'Not about my presence and not about Mr Paterson either. He seems to not want to take any side, certainly after he was the one to alert us to the missing scalpel...'

'He's the doctor – he doesn't have a side to take. And it was not Dr Faulkner who informed the captain.' Courtney glanced down the table but Pascoe was engaged in conversation with Godfrey. 'I don't believe Mr Paterson took it,' he admitted quietly.

'Nothing was found in his possessions,' Nightingale said.

Even Bryant could not deny that. Courtney did not know what the captain intended to do with Paterson. Perhaps he planned to hand him over the authorities at Gibraltar, but that seemed a large step for a crime that was not even certain and had no evidence. Perhaps he wished for the man to break in the dingy hold. Perhaps it was simply a statement of his power; some captains revelled in the authority they gained once they had a coat to separate them from the rest.

Courtney knew that power made men believe strange things about themselves and others.

He tried to concentrate upon the *Lysander*. Despite the tension on her decks, she settled nicely in her place alongside the *Fantôme*. Courtney slowly became accustomed to her quirks and which tack and trim she preferred. She was remarkably sprightly when running before the wind, responding well when a breeze veered, something that would aid them if she ever needed to scud in dirty weather. Courtney prepared himself for it, keeping a close eye on the falling barometer that threatened worse skies.

By and large, the two vessels were able to lay their courses, but the practice of working to windward allowed Courtney to keep the crew lively and prepared. Across the water, sometimes within hailing distance, sometimes further astern due to her heftier weight, the *Fantôme* remained dependable and weatherly.

Courtney had not told Bonfils about the issue with Mr Paterson. He hoped the problem would blow over before it became serious enough to alert their French companions.

When it next came for him to visit the *Fantôme*, Bryant deigned to accompany him, trailing Godfrey also. This time, instead of Courtney speaking to Bonfils alone, all of the officers assembled in the *Fantôme's* great cabin, standing amongst the deep-red decoration and glimmering trinkets. Even Geneviève Baptiste joined them, sitting primly at the head of the table. With Gabriel shuffling about amongst them, setting down wine and cigars, Bonfils spread out the charts of the Mediterranean, from the Strait of Gibraltar to the small dot of Malta.

'Should he be party to this?' Bryant asked, glancing at the little cook.

Bonfils laughed. 'Gabriel does not speak a word of English, Captain. Consider him as invisible as a phantom.'

Bryant looked towards Godfrey, obviously expecting him to turn and share Bryant's expression of reproach, but the second lieutenant did not bite at the bait. Courtney respected him for it.

'We shall reach Gibraltar in three days,' Bonfils continued, seeming not to have noticed. 'I have been given the authority to decide whether setting a man down to discover any further information would be a viable course of action. Perhaps to move along the coast.'

'Our ships may not be in frequent communication with the shore,' Bryant said. 'The European coastline, following the shores of the Balearic Sea and further east, is some distance from our areas of search. And it would be far too perilous to set a man down on the Barbary Coast of North Africa.'

'I am in agreement with you, Captain. I do not see the benefit of a search on such a potentially distant shore. I believe we can glean more helpful information in Gibraltar itself.'

'Gibraltar is a British colony.'

The implications of that hung for a moment, Bryant's distaste of allowing a French ship to potentially sully the port. But they were at war no longer.

'I am very familiar with Gibraltar,' Courtney interjected. 'There are always sailors stationed there. At least some will have seen the *Loyal*.'

'Yes.' Bonfils nodded. 'We have already received information that she has been seen from the port.' He paused as Auclair spoke up. 'My lieutenant is also familiar with the area,' he translated. 'He fought under Linois when our squadron from Toulon attempted to reach Cadiz a year back.'

'I dare say many of us are familiar with Gibraltar,' Bryant dismissed. 'Additionally, I needn't remind you gentlemen that our voyage is a secret one.'

'We can inquire in a way that does not reveal the entire truth.'

'My brother is an acquaintance of the governor. I dare say I may be able to arrange a meeting.'

That was not quite the kind of contact that Courtney had had in mind. Privately, he doubted the governor would have had the same eyes as the regular sailors who frequented Gibraltar.

'I should like to go ashore also,' Geneviève suddenly said. 'I am anxious to know of my husband.'

'Then I shall certainly accompany you, Madame,' Bonfils replied, tilting his hat to her.

Bryant said nothing.

After further talks of Gibraltar, the meeting of the officers finished and Bonfils herded them back onto deck, Geneviève on his arm. The skies had darkened since they had entered the great cabin and a colder wind rose from the south-east. The chillier weather reminded Courtney that autumn approached – and Jane's wedding. There still seemed so much of the voyage to complete, shadows lurking about every corner.

'Madame Baptiste was telling me of your last visit to the *Fantôme*, Lieutenant Courtney,' Bonfils said. Courtney split from his troubled musing.

'Oh,' he said. 'Yes, thank you, Madame.'

She smiled, lowering her head. Courtney noticed that the red mark on her forehead had nearly faded, although that could have been a result of her powder.

'She said that she enjoyed her tour of the *Lysander*,' Bonfils continued. 'Perhaps soon, I shall see her also.'

Bryant bristled as he, Courtney and Godfrey descended down to the waiting cutter. Harris, at the tiller, looked at the captain's flushed face and then promptly looked away.

'The cheek of the man,' Bryant hissed to Courtney. 'I shall invite him across to dinner when I see fit.'

'Yes, sir.' Courtney did not want another argument.

'You shan't mingle with that French woman anymore either, Lieutenant. It is obviously giving her and Bonfils ideas.'

Courtney kept his eyes ahead on the sails of the *Lysander*. 'She is Monsieur Baptiste's wife, sir, and Capitaine Bonfils's guest. She was simply interested in the ways of an English ship.'

Bryant huffed. 'I know women, Lieutenant.'

Courtney did not comment. He held no true separation when it came to the sexes, whether for friendship or attraction. Growing up, there had been more important matters than the proper interactions of boys and girls. Poverty and welfare held no distinction.

'I shall be speaking with Mr Paterson again today,' Bryant continued. 'I still do not believe he is entirely free from guilt.'

'We found nothing on his person or in his possessions, sir.'

'They have ways, sailors, all of them. I have confiscated many a bladder of rum and gin, brought onboard in the most peculiar of ways.'

That was something Courtney could not deny. 'This is not drink, sir,' he still said, retreating on his assertion that he did not want to argue. 'He cannot simply swallow the evidence and try and hide his drunkenness.'

'Where do you assume he has hidden the contraband then, Lieutenant? Surely you must have experience. Your wayward youth could be of benefit to us.'

Courtney bit his tongue. 'I do not believe he has hidden it, sir.'

'Then he must be in league with another. Mr Arnold perhaps. I shall speak with him also.'

Within the hour, both Paterson and Arnold stood before Courtney and Bryant. Neither of them could add any more to what was already known. Dr Faulkner's scalpel remained missing; Paterson's belongings remained in a mess; and Paterson himself remained punished. Bryant finally allowed the man out of the hold but he still docked a chunk from his pay and stopped his grog. As if wanting to keep him away from his friend, he was also sent to the masthead immediately after their interrogation.

Courtney did not agree with Bryant's decision to make the man suffer. It was obvious to him that Paterson was innocent, perhaps not of causing disruption, but at least of this offence.

At the end of the day, with Paterson down from the stomach-turning masthead, and with Courtney's watch complete, he retreated to the sanctity of his cabin. The cot Nightingale slept in was empty, but Courtney still clambered into his hammock and hoped Bryant did not call him back to duty. With a note of paper in hand, he tried to compose the letter to Jane that he still had not started. The brief docking at Gibraltar might allow him to post it to her. Half of him wished to assure her that she could continue with her wedding plans; another selfish part wished she could delay them again for his attendance.

He told himself he was being ridiculous. But the anxiety of it still tugged at him.

He had only written the first word, a scrawled 'Dear', before Nightingale entered. He paused as Courtney sat up. 'Oh, I did not realise you were here, Arthur,' he said.

'It is your cabin as well, Hiram. What is it?' he added, as Nightingale had barely responded. The look on his face echoed what Courtney thought must be on his.

'Captain Bryant must have heard of my visit to Mr Paterson,' Nightingale said, perching on the cot.

'And what business is it of his?' Courtney asked, although he knew the question was ridiculous. The man was the captain.

'Arthur, don't.'

'What? Did he reprimand you for it? You are a guest onboard the *Lysander*. It is your father-in-law who has gone missing. He cannot order you.'

'Arthur, you know he can.'

'I shall speak to him.' Courtney realised he should not, but he was already swinging his legs out of the cot.

'And say what to him, precisely? Don't make this difficult.'

'He near-insulted Capitaine Bonfils today, and it is not the first time.'

'Arthur, don't be rash. And let me finish—'

But Courtney had already left the cabin and Nightingale in his wake. He climbed through the decks to the great cabin, passing Arnold on the way. Steeling himself, he knocked on the door and was answered by a begrudging call to enter. Bryant glanced up from his paperwork.

'Oh, Lieutenant Courtney,' he said, promptly looking down again. 'What do you require now?'

Squeezing his hands behind his back, Courtney said, 'I wished to inform you, sir, that it was my idea for Mr Nightingale to visit Mr Paterson in the hold. He should not bear the blame for it.'

'That is very noble of you, Lieutenant, but the fact of the matter is that he did visit him. The man is forty-two, able to make his own decisions. We all know he is not afraid to make...questionable choices.'

'I wished to know that Mr Paterson was well, sir. As I was occupied in my duties, I thought Mr Nightingale would be an acceptable substitute.'

'Mr Paterson was in chains. His wellbeing did not matter.'

'Men do not like being kept in chains, sir.'

'Is that a warning, Lieutenant?' Bryant looked up, laying down his quill. 'I do not take seditious behaviour lightly, as you have seen.'

'No, sir. I was not questioning—'

'I have been disappointed at your behaviour, Lieutenant. You continually act above your station, not to mention your instruction of Mr Smythe, a responsibility that should be mine.'

Courtney opened his mouth to argue, quickly decided better of it, but Bryant kept going.

'Mr Pascoe informed me of Mr Smythe's comments about the *Lysander* and her comparison to the *Scylla*. I do not like any reminders of that old ship which you and I both know has now been broken up. You are on the *Lysander* now, and cannot keep to your old fellows, but must give yourself to the present.'

'I believe that she has only been mentioned directly by Mr Smythe once, and he meant nothing of it, sir.'

'I should hope not. And ensure that Mr Nightingale does the same. This is my ship and he agreed to obey my directives. Do you know...' Bryant sat back, folding his hands across his stomach. He eyed Courtney as if weighing up whether he should speak the next words, and then did, with the subtle hints of a smile. 'I have a mind to set him down in Gibraltar. He is obviously a distraction to you and he serves no true purpose here.'

'Sir.' Courtney now looked him in the face, rather than the spot above the gallery windows where he had been staring. 'His father-in-law is missing.'

'Yes, I am aware of that. Yet I can't help but feel a better place for him would be at his wife's side in England. She has potentially lost her father.'

Courtney shut his mouth. He could not deny Louisa's loss – and the mere thought of her sent a chill over his skin. Nightingale should be with her. That was the fear that had bloomed in him again and again. They had a marital bond. What did he and Nightingale have?

'I see you agree with me,' Bryant said before he could say anything more. 'That will be all, then, Lieutenant. Please, leave. I shall consider Mr Nightingale's place on the *Lysander* very closely.'

Courtney could only obey. He returned to the gunroom and his cabin where Nightingale looked up at him but did not utter a word. Courtney rolled back into his hammock, glanced at his pathetic letter to Jane, and decided against writing any more.

Instead, he stared up at the low timbers above him and listened to the ambience of the *Lysander*: the aching of the ship, the waves outside, and the whistle of the rising wind down through the decks. He knew he could not act any further against Bryant, risking himself, his career, Nightingale, and the crew.

Yet he was beginning to realise that Bryant resembled himself in some ways – not in background or social hierarchy, but in stubbornness.

They had both dug their heels firmly in the unyielding ground.

–

'You're hurt again.'

For the past two weeks, Courtney had been trying to ignore the bruises to Walker's face and limbs. The boy had been walking stiffly, avoiding putting any weight on his right-hand side, and sometimes when he leant down in his hammock or against a bulkhead, he would wince. Courtney had mentioned it once or twice, perhaps more, and been swiftly silenced.

But the cut to Walker's bottom lip and the swollen nature of his jaw could not be so easily quietened.

In the dim berth deck, Courtney hoped he imagined it. Walker's reddening face and his turned cheek confirmed that he hadn't.

'Another fall?' Courtney asked, using Walker's usual excuse. 'You really should watch where you put your feet.'

'We've had dirty weather,' Walker said lamely. 'I'm not a born sailor, you know that, Artie.'

Courtney sighed and plucked out the handkerchief in Walker's belt. He doused it in the small mug of water he had intended to use for shaving. As he grew older, hair had started to grow about his cheeks and chin. For Courtney, this was not the stepping-stone into adulthood. He had become a man at eight or younger, protecting Jane as she grew.

He soaked the fabric and raised it, intending to press it against Walker's injured face. The boy flinched.

'I won't hurt you,' Courtney insisted. 'I can be gentle.'

Walker hesitated but slowly nodded. Silently, Courtney laid the handkerchief against Walker's skin and wiped at the dried blood. It spotted his delicate jaw and reached down his throat to where a neck-cloth was elegantly tied. Courtney wiped as softly as he could muster, paying attention to any of Walker's pained winces. Trying to ignore the anger his suffering stoked in him, he said, 'You're always so tidy. Are those your initials embroidered on your handkerchief?'

Walker nodded again.

'You said you're not a born sailor,' Courtney continued. 'What are you then? Why are you here?'

Walker did not speak for a moment. He gritted his jaw as Courtney ran the fabric tenderly up the line of it, eyes lowering. 'I'm nothing,' he finally managed. 'Not anymore.'

'You were, though? Before coming onboard the Grampus?'

Courtney thought back to what he had overheard from Midshipman Lowe. He probably should have closed his ears to such talk from the officers, but the young lad hadn't exactly been quiet. He had started to get the impression that it had been connected to his Walker. The neat clothes, the embroidered fabric, the knowledge the boy had about academic subjects… He was no normal deckhand, impressed by a gang or drawn from the hard work of fishery and merchant shipping, but more like someone from Lowe's set. No doubt that was a reason why the other boys singled him out for sniping and attack.

'I come from Plymouth,' Walker eventually said. 'My family owned a number of mines along the coast of Cornwall. My elder brother often had a direct hand in them and enjoyed overseeing the day-to-day working. But, as a family, we were not miners ourselves. We simply reaped the rewards of it. We owned a comfortable house and made a handsome living each year. I had an upbringing which many boys would have envied.'

Courtney knew he would have. He could barely recall having a stable place to sleep and live, not until Mr and Mrs Woods had taken him and Jane in. Luxury had been a distant dream.

'But one year, not long ago, disaster struck our business. A dreadful collapse happened in one of our mines and the profits plummeted. We tried to put more finance into our remaining mine but it did not work. We found no tin or copper. And then, perhaps because of the strain we put upon the structure, perhaps because of sheer misfortune, the same disaster happened to our second mine, though this time, many good men were killed. Including my brother.'

Walker fell quiet again. Courtney had stopped cleaning the blood from his face and now peered into his soft, sad eyes. Walker obviously still looked through the past at that destroyed mine, realising that his brother would not return from its ruin. Courtney imagined losing Jane to such tragedy, and his heart ached.

'My brother had gone to help,' Walker continued brokenly. 'The mine flooded. His body was never found. No one cared for our plight. People we had thought were friends turned against us and we were left on our own. We had to abandon our home and all that we knew. My family could no longer support me. So I was taken from my life of education and promise, and sent here. Into the navy.'

'I'm sorry,' Courtney said quietly.

Walker shook his head. 'I don't belong here, I know that. But I don't belong there either, not now. And it…keeps coming to haunt me. There are men here who knew of us in Plymouth, men who we never had a chance to pay, whether we employed them or were in debt to them.'

Despite their differences, Courtney knew that sensation — both of being indebted to others and feeling lost. Though the Grampus *felt rigidly hierarchical, it was still populated by men caught between worlds, lost and trying to find a place for themselves. Courtney did not know what future lay ahead for himself. Those crossroads looked dim and hazy.*

'I ran from home too,' Courtney admitted. 'Not in the same way that you did, but I was fleeing wretched people and a lot of troubles. I took my sister with me, as far as I could, and then I came here. I hope to send money back to her. She's safe, for now.'

'Your sister? Jane?'

'Yes.'

'That was who I helped you write to.'

'That's her.'

Courtney saw understanding cross Walker's face, perhaps an acknowledgment of a shared bond. For some reason, he realised there was relief there too. It warmed him, made him think he had been successful in providing the boy with an ally.

'I thought she was your sweetheart,' Walker said unexpectedly.

Courtney found himself chuckling. 'No. No sweetheart.'

Walker smiled. It was the first time he had smiled in days, and Courtney treasured the look. He could almost forget that there was blood on those cracked lips. The air now lighter between them, he finished cleaning off the marks and then soaked Walker's handkerchief again, hoping that the stains would vanish. When he tried to hand it back to Walker, the boy shook his head. He reached out and curled his fingers about Courtney's fist, closing it around the fabric.

'You keep it,' he said. 'I don't need such a fanciful thing anymore. It reminds me too much of home.'

Courtney did not know what to say. He held the fine gift in his rough hand and gently tucked it away in his shirt. He kept it there even when Walker had left, returning to his position in the waist of the Grampus. *As well as the gloves from Walker, this was one of the first physical offerings he had even been given. It was far worthier than he deserved, but he could not deny the flutter of warmth it gave him. They were allies, truly, he thought, and perhaps friends.*

Chapter Thirteen: Tie Mates

'Arthur.'

Someone rasped his name. At first, Courtney thought it was Walker. He had been floating in his thoughts recently, pulled back to the surface by the events of the present. Courtney wanted to push him down again but he kept returning, no matter what he did.

'Arthur.'

He did not sound as he once had. Perhaps this was the Walker of now, after they had been parted on the *Grampus*. It had been so long ago, although it only felt as if it happened the year before, or even sooner.

'Arthur!'

Courtney jerked awake. A hand grasped his shoulder, wrenching him from the fragments of the bad memories. In the darkness of his cabin on the *Lysander*, Nightingale leant over him. Courtney scrambled upright.

'What is it?' he asked, grasping Nightingale's wrist. He was briefly relieved to feel the calmness of his pulse. Sometimes, Nightingale still awoke from night terrors and intrusions of his past. 'Are you well?'

'Yes. Yes, I'm fine. But the marines are about. I heard Pascoe's voice.'

'Good God...'

Courtney rolled from his hammock, reaching for his drawers and trousers. He pulled them up beneath his nightshirt and let Nightingale drape his uniform coat around his shoulders. In the gunroom, Smythe peered blearily out from behind his door. Marine Sergeant Dawes's cabin was empty.

Tugging on his sword-belt, Courtney grabbed a lantern and made his way through the deck. He had not checked the time, but only a cold stream of moonlight struggled through the hatches. It illuminated his path through the gently swinging hammocks. Every now and then, dark faces peered from the cocoons. He tried to keep his expression impassive, but his heart throbbed. Any mention of marine activity drew up immediate thoughts of the worst – murder, mutiny...

A figure rushed out of the shadows. Courtney grasped the hilt of his sword, only for Pascoe to snatch his arm.

'Mr Pascoe,' Courtney breathed, glad and angry at once. 'What the devil is happening?'

'Those wretched mongrels,' the master hissed. 'Didn't I tell you they were wrong 'uns?'

He all but pulled Courtney down the companion-ladders towards the hold. There in the gloom, Sergeant Dawes had Paterson in his brawny grip. Across from him, a private held Arnold. Even in the low light, Courtney could see the terror on their faces. They jumped like rabbits as Courtney and Pascoe approached, shying away from the finger Pascoe waved at him.

'These...animals,' he growled. 'Behaving dirtily!'

'Mr Pascoe,' Courtney snapped. 'Calm yourself, man. What exactly is the issue here?'

'I found them, sir. In the dark. Together like man and wife.'

Courtney's heart dropped from his chest. He felt it hit his stomach, coiling it into a tight knot. Praying his voice did not wobble, he asked, 'What precisely did you see, Mr Pascoe?'

'It doesn't bear repeating, sir!'

'You shall have to repeat it. Never mind your sensibilities, man.'

His anger balanced his dread. Pascoe shook his head, again turning on Paterson and Arnold. 'Never in all my ships...'

'This is not your ship, Mr Pascoe. Come away and tell me what you saw. This is a serious accusation to make.'

'Do you think I would jest about it?'

Courtney turned to Dawes. 'Keep the men under watch, Sergeant. I shall take Mr Pascoe away and find out the truth of this.'

'I shall go to the captain, Lieutenant Courtney. I apologise for suggesting it is my vessel. He shall know what justice awaits these damned buggers.'

Fuelled by his emotions, Pascoe stamped up the ladder. Courtney followed, furious at Paterson and Arnold, furious at Pascoe, furious at himself for not realising. Those bleary faces turned to them throughout the gun deck again. A few men sat at the edge of their hammocks, muttering amongst themselves. Courtney noticed some of Paterson and Arnold's messmates. Obi stared at him, stood beside his berth and seemingly about to approach. Courtney shook his head and he stepped back again.

'Lights out!' Courtney ordered. 'Or I shall find you a comfortable place on the tops before your watch begins!'

Nightingale had hurried from the gunroom and stood at the companion-ladder with a night-gown thrown around his shoulders. Seeing him there, handsome with his auburn hair unbound, the man Courtney would have crossed oceans for, nearly broke Courtney's façade. They shared Paterson and Arnold's crime.

Bryant's reaction, barely veiled disgust as he curled his lip, was the reaction Courtney knew he also would receive.

'Have them brought to the cabin,' he seethed. 'Now! Before they have had a chance to conspire and invent all manner of lies. Sergeant Dawes shall accompany them. Lieutenant Courtney, Mr Pascoe, remain with me. You shall observe.'

Part of Courtney felt relief that he would be here at this hastily convened interrogation. He wished to keep the worst of Bryant and Pascoe in check. But he knew he must tread carefully. Any vigorous defence of them would turn eyes upon himself – moreover, it would turn eyes upon Nightingale. He would not allow the man to suffer any more grief for the feelings in his heart. Those terrible scars on his back were more than anyone should bear.

Dawes arrived with the two aghast men. Their parade through the curious gun deck would have stirred rumours. Courtney knew what it was like to watch a man in trouble, wondering what his allegations were. He was sure other sailors had once looked at him in the same way after the trouble he had caused. *Walker*, he thought. That boy, and all they had done, still haunted him.

For the first time, Courtney truly observed Paterson and Arnold. They were at least a decade older than him, although their weather-beaten browned skin could have added more years. Their long pigtails matched, one dark, one blonde. Doubtless they had been tie mates, comrades who would stick together through all, including plaiting the other's winding hair. The twin tattoos made sense now: perhaps a mark of a former ship. Courtney had noted all this down when they signed on, but now, there were faces and lives attached to those paltry details.

He did not want to note them down in the muster as deceased.

'Mr Paterson, Mr Arnold,' Bryant announced. He stood before his desk, his uniform gleaming in full, the entire power of his rank behind him. 'Please tell me what Article Number Twenty-Nine entails.'

Neither man responded, as if to speak the Article meant its truth.

'Article Number Twenty-Nine,' Bryant continued. 'If any person in the fleet shall commit the unnatural and detestable sin of buggery and sodomy with man or beast, he shall be punished with death by the sentence of a court martial. Tell me what you were doing in the hold of the *Lysander*.'

Paterson did not even glance at his companion, as though he were in an entirely different room. Death by court martial. Courtney had seen that sentence carried out before, the mutineers of the *Ulysses* hanging from the *Leviathan*'s yardarms.

'Mr Pascoe, please state what you witnessed in the hold.'

Pascoe cleared his throat, shuffling uncomfortably. Courtney hoped he was reconsidering what he had already told Bryant. 'I saw them in the darkness. Fumbling. Their mouths upon each other. Their hands upon each other. Their bodies upon each other. He—' Pascoe had riled himself up with the account and now pointed a sharp finger at Paterson. 'He was within him, like mating animals.'

'Do you deny it?' Bryant asked.

Still, nothing. Perhaps that was the most sensible path, perhaps it was not. Either way led to a trial by court martial.

'I have no choice but to hand you to the military authorities at Gibraltar. First, you cause disruption through your fighting, then Mr Paterson, you are accused of stealing from the ship's stores, and now, this ugly crime. I have been far too lenient with you. Lieutenant Courtney, do you have any questions before I put them back in irons?'

It was simply protocol that made Bryant hand this opportunity to Courtney. Bryant was the captain; although he had his broader orders, the standing regulations for the ship were his authority. Courtney took a breath. 'What was your purpose in the hold, Mr Pascoe?' he asked.

Pascoe turned to him. 'I was there to look over the ship's ballast. You and I have both seen the barometer's readings. We know that a storm may be approaching.'

'I assume that you took a light with you.'

'Pardon?'

'The hold is very dark.'

'Of course it is.' Pascoe gritted his jaw. 'Sir.'

'Then how can you be sure of what you saw?'

Pascoe fell silent. Both Paterson and Arnold dared to look at him. 'I took a lantern,' Pascoe finally said. 'I know what it was that I saw, Lieutenant Courtney.'

'Lieutenant, the cross-examination shall be the duty of the court martial,' Bryant cut in.

'I am simply trying to ascertain if...'

'We can ascertain nothing, other than these men have offended before. They do not have much firm ground to stand upon. A court martial must be convened and the sentence must be carried out.'

The statement ended the impromptu investigation. Amongst the governance of the navy, no infraction other than mutiny could stir such feeling as sodomy. In the lower berths, such suspicions were often kept quiet, as long as the hands performed well in the yards and about the ship. But the dismissal of the regular sailors did not extend to the Articles. Paterson and Arnold could be hanged, as they would be on land, or they could be flogged around the fleet. Both options entailed humiliation for the accused and their families.

Any impassive façade that Bryant wore dropped as soon as Paterson and Arnold had been escorted out. He sat back down behind his table and shook his head. 'This,' he hissed, 'is a grand spectacle we are showing to our French allies. Theft and buggery and insubordination!'

'We cannot be sure of theft or buggery,' Courtney tried.

'Have you never encountered such crimes before, Lieutenant?'

Courtney said nothing.

'Of course they did not admit their guilt. But that does not mean they are innocent.' He huffed, flushing an angry red. 'I cannot be seen to do nothing. As I said, I have already been too lenient. The men and the Frogs must see that we do not stand for this.'

'They are already sentenced to a court martial.'

'I should have had Paterson flogged for the thievery.'

'You will have them flogged even while waiting for a trial? The men will not like that.'

'It is not their place to like it or dislike it. Crime requires punishment, as is stated in the Articles. By stepping on a naval vessel, they all agree to obey or pay the price.'

Courtney looked to Pascoe but he remained silent, only nodding in agreement. He and Bryant had not seen eye to eye yet in this, they were united.

'Have some mercy, sir,' Courtney said. He knew it was too far as soon as it had left his mouth.

'Mercy? Upon these men? Why don't I go a step further and allow them into my cabin to make the decisions for the ship? Why don't I allow them to wear the uniform of their betters? I had my fill of Revolutionary sailors in Spithead. You, Lieutenant Courtney, sound more and more like our French neighbours.'

Courtney stood. For a moment, surprise, even fear, crossed Bryant's expression. Such an accusation would have been enough to have him called out on land, but Courtney had to accept it. His position in this hierarchy demanded a closed mouth.

When he responded no further, a smile touched Bryant's mouth. Courtney knew he wanted him cowed and obedient. 'But,' Bryant said, 'perhaps you speak some modicum of sense, Mr Courtney. If you are so concerned with the men despising my actions, then I shall adapt accordingly. I shall not have them flogged. I shall pass the baton into the hands of the crew. I will have Mr Paterson and Mr Arnold face the gauntlet.'

Courtney's stomach tightened. More than flogging, the gauntlet was a terrible thing. 'The gauntlet is for theft.'

'Which Mr Paterson is already accused of. It is for any crime that affects the entire crew. Their name has been marred. You cannot disagree with that assessment. And now that I think of it, you came to me last night, speaking of Mr Nightingale's actions when he visited Mr Paterson. If I was not a man above speculation, I would suggest that you and your friend are in alliance to distract me from the blackguards in my ship.'

'Sir!' Courtney tried to bite his tongue. 'That was not my intention.'

'As I say, Mr Courtney, I am a man above speculation. I was simply warning you about your behaviour.'

There was nothing else Courtney could say. Bryant and his brother at the Admiralty Office could have him dismissed without a second thought.

'Very good,' Bryant said at his silence. 'I see you understand. Therefore, you shall be the one who guides them through, Lieutenant. They are your men.'

The relief at finally leaving the cabin sank upon Courtney like a physical weight. In the corridor beyond, he felt his composure wobble. He had not expected to be confronted with such a thing as sodomy amongst the men on this ship; perhaps he had been naive to think he could weather his entire career as an officer unscathed. Before then, he had seen those accusations from another ground. It had been the first time, but not the last. All he wanted to do was to protect those on the other side of such charges; he would defend Nightingale to his dying breath. But to speak up further would endanger them and his own future in the navy.

Smythe was gone from the gunroom when he returned. Courtney pulled Nightingale into their shared cabin and felt the frustrated, angry tears creep upon him. 'They are accused of sodomy,' he managed to say.

'Ah.' Nightingale lowered his eyes. 'I worried that... I had the idea that they might be...'

Courtney grasped the hand that Nightingale had lifted, stopping it from cupping his cheek. 'Why didn't you tell me?'

'I could not. One cannot make such an accusation without truth.'

'I could have helped them.'

'How? By revealing your own life to them? Arthur...' Nightingale pushed against Courtney's hand and despite his protests, made him look at him. 'I have lived forty-two years. Do you think I have not ever been tempted to step in? My... Tom, he was hanged for it. I have watched men flogged. I have heard their death sentences read out. You and I, men like us, we have to live in the shadows. We cannot help.'

'I cannot...' Courtney shook his head. He had wanted to speak to Nightingale of what they had; he had wanted to admit all his fears and all his blessings. They had not spoken of intimate things, of how their future laid. Now, it was racing upon him in a veil of crushing emotion. 'I cannot condemn them for loving each other in the same way that I love you.'

Nightingale stopped. He searched Courtney's face, green eyes widening. A breath passed between them with only the creaking of the ship and their secrets. 'Love?' he whispered.

'Yes. Of course. Of course I love you.'

'I...' Nightingale lowered his hand, letting it brush Courtney's neck and rest on his chest. Courtney felt his ring, the tie that bound him to Louisa by law and by tradition. It was something they could never have. 'I wish we were not here,' Nightingale muttered.

'But we are. And he is going to have them run the gauntlet for it. I... I'm sorry, Hiram, I cannot be here. I cannot...'

Look at you, he was about to say. With the passion still churning in his breast, Courtney swept past him and out into the gunroom again. He did not turn back, only ascended to the deck where the stars still hung in the sky. There were too many shades in this ship, emerging from places Courtney had not expected to confront. They enmeshed with Nightingale, with Paterson, with Arnold, with Courtney's hatred of injustice and brutality. But he could not give voice to them, not now. Once, upon the *Grampus*, he had tried – and been punished harshly for such a thing.

Now, he could not stand firm as he once had. Bryant might have been a tartar but Courtney was no longer the sailor at the bottom of the pile.

More than a decade later, he had so much more to lose.

Chapter Fourteen: The Gauntlet

To Courtney's right, Captain Bryant stood, bedecked in his full dress uniform, and to his left, he could feel the eyes of all of the Fantômes. In these light airs, with the coast of Spain to larboard, the two ships sailed under topsails alone. Enough men had been left to handle the sails and the helm. The rest occupied the deck from the aft boat davits to the forecastle. It had not been sufficient humiliation to face their fellows alone; the French crew would also bear witness to Paterson and Arnold's punishment.

Despite the chill, Courtney could feel sweat beneath his collar. He kept his eyes ahead, not listening to the trampling steps of the marines as they accompanied the prisoners from the hold. But in the corner of his vision, he could see the glint of Bryant's epaulettes and golden buttons. His best uniform represented all the authority he wielded over these condemned men. He had the power to accuse them, to throw them into the hold in chains, to send them to a court martial, to eventually mean their death. Yet this…this additional abasement before their mates was not for his power.

It was cruelty, plain and simple.

Paterson and Arnold emerged from below. Manacles still ensnared their wrists. Even after only two days of imprisonment, they walked with bowed backs and trembling legs. No one but the officers had been told of their crime, but hearsay spread like fire in the confines of a wooden ship. There could be little other reason for two men, two close friends, to be so treated.

Whatever the mill of rumours in the decks below, Bryant addressed the crew now. His steward had placed the Articles on the rail before him and Courtney could see that dreaded number. Twenty-Nine. He gritted his teeth and tried not to react as Bryant read it aloud to all. Article Thirty followed. Robbery. Two crimes, Bryant said, that blackened the entire ship's name and put all of them into ignominy. The words washed over Courtney as if from a distance. He only watched for the crew's responses.

They did nothing. Perhaps the shock of standing there, knotted ropes in hand, had struck them dumb and mute. Never in all his time at sea had Courtney seen the gauntlet being run. It was not in the way of an impersonal flogging. Every strike would unite them in condemnation. The men who had signed on with Paterson and Arnold, including their fellow, Mr Lynde, would feel the barbarity of this the most. Courtney's eyes drifted from them to Obi, a man scarred by such savage whips such as the ones they now carried. God above, it was so needless. As the officers overseeing it, Godfrey, Smythe and Faulkner had been spared from participating. Nightingale stood apart from them, watching from the forecastle. Nothing had been said about his own involvement, but he was not one of the crew, doling out the punishments – and even Bryant could not deny the social standing that separated Nightingale from such base discipline. Despite their disagreement, Courtney wished Nightingale did not have to see this.

'Lieutenant Courtney.' Bryant was saying his name. Courtney took a breath, but did not look at him. 'Please take your place.'

Hand about the hilt of his sword, Courtney stepped down from the poop deck and towards the hatchway where Paterson and Arnold waited between the marines. The red-coated soldiers had been posted at each possible exit point, even at the gunwales, in case either of them tried to flee. The briny sea would be kinder than this, Courtney thought.

Paterson and Arnold looked at Courtney, fear in their eyes, and Courtney felt he had failed them. Nightingale's words reverberated in his head. He could not help everyone. His morality had to bend the knee.

But he knew, if he could, he would have taken the blows himself.

Silence rang as a cord was tied about them. With their shirts pulled from their bodies, Paterson took the lead position, Arnold behind. Courtney stared at Paterson and his weather-beaten face, stepping careful paces backwards until he was between the first lines of the crew. The two rows faced one another, ready with their weapons. Courtney unsheathed his sword and raised it so the point glimmered at Paterson's throat. Sergeant Dawes echoed him, his bayonet wavering at the base of

Arnold's skull. Even the stout marine officer seemed unsettled by this brutality.

Courtney curled his fist until the whorls of his sword hilt dug into his palm. Down the steel blade, Paterson's expression hardened. Wicked, hot hatred bloomed in Courtney's chest – not towards him, but towards the man who ordered this, the society that deemed it correct.

'Begin,' Bryant said.

Courtney stepped backwards. A second passed where he thought the men might refuse, then he felt the sharp wind of a rope whipped into the air. The knotted end slashed into Paterson's left shoulder. He winced, but at the last moment, stopped his mouth. No cry emerged from him.

Another attack came, this time from the opposite side. It cut a twin divot in Paterson's right shoulder. He set his jaw as hard as an anvil, refusing to even whimper. Courtney respected him for it.

Now the first blows had been struck, the dam broke. Courtney walked slowly backwards, watching the point of his sword. Behind Paterson, the assaults also fell upon Arnold. The man tried to remain as stoic as his friend, but the agony of strike after strike was fired by the humiliation. Courtney counted the beatings and where they fell: on shoulders and chests and backs and even one, a missed aim, slashing Arnold across the cheek. That was the hit that broke him. He whined and at the next impact, gave a plaintive howl.

Courtney kept staring at Paterson. Tears had gathered in the man's eyes, his brow furrowed in pain. He bore Courtney's gaze but his mouth twitched and throat convulsed around desperate swallows. Hearing Arnold's sobs fractured his spirit. He wept silently, until one of his messmates lashed a red-raw laceration across his chest and he cried aloud. The sound pierced through Courtney. But all he could do was to keep stepping backwards. Attacks pummelled Paterson's and Arnold's naked torsos and backs, slicing open wounds and arousing them again and again and again. By the time they reached the end of the first row, both were as subdued as whipped boys. Gasps shuddered from their lungs, every limb trembled. A ferocious tangle of emotions ignited their expressions.

Courtney stopped. They were free from the initial punishment – but the second row still remained.

'Proceed, Lieutenant Courtney!' Bryant called from the poop deck. The captain had not looked upon Paterson and Arnold's faces, only their wounded spines. With this next row, Courtney would lead them backwards towards the stern, straight beneath the captain's eyes. He hoped he saw them and felt a shred of humanity.

With sword and bayonet guiding them, the two men shuffled to their next abasement. Splatters of blood stained the deck. Courtney smeared some away with his boot. It was a ridiculous motion: more of the stuff had splashed across his coat and shirt, and some of it stuck on his face and in his hair. He would scrub himself clean later, for all that it mattered.

In the second row of men, the next sailor had barely raised his arm to strike when Bryant suddenly spoke again.

'Lieutenant Courtney!' he called. Courtney raised his eyes, barely trusting himself to move any further. 'A man is missing. Mr Nightingale does not have a cord.'

Now, Courtney turned. Nightingale, close to him at the forecastle, met his gaze, mouth opening. Shock crossed his face. With Arnold and Paterson shuffling and stretching their mutilated muscles, trying to relieve at least some of their pain, he left his position and hurried to Bryant's side. The captain looked coolly up at him.

'A cord, Lieutenant,' he repeated. 'Did you not hear me correctly?'

'Mr Nightingale is not part of the crew, sir,' Courtney said lowly. 'Like the officers, he should not have to—'

'He agreed to obey my orders upon joining us. And he is not one of the officers, not anymore. He quite cast himself out of that net with the *Ulysses* affair.'

'He shares the gunroom with the officers. You cannot ask him to—'

'I am not asking him, Lieutenant. I am ordering him. He may be your friend, but he is not yours to command. He has already tried to interfere in the workings of the *Lysander*. So, fetch him a cord.'

As Courtney stared, unbelieving, at Bryant, he knew that it was not for any protocol that Bryant gave the order. This was another cruel, twisted game, a reminder of each man's place in the hierarchy, most of all Courtney's and Nightingale's. Courtney thought of Bryant being sent ashore because of the Spithead mutineers' dislike of him. Many a captain had been driven mad by the thought of mutiny. Was this a way of striking Courtney and Nightingale for possible disruption to his ship?

Heart thudding, Courtney turned and marched over to the first row of men. Mr Lynde stared mutely at him. He was one of Paterson and Arnold's messmates, a man who had signed on with them. Courtney wrenched the cord from him and stood, for a moment, with it grasped in his hand. A sickening thrill went through him, an idea to hurl it to the floor or overboard.

But this one second of anger could unseat his entire career. He did not act only for himself now.

Anger churning, he returned to Nightingale. For the first time, he could not read Nightingale's expression. He was trying to remain as stoic as Paterson had for the sake of his tie mate. Courtney thrust the cord into his hand and turned immediately away.

Bryant loomed over them all. 'Begin,' he said once more.

Raising his sword, Courtney fought with himself not to look at Nightingale. He had been made to join the line of the gauntlet, the man at the very end.

Courtney kept his eyes upon Paterson, who now wept openly. The blows scoured his already scarred flesh, whipping more and more blood into the air. More than once, Courtney felt it splatter against his uniform. He wore it like a brand, only flinching when another drop splashed upon his cheek. The men did not diminish their lashes; a few times they came close to Courtney's wrist.

He counted his steps backwards, knowing that each one brought him closer to Nightingale. They felt awfully united in this. Courtney had once kissed the scars on Nightingale's back, ones which had been ordered by his own father in retribution for finding him with Tom, the stable-boy. Courtney too bore injuries from past pain. And now, together, they would wound two more innocent victims.

Finally, Nightingale was there, in the corner of his right eye, at the end of the line. His blow would be the last, the one that lingered the longest on Paterson and Arnold. The seconds stretched on. Courtney waited.

Then, in a sharp movement, Nightingale's rope came down. It struck Paterson's arm where no wound yet festered. The same fell on Arnold, onto the crease of his elbow which only jerked it back but did not welt. Such was their pain, though, that the two sailors still cried. They staggered away from their punishment, finally over, dripping sweat and tears and blood. Courtney kept his sword-point upon them, but he could not help glancing over at Nightingale. He had his head lowered, mouth drawn tightly. Courtney's chest ached as if his sabre had been driven into his own flesh. When he had first met Nightingale, he had been cowed and abused. They had both come through hell together and Nightingale had dragged himself onto the path of recovery.

It would be easy to tumble off it again.

Courtney would not allow Bryant to be the architect of his despair.

But now, the humiliation was finished. Dr Faulkner came forth, just as Paterson's legs gave out. The strength he had been wearing collapsed. Faulkner caught him about the arms, but his head still lolled in a dead faint. Arnold made a step forward, only stopped by the shame of their accusations and Bryant's shouted command for neither to move. Courtney felt the same, torn between his duties to himself and the ship, and to the man he cherished.

Why did it always have to be a sacrifice?

Bryant, still observing from the poop deck, crystallised his resolve. Courtney straightened his spine, re-sheathed his sword, and only watched as Faulkner tried to support Paterson back to his feet. Blood dribbled down his back and from the wounds on his torso. Even if the men were spared the noose, those marks would never fade.

'Take the prisoners below, Dr Faulkner,' Bryant ordered. 'Tend to their injuries but make certain that they are awake and alert when you do so. Sergeant Dawes, please accompany the doctor and ensure Mr Paterson and Mr Arnold are returned to irons afterwards. Lieutenant Courtney, you may dismiss the men by their divisions.'

Courtney did so without thinking or feeling. He only kept the waisters of the larboard watch behind. As soon as the deck had been cleared, they got on their knees and scrubbed and mopped at the stained timbers. All that remained of the punishment was the blood and shreds of skin on the knotted cords. Courtney did not realise he was still standing at the mainmast, staring down at the gore, until Godfrey appeared at his side.

'Lieutenant Courtney,' he said lowly. 'I did not think it was your watch.'

Courtney blinked. The scraping of the holystones and the swabbing of the sweepers seeped into his ears. 'No,' he said, throat dry. 'It is not. Thank you, Lieutenant.'

He manoeuvred around the men, making his way to the companion-ladder. For the first time, he glanced starboard to the *Fantôme*. He did not know what he expected to find: a marker of sympathy, cold-hearted resolution, thinly veiled disgust? As it was, the Fantômes worked just as the Lysanders did, preparing to crack on towards Gibraltar and leave this punishment behind them. Except Courtney knew it could not be left behind. Bryant would convene a court martial, and the agony would continue.

Now, Courtney descended to the gunroom. Smythe occupied it, writing in his logbook. Many officers kept their own additional journals, noting down decisions and orders to refer to in their later commands. Courtney hoped he did not follow that day's example.

'Where is Mr Nightingale?' he asked, and Smythe looked up. He sprang to his feet, giving a quick salute.

'I think he went to the orlop to aid Dr Faulkner, sir.'

Courtney knew that Captain Bryant would not look kindly on that. He resolved to head straight to the sickbay but the look on Smythe's face stopped him.

'Thank you, Mr Smythe. Are you well?'

'Yes, sir.'

Courtney could see that Smythe's hands were shaking and his eyes were red-raw from recently shed tears. Courtney felt a wave of sympathy for him; despite the schism in their ranks and stations, they had a wealth of shared dramatic experiences. He looked on him with the affection of an elder brother.

'Are you truly well, Mr Smythe?' he asked.

'Truly, sir,' Smythe lied. 'I have... I have simply never seen the gauntlet being run before.'

'Nor I, Mr Smythe. Let us hope we do not have to witness it again.'

'Indeed, sir.'

'Perhaps you should breathe in some fresh air. The deck has been cleaned now. Lieutenant Godfrey has the watch and he would not look unkindly on the company.'

'Thank you, sir.'

Smythe saluted again and hurried past Courtney, perhaps eager to get away from the shame of his tears. Courtney wanted to tell him that he had nothing be ashamed for. If he were not so angry, he might do the same.

Instead, he left the gunroom for the dingy orlop. For all the tension on her decks, the *Lysander* had been fortunate to have minimal physical injuries and sickness. The space was empty but for the doctor himself, tending to his two new patients, Nightingale, and, surprisingly, Obi. Arnold lay out on a makeshift table, seemingly unconscious. A patchwork of weeping, ugly lashes cut through his bare back, softly wiped by Nightingale and Obi. Paterson sat in the corner, head against the bulkhead, staring up at the timbers.

Courtney quietly cleared his throat. Obi rose to his feet, as did Nightingale.

'As you were,' Courtney said. 'I...merely came to see how Mr Arnold and Mr Paterson were faring.'

Dr Faulkner looked up from where he prepared poultices to ease Arnold and Paterson's wounds. His eyes were a little cloudy, no doubt from dabbling in his own stores. 'They will recover, Lieutenant,' he said simply.

'I am glad to hear it.' Courtney glanced to Nightingale, who immediately looked away. Courtney opened his mouth to speak but Nightingale cut him off.

'I shall fetch some more water for them, Doctor. I shan't be long.'

Nightingale went to leave. Courtney stood in his way for a moment.

'Pardon me, Lieutenant Courtney,' Nightingale said lowly. Courtney's heart sank at the use of his rank. He would have given anything to be called 'Arthur' in that moment.

'Captain Bryant will not like this, Hiram,' he said quietly.

Courtney hated that he had to say it. All he wished to do was protect Nightingale. He knew he had failed when Nightingale whispered, 'I don't give a damn,' and strode past him.

Courtney let him go. The others in the room had not heard his words, or if they had, they made no sign of it. Feeling humiliated and guilt-ridden, Courtney moved towards the doctor's slab, made of chests lashed together. Arnold slumbered, mercifully free from his pain for now. At Courtney's permission, Obi sat again, retrieving his bloodied cloth and resuming his gentle anointing of the man's wounded back. Courtney thought of the *Grampus* and his own careful tending of Walker.

'It is not your watch, Obi,' he said. 'You are not expected to aid Dr Faulkner.'

Faulkner did not respond to the comment. Obi nodded and replied, 'No, sir. I chose to aid him. Mr Paterson and Mr Arnold are in my mess and they've always been kind to me. I have experience in dealing with wounds like these.'

No doubt he had, considering his dreadful past. Courtney also couldn't help but notice how he referred to Paterson and Arnold as 'they', a united force together. 'That is very noble of you, Obi. I shall ensure Captain Bryant hears of it.'

Or perhaps he would not. He had no faith in Bryant's ability to recognise good men. Not wanting to dwell further on those almost-mutinous thoughts, Courtney continued, 'I am glad to hear that the *Lysander* is treating you well.'

'Thank you, sir. I am grateful you allowed me to come aboard.'

Such thanks were not needed, or expected. Courtney's place was not with the hands; his job was to keep them in line and oversee their efficient work. But he still felt he had a foot in their world, just as he had had when aiding a similarly wounded boy on the *Grampus*. That past kept rising to meet him, again and again. And Obi was a remnant of the *Scylla* – another ship he had to lay to rest.

'I had no other place to go after the *Scylla*, sir,' Obi said. 'She was my home for many years. Mr Smythe was too kind in offering me passage with him back to England. I had never been there before. I think I have spent more of my life at sea than on land.'

Courtney thought the same about himself. These ships were more than wooden vessels, just as he had said to Madame Baptiste. He hated to see such a place distraught and turned upon its head.

'The sea will always have a place for you,' Courtney said, and wondered why he did. It sounded pathetic, and he knew he could not promise such a thing, not for any man. The sea and her ships were fickle. Men could not truly abandon all of their issues and prejudices from the land. They followed them everywhere.

For now, Courtney left Obi with Dr Faulkner, before Nightingale could have a chance to return. He went back to his cabin where his letter to Jane, that note of indecision and worry around her wedding, still sat on his cot. He moved it and sank down onto the unyielding surface. In the little shaving mirror on the side, he saw his expression: haggard, blood-smeared, pale. A year before, in the Caribbean, he had appeared the same, thrown into turmoil after Robinson's death. That mire had been worsened by Captain Bryant, as this present disaster had been.

But once more, Courtney was the dirty one.

Perhaps he raged against a system and a hierarchy which would never be changed. It did not stop it from hurting.

Thinking of the court martial still to come, Courtney put his head into his hands and wept in fury and helplessness.

–

The dimness of the Grampus' *hold, despite its aroma of stinking water and soaked timbers, was a blessing. Courtney knew the patterns of the petty officers' and commissioned officers' watches and between which bells the space would be empty of living souls aside from the nesting rats. In a ship of so many men, the quiet shadows, away from the noise and tumult, felt like a secret for only him — and Walker.*

The boy lay against him, his head upon Courtney's shoulder. The side of a barrel supported them both in a secluded and furtive haven. Here, though Courtney only wore his thin shirt and trousers, the cold did not penetrate. Warmth still licked Courtney's chest and limbs in the aftermath of his and Walker's quick, fumbling passion.

He shifted his arm about Walker's shoulders and caressed his hair. Walker let out a slow breath, accepting the touch for a long moment. He had barely needed convincing to receive and enjoy this congress. It did not feel wrong, or unnatural, simply an extension of the intimacy and friendship they already shared. What had started with Courtney's attentions and Walker's gift of his handkerchief had led to lingering touches, understanding glances, and something unspoken. Courtney had no words to define it, not yet, but he was not ignorant of the world and of men who did such things.

He waited, each time he and Walker met, for the shame. He waited for the regret and the fear. It never came. Perhaps, he thought, there were other things in his life to be afraid of: pain and poverty and hatred. Not this.

Walker moved and looked into the dull darkness. They could not see the companion-ladder from here, and nor could the companion-ladder see them, but they needed to move soon. Watches would change.

'Will we do this again?' Walker asked softly, as he always did.

'If you would like,' Courtney replied. 'I won't be one to complain.'

Walker nodded. 'We shan't have long,' he said. 'When we are men, we shall grow out of it.'

Courtney did not know if he would. Walker had not said such a thing before. He did not reply, only helped Walker to sit up and re-do his buttons. As he did, his shirt slipped a little and revealed the pallid skin of his lower back.

Courtney paused.

'What are these?' he asked.

Walker stiffened. He hastily tucked his shirt into his trousers and put some distance between himself and Courtney. 'They're nothing,' he said.

'No. That is not true.'

Walker had not allowed Courtney to remove his shirt any of the times they had descended to the hold. Courtney had always agreed, knowing that to be almost fully dressed would save their necks if the worst should occur and they were found. But now, he neared Walker again and reached out to touch the fabric. Walker grasped his wrist.

'Don't,' he said. 'Do not ask me about them.'

No matter what Walker said, Courtney had seen the scars. They were not the kind that had appeared on Walker's face: the split lip and the bruised cheek and the swollen jaw. The long, twisted wounds were more than that, like beatings from a starting cane, but uglier and more vicious.

'Who did this to you?' Courtney asked, anger rising in his throat.

'I fell,' Walker insisted.

'Fell onto a lash?' Courtney shook his head. 'Someone has beaten you.'

'No.'

'Don't lie to me.'

'I am not lying.'

But the crack in Walker's voice said what he did not. He stopped, released Courtney's wrist, and began to stand. His legs wobbled and Courtney quickly rose to support him.

'You've been beaten,' he repeated. 'Was it one of the hands? One of the boys who have been mocking you and mistreating you?'

'Artie, don't ask me these things.'

'What did they do to you? How did they — what did they even use to hurt you with?'

'They didn't… Nothing has happened. Artie, I am well.'

'You're not well. I tried to ignore it when you were hurt before, but I can't ignore this. I am your friend, Garrick. We are allies here.'

'My friend…' Walker seemed to be about to say more, but stopped himself. 'Don't involve yourself. I am fine as I am.'

'You are not fine!' Courtney did not realise his voice had risen. He glanced to the ladder, but the motions of the ship continued as distantly as they had for the last twenty minutes. 'Tell me. Please. I won't be able to rest.'

Walker stared at him, mouth moving silently. His eyes darted about Courtney's face and he suddenly looked so young and vulnerable in the midst of this lumbering, dark old ship. 'I can't…' he whispered.

'You can,' Courtney insisted. He grasped Walker's hand and cradled it. 'I won't do anything foolish.'

He knew he could not promise that, but it seemed to placate Walker a little. He swallowed, fist twitching in Courtney's. 'It was… It was not the boys,' he admitted softly. 'Not one of those damned boys, not alone anyway.'

'What do you mean?'

'They were ordered. To do it. To hurt me.'

'By who?' Courtney must have said it too aggressively for Walker flinched and tried to back out of the conversation again.

'I cannot tell. I must not. It will only bring more trouble, and I cannot be sent home.'

Courtney grasped on as Walker tried to pull away. He wanted to shake him and ask him to give up the name, to confide in Courtney as he hoped he had made him comfortable enough to do, but the boy only gave a sob. Courtney's stomach chilled as tears fell.

'I'm sorry,' he stammered. 'I didn't mean to make you cry.'

'No,' Walker wept. 'It is not you. It is this ship. These boys. This navy. I don't know what to do.'

Courtney ceased his tight hold on Walker and allowed him to slip away, sitting down upon a barrel. He wished to embrace him again but thought Walker would reject him.

'I wish I was away from this,' Walker said through shuddering breaths. 'I don't know where, but…not here. The navy doesn't care for me. It doesn't care for my family. It will never help me. And he… No justice will come for him.'

Courtney knew what it was like to be mistreated by someone who would never feel any retribution for it. He listened silently to Walker, chest tight.

'What I would do if I was away...' Walker continued. *'I would punish them all myself. I would ensure that they know how it feels.'*

The sudden venom in Walker's voice surprised Courtney. He sat down beside him, thigh almost touching his. 'Tell me what to do to help you, Garrick. I want to help you.'

'You can't help me. No one can. Perhaps I should simply jump off the edge of the ship.'

'No.' Courtney grasped Walker's hand again. 'For the love of God, don't do that. Don't let them put those thoughts into your head. That is what they want.'

'Perhaps I should push them over the edge of the ship.'

His tone was too harsh for Courtney to tell whether he said it in seriousness or not. He decided not to respond, only cradled Walker's soft hand and wished that he did not have to experience the brutality of the world. He stayed still until Walker pulled his hand from his grip and lurched to his feet again. Head bowed, and not only because of the low timbers, he headed towards the ladder without a further utterance to Courtney.

But his words still echoed in Courtney's head. Suspicion festered within him, the unspoken knowledge of who Walker referred to as his abuser. If he was correct, there was little either of them could do. It only served to aggravate Courtney's regret and anguish. He sighed and picked himself up off the barrel. The watch would change soon. Such pleasure with Walker had to be consigned to the hold, but more and more, it bled into the rest of his days, churning in his thoughts and heart. Along with it, further feelings than simply carnal satisfaction were rising, equally as strong.

Courtney did not know what to do.

Chapter Fifteen: Gibraltar

15 September 1802, Gibraltar

Courtney held onto his bicorne hat as the wind increased. He flinched and spluttered when a gout of rain suddenly sprayed into his face. It blinded him for a moment, but with a frustrated wipe he cleared his vision and found the little pilot boat again, guiding the *Lysander* through the crowded anchorage of Gibraltar. The waves bobbed the small schooner; much more and the larger *Lysander* would have a job to moor safely. The masts already supported as little canvas as sensible. Courtney could barely wait to have this wretched business done.

But with the end of one began another. Courtney was not a man of God, yet this worsening weather seemed an omen of things to come.

Shouting directives, he observed as the best bower anchor was let go, the cables racing through the hawse-holes. When secure, the small bower followed and the capstan bars were shipped. Moored head and stern, the *Lysander* moved into the tide, quivering but safe. Courtney finally breathed, as much as he could in the sheet of rain, and took a moment to look at their new station for at least the next twenty-four hours. Twenty-four hours, he reminded himself, away from their voyage.

Courtney had visited Gibraltar many times before. In his youth, the grand, imposing rock had impressed him. It had been green and swarmed by migrating birds. There he had walked with Sara Foster, the girl he had promised to marry to take her away from her cruel brother, and she had known all the names of the squawking creatures. Courtney had failed to remember them all, just as he had failed to wed her. The next time he had come to Gibraltar, his ship struggling through reams of fog, his attention had been robbed and he had been unable to locate Sara or her brother.

Now, the rock of Gibraltar was not lush and green, nor shrouded in mist. It was simply grey and miserable, an ugly slab of land that loomed over the colourless town. The weeping heavens had bled all the hues from the markets and houses, leaving them cold and plain. That was precisely how Courtney felt too, shivering in his pea jacket and boat cloak.

Through the downpour, Bryant stamped, scowling. Sergeant Dawes followed him, trailed by Paterson and Arnold. Dr Faulkner had tended to their wounds, with Nightingale and Obi as his helping hands, but Courtney could still see drops of blood on their trousers from the lashings. Word had already been sent to the governor of their imprisonment and the details of the incident, but no other post had yet gone ashore. Courtney's letter to Jane remained on his cot.

'Capitaine Bonfils will join us soon,' Bryant said, drawing Courtney's focus. 'He is anchoring further out. This is a British colony.'

A British colony which no longer was at war with France, Courtney wanted to point out.

'You shall attend to the port-captain, Lieutenant, to deal with the necessaries,' Bryant continued. 'I shall speak with the governor and see if any more information is forthcoming. I will also inquire whether our testimony for the trial can be taken beforehand.'

'I can go to the taverns,' Courtney commented, gaining an incredulous look from the captain. He had endeavoured to say as few words to Bryant as he could muster, but now he could not ignore him any longer.

'This is not the time for drinking, Lieutenant,' Bryant snapped.

'To ask the sailors if any of them know more than we do now,' Courtney clarified.

Bryant glanced around him but no one lingered nearby – or rather, no one who could have heard over the rain. 'I needn't remind you of the secrecy of our voyage,' he said lowly. 'The *Loyal*'s absence cannot be spoken of beyond trusted associates.'

'I shall not mention her by name, or mention any ship at all. But Capitaine Bonfils said she had been seen off Gibraltar. He himself said he had been given the authority to ask questions.'

Bryant paused, seeming about to argue further, but then nodded. 'Meet me at the governor's house at two,' he said, flicking his pocket-watch open and closed.

'You do not wish for me to accompany you to the governor?'

Another dubious expression crossed Bryant's face. 'He is the Duke of Kent, Lieutenant. The son of King George. He is very particular about the discipline and governance of Gibraltar. No, I do not wish for you to accompany me.' Bryant sighed. 'Oh, and Mr Courtney...' Courtney paused as he was about to leave Bryant to fetch the ship's paperwork. 'Do not forget what I suggested about Mr Nightingale. I am still of the mind to set him down. While you are below, fetch him and send him up to me.'

Courtney gritted his jaw. He had not spoken to Nightingale since he had helped Dr Faulkner. 'Yes, sir,' he said regretfully.

With the paperwork beneath his arm and Nightingale dispatched to Bryant, Courtney visited the port-office and then navigated through the busy streets. The skies still threw their tantrums around him, lashing him with wind and rain. Only the red coats of the resident soldiers split the monochrome of the grey buildings and the dusty roads. He did not envy them. Gibraltar was a bustling, lively economy now, the result of the open and varied trade, but being stuck in a space which could be walked across in a few hours would have driven him to madness. He supposed there was an irony in that, being an officer of a naval ship, yet at least that was with the knowledge of constant movement.

Courtney hated feeling entrenched, unable to move any further. It allowed doubts to creep in.

Yet that was how he had felt for many a month and he feared having to confront it.

He wished he had a companion, but Bryant had not allowed any shore leave yet – perhaps in the hope that the *Lysander* would leave soon. Alone, Courtney made his way through the market, past the smells of spices and wet rugs and fresh fish, towards the taverns lining the shore's edge. Already he could identify the men who were sailors, their loose trousers and bandannas and long hair setting them apart, along with their tolerance for this disgusting weather. A Briton could not be told by his accent, but by his sufferance of rain and hail.

Courtney pulled his cloak tighter around himself as he entered a tavern named the Royal Oak. Even though the press-gangs were not in action, an officer's presence in a public house could still be unwelcome. Yet an hour remained before he had to meet Bryant at the Convent where the governor resided, enough time to sit and listen to the men.

No one marked him as he took a seat in the corner. The small common room stank of salt, sweat and ale and it was thronged with noise. He bought a cheap bottle of gin and looked out over the crowd. With the peace, many men had little to do. It was as though all of England had been granted shore leave at one time, a state sure to lead to penniless, drunken, desperate strays. Courtney did not think it with any malice towards them. Once upon a time, he might have done the same. What was the difference now, he wondered. He still had no fortune to his name, no certain future. Sometimes, he still felt locked in the frame of mind he had been in as a youth, raging against the same things.

Was it so terrible to want to speak against those same issues? In the eyes of others, perhaps. He knew it would do him no favours, but he could not help it. He could not stand to see Bryant's cruelty and the whipped flesh of innocent men.

In the Royal Oak, Courtney tried to push those frets away. He attempted to concentrate and listen into the conversations of the sailors about him, but he had barely been sitting a few minutes when a woman approached him. He saw the flash of her blonde hair from the corner of his eye and decided not to look up. 'I'm sorry, ma'am, but I'm not interested in…'

'It is you! Oh, Artie!'

The woman sank down into the chair opposite him. With a start, Courtney recognised her: the girlish red cheeks, the wide blue eyes and the soulful mouth. She had been little more than a thin rake when he had last seen her, but now she was healthily round in the face. 'Sara,' he breathed. 'Miss Foster. You are still here?'

'I am.' She smiled widely and reached across to touch his hand. Courtney gently retracted it.

'How are you? Is your brother…?'

'Gone. He joined the navy too and sailed for the East. I haven't heard from him in years.'

Courtney felt a guilty thrill for it. Sara's brother had been an evil wretch, one of the reasons for her hollow and haunted appearance. 'That is good news. But you are still in Gibraltar?'

'Yes. I know it well, and being here makes me feel closer to my husband.'

For the first time, Courtney noticed the ring upon her finger. Relief flooded him. He had sometimes worried that his departure had thrown her to the lions, alone and vulnerable in the world. 'Someone succeeded in the task then.'

Sara laughed. 'I wanted to wait for you, but I knew that you would have only married me out of pity. Pity for Aaron and his wrath. Nathan, my husband, is another sailor. He is gone now, to who knows where, but being here, amongst his kind, allows me to hear news of him. Sailors talk like gossiping old women.'

'That is true. I am very happy for you. I always wondered what became of you.'

'And what of you? Nathan and I read in *The Times* about the *Ulysses* and the *Scylla*. Your captain mentioned you in such an impressive way.'

Courtney flushed. Nightingale had indeed written a beautiful report of the battle, although it had been buried beneath the aftermath of his own actions and the court martial. 'I am still a lieutenant,' he said.

'Even after the events of the mutiny?'

'Yes. It was not all glorious.'

Sara said nothing more about it. 'Then, what brings you to Gibraltar? I would expect you to be on leave in England during the peace.'

Courtney chose his words carefully. 'We are searching for a ship.'

'Another? What is her name? I may have heard something of her whereabouts.'

Bryant had impressed upon him the importance of secrecy, as had his brother at the Admiralty – yet Capitaine Bonfils had the authority to ask questions. Courtney could not see another way of gaining information. Taverns were as good a heart of information as the governor's offices. 'The *Loyal*,' he said quietly, glancing around at the crowded room.

Even in the din, all Courtney heard was Sara's little hitching breath. The colour drained from her flushed cheeks. She sat back in her chair, putting a hand to her stomach. 'Oh God,' she whispered. 'Is the *Loyal* missing?'

Courtney had already made the awful connection. 'Nathan is on the *Loyal*,' he stated.

She nodded. 'That is all I know. He sails all over the world. I don't know his destination or purpose. I was only happy he had managed to sign on during peacetime, even if it meant he was away... Oh God.'

'We do not know what has happened to her yet,' Courtney insisted, moving closer and taking her hand. 'It may be innocent. All we know is that the ship was last seen off Gibraltar.'

'Here? Oh, I could have stood on the docks and seen him pass. I could have waved at him. Now...'

She shook her head. Tears welled in her eyes but with a quick glance around her, she bravely swallowed them down. Courtney found his handkerchief and she dabbed at the wetness in her lashes. 'Do you have any letters from him? Anything that might help us?' he asked.

'No. I have not heard from him since... Oh, Portsmouth. I believe that is where he sailed from.'

Perhaps that was due to not meeting a packet; perhaps it was due to the nature of their voyage. Either way, Courtney felt for Sara. The *Loyal* did not only include Sir William and Hugo Baptiste, the diplomats who the Admiralty were desperate to find; around two hundred men also crewed the ship. Two hundred families who could be destroyed if their husbands or brothers or fathers or sons were not found. A sailor's pay might not be much, but it could be the difference between going hungry and eating another meal. Not all of them threw it away on gin and women.

'Oh,' Sara sighed, clutching his fingers. 'There is something... Now that I think on it. A little while ago, perhaps a week, ten days, there was a terrible blow. It came across us here, rattled the ships in the harbour. I thought of Nathan then, but I did not imagine... Do you think they might have sunk?'

'I don't know.' The information settled with an idea that Courtney had thought of. Any ship, cast on the waves, could founder. Nature could not entirely be conquered. 'But I shall find out.'

'Please,' Sara breathed. 'I thought once I would forever be in your debt, when you said you would take me away from Aaron. But I did not feel any malice for you when you did not come to me. I saw the fog that surrounded Gibraltar that month, I knew your ship would have struggled, and you had so many other things on your mind. But now... I truly would be in your debt, Artie. The last – the last letter I wrote to Nathan, I told him of my condition.'

Sara indicated her stomach, and Courtney realised another reason for her healthy size. He nodded and squeezed her hand.

'We will find the ship,' he promised. 'I'll bring him home to you.'

Courtney knew he sounded like Nightingale, who had so kindly believed in their ability to find Jane and rescue her from the *Ulysses*. The thought of Nightingale's goodwill stirred in his chest. He had spoken badly to him on the *Lysander*, and could not ignore the thrum of guilt for his involvement in the gauntlet, the way Courtney had been unable to protect him from Bryant's spite. Facing the girl he had perhaps once loved, he knew he had to speak to Nightingale – before Bryant set him down upon Gibraltar and severed all ties with him.

Now, though, Courtney had to face the captain himself. The hour had not yet reached two but Bryant was already pacing outside the governor's house, stamping through the dirty puddles of rainwater. Bonfils sat upon a stone bench, watched over by the two red-coated sentries, alongside Geneviève Baptiste who had come ashore to hear of any news of her husband. Courtney tipped his hat to her.

'Lieutenant, there you are,' Bryant snapped. 'Where have you been?'

'I have been where we discussed, sir,' Courtney said, but Bryant waved his hand in dismissal.

'I have spoken with His Lordship the duke,' he continued, only for Bonfils to correct, 'His council, not the duke himself,' and receive a scathing look from Bryant. 'Lord Keith, the commander-in-chief of the Mediterranean, is on leave in England. But in any case, the duke and his council will not allow us to give testimony without our presence. They must convene a court martial. They say it shall not take long for the captains to convene.'

Courtney was unsure of that. 'I spoke to someone,' he began.

'You spoke to someone? Lieutenant, I told you—'

'She has a husband on the *Loyal*, sir.'

'She?' Bryant seemed not to know what to be more confounded over. 'How – how did you find this woman?'

'I knew her from a while ago, sir. She works at a tavern by the dock and knows all that the sailors say. Around ten days ago, she says there was a storm that blew into the port. Perhaps it swept in from the east and had already caught the *Loyal*.'

Bryant considered it. 'If it were a storm...' he started but did not finish.

'Perhaps they have all perished,' Bonfils interjected. 'Your *Royal George* went down with many hands and civilians aboard.'

'She was in sight of land when she did. If the *Loyal* has foundered, we would not know unless the same occurred.'

'No one has reported any wreckage,' Courtney said. 'And no survivors, either. We cannot be certain unless we follow her course, but even then, a thousand things could have made her stray from it. She could be anywhere between here and Malta.'

'Yes, I'm quite aware of the hardships we face, Lieutenant,' Bryant said sharply. 'Well, standing here and being tied to Gibraltar is not helping us. If Paterson and Arnold had not forced us to bring them to trial…'

Courtney said nothing.

'I have a suggestion to make,' Bonfils intervened. 'The *Lysander* has to stay, but the *Fantôme* could continue. We have no bearing on this trial. None of my men or officers are witnesses. We can continue the search while you perform your legal duties.'

Bryant opened his mouth to tear such an idea down, but even he then had to pause. What Bonfils offered was sensible, Courtney could see that – and this was a quest for both of the ships, not simply the English *Lysander*. The only reason Bryant could refuse could be from sheer prejudice. 'I…understand your point, Capitaine,' Bryant relented, though the twitching of his jaw revealed his true feelings.

'I suggest that we set down a point of rendezvous and an approximate date.'

'Very well. We shall discuss this further in my cabin. We have left the *Lysander* for too long. Surely it will be crawling with traders and women and bum boats now. Come.'

They returned to the *Lysander*, crossing back through the crowded marketplace. Despite the awful weather, Bryant was correct: many of the traders from the town had rowed out to the *Lysander*, a new and ripe target for their wares. Bryant had to snap at Harris, the coxswain, to manoeuvre through the zealous vessels, threatening to beat them back with the oars. Courtney had refused at least ten bottles of different spirits before he clambered back onto the deck with a furious Bryant and an amused Bonfils. With an order to Sergeant Dawes to threaten all the merchants back to the town, they descended to the great cabin and laid out the final plans for the *Fantôme*.

The following morning, at the change of tide, the French frigate would set a course for Malta where the *Loyal* had been expected. Two weeks on, the *Fantôme* and the *Lysander* would aim to rendezvous off Palermo, dependent on tide and wind and weather. The Kingdom of Sicily was a prime British base of operation, and therefore another powerful opportunity to uncover information about the *Loyal*. Spelling it out with the aid of charts and maps, it all sounded so simple. Courtney knew that would not be the reality.

Once finalised, Bonfils and Geneviève began to depart. Before they could, on the waterlogged deck, Bonfils signalled for Courtney to step aside. Bryant had not joined them from the cabin, so Courtney did so without concern of the captain. 'I know,' Bonfils said lowly, 'that you have your feelings against Captain Bryant.'

'Oh, I...' Courtney did not want another officer, no matter if he was French, to think he planned anything against Bryant.

'I understand the frustration. I come from your world, Lieutenant. A world in which I never hoped to attain the career I have now. May I suggest something privately to you?'

Men surrounded the deck, but all of them were engaged in the continuing chaos of ushering boats away or, in other cases, surreptitiously buying and selling goods. Courtney thought he should probably put a stop to that. He tried to move away as an excuse, but Bonfils stopped him.

'Geneviève is fond of you,' he said with a glance at the lady, waiting for him. Courtney looked over and she lowered her head. 'She speaks highly of your conduct and behaviour. You, Lieutenant, would be welcome aboard the *Fantôme*.'

Courtney froze. He had to loop the words again around his head to fully understand their meaning. 'I... My commission is here, on the *Lysander*,' was all he could think to say.

'I understand that, Lieutenant, but—'

Courtney had to halt this discussion before anyone received the wrong impression. 'I also have to give testimony at the trial, sir,' he said, hoping Bonfils did not take offence at his interruption. 'I cannot leave the *Lysander*. I am a British officer.'

Bonfils considered him for a moment and then, as if they were only exchanging pleasantries, he laughed. 'Of course, Lieutenant. My apologies. I would never be so bold.'

Courtney gave a thin smile as Bonfils tipped his hat to him and walked away. No one else had marked the conversation and for that,

Courtney was glad. If Bryant heard anything of it, he'd have his head. Now, he watched Bonfils leave and wished him fortune. He hoped the *Fantôme* met with good news and the *Lysander* reconvened with her side by side with the *Loyal*. Many lives hinged on such a thing.

And, for good or for bad, Courtney knew his place remained on the *Lysander*.

Chapter Sixteen: Changing Tides

'Are you certain you wish to do this? It may be some time before the *Lysander* meets the *Fantôme* again.'

Courtney lingered at his cabin door as Nightingale pulled on his overcoat. The little room, though only small, seemed even barer now his sea-chest had been taken up. Only Courtney's meagre belongings were left.

'I am certain,' Nightingale said. 'My father-in-law is still missing. I cannot sit here while he may be in danger.'

'You do not speak French very well.'

It was a paltry statement, more of a desperate attempt to change Nightingale's mind about going aboard the *Fantôme*. Courtney knew he did not have much in his arsenal to convince him. He intensely regretted mentioning to Nightingale that the *Fantôme* would be departing soon. As soon as he had done so, Nightingale had settled on the notion of joining her.

'Capitaine Bonfils and Madame Baptiste are proficient in English,' Nightingale continued. 'We shall understand each other.'

'It seems so—'

Courtney stopped. In truth, Nightingale's idea to go ahead with the *Fantôme* was a sound one. Though he had visited Paterson, he had no true bearing on the upcoming court martial, not so much that his testimony could give any weight. It would be for the officers and crewmen to take the stand. And Bryant himself had suggested setting him down on Gibraltar. The captain had not refused Nightingale's absence, especially with the secondary agreement from the governor, and the knowledge that Nightingale was Sir William Haywood's son-in-law. But it did not mean Courtney liked the idea.

'It seems so drastic,' Courtney continued weakly.

'I told you before, Arthur. I feel so very useless on this ship. I have no real role. Standing around idly is not helpful for me, or for anyone else. If I accompany the *Fantôme*, there shall at least be one Englishman who knows the navy of the vessel we search for.'

Courtney sighed. 'This isn't because of what happened, is it? The gauntlet, and what I said to you before?'

He hated to voice that doubt – but it had lingered in his head ever since he and Nightingale had argued. Nightingale looked down, focusing on buttoning his cloak. 'There was nothing else you or I could have done, Arthur.'

'Are you angry with me?'

'Of course not. But Captain Bryant...' Nightingale shook his head. Perhaps he had been on the verge of breaking his neutrality, doing what he had warned Courtney not to.

'At least you can escape him,' Courtney whispered, and regretted it.

'I shall see you again, when we rendezvous in Palermo. I shall hope for a merciful outcome for Paterson and Arnold.'

Courtney said nothing. They could hope, but he knew it would be in vain. There was nothing he could do about that, though, just as he could not raise a hand to stop Nightingale. Instead, he came forward and helped Nightingale to loop through the ties of his cloak. In a flash, he remembered doing something similar that night in Trinidad, unbuttoning Nightingale's waistcoat before first placing a kiss upon his shy lips. He still felt the same emotion for him, even greater now. 'Be careful,' he said, attempting to voice it again.

Nightingale nodded, wordless.

'Sir?' Rylance appeared in the gunroom. Courtney stepped away and let Nightingale walk past him. 'Your dunnage is in the cutter, sir. The *Fantôme* is ready to receive you.'

'Thank you, Rylance. I'll be there directly.'

Rylance nodded and disappeared back up onto deck. Before following, Nightingale gave Courtney one last smile, reaching out to squeeze his arm. Then, with nothing more to be said, he was gone.

The following morning, as arranged, the *Fantôme* left too. Their point of rendezvous suddenly seemed even further away now Nightingale had departed. So much could change in the next fortnight. Courtney stood at the stern of the *Lysander* and watched the sails of the *Fantôme* disappear. Despite being surrounded by the busy crew, he had not felt so alone in a long while. Mr Midshipman Smythe was an old ally from the *Scylla*, but a gulf separated a junior and senior officer.

Courtney had only been a mid for a short while, but he remembered that uncertainty and fright in the build-up to his lieutenant's examination. He had not been entirely honest with himself, or with others, at that point in his career.

Watching the empty horizon, he was suddenly filled with an urge to have told Nightingale every bit of that truth: about Walker, about the *Grampus*, about the lies he had told in his past – and about the future he wished to have. Nightingale should be a part of it all.

In the way of Jane stepping away from her troubles alongside Lieutenant Wainwright, he wanted to have the same.

The thought of his sister spurred Courtney back to the present. His letter still sat in his cabin, unsent. He had prevaricated over whether or not to send it. He had tried to ask permission to take the rest of the post ashore, if just to escape the atmosphere on the *Lysander*, but Bryant had refused. He still had a sore head over the *Fantôme*, over the court martial, over the delay, and all else was felled under his irritation.

It wasn't until the afternoon watch the next day that any man was allowed to leave, and even then, it had to be performed under marine guard. Poor Sergeant Dawes appeared thrilled to have to trudge through the wet streets of the town, acting as a sentinel to the small landing party on their way to buy stores for the ship. Courtney joined them, cowering under a boat cloak and with the ship's letters secured safely beneath his coat.

He left the marines and their wards at the market to organise the post. The office was not located far from the port but he was already soaked through by the time he reached it. He dealt with the package of letters then lingered in the sheltered room, looking out into the deluge. He had barely been able to dry his wet clothes from the last time on shore, and he feared a feverish chill was on the horizon. He decided he could wait a moment to see if the worst of the rain would pass.

A mere few minutes had elapsed when a figure emerged into the lane. Courtney could not tell why he marked him, but he knew, at a glance, that the man was searching for someone. No sensible person would rush so hastily on such wet cobbles. He was not dressed for the downpour, in a thin brocaded coat and waistcoat, his buckled shoes dangerously heeled. Predictably, that unsuitable footwear slipped and fumbled on the ground and in a mere few long strides, the poor sod collapsed in a heap.

Courtney drew his cloak about himself and hurried over. He extended a hand and the man, his cheeks flaring, took it.

'Didn't break anything, did you, nipper?' Courtney asked as he brushed himself down.

'No. I don't think so. Thank you, sir.' The man paused, his eyes falling on Courtney's uniform beneath his cloak. 'Are you from the *Lysander*, sir?' he asked in a dash.

'Yes. I am her lieutenant.'

'I am a clerk in the governor's office. I have a missive for your captain!' The damp clerk felt in his coat and extracted a folded piece of paper addressed to Captain Bryant. The edges had gone a little transparent in the man's fall. 'You must make haste to him! I was told it was of the utmost importance.'

Courtney looked down at the paper and nodded. 'Thank you, sir. I will ensure he receives it.'

Feeling a little guilty that the clerk had had to face the dirty weather, Courtney pocketed the note and rushed for the marketplace. Across the throng, he caught sight of Sergeant Dawes's tall stature and red coat. Raising a hand, he alerted Dawes, who easily found his way through to him. 'I have a message for Captain Bryant,' Courtney said. 'Are the men almost ready to depart?'

'They will be soon, sir.'

If the clerk was correct, then they could not delay. Courtney hurried to the harbour, hailed Harris, who had miraculously been able to keep his smoking pipe dry, and returned to the *Lysander*. Bryant looked up with a frown as he knocked on the great cabin door and entered with his note.

'Have you sent the post already, Lieutenant? I did not hear the men return.'

'A clerk from the governor's office found me, sir. He had a message for you.'

Bryant reached out and Courtney laid the letter in his hand. The captain opened it and frowned. 'This is barely legible, Lieutenant. Did you drop it in the sea?'

'No, sir. The clerk took a tumble.'

'Into the sea?'

'No, sir.'

Laying the paper flat on the table, Bryant read. Courtney did not know what he anticipated but he had not expected Bryant, in a mere minute, to slam his hand down on the desk and curse. 'They decide this now?' he asked, nostrils flaring and face flushing. 'After the *Fantôme* has already departed?'

'Sir?'

'Read it. You may as well, Lieutenant.'

Bryant thrust the letter into Courtney's hand and strode past him. As the captain bawled for Lieutenant Godfrey and Master Pascoe's presence, Courtney read as quickly as he could. His stomach tightened. For the first time, Bryant's fury seemed justified. He looked again over the words, wondering if he had misinterpreted them, but he had not: suddenly, it had been decided that to wait for the arrival of the captains for the court martial would take too long. There was not the required number currently in Gibraltar, many having taken leave. Such a thing could take a fortnight, perhaps three weeks.

And the *Lysander* had been languishing in port in the time it had taken the governor's office to decide that.

Bryant returned with Godfrey and Pascoe. They listened in silence as he regaled to them the change of their plan, not even attempting to hide his frustration. Godfrey nodded placidly along, but Pascoe's eyes reflected the same rage as his captain's. A curious alliance had formed between them, something Courtney could not yet understand the crux of.

Finally, in the strained quietude that followed, Pascoe ventured, 'What are we to do now, Captain?'

Bryant slammed his hands behind his back, straightening his shoulders. 'We must make haste to catch the *Fantôme*,' he said. 'And pray our delay has not cost us anything.'

Chapter Seventeen: Deluge

24 September 1802

The desire to catch up with the *Fantôme* drove the Lysanders to loosen all sensible canvas. As Courtney paced the quarterdeck, he listened to the sounds of the waves flowing alongside the hull. In this last hour, the seas had increased until he could feel the dip and climb in and out of the watery troughs. Slowly, the masts would roll, tilting to larboard then upright again as the vessel corkscrewed handsomely. Each time, he felt his stomach tense, but each time, the *Lysander* regained her feet. Captain Bryant pushed her to the edge of her ability in the rising wind.

Palermo awaited. With thirty-six hours between the *Fantôme*'s departure from Gibraltar and the *Lysander*'s, Courtney hoped they could meet them before Sicily. The *Fantôme* was a frigate: heavier than the *Lysander*, potentially slower. Yet she did not know the *Lysander* had left. Her eyes would be forward, searching for the *Loyal*. In that time, she could even have found the missing vessel. Courtney almost wished she had.

The other part of him feared the discovery. This long without word could only imply disaster. He had not said such a thing to Sara, but her mention of the storm stuck with him. They could not expect to find the *Loyal* if she had gone down in the Mediterranean.

Yet other tragedies also loomed in his mind. The *Ulysses* had mutinied. The *Fénix* had been struck by lightning. The *Cygne*, Bonfils's own ship, had caught fire. Destruction and danger followed every vessel upon the sea, no matter if war or peace reigned. The ocean recognised no treaties.

The frustration of the unknown churned in him as he looked towards the horizon. Grey clouds gathered there. They had left the worst of the downpours in Gibraltar, but the sandglass could barely turn without a drizzle of rain interrupting the watches. In the last two hours, Courtney had felt the wind increase and he had updated the log to reflect so, noting down a strong breeze. Simultaneously, the barometer had been steadily dropping. All threatened a dark horizon ahead and so, under Bryant's permission, he had ordered preparations for the encroaching storm. Yet the captain had barely alighted on deck.

By the time the guns and anchors had been secured, preventer braces rigged, and tackles hooked to the rudder, the first watch approached. Courtney's duty was coming to an end, but he was loath to go below with that blackening sky and leave Lieutenant Godfrey to it. He did not like the look of it, or how quickly it loomed.

Courtney found Bryant in his cabin, seated at his writing desk. He stowed the note away as Courtney entered.

'Yes, Lieutenant Courtney?' was his curt response.

'A dark sky is approaching, sir,' Courtney said. 'Permission to send word to make ready the storm canvas?'

Bryant glanced out the gallery windows. 'I shall be on deck directly, Lieutenant. Give me a moment.'

'All else is secured, sir.'

'Yes, Lieutenant. I heard.'

Courtney wanted to wait, to ensure Bryant followed him up, but the man made no move. He opened his mouth to say more, but was interrupted by a cry above.

'Sail! A sail off the starboard quarter!'

The cry finally wrenched away Bryant's attention. He could not ignore that call to the deck. With Courtney close behind, he hurried up. Above, on the masts, the topmen stood upon the footropes, pointing out over the sea. Bryant trained his spyglass in that direction whilst Courtney squinted in an effort to make anything out. The black clouds had closed in on them since he had been below, throwing the sea into shades of dark grey, topped with white foam. Water and sky blended in monochrome palettes, difficult to make out where one ended and the other began. Courtney could see no vessel.

'Lay aloft, Lieutenant Courtney,' Bryant suddenly said. 'The sail is strange.'

Courtney did not relish the idea of climbing but the odd statement intrigued him. He hurried to the shrouds and swung himself onto them. The ratlines felt damp beneath his palm, something he attributed to his nerves until he sensed drops of rain upon his cheeks. By the time he reached the futtock shrouds, leaning out over the expanse of dull water, the heavens wept in earnest. He gripped tighter to the heavy rope, wishing he had removed his boots which slipped dangerously on the rigging. He had been too hasty in thinking that they had left the dirty Gibraltar weather behind.

Fighting through the discomfort of the head-spinning heights, he found his way to the top and balanced upon the main yard. It was not sufficient to see the unknown vessel, so he braced himself and climbed higher, up to the crosstrees and main-topsail yard. As he felt for his spyglass, the *Lysander* gave one of her kicking lurches, bobbing into the depths of a wave. He gripped a backstay for dear life and peered through the lens. The world rolled and rocked as though he sat atop a spinning windmill.

Eventually, after wildly scanning the horizon, he found the sail. It jumped in and out of his view, but he focused enough to know one thing. It could not be the *Loyal* or the *Fantôme*. She only carried two masts, a brig-rigged sloop perhaps, and he could not make out her colours.

He opened his mouth to shout down to Bryant, only for dazzling light to strike him blind. He jerked backwards, vaguely hearing a cry of alarm ripple through the ship. It was drowned out by a deafening crack of thunder.

Disoriented, Courtney clung to the rigging. He blinked, furiously trying to clear the haze in his vision. A lightning strike had lashed the ocean a couple of cables away from the *Lysander*, and now, another flashed. For a moment, it illuminated the entire vista in white, showing the black punchbowl of the ocean and that distant, scudding vessel. Courtney tried to concentrate but his head rang, hairs standing on end. Somewhere below, Godfrey shouted, ordering sails to be taken in.

Courtney forced himself back to his senses. He could hear the canvas straining in the sudden gust, ballooning out before the wind. Below his feet, the main course flapped and tugged at its clews, threatening to unbalance the yard. Not giving a damn now about the sheer height, Courtney scurried down to reach the spar where men already crowded. Balancing on the footropes, he joined them. The wind buffeted them from aft, throwing forward spates of rain.

'Ease off tack and bowline!' he shouted, unnerved how much he already had to raise his voice. The weather clew struggled up, followed by the lee as the clew-garnets and buntlines were hauled. The leeches crumpled, inch by inch reducing the area of the canvas, but Courtney could still feel the ship rebelling. She carried too much at her head and stern, the wind throwing her around like a ragdoll. If it grew too heavy for even close-reefed topsails, Bryant would have to order the trysails set. They had only drilled for that a handful of times.

Now, Courtney groped for the gaskets with the topmen to lash the sail to the yard. The course had been furled as quickly as possible, but it was not enough. He scrambled back down the shrouds and leapt upon the slippery deck. Bryant squinted in the fierce rain, clinging to his hat. Above, the fore course was still being clewed up, the mizzen carrying only her topsail.

'We may have to resort to storm canvas!' Courtney yelled at Bryant. 'The staysails, sir!'

'She will bear it, Lieutenant!' Bryant replied. 'Did you see the vessel?'

'A brig, sir! I couldn't see the colours!'

'Not our quarry, then!'

Courtney glanced back to the horizon, but the churning waves had completely obliterated any hope of seeing the other ship. He thought of the *Loyal* out there, perhaps having already weathered a gale. 'We should batten the hatches, sir!' he shouted. 'These waves are increasing! If one breaks over the deck—'

He had not finished the sentence when the sea collided with the hull. Courtney was thrown forward, tumbling forward onto his knees. His chest struck the steps down to the quarterdeck, blowing the wind from him. Next to him, Bryant groped for the rail. Gasping for breath, Courtney raised his head in time to see a furious wave roll along the length of the *Lysander*, lashing up over her sides. Men lost their footing, grabbing for belaying pins and braces as they were swept towards the angry sea. In a jerking movement, the *Lysander* pitched forward and then to starboard, masts tilting, canvas heaving.

Courtney scrambled to his feet. 'We must strike the mizzen-topsail!' he shouted, hating that it had not already been done. 'We must have her under main- and fore-topsails, only, and put her under storm staysails, Captain! She'll be brought by the lee if we're not careful!'

'We must—' Bryant began, but was interrupted by a cry from below-deck.

'The gallery windows, sir!' Mr Lynde raced up through a hatch which still needed to be battened down. Despite being below, water poured from his hair and clothes. 'The sea's coming in!'

Courtney followed him down the companion-ladder. He leapt from the bottom of it into freezing water up to his shins. The blackness of the day had drowned the ship in low light but in the flashes of lightning, he could see water swamping his feet. Aft, the great cabin's door was beating the wall as the *Lysander* rolled back and forth. All of the gallery windows had been smashed, fragments of glass swimming in the deluge, alongside overturned chairs and lanterns and books. The flood had already reached down the gun deck, lapping at the cannon carriages and sucking up men's possessions. Chests and bags and scraps of paper floated past Courtney as he waded through.

Water spilled down the ladder to the next deck. In the gunroom, the officers' cabins were ruined. But such inconvenience barely touched Courtney's thoughts. Waves kept rising, lashing in.

'All hands to pumps!' he cried as he dashed back up. Bryant still lingered on the poop deck, gripping the rail. 'Captain Bryant, we must batten the hatches now! We need some kind of barrier to stopper the gallery windows! She'll go down by the stern if much more water gets in!'

'Yes.' Bryant finally spoke. 'Yes, yes, the windows, Lieutenant. And the staysails. The staysails!'

Courtney left Godfrey to order the setting of the storm staysails, more robust canvas that ran fore-and-aft along the stays. He called for the carpenter, Brooks, who immediately assembled his mates to throw some makeshift timber against the yawning windows. Other crew not employed on the yards Courtney grouped together to man the multiple pumps. Just as he had in the tops, he joined them, straining over the handle to turn the chain and shift the water from below and over the side. Despite the direly cold seas pouring in, he felt sweat quickly form on his aching muscles. The handle rebelled and stuck, making all of them push and heave with all their might. Courtney had heard of men dying from exhaustion at the pumps, or at the least greatly injuring themselves.

But such a death was hypothetical. If they did not clear this water, they would all die for certain.

The *Lysander* lurched around them. Some men slipped in the deluge but still they got to their feet again and kept pumping. Lightning lit their red faces, long enough to give them a view of the ruined deck. It was sufficient to keep their determination up, twisting, turning the stiff handle. Courtney did not know how long they laboured; the sound of the watch-bell was drowned beneath the furious storm and the noise of blood roaring in his ears as he worked.

And then, overhead, just as they made progress: 'Helm!' Bryant shouted, somehow rising above the chaos. 'Hard a-larboard! Avert your course this instant!'

Harris's voice could not be heard.

'Avert your course!' Bryant yelled again.

Courtney ran up, past the men still crouched over the hatches, trying to lash the tarpaulin down. They were frozen in place, staring out to sea.

Courtney's heart left his chest. Two terrible sights greeted him: the curtain of rain pulling back, revealing the sharp teeth of deadly rocks, the perilous gateway to an island – and to starboard, thrown back and forth by the seething waves, that unknown vessel towered above the *Lysander*. She bore directly down upon them, masts scraping the furious sky. In terror, Courtney realised she was no two-master; she was a frigate, her mainmast severed, her fore leaning perilously to larboard.

Bryant grasped his speaking-trumpet as if his life depended upon it. Courtney, forcing his legs to move, climbed up to him. In the glimpses of the other ship between pitches, he saw only a handful of men staggering about on her deck. They could not avert course, even with a whole crew.

And nor could the *Lysander*. Godfrey's orders swept over the waters. No hauling on the braces or wrenching at the wheel affected the vessel. She was at the mercy of the storm, thrown along by the wind.

Above, men started to scamper from the yards. Bryant shouted at them to stop, but even at the waist, the crew ran, hurrying for the stern and the forecastle. The frigate aimed directly for her hull, bowsprit bouncing into the air, threatening the hempen maze of the *Lysander*'s shrouds.

'Hold fast!' Courtney shouted, winding his fist in a stay. 'Brace for impact!'

Men screamed. The full weight of the frigate slammed into the *Lysander*'s flank. Courtney crumpled, the impact knocking all the breath from his body. The *Lysander* tilted beneath him, falling to larboard, masts careening madly. Beneath the awful crunching, he heard the thumps of men plummeting to the deck whilst others became caught in the tangle of rigging. He dug his fingers into the seams of the timbers to keep his grip, the world going dark. For a moment, he thought he had fainted – and then realised it was the shadow of the frigate's bowsprit. The frightful spire sliced across the deck, driven back and forth by the waves like a mad dog shaking its prey. Courtney tried to scramble up but the other vessel's figurehead slammed into the *Lysander*, chips and splinters raining around the men. He looked up to see the mizzen stay shivering. The damaged cap, troubled during the squall in the Bay of Biscay, trembled. He only had a moment to throw his hands over his head and then the timber plunged down.

It came within inches of his body. He feared it would break the deck but he heard no damage, only a dull thud. He raised his head, seeing the frigate still entangled, the shadow of the rocks ahead – and beside him, Bryant's prostrate form.

Stomach swooping, Courtney crawled over. The *Lysander* reeled again and he smacked his chest on the deck. Winded, he reached Bryant. Chunks of the mizzen cap had collided with Bryant's head and blood poured in rivulets over his eyes. He was not even twitching but as Courtney frantically felt for a sign of life, he found his heartbeat – slow, but present.

Lieutenant Godfrey raced up to them. Smythe was at his side, rain soaking his uniform through. They both stared at Bryant, waiting for Courtney to say something, anything.

'Fetch Dr Faulkner,' Courtney ordered, getting to his feet. 'Captain Bryant will have to go below.'

'Is he...dead, sir?' Godfrey managed.

'No, he's still breathing.'

'The mizzen cap should have been repaired,' Godfrey said inanely.

But there was no time to affix blame, not yet. As Godfrey hurried to retrieve Dr Faulkner, Smythe lingered around Courtney. 'Get your heavy-weather gear, Mr Smythe,' Courtney said, not wanting the boy on deck in amongst this danger. The frigate still assaulted the *Lysander*. Only for a moment did she pull away and then she returned, yawed by the force of a wave. She charged with the strength of a broadside, pummelling the *Lysander* quicker than the crew could trim her yards and divert her course. The men ran now, ignoring the danger, balancing themselves as each resounding smash rocked the ship. Shrouds and braces snarled, wrapping and twisting in a cat's cradle. The frigate's fore yard matted into the *Lysander*'s main, threatening to snap it from its supports. Caught in the web of rigging, the ship would drag the *Lysander* into the looming rocks.

Courtney had to help. With Faulkner and Godfrey hurrying back to deck, Courtney left them, and found himself running towards the imprisoned frigate. At every second, he expected to hear the sickening crack of snapping timbers as the *Lysander* was mauled.

'Cut her away!' he yelled. 'Cut her loose!'

On the other ship, the scanty crew echoed the Lysanders. They climbed into the tops with axes and boat knives and marlinspikes. At the foot of the mainmast, Courtney noticed Obi, drawn from the pumps by the sound of the collision. He shouted at him to follow and then scampered into the shrouds. Behind him, the frigate tossed and shook, each wave throwing her remorselessly into them. Her running rigging – what remained of it – was a web which groped at Courtney's unsteady feet. He kicked away from it, leaning back to get into the futtock shrouds. In the rush, his boot slipped. For a moment, he hung, clinging to the cordage, dangling above the wild waves. A hand thudded against his spine and shoved him back into place. Through the rain, Obi gave him a reassuring nod. Courtney swallowed his fright and continued to climb.

Bowlines and clewlines had flown free. The reef-points of the *Lysander*'s main-topsail had half-unravelled and the canvas sagged. Courtney set men to furling it in again, whilst dealing with the yardarm. The frigate's jib hung raggedly, flapping in the mesh of stays. Courtney could have almost leapt onto her jib-boom as it jabbed and tried to maim the *Lysander*.

He reached over to attack the mass of cordage and spars. The men of the frigate did the same mere feet away, balancing over the perilous drop. One slip and anyone could be crushed between the two heaving ships.

Back and arms screaming from the time at the pumps and now bent unnaturally over the *Lysander*'s spars, Courtney took a second to look ahead. The rocks neared, jagged and black. White foam lashed them, the waves licking their tops before retreating and revealing ominous craggy depths. The ships would be gutted by them.

He returned to the yard, hacking desperately at the frigate's tangled rigging. She no longer smashed into the *Lysander,* but scraped and whined against her hull. It seemed all of the frigate's available men had scrabbled onto the bowsprit to free her. Driven furiously by the sea, they worked as one, inch by inch releasing the spars and ropes.

Then, finally, the very edge of the *Lysander's* topsail yard began to split, overstrained by the tangled rigging. As it broke off, yanking against stays, it took down a great chunk of the frigate's bowsprit. The frigate's men let it fall, splashing into the deep waves. The *Lysander* was loose for one blessed second.

'Get to the deck!' Courtney yelled at the opposite crew. 'Away from the bowsprit!'

Then, when they had raced away, he screamed, 'Hard a-larboard!', praying Harris and his mates could hear. He imagined the two burly crewmen fighting for control of the spinning wheel. The wild wind slapped against the back of the topsails, shivering along the staysails, and the *Lysander* finally turned, minutely, but enough. Her stern lifted in the waves. She slammed into the frigate's waist. The movement jerked her, throwing her away from the *Lysander.* In the impact, her bowsprit snapped entirely with a deafening crunch. Canvas and hemp and timber plunged into the churning sea. With half her masts impotent, she had no control.

Courtney watched her veer, thrown onto her beam-ends by the sea. Her remaining crew scattered across the deck, unable to hand, reef, steer; anything that might save their ship. As the *Lysander* worked to heave aback, the frigate heeled over, her keel rising from the waters. Dashed like a cork bobbing from wave to wave, her crew teetered, clinging to the soaked rails and timbers.

Silence fell over the *Lysander.* All hands stared at the awful sight. Courtney gasped for breath, still bent over the yard. The world suddenly moved so slowly, every wave, every crash of thunder, every burst of lightning, every movement of that doomed ship passing by in fractured images.

And then, a terrible crash. The frigate's bows arched, timbers flying. Her foremast tilted, raining down showers of blocks and ropes. Black, razor-sharp rocks punctured the hull as the ship came to a sharp, brutal halt. There, slaughtered on the edge of the island, she lay.

And finally, through the veil of the storm, Courtney saw her stern lettering.

'My God,' he said. 'It's the *Loyal*.'

PART II

Chapter Eighteen: On the Rocks

For hours, the Lysanders could do nothing but stare at the ruined *Loyal*. The fury of the storm kept them from lowering boats to help or approaching the wicked teeth of the rocks. Courtney's attention was wrenched between many different matters: the damaged *Lysander*, the wrecked *Loyal*, his own men, and Captain Bryant. Dr Faulkner and Lieutenant Godfrey had transported him below but Faulkner's tentative reports were not promising. The falling mizzen cap had grievously injured him and, despite Faulkner's best efforts, blood kept flowing. The captain had woken for a few seconds before dropping back into a death-like state.

Courtney knew he could not do any more. The *Lysander* had been as marred as her captain, but he had ways to fix her. Brooks and his mates had done all they could for the smashed windows. Their main focus now became the harm to the ship's masts and yards. In the tangle of spars, the *Loyal* had wrenched at the *Lysander*'s main-topsail yard, a deal of which now lay on the deck. The missing timber had almost scuppered the men's ability to lay the *Lysander* to, but running up a jury-rig from the cut-away wreckage had soothed her.

Fortunately, in the collision, the *Loyal* had not breached the *Lysander*'s hull. With the hatches finally battened down, the pumps dashed water out of the lower decks. The *Lysander* was wounded and drowned but she would survive if she could weather this storm. When the dirtiness finally cleared, a fothered sail might see them right.

In between aiding the men at the pumps and scouring the damage to the *Lysander*, Courtney kept coming to deck to look over to the doomed *Loyal*. The wind and waves had crushed her against the jagged island which ate through the hull. With some mercy, her masts had been thrown to the landward side and her keel had been half-lifted from the deadly water. Even with the wild weather, the sea was not pouring in quick enough to sink her.

Not yet.

Men crawled from the desecrated ship to take shelter on the rocks. They had tried to risk a cutter themselves but the tempest had soon smashed it apart. Now, they ferried chests and possessions out of the *Loyal* to save them from the churning waters. Both through a speaking-trumpet and at the signal halliards, the Lysanders promised to aid them once the storm had abated.

Eventually, night came down. Ascending from the back-breaking work of the pumps, Courtney came on deck to see stars flickering in the sky, freed from the grasp of the black clouds. The rain had dwindled into weak spits whilst the wind had died, finally chasing the storm over the horizon and away from them.

Across the calmer seas, lights burnt as the Loyals manoeuvred over the rocks. They had been there, beaten by the elements and the dread of an imperilled ship, since the start of the first watch. The time approached one in the morning now, a total of nearly five hours.

Courtney had worked without rest, but he could not stand idly by and watch the Loyals suffer on the rocks. Answers as to what had happened to them would come later.

For the first time in a while, he visited Bryant's cabin and found where Faulkner had laid him out in his cot. The captain's face was pallid, aside from the dried blood along his temple. Faulkner had at last managed to stem some of it with bandages swaddled about Bryant's head. He was delicately compressing the linen against Bryant's wound as Courtney lingered on the threshold. Faulkner's hand slipped every now and then, fingers fumbling the points where the material was tied. Courtney had never seen the man entirely sober.

'Is he awake?' Courtney asked, knowing the answer.

'No, Lieutenant.'

Courtney did not want to question if he would arouse himself again. 'I came to ask his permission to lower a boat and fetch survivors from the *Loyal*.'

'I do not think he shall be making any decisions soon, Lieutenant.'

If Faulkner became clear-headed enough to declare Bryant unfit for duty, the responsibility would fall to Courtney. It would not be the first time Courtney had assumed command because of tragedy or misfortune. Captain Carlisle had died of yellow fever; Nightingale had been shot by Lieutenant Hargreaves; Captain Robinson had been killed by a cannonshot. Perhaps his eagerness for advancement brought it forth from the world in the ugliest of ways.

'I am going to go across to the *Loyal*,' Courtney rephrased. 'I have to know how many survive.'

'Yes, Lieutenant. I shall still be here.'

Like himself, all the men had been on watch for more than their allotted share, but Courtney barely needed to request volunteers. He gained thirteen to crew one cutter and another thirteen to work in another under Smythe. The midshipman, now wrapped in a cloak, descended into the launch without a word of complaint. The lad had seen more in his short career on the sea than many others would ever dream of. Courtney had previously wanted him off the deck when the *Loyal* had collided, but he could not turn Smythe away this time. He needed people he could trust – and that was why he was glad to see Obi amongst the numbers too. The able seaman joined Smythe's thirteen.

Remembering the burning *Cygne*, Courtney sat amongst the banks of oars and helped to row across to the stricken *Loyal*. His muscles ached from winding the handle of the pumps but he worked with the rest of the men, bumping across the waves which still dipped and lurched. Seeing the boats approach, a cry rose from the rocks.

'Stay where you are!' Courtney shouted through the speaking-trumpet. He could not face men plummeting to their deaths when they were so close to rescue.

The *Loyal* towered above them. The rocks had lifted her partially from the sea, revealing her copper-sheathed bottom. Debris surrounded her: gun carriages, cannons, sea-chests, planks and spars. The entire jib-boom with scraps of sail still attached bobbed past Courtney's cutter. He shoved it away with his oar.

His men reached the rocks before Smythe's. By the glow of a lantern, he peered up onto the jagged pile. Waves kissed up against it, making the entire surface slippery and miserable. He hoped the dim illumination was obscuring his sight – for he could not see many men clinging to the small island. There had been only a paltry few on deck, too.

Watching his feet, he climbed out of the cutter. His boots skidded a little but with one hand groping amongst the rocks, he made his way up. The boatsmen followed. Pale faces appeared out of the gloom. Some of them struggled down the rise to meet him, but others waited for him to approach. He could see no officers, only sailors wrapped in anything that they had grabbed from the ship: tarpaulin, spare canvas, coats, blankets. They shivered, drenched in the cold waters that had lashed them. One man was laid out on the sharp ground, a tourniquet bound about his leg. Others had blood dripping from head wounds, arms hanging uselessly at their sides, clothing torn and red.

Courtney approached the prostrate sailor. Another man, not dressed in naval garb, crouched over him. His long fair hair was plastered to his cheeks, linen shirt and waistcoat clinging to his trembling body, but he still held the seaman's hand in a tight grip. Whilst the Lysanders helped the Loyals down to the boats, Courtney knelt beside him.

'I am Lieutenant...' he began, but stopped when he saw the injured sailor. He was as white as a sheet, eyes staring at the night sky. Blood from his leg still dribbled down the rocks. Courtney cleared his throat. 'Sir,' he said to the civilian. 'He is dead.'

'Hm?' The stranger looked up.

'That man is dead. You can... You can let him go now.'

Silently, the man turned to the dead seaman. After laying his fingers against his neck, he nodded. Courtney reached down to offer him his hand, helping him to his unsteady feet.

'My name is Lieutenant Arthur Courtney,' he said. 'I am from His Majesty's Ship *Lysander*. We were sent to find out the fate of the *Loyal*.'

But the man only nodded again. Courtney realised there was no point in getting his story until he was warm, dry and fed.

Holding onto his arm, Courtney guided him back down the rocks. Smythe, Obi and the others had nearly filled the spare cutter, the Loyals shivering and dripping amongst the oars. More still waited on the crags but they had been offered blankets and coats to ward off the worst of the chill. Courtney counted them quickly: fifteen in the launch, perhaps another forty to transport. Where had the rest of the crew vanished to? This was barely enough to man half a watch.

'Take them across,' he said to Smythe. 'I'll stay with the men.'

Smythe stared at him as if he was mad. But he eventually nodded, garbled a, 'Yes, sir,' and returned to the boats.

Courtney picked his path back up the rocks as they rowed away. He could not simply leave the dead man there to be beaten by the elements and eventually bleached in the sun. A group of his comrades surrounded the corpse when he reached him. One man had laid canvas over his deathly white face.

'What is this man's name?' Courtney asked.

'Darius Wade, sir,' someone piped up. 'We shared neighbouring hammocks.'

'I am going to commit him to the deep.'

Courtney had never performed such a thing before, although many funeral services had taught him the procedure. The men did not refuse. Together, they lifted the heavy, waterlogged sailor from the rocks and between them, carried him down the steep, jagged rise. With the hull of the *Loyal* looming beside them, they laid him down again, swaddled in tarpaulin. There was no shot to weigh him down but as they placed him at the water's edge, the waves, growing again, took him. Courtney watched the white form consumed by the sea.

'...looking for the resurrection of the body when the sea shall give up her dead,' Courtney finished, feeling his chest constrict. He did not know the man, but deaths in this way always choked him. Demise in the service of England was what every Royal Navy man expected – a glorious end for a higher purpose. But so often, this was how a seaman lost his life: storms and rocks and deadly accidents. It all seemed so needless, so cruel.

As they returned up the rocks, he glanced over to the waiting *Lysander*. The boats had not yet reached her side but lanterns burnt to show them their way.

A distant pounding distracted him. He thought for an awful moment that Wade's body had returned but the other sailors were looking back towards the stranded *Loyal*. Something was hammering from the inside. Courtney stopped.

'Are there men still in there?' he asked.

'We thought they were all out,' a *Loyal* man said.

It could have been debris swilling around in the bowels of the *Loyal*, but Courtney could not bet upon that. Before he had time to debate, he hurried to the side and latched onto the ladder. Parts of it had flown off in the collision but the gunports had sprung open, allowing him to scramble between the makeshift footholds. Behind him came two Loyals.

The deck of the *Loyal* tilted down towards the churning cradle of the sea. Her bows had lifted partially into the air whilst her stern was in danger of being swallowed. Courtney carefully pulled himself over the rail, feeling for a stable point to put his feet upon. Fragments of the deck had risen, pushed upwards in the force of the smash. He balanced on the large splinters, making his way to the foremast. The foreyard hung at a steep angle with its rigging loose and tangled. A crack splitting the middle told how it would not last long.

Hatches had not been battened. Courtney signalled for his two companions to head that way.

'My name is Lieutenant Courtney,' he suddenly thought to say. 'You are?'

'Owen Ingram, sir. Forecastle division.'

'Radley Addison. Forecastle division, also, sir.'

'Follow me.'

Courtney led them down the first hatch into the gun deck. He had thought the gunports had burst open in the collision but he saw that some of the cannons were still run out. Fire buckets and powder horns lay scattered around the carriages. Some of them had turned over completely, balancing treacherously against each other or the bulkheads. If they fell down the incline of the deck, they could break through the stern or down into the lower spaces.

'Is anyone here?!' he shouted into the gloom. He could see no human form amongst the smashed mess tables and detritus that had spilled from the galley. Lanterns swayed as he manoeuvred through the debris, startling him as he brushed past. 'Is anyone here?!' he called again.

No one responded. Above, the wind whistled, stirring the wrecked yards and remaining canvas. If the weather worsened, the *Loyal* would be claimed by the deep as Darius Wade had been.

And then, muffled below, that thumping sound again.

'Who's there?!' he shouted as loud as he could. Without complaint, Mr Ingram and Mr Addison followed him down into the berth deck. A bottle rolled beneath Courtney's foot as he found the tilted floor. He kicked it away and heard a splash down in the shadows. Through the moonlight struggling through the aftermost hatch, he saw a sheen of water. The sea was already coming in.

His stomach twisted. If they did not find these men, they would be at the mercy of the water or the breaking *Loyal*: whichever came first.

Courtney fumbled his way down to the gunroom. The partition walls were still down, letting him see into the space. A growing lake lapped at the cabins, swilling paper and books and clothes in its blackness. The seams of the *Loyal* had bowed, the caulking had wetted, and now they seeped. As he looked up, he could see the gundeck through a hole in the low timbers. The wheels of a cannon in the captain's great cabin teetered in the gap.

But there was no one there.

He turned to see Ingram and Addison making their way aft. 'Down,' he called. 'We must go down.'

The smell of the hold took Courtney's breath away. Barrels had split open in the crash, spilling fish and bread and spirits. They all bled into the pool of freezing water that sluiced between the store rooms. Even near the bows, Courtney sank up to his knees. Chunks of the *Loyal*'s hull floated past. Sharp rocks had punctured through, gouging and raking the poor ship.

'Is anybody here?!' he shouted. This time, a muffled cry sounded from aft, past the aisles of barrels and ballast and in the direction of the powder magazine. Something struck against the bulkheads again. 'I'm coming! Keep shouting!'

The only light came through the wrecked hull, minutely illuminating the water and debris. He had to climb over the barrels that blocked the way aft, shoving bits of ballast and cordage away. The water deepened until he found it difficult to touch the timbers with his feet. The surface lapped at his waist then higher towards his chest. In the shadows, he could see collapsed bulkheads. The decks above had partially fallen in on themselves, strangling the stern of the *Loyal*.

The cry came again, trapped behind a heap of barrels which had come loose from their lashings, heaped together with broken partitions and chests. Courtney could not scale them in the tight squeeze. He held his breath and dipped under the water. The chill of it immediately seized his bones and muscles. Murky gloom stretched around him – but as his eyes adjusted, he could see a gap where the barrels had not quite wedged against the hull.

Ingram and Addison still knelt on the wet ladder as he resurfaced. Their pale faces stared at him in the lantern light.

'Come here,' Courtney urged. 'Pass me that rope.'

Both of them braved the cold, grasping a line of cordage. For men who made their living off the sea, sailors hated the water. Few could swim, believing it to be bad fortune. Courtney had learnt young, and on the *Scylla* had taught as many he could, in the safety of a sail overboard.

But this flooded hold was not safe. At any point, the ruined masts or that gun carriage above could fall through the decks. Then all of them would be trapped in this watery grave. He had to act quickly.

Pulling off his coat and waistcoat and thrusting them towards Ingram, he looped the thick rope about his waist. 'Keep a firm hold, lads,' he ordered, trying to hide his chattering nerves. 'If I tug on it three times, start hauling.'

'Yes, sir,' they said.

Courtney did not know what awaited him on the other side. He knew it could not be entirely flooded, for the voice kept shouting, but before he ducked beneath, he sucked in a deep lungful of air. The frigidness shocked him again. He fought against it, groping his way to find the gap in the blockage. When his hands located the space, he followed with his body, kicking his feet off the floor and praying nothing trapped him.

A floating halo of debris met him. He pushed away ropes and canvas, ensuring they did not tangle with his own line. The thick pool, choked with shimmering lantern oil and beer, swarmed about him. It was impossible to see. He aimed for the surface and broke it with a gasp. In the small space, he could lift a hand and touch the beams above. Before him lay a maze of detritus from the collision. He coughed, tasting the noxious mix of food and drink in the water, and managed, 'Who's there? Keep shouting!'

The voice struggled out, emerging from a heap of timber lodged further aft. He waded through, the water deepening. Two hands sprang out from behind the mess. Courtney grasped one and beat a chokehold of litter away. He made out a duo of pallid faces, pressed against the bulkhead and only just bobbing above the surface. The hand he held shook like a leaf on the wind. Much longer and they would die of the cold.

'I'm going to get you out,' he insisted. 'Can you move?'

'There's a chunk of wood holding us down,' one of the men replied through gnashing teeth.

Courtney saw it, jammed against the wall and plunging into the water. He grabbed it and gave it a forceful shove. It did not budge. The two men helped but they had been drenched for hours, perhaps, and had no strength remaining.

'Mr Ingram, Mr Addison!' he called. 'One of you come through!'

He did not know if they would, but with his comrades' lives in danger, Ingram appeared, following Courtney's line.

'Help me with this,' Courtney urged.

They scrambled in the water to find something to lever the timber up. As they moved it into position, Courtney heard a deep groan from above. Something cracked, dropping onto the decks. For a moment, the entire ship shuddered. He swallowed his fear. He would not move until these men were out.

Side by side with Ingram, they fell upon the leverage, straining with all their might to shift the fallen block. It was only then that Courtney realised his exhaustion, hours spent at the pumps catching up with him. Still, he dug into his reserves. The sight of the two men, trapped and freezing and terrified, thrust him onwards.

He felt the timber move – only an inch, but it was enough. Impelling Ingram on, he gave another hard push, shoving down from his aching shoulders and through his soaked muscles. Another inch. And another. And another.

The two men slipped to the side. 'Come on through,' Courtney gasped. Together, they ducked beneath the water and beneath the lifted timber. Once they were at Courtney's side, he and Ingram let it fall with a rush of breath.

Above, the ship moaned again. Outside, the sea lashed at her, soaking in through the breakages. 'We have to move,' Courtney said. 'Quick, back through.'

Ingram led them, ducking back through the gap. One of the rescued Loyals followed but the other hung back, wincing. Courtney noticed blood swilling in the water. 'You're wounded,' he managed, cursing himself for not realising.

'It's nothing. Just a scratch where the timber fell.'

'Hold on to me. I'll see you safe.'

Courtney unlooped the rope from around his waist and lashed it around the other man. Guiding him, they reached the barrels and found their way back through. Addison met them, pointing to the upper decks. 'More water's coming through, sir,' he said. 'The mast or something big's come down.'

'All of you, onto the rocks. The *Lysander* will be sending the boats back over. You'll be warm and safe soon, I promise.'

As fast as possible with the *Loyal* man's arm about his shoulders, Courtney led them back up. More debris had rolled along the decks since they had been in the hold. The foreyard had toppled completely onto the main deck, dragging with it a wedge of the mast. The upper yards teetered dangerously.

'Go, go, onto the rocks,' Courtney pushed.

Ingram and Addison helped their injured comrades to the rail, then over the side. Courtney was the last to go. He looked back, saw the foremast arcing backwards. Below, at the same time, something snapped, perhaps that gun carriage finally breaking through. The *Loyal* wailed and trembled. It was enough to unhinge the unstable spars.

Now that the other men were safely off, Courtney vaulted the rail. He found a porthole lid, and another, then leapt the rest of the way. Behind, the waves lashed the *Loyal* as she began to split. Her seams bowed, her decks rent asunder, and the sea began to consume her.

Courtney and the others scrambled up the rock face. They turned to watch the final destruction of the *Loyal*. Wrapped in their fellows' coats, the two they had rescued trembled with tears running down their faces. A minute more and they would have all been taken down with the doomed *Loyal*.

Courtney looked down, feeling as though he performed another service for the dead. They had their answer for where the *Loyal* was – but her reasons for being so wrecked, he did not know.

'Thank you, sir,' one of the men finally gasped. He held out a shaking hand and Courtney felt an upwelling of emotion: exhaustion, relief, terror at last taking hold. In answer, he grasped the other man's palm.

'What are your names?' he could only think to say.

'I am Mason Dunn.'

'And I am Nathan Waters,' the injured sailor managed.

'Nathan Waters.' Courtney could barely believe it. 'Sara's husband?'

His eyes widened. 'Yes, sir. How – how do you know my Sara?'

Courtney smiled. 'She is my friend. I spoke to her not a few days ago in Gibraltar.'

Waters laughed. Courtney joined in, gaining the grins of the other three men.

Across the sea, the *Lysander's* boats were returning: the promise of safety and warmth – and of answers.

Chapter Nineteen: Answers

Courtney shivered, his feet in a bowl of warmed water and a blanket wrapped about his shoulders. A draught kept winding down the decks, drifting past his clammy skin and making him prickle. He had thought that, before leaving Gibraltar, he would be lucky to escape a chill, and now it was creeping up on him.

It was only when reaching the *Lysander* again that Courtney realised his coat and waistcoat still floated in the bowels of the *Loyal*. Nightingale had paid for them both. He hoped the man could forgive him. The thought of him, out there on the *Fantôme*, made Courtney feel even more deathly.

The *Fantôme* now chased a phantom itself. The *Loyal* was wrecked. All her remaining people had been ferried off the rocks, but when counting them and taking their names, Smythe had found there were only forty-seven of them. The rest of the *Loyal's* crew, as well as Sir William Haywood, remained somewhere else.

Now that the surviving Loyals were being fed warm broths and grog and the injured men were in the sickbay, the officers could receive the answers they had travelled for weeks to find. The only absent man was Bryant himself, attended to by Dr Faulkner in his cabin. He had said no more about the state of the captain's injury.

It had only been a short while when a knock came at the door. It was opened to reveal the civilian who Courtney had pulled away from Darius Wade. He had been checked over by the doctor and now stood a little firmer, the shock having ebbed to a small degree. He wore only his frilled shirt, breeches and boots, but Courtney could tell he was a man of standing. He bowed neatly to him and came to sit at the table where a mug of coffee awaited him.

'Thank you for your aid, sir,' he said to him. Courtney managed a nod, only then noting the man's French accent.

'Monsieur Baptiste?' he asked. 'You are Monsieur Hugo Baptiste?'
'I am.'

Courtney cleared his throat, suddenly feeling a cough rattling up it. He extended a shivering hand. Baptiste took it, again bowing his head. He was an older man, silvery hair pulled back into a neat tie and with an air of natural authority to him.

'I apologise for the captain's absence, Monsieur,' Courtney said. 'He was wounded during the storm. I am, as you know, Lieutenant Courtney. Our ship, the *Lysander*, has been sent from England to locate you and the *Loyal*. The Admiralty has been extremely concerned about your wellbeing. We thought that perhaps foul play had occurred. That suspicion may have driven both of our sides quicker to conflict again. A French ship, the *Fantôme*, has also been sent out.'

'We were supposed to reach Malta in the second week of August,' Baptiste stated calmly. 'Alas, we did not. I had no way of contacting anyone to tell them of our condition or our whereabouts. I do apologise for the strain we have put you gentlemen through.'

'What on earth happened to the *Loyal*?' Courtney asked. 'Her state, even before she hit the rocks, was...atrocious.'

Baptiste lowered his eyes. 'Fortune did not follow the *Loyal*.'

All manner of awful situations raced through Courtney's head. Finally, after taking another long sip of his coffee, Baptiste began. 'We passed through the Strait of Gibraltar at the beginning of August. With the wind upon on our side, Captain Myles said that we would reach Valletta in a short while. We had no reason to doubt him. Our countries have laid down their arms and we expected no conflict.

'The Balearics passed to our north, and we were south of Corsica when the storm struck us. We had weathered a gale on the journey past Spain but nothing like the one we encountered there. I became dreadfully seasick, as I had before, and locked myself in my cabin below. So I do not know how it began.'

Courtney leant forward, waiting. Baptiste closed his eyes briefly, shuddering at the memory, perhaps of the storm, perhaps of the seasickness, perhaps of worse.

'The first I knew of it was the sound of the *Loyal*'s cannons. I wondered if it were some English trick to outwit the weather. I had known of guns being heaved overboard before. But the fire kept echoing through the ship. I heard a collision, and then the noise of the *Loyal* being torn apart. I could not stay in my cabin, despite my illness.

'I ran out as a ball split through the hull. It came near to my leg, so close I could feel the air of it as it flew past. I hurried out of my quarters into the gundeck. All the men had been roused and parties of them manned the guns. I wanted to ask who it was we fought. We are not at war, I thought. Sir William Haywood found me first, not the officers who were on deck. He told me to go below. Lock myself below and not come out until one of the *Loyal*'s crew told me it was safe.'

'What happened to Sir William?' Courtney asked.

Baptiste shook his head. 'He was so brave. He did not lock himself away with me. He fought.'

Courtney braced himself for the next words. When he could not bear Baptiste's pause any longer, he asked, 'Did he die?'

'I do not know. I did not see him again after this. I obeyed his orders and locked myself below in the hold. I listened to the cannonfire and the shouting and the screaming and the destruction of the *Loyal*, thinking that at every moment my death would come. But I was preserved until a seaman, Darius Wade, let me out.'

Baptiste's eyes welled with tears. He searched for his handkerchief but could not find it. Smythe handed over his own. 'The young man died on the rocks,' he continued. 'I wish I could have saved him, but his leg was crushed by falling timber and he was injured upon his head, too. Those poor *Loyal* men.'

'Where are the rest of your crew, Monsieur?' Courtney asked. 'Who did you battle?'

Baptiste sniffed. 'They came from Tripoli. Pirates. They stole our crew and nearly stole our ship.'

Courtney felt a chill down his spine. The idea of pirates had crossed his mind briefly. He had heard horror stories as a child on the English coast. Long ago, raids had come as far as Cornwall, capturing innocent men, women and children and holding them for ransom or selling them into slavery. The idea of bondage made Courtney's skin itch. Living in the Caribbean for years had made him intimately aware of it, even more intimately due to the former slaves who had served on the *Scylla*. Obi had been from a plantation in Antigua, something Captain Carlisle, and then Nightingale, had turned a blind eye to. Courtney had only very reluctantly and very harshly bitten his tongue about the trade, and when he had spoken up, Lord Fairholme, that bastard, had nearly threatened him for it.

'Pirates,' Courtney breathed, sinking back in his chair. He glanced at Smythe and Godfrey who looked as horrified as he felt. 'They are bold to attack an English frigate. But...we are not at war now. Even the *Lysander* does not carry as many men as she would during conflict. There is less crew to man the guns.'

Certainly during a storm, he did not add. The pirates had been crafty to attack the *Loyal* when she was so maimed and strained.

'They took us unaware,' Baptiste continued, confirming his thoughts. 'We should have been able to destroy them. They are a menace which, even in war, could unite our two sides. They have no discrimination between English, French, Spanish, Italian, African, or Arab... Four years ago, nine hundred were taken from near Sardinia.'

Courtney opened his mouth to ask more, but Baptiste continued, 'The *Loyal* escaped, but not for long. The pirates fell upon us again within days and we battled her, a running fight that lasted for... God only knows how long. We were taken, escaped, re-taken... What a nightmare it all was.'

'But you escaped again?' Courtney prompted.

'Regrettably so,' Baptiste unexpectedly said. 'We had to leave crewmen behind. Captain Myles and many others are still in captivity with the pirates. The battles took their toll on the *Loyal*. You saw her damage. She was mortally wounded. There were not many of us left, but we sailed her as far as she would go, hoping to reach Sardinia. We could barely guide her without her mast and with her damage. And then the next storm struck us...'

That had been when the *Lysander* had encountered her. She had been limping already; any rising wind would have troubled her without her spars, let alone a fierce gale. Courtney was impressed she had made it as far as she had.

'The Americans are at war with Tripoli,' Godfrey said. 'They have been seizing Tripolitan ships and battling them since last year.'

'Many of the *Loyal*'s crew are still with them,' Baptiste confirmed. 'The pirates' ship was quick and powerful.'

Many of the *Loyal*'s crew, and Sir William Haywood. They had their answers now, but those poor men, and the *Fantôme*, were still out there.

'Those men will be sold into slavery,' Courtney stated, his bones chilling at the very thought. He imagined Mrs Nightingale, back home, forever fretting of her father's fate. But Britain was not at war with Tripoli, not as the Americans were. Any action now would be dangerous. 'Our original plan was to head for Sicily,' he continued. 'That is where we agreed to meet with the *Fantôme*. She has to be told what has happened to the *Loyal*.'

Their mission had been secret because of the fact it could have brought war between France and Britain. Now, they risked the wrath of the Barbary states also.

Yet those poor *Loyal* men would expect rescue. Courtney could not leave them.

'I shall speak with Captain Bryant when he is awake.' *If he awakes*, he thought privately. 'The *Lysander* is damaged. She needs a harbour to finish her repairs, and we are two days from Palermo.'

Smythe and Godfrey nodded. They had found the *Loyal*, but the seas to Malta and around the Tripolitan coast were still vast. The captured seamen and officers could be anywhere, en route to the slave markets or to be ransomed for a high cost.

'Thank you for your time, Monsieur,' Courtney said. 'I appreciate that you are tired. You acted very bravely on the *Loyal* during the storm. But your reward will come soon. When we reconvene with the *Fantôme*, you shall be reunited with your wife. She requested passage on the *Fantôme* and Capitaine Bonfils has been looking after her well.'

For the first time since leaving Darius Wade, emotion swept across Baptiste's face, as if the weight of his story finally found him. 'My wife?' he rasped.

'Yes. Madame Geneviève. Not long ago, she came across to the *Lysander* to inspect her. Capitaine Bonfils on the *Fantôme* has been looking after her.'

Silence rang. Baptiste sat back in his chair, tears spilling. 'She is too bold,' he managed. 'I do not deserve her.'

Courtney smiled. 'She is a remarkable woman.'

Having been rocked enough by this storm, Monsieur Baptiste was sent below again to finally sleep, if he could manage to do so. Courtney wanted to retire to his cabin also, but the weight of responsibility loomed heavily over him. He had to try to speak with Bryant again. Godfrey and Smythe looked at him expectantly. Courtney tried to gauge the looks in their faces. Whilst Bryant was down, he was their commander. Wasn't that what he had wanted?

Finding his stockings and boots, Courtney dressed again and threw the towel from around his shoulders. Listening to the sounds of the men still pumping the water and the hammering of the carpenter and his team, he made his way to Bryant's cabin. A knock brought Parker's stooped form to the door. Behind him, Courtney could see Dr Faulkner laying dressings out on the table.

'Is the captain awake, Parker?' he asked, feeling his stomach tighten.
'Just, sir.'

Relief flickered in Courtney. As much as he disliked Bryant, he did not want him to die. 'May I see him?'

Parker turned to Faulkner. The man was bleary-eyed still, not in a state to treat a head wound.

'Yes, Lieutenant, you may,' Faulkner said. 'But you must be quick.'

Courtney did not know if that meant Faulkner wished to continue dousing him, or if it meant Bryant's strength was fading fast. He found him in his cot, propped up on a pillow, bandages wrapped about his head. Fresh blood stained them. Courtney swallowed.

'Sir,' he said softly. 'I have spoken with Monsieur Baptiste. He was one of the men we saved from the rocks. The *Loyal* is gone.'

'Mmm,' Bryant managed. His eyes fluttered as if he barely understood Courtney. 'What…happened…to her?'

'She was attacked by Barbary pirates. Sir William and many of the Loyals are still missing as captives.' Bryant did not respond. 'I am going to see the *Lysander* into Palermo and meet with the *Fantôme*. But we must find the missing men. We cannot return to England knowing their fate, and Sir William's, without acting.'

'No orders,' Bryant croaked. 'No orders to cover this.'

Courtney knew that. He glanced at Faulkner, who was lingering at the door, towels in his hand Courtney knew a few dressings would not cure Bryant. Seeing him so helpless and wounded threw his new role into sharp relief. The *Lysander* and her journey were under his command now. 'You shall be treated better ashore in Palermo, sir,' he said.

'Faulkner,' Bryant mumbled, then seemed to drift into a short slumber. Faulkner stepped forward but Bryant jerked awake again. 'The doctor…needs to claim me…unfit…before you have—'

'I know, sir.'

'—before you have my command…'

Courtney looked down. 'Your health is our concern, sir. Focus upon that. I shall see to the *Lysander*.'

Bryant muttered incomprehensibly. Courtney returned to Faulkner, who was rocking slowly on his feet, twisting the towels in his grip. He dismissed it as drunkenness until the doctor said, 'I cannot do anything more. He was saying about declaring him unfit but… I have never done such a thing. Do you think that I should?'

Courtney did not like that question being laid at his feet. 'That is not my place, Doctor. Just…look after him. We shall be in Palermo soon.'

Pascoe waited outside the cabin as Courtney left. His eyes peered curiously in but Courtney shut the door behind him. 'Is he well?' the master asked.

'No. I don't know if he'll survive the night. I've seen head wounds like that before.'

'What did you tell him?'

Courtney did not like the lack of 'sir' in Pascoe's speech. The man had had a strange rapport with Bryant, no doubt being party to all of the captain's distaste for Courtney. Now the hierarchy had been rattled a little, he was testing where he stood. Courtney knew it, because he had done it before.

He swept past Pascoe, wanting to rest but knowing that, despite his aches and creeping chill, he would be arranging the ship and her journey for the rest of the night. Pascoe hurried into step beside him.

'He did not give any orders for his successor in command.'

'I'd advise you not to listen at the keyholes of officers' cabins, Mr Pascoe.'

'What shall you do?'

'Now?' Courtney stopped. 'I have no other choice. I shall see the *Lysander* into Palermo and have Captain Bryant properly cared for. She still suffers damage from the storm and the collision with the *Loyal*.'

'And beyond that? Captain Bryant has not been judged unfit for duty, and you are not of the rank to command my – this – ship.'

'Mr Pascoe,' Courtney tried to say levelly, not liking Pascoe's tone or the way his questions stirred up his own uncertainty. 'You are no longer the master of this ship. I'll assume this is shock from the trying day we've both had, so I recommend retiring to your quarters and sleeping off your discontent. Tomorrow, we shall investigate this ship from bilge to skyscraper and make an accurate reading of her state and location. Good night.'

Sensibly, Pascoe did not follow. As he returned to the gunroom, Courtney thought of his first interactions with Nightingale. Frustrated over Courtney's insubordination and questions, Nightingale had said a similar thing to him once, telling him he was no longer the sole commander of the *Scylla*. Courtney felt an ache in his chest as he realised how much he had absorbed from Nightingale. He was still out there with the *Fantôme* somewhere. He could barely wait to see them again in Palermo. Then, a better decision could be made.

Then, they could all plan.

Chapter Twenty: Grey Waters

The *Fantôme* was nowhere to be seen in Palermo. From the moment they raised Monte Pellegrino, Courtney kept his eye through the spyglass, searching the forest of masts in the harbour. British ensigns flew, a result of the British protection from Napoleon afforded to the island, but Courtney could not find the French frigate. And neither was she anchored further out in the bay. She would have stood out sorely in amongst these vessels.

Hiding his concern, Courtney saw the *Lysander* into her moorings. They had fared well since they had left the wreck site of the *Loyal*. The ship had borne the journey bravely, though Courtney and Pascoe had found her seams leaking still and her hull scarred like an old, harpooned whale. A sail, thrummed with yarn and fibres, had been fothered over the worst puncture in the *Lysander's* starboard flank, a temporary solution until they reached a harbour. The pumps had not stopped. All of the men's possessions had been marred in the churning waters, with no distinction between officer and regular hand. Pascoe's personal chest had lost its lock and nearly been stove in, Courtney's effects were waterlogged, and the starboard division's hammocks had needed hours of drying.

Courtney had joined the men at the pumps and with the repairs, appreciating the back-breaking work as a distraction from Bryant. He had not yet awoken. Whilst the *Loyal* survivors recovered slowly in the tentative care of Dr Faulkner, Bryant lapsed into a deep comatose state. There was little they could do for him other than mop his brow and check in on him during the day and night.

'Surgery may be necessary,' Faulkner had said to Courtney. 'But I cannot even think of doing it aboard this ship. One slip and I would kill him.'

Courtney was not sure he trusted Faulkner to perform it on dry land, either. Under the constant strain, he had nursed a bottle of gin as if it were the only thing keeping him upright. Courtney would be glad to set Bryant down in a hospital.

It was the first thing he supervised after reporting to the port-captain of Palermo's harbour. With no record of the *Fantôme*'s arrival, Courtney did not know how else he was supposed to proceed. Bryant was down. Bonfils had vanished. The *Loyal*'s Captain Myles had been captured by pirates. Responsibility fell upon Courtney like a millstone.

Bitterness churned in his throat as he accompanied Faulkner and Godfrey with Bryant. Waiting within the imposing walls of the grand hospital, the second lieutenant paced restlessly whilst Courtney sat, trying to ignore the pounding in his head. His chill from diving into the drowned *Loyal* had worsened, worming right between his eyes and upon his chest. He pushed through it for the crew. They all needed him, not to mention the missing Loyals somewhere out in the blue.

'Will he die?' Godfrey suddenly said. Courtney blinked, shielding his eyes from the winter sun pouring through the colonnaded walkway.

'I don't know,' he replied truthfully. 'Dr Faulkner did not have high hopes. But the men here seem capable.'

'I served with Captain Bryant in the Caribbean. The incident with the *Meridian* was…unfortunate. He was always unsettled by having to sail alongside the *Scylla*, after her history. I think he knew that he would not be able to achieve that kind of notoriety.'

Godfrey seemed to be already composing Bryant's eulogy. 'The *Scylla* had a reputation,' Courtney remarked. And never again, he thought, would he have that same long-term understanding of a ship and crew.

'What shall happen if he does not recover?'

The question had plagued Courtney ever since the cap had injured Bryant. The pathway ahead was not clear. As the first lieutenant, he would be expected to care for the *Lysander* and her men if the captain fell. But they operated under strict instructions and tentative, fragile diplomacy. One wrong move could upset everything.

He was saved from answering Godfrey's question by Faulkner emerging from a door, accompanied by a hospital doctor. Courtney rose from the seat, heart sticking in his throat. 'How is he?' he asked.

'Very unwell,' Faulkner replied. 'We shall have to operate if he has any chance of survival. The skull is fractured and putting pressure upon his brain. We cannot be sure what his state will be if he does recover.'

Godfrey removed his hat, sighing deeply. Courtney nodded, uncertain how to feel. A thousand emotions churned within him. But Faulkner's statement brought confirmation: he no longer operated in a purgatory, caught in half-command of the *Lysander* and her men. Courtney, the boy from the lower berth of the *Grampus*, was now the highest-ranking officer.

He reminded himself that that was what he had wanted.

As he and Godfrey walked away from the hospital, heavy with the knowledge they had to break to the men, Courtney tried to separate out the options he now had before him. The *Loyal* men were missing. For all he knew, the *Fantôme* still searched for her – but surely, she would have been able to reach Palermo before the *Lysander*, having left Gibraltar days before. He could either assume that she was still on her way, delayed by time and tide, or he could search for her and potentially miss her arrival.

Yet the idea of sitting dormant in Palermo, with the Loyals in the clutches of pirates, potentially on the cusp of being sold into slavery, made him ache.

The Admiralty's orders now became his responsibility, but there were grey waters that Courtney was unsure he could tread. He had never battled pirates before, though he had often heard of their scourge along the Barbary Coast. Whether he would cross any lines that he could not step back over was a dear question.

The mantle of command already weighed upon him.

Sitting in the gunroom with the officers, he snivelled and coughed through his news about Bryant. In the absence of Parker, caring for Bryant at the hospital, Andrews, the ship's cook, made coffee which tasted of burnt beans and the tang of the pot's metal. It did not warm Courtney and, after the first sip, the others gave up too. They nodded silently, perhaps having already thought the worst. Only Pascoe met Courtney's eyes as he looked around at them to judge their thoughts.

'What do we do now?' he asked when Courtney prompted any questions.

Smythe and Godfrey shifted uncomfortably. Courtney paused, sifting through all the possible trials and dangers and reprimands that awaited him.

'We,' he began, then had to clear his throat. 'First of all, we must repair the *Lysander*. She will struggle if she leaves Palermo in this state.'

With that at least decided, Courtney could focus on another task. Brooks at his side, he prepared lists of wounds in the poor *Lysander*. He shepherded Smythe around with them, allowing him to take note of the *Lysander*'s issues and prompting him for what he would decide in such a situation. Dramatics or not, the boy was still on his path to becoming a full officer, and Courtney was his guide now – not that Bryant had taken much interest before.

They scoured the ship's interior and then had Harris row them about her to make sure they had not missed anything on her hull. They sourced a glassmaker in Palermo for the mending of the great cabin's gallery windows, and set to work with them and her damaged timbers. Reports had to be written, letters had to be noted, both official and private. The lull gave him time to add to his letter to Jane, still unsent, but his mind kept floating away, over the shrouded Mediterranean towards wherever the *Fantôme* and the Loyals might be.

The watches passed him by. Though they were not at sea, he kept the men to the regular routine they were used to and only allowed small parties to go ashore under the eyes of the marines. Palermo was exotic, beautiful, appealing, and he did not want to lose any of them to its wilds. Walking amongst the crew, he hoped they remained at his side, but the shock of the storm and the possible demise of their captain meant the hierarchy was shaken. His first days in command, whether it be temporary or not, would show everyone where he, and they, stood.

In between assisting the supplies and repairs over the next day, he visited the hospital. Bryant did not awake. Faulkner and the resident surgeon prepared to cut into his head and Courtney, for all his stomach, did not want to be there when they did. The perils of not knowing, though, ate at him: not knowing about Bryant, not knowing about the missing ship and sailors, not knowing how far his new command would stretch. When he lay awake in his cabin at night, he almost damned Bryant for his decisions in the storm and for all the other decisions before that.

But, below all his uncertainty and anger, he knew where the core lay. Nightingale was gone. With every hour that crawled by, the horizon never broken by the form of the *Fantôme*, he thought of him on that strange ship with a strange crew. He wished he had been forceful in making Nightingale stay on the *Lysander*, but he could not command the man. Nightingale was capable, he told himself. He would be fine.

Yet, before Nightingale had departed, they had argued. Courtney knew what Nightingale was like; he would be stewing over that, just as Courtney did.

He simply wanted to see him again.

On the second day, laid up in port, Courtney sat with Baptiste at the taffrail. Courtney's chill had cleared a little, but the cool air still stuck in his lungs. The French diplomat, after being examined by Faulkner again, had no lasting wounds on his body. The strain of the *Loyal's* struggles still weighed on Baptiste, though, and Courtney felt guilty that he had been cooped up on the *Lysander* with his troubled memories.

'You are not one of our men, Monsieur,' Courtney said. 'You are free to go ashore.'

Baptiste offered a weak smile. 'I would prefer to stay aboard, Lieutenant. Dr Faulkner and your men have looked after me kindly. I assume that you are going to go ahead and search for the missing men.'

He may have assumed that, but Courtney had come to no concrete decision. The sensible course would be to turn for Gibraltar once the *Lysander* had been repaired and await new orders.

'To be perfectly truthful, Monsieur, I am not sure,' he admitted.

'Well, if you do, I want to be with you. I would like to rescue the men who were taken. It is only through fortune that I was not.'

'It may be very dangerous.'

'I have already composed my letter to the officials at Malta, Lieutenant. They shall know of our fate. I wish to accompany the *Lysander*.'

'That is very brave of you, Monsieur.'

Courtney thought of the Frenchmen he had met throughout this voyage. None of them had conformed to the prejudices of the English. They had been courageous, astute, and skilful upon the sea. He wondered, if the wars returned, how he would feel fighting them as the opposing side again.

By the end of the day, another nationality made its appearance in Palermo. Into the harbour came a brig, the colours of the American stars and stripes flying at her stern. Courtney watched her in fascination. He had seen very few ships of the US Navy before. Only a handful had ever crossed the *Scylla*'s path in the Caribbean, and of American sailors, he had little experience beyond Ransome, the mutineer who had so terrorised the *Ulysses*.

But he watched the brig's men moor the brig smoothly and approved of their handling. Upon her stern, he read the name '*Franklin*'.

Within the next hour, as the night came down upon the bay, Courtney descended to the gunroom. Unusually, no one else occupied the space. By the light of a guttering lantern, he scribbled the rest of his letter to Jane.

Ever since laying pen to paper, he had oscillated between wanting to ask her to delay her wedding, and telling himself he was being selfish. He greatly desired to walk her down the aisle to Lieutenant Wainwright. But he could not command the heavens and the seas, and who knew how long this voyage would stretch? The most important matter was her happiness. He would return one day and see her again.

Instead of dwelling on his own turmoil, he wrote to her of the sights of Palermo and how she would love the grand cathedral and the mysterious grotto sanctuary atop Monte Pellegrino. If they had to stay much longer in the city, Courtney would ensure his descriptions were not so vague. Once, he and Jane had shared everything; she had worked alongside him as a child on the fishing boats and on the farms, and when they had journeyed to the Caribbean, they had explored Antigua from coast to coast. She had even tried to join the navy with him. Now, she seemed so far away. He did not have to look after her any longer, but he would never cease wishing her every joy.

'Sir!'

Smythe's voice startled him. The midshipman hurried to the gunroom, staggering to a halt at the entrance.

'What on earth is it, Mr Smythe?' Courtney asked, tension crossing his chest.

'The *Franklin*, sir, it's the *Franklin*,' the midshipman managed to say. Though his voice had deepened almost to that of a man, he still had his childlike energy. 'Her captain, sir—'

He paused for breath and Courtney sat him down at the bench.

'I'm sorry, sir, I ran all the way here from the timber yard. Couldn't wait. The *Franklin*, sir, her captain – he said he'd just fought pirates. Pirates from – from Tripoli, sir.'

Courtney paused with his hand on Smythe's shoulder. 'Are you certain?'

'Yes, sir. I overheard him and his first mate talking. They were in the yard with us because their ship has been damaged too.'

'Did he say if he'd seen any other vessel?'

'No, sir. Don't know, sir.'

Courtney had to speak with him. Abandoning his letter and pulling on his boat cloak, he left the gunroom and found Godfrey on deck. Hurriedly explaining to him where he was going, he fetched Harris, was rowed across the harbour, and stepped onto the dock in a matter of minutes. Procedure called for something more organised, perhaps a meeting arranged between two officers, but Courtney had no time for formality. He rushed to the timber yard, only to spot a decorated man walking along the city's fortified walls. He wore a deep blue uniform with gold buttons, shining epaulettes on each shoulder.

Courtney raised his hand to hail him. 'The captain of the *Franklin*?' he managed, realising he did not know his name.

The man stopped, looking Courtney up and down and laying a hand on his sword as if he were threatening him to a duel. 'Do I know you, sir?' he asked. Courtney heard the distinct accent that shared the same heavy 'r' sounds that his own did.

'No, sir. I am Lieutenant Courtney of HMS *Lysander*. You are the captain of USS *Franklin*?'

'I am. Captain Kelly.'

'May I speak with you about a sensitive matter? It involves piracy.'

The man frowned, but Courtney could see he was intrigued by the mention of the pirates. He glanced to his companion and nodded. 'You may walk with me, sir.'

Courtney walked in step with him along the harbour, realising he must appear quite shabby next to Kelly's glitter. 'I apologise for my looks, sir,' he said with that in mind. 'I lost my coat when rescuing some men from a sinking ship. That is what I wanted to speak to you about. We have only recently pulled survivors from a wreck. They say they were attacked by Tripolitan pirates, and their comrades were taken.'

He tried carefully not to reveal too much about the *Loyal*, if secrecy was still the concern of the Admiralty. He had a feeling he would be wading in murky waters soon and he wanted as little ammunition against his actions as possible.

Kelly nodded, his face showing nothing.

'I understand your nation is at war with Tripoli, sir,' Courtney said. 'My midshipman overheard you mention it. I wondered...'

'If we had seen any sign of your missing men?'

'The ship that accompanied mine is also missing, sir. She was supposed to wait here in Palermo for us but we've seen neither hide nor hair of her.'

'I am afraid I may have bad news for you, Lieutenant Courtney.'

Courtney's stomach swooped. 'You've seen nothing?'

'No. Quite the opposite. That is why we have had to make port in Palermo where the Kingdom of Naples has so kindly allowed our navy to operate from. It is fortunate that it is so close to where the *Franklin* was attacked.'

'You were attacked too?' These pirates were bold, even bolder than Courtney had assumed of them.

'Yes. Damaged our rudder and mainmast. At first we thought that they were two Barbary ships. But only one fired and came in so close we thought they meant to board us. She was a polacre, the kind we have seen many a time before. But she was well-armed and seemingly very powerful. We escaped and it was only afterwards that I thought about that other vessel with her.'

Courtney could barely breathe. He prepared himself for the worst but hated to say, 'She was of a French design? The *Fantôme*?'

Kelly nodded. 'I believe she had been boarded by the pirates previously and was being commanded by a prize crew.'

'Where were they? Where were they headed?' Courtney could not get the questions out of his mouth quickly enough.

'I can point to their location on a chart. We have heard of the experience of the Barbary slaves. Many are pressed into service on the corsairs. Others are sold or ransomed for high prices. I have seen the markets in Algiers and Tripoli.'

'I served in the Caribbean,' Courtney heard himself say. 'I'd string all slavers high if I could.'

Kelly looked sidelong at Courtney. 'You do not talk like any lieutenant I have known.'

'I have heard that before.' He looked across the harbour where the masts of the *Lysander* broke the moonlit night. 'Can you show me where you encountered the pirates?'

'I can. Where is your captain? That is a frigate, is it not? Not the kind of ship a lieutenant commands.'

'My captain is severely wounded. It is not certain if he will survive. I command the *Lysander* for now.'

An hour later, having perused the charts with Captain Kelly, Courtney finally sat again, his mind spinning. He had answers now and he hated the way they fell. When he sat with the other officers upon the *Lysander* and told them what he had discovered, he saw their faces drop. He rushed through the explanation, hating that he could not give a clear answer of what they would do now. Despite what he had said to Kelly, his command was an impotent one.

'They will...they will survive, won't they, sir?' Smythe asked him in a small voice once Godfrey had retired under a black cloud.

Courtney wanted to say 'yes', if only to assure them both, but he found he could not bring himself to do so. His thoughts, so tangled, kept racing to Nightingale. Over and over, he pictured him as a captive, as a slave. Courtney's chest tightened. For a moment, he could not breathe. His fingers fumbled as he tried to pick up his mug of coffee.

'I don't know,' he admitted, knowing it was the wrong response to give to a boy like Smythe. He would be looking for a figure to look up to for inspiration and assurance.

'They will, sir,' Smythe insisted. 'I know that they will.'

Unsurprisingly, Courtney did not sleep that night. He lay in his hammock, then the cot, tossing and turning. It felt so long ago that he and Nightingale had slumbered in each other's embrace in the cottage on the Isle of Wight. He would have given anything to return there with him. With all the burden of command and ideas of his career and the missing *Fantôme* stripped away, the heart of Courtney's troubles centred on Nightingale. If anything happened to him...

Courtney could not bear to even allow the thought.

In the cold light of day, determination and certainty at last dawned upon him. He had not acted when Paterson and Arnold were condemned. He had allowed Nightingale to go off to the *Fantôme*, to his doom. He could not allow the *Fantôme* to be as wrecked as the *Loyal* had been.

Yet, on the morning of the next day, another unexpected note arrived onboard. Courtney opened it, fearing that he would find the words he dreaded, yet anticipated: Captain Bryant's untimely death.

The captain still lived.

And Courtney no longer operated in grey waters – for the *Lysander* had been recalled to Gibraltar.

Paterson and Arnold's trial was to begin.

Chapter Twenty-One: The Outsider

The bulky form of HMS *Mallard* now sat in Gibraltar's harbour. With the commander-in-chief of the Mediterranean, Lord Keith, on leave in England, Courtney assumed this old fifty-gun fourth-rate was the best that could be mustered. He looked at it as the *Lysander* returned to her moorings in the harbour, remembering the court martial aboard the imperious *Leviathan*. He had hoped to never again be tangled in the world of naval law and punishment.

Yet here he was, ordered back, torn away from the search for the *Fantôme*.

The journey across the Mediterranean had been less eventful than the *Lysander*'s previous crossing, although it felt she was being pulled back and forth like a ragdoll. No storms plagued them – fortunately so, as the *Lysander* had only recently been patched up in Palermo. The men had handled her handsomely and to fill the low times, Courtney had them drilled in every manoeuvre possible. He had barely stopped, hardly even slept. To do so would be to allow the thoughts and fears to creep over him. Many of them, too many, lurked beneath the surface – about the *Fantôme*, his career, the men, but more than anything, about Nightingale. So, as they ran out the great guns, or laboured over the carronades, or tacked in calm winds, or set and then furled the sails, he kept his eye on the waters. No *Fantôme* appeared, and no Barbary corsair.

But now, whilst he gathered together the logbooks and journals to hand over to the court martial's panel, he could only think of Nightingale. He could be anywhere: pressed into service on a corsair, forced across the burning Tripoli landscape to market, chained up for ransom. Before testifying, Courtney had to know where his own position lay.

He had to know the orders. He was already treading unknown depths with the absence of Bryant.

Barely two hours after mooring, a message from the *Mallard* arrived. Her commander and the president of the court martial, Easton, invited the captain of the *Lysander* to dine aboard with the fellow officers. Courtney, who had been spending most of his time in shirt-sleeves since losing his coat on the *Loyal*, finally opened the chest containing his dress uniform. The water had seeped in during the storm so it emitted a mouldy, acrid smell as he brushed it down. In the end, it was only with coarse soap and a quick soak that he could rid some of it.

During the first dog watch, he left the *Lysander* under Godfrey's command and had Harris row him across the harbour. Climbing the high sides of the *Mallard*, he heard the trilling of the bosun's pipe announcing the arrival of a captain. Confused faces greeted him. A tall and broad grey-haired post-captain in blue and gold, who he assumed to be Easton, looked him up and down.

'Lieutenant?' Easton asked.

'Lieutenant Courtney of the *Lysander*, sir,' he said, removing his hat.

'Is Captain Bryant ailing?'

'Yes, sir. He is still in Palermo at the hospital. A fallen chunk of the mizzen cap damaged his skull.'

Easton lowered his eyes. 'I am sorry to hear that. You have been commanding the *Lysander* in his absence?'

Courtney detected a hint of disbelief in his tone. He wondered if he had done something wrong by assuming command. 'Yes, sir. In fact, I wanted to ask you...'

The arrival of another captain interrupted him. Easton's eyes drew away from him and an officer's steward, standing at the door of the great cabin, guided the waiting men inside. Courtney had no choice but to shut his mouth and join the parade into Easton's richly furnished space where glasses and cutlery and china plates adorned the polished table. He knew none of the men there, not even by name as they were introduced. He had spent the last few years in the Caribbean, a place where sailors, both officer and deckhand, feared to serve due to the lethal fevers. A posting there, for many, was a death sentence. He had done his best to keep up with events on the other side of the world, but they had felt so very distant.

As he had on the *Fantôme*, Courtney wished Nightingale were there. He knew how to act in these circumstances, the correct thing to say, and the appropriate way to drink and eat. Fortunately, no one looked in Courtney's direction for much of the meal, talking amongst themselves and sharing stories which each officer seemed to already know. Courtney listened to tales about politics, about London, about the annual countryside hunts, as if they were here in Gibraltar for a social occasion and not the awful task they had convened to complete.

He wondered if Paterson and Arnold ate so well – or if the Fantômes and missing Loyals did. The thoughts turned Courtney's stomach, and he found he could not bear another morsel of the rich pie topped with dense, viscous cheese. He stuck to sipping at the Madeira, though the sweetness burnt his throat.

When he was eventually acknowledged, it became no easier. The captains wished to know about the *Scylla*, probing for sensational details about life aboard her and her tumultuous history. Courtney hated to talk about Nightingale to people who would never understand his actions, and it pricked his heart to know he was out there, and Courtney could not address those fears. He wanted to speak to Easton about their voyage yet he had no chance amongst the inane chat – and he was still not entirely certain where he stood.

Fortunately, the dinner did not last for as long as some Courtney had attended. Once the king's health had been drunk multiple times, Easton allowed his guests to take the air on deck. The captains began to file out of the door but Courtney hung back. At last, he managed to catch Easton's eye. Plucking a cigar from the case his steward had brought in, Easton approached him.

'Are you well, Lieutenant?' he asked. 'You were very quiet during dinner.'

Courtney had known he had not excelled socially. 'I was thinking about my men, sir,' he said. 'They've been through a hellish time of it recently.'

'Ah, yes.' Easton exhaled a stream of smoke. 'I have been told.'

A flicker of relief sparked in Courtney. 'Told, sir?'

'I was informed, when it became possible that I would set my feet in Gibraltar, of the *Lysander*. I was briefed – albeit shortly – about her mission.'

Courtney breathed out, the weight lifting from his shoulders for a moment. From overhead, he heard one of the captains laughing and then the sound of a hornpipe beginning. 'That is what I wished to speak to you about, sir,' he said, knowing he would only have Easton's ears for a short while. In the absence of Lord Keith, the commander-in-chief, Courtney did not know who else to turn to. 'We ascertained the fate of the *Loyal*. I have sent it all in a report. She had been attacked by pirates and her crew kidnapped.'

'Pirates?' Easton drew the cigar from his mouth.

'From Tripoli, sir, according to the crew we interviewed. They descended upon the *Loyal* and the remaining men were lucky to escape with their lives and the ship. It is only through sheer chance and fortune that we found her – or rather, she found us. We collided in a storm and she became wrecked. I rescued who I could but...' Courtney shook his head.

'Go on, Lieutenant.'

'When we reached Palermo, I spoke with an American captain. He said he had seen Tripolitan pirates only recently and they had been in possession of another ship. I believe that other ship was the *Fantôme*, the French frigate we sailed with. She had been captured too.'

Easton looked away, considering all of this. Courtney almost felt guilty to dump it into his lap too – but his report could be anywhere: perhaps on the desk of Sir Rodney, perhaps still on a packet ship, perhaps on an overland coach. He only knew for certain that men were in danger.

'There are still English seamen in the clutches of these pirates?' Easton finally asked.

'Yes, sir. And an entire French crew.'

'We are not at war with Tripoli, Lieutenant. In fact, Gibraltar and the Mediterranean fleet rely on the Barbary Coast for supplies. That is why we tolerate her as an uneasy neighbour. The Americans began their war because of the upset to their shipping, but we do not have the freedom of that response.'

'And yet they have attacked us. There could have been no mistaking the nationality of the *Loyal* or of the *Fantôme*.'

A forecastle man started to sing above them, crooning 'Coasts of High Barbary' to the night sky. Courtney listened to the words and felt a chill for their appropriateness.

'If they are not pleased, we would risk cutting off an important source of our supply,' Easton continued.

'But men are in danger, sir. They may be sold into slavery.'

Yet, even as he said it, Courtney knew such things did not matter in the face of fortune. He had thought the same thing many a time about the African slaves in the Caribbean. Sentimentality and justice bent the knee when remuneration was involved.

'You say you have sent your report, Lieutenant,' Easton said. Courtney nodded. 'Then I should wait for further orders. This is a very sensitive matter and one that we officers would do best to obey our instructions in. And, without sounding indelicate, Mr Courtney, you are a lieutenant. Your rank can command an unrated sloop, but not a frigate such as the *Lysander*.'

Somehow, Courtney had known that Easton would tell him that. Of course he must wait; he was but a cog in a huge contraption. It was not for him to decide the direction of the machine. But the confirmation of it flooded his mouth with bitterness. So much so that when he and Easton ascended onto the deck, he could not face talking to and associating with the rest of the captains. He looked instead to the men upon the forecastle, singing and dancing to the tune of the pipe. He had been one of them once. He had made shaky steps up the ladder of the naval hierarchy, but he still felt as powerless as an able seaman.

Easton nodded to him as he requested permission to leave. Harris arrived again and as they rowed across the harbour, Courtney watched the form of the *Mallard* fade into silhouette against the moon. He did not give directions to return to the *Lysander* – not yet. With the night still weighing heavily on him, he returned to dry land and navigated the dark streets of Gibraltar. More sailors occupied the dense warrens: men given leave from the new ships in port. Each one reminded Courtney of the trial still to come. Trouble in the past, trouble in the present, and trouble in the future, he thought. That was what awaited him – and no clear path through.

Paterson and Arnold were still in the gaol. Procedure usually dictated a condemned man was to be kept in irons on his ship, but with the *Lysander* away and the *Mallard* only having recently arrived, they had been locked in the public cells. A red-coated soldier guided Courtney through the dim aisle, surrounded by bars and imprisoned men and women. Courtney remembered sitting in such stinking holes as a child, sleeping on the hard ground and listening to the drip of fouled water. His faith in the systems of justice had only improved after the *Ulysses* trial when the innocent men, and Jane, had been spared. Now it was being shaken again.

The guard pointed to two tiny cells at the end of the row and then moved, pistol in hand, back to his post. Courtney said nothing to him. He stepped closer to the bars and saw movement in the filthy shadows. Paterson turned to him first. The crags in his rough skin had deepened during his time off of the *Lysander* and Courtney felt he looked at a man at least twenty years beyond his true age. Arnold was the same, beaten down not only by the accusations upon him but by his looming fate.

'Mr Paterson, Mr Arnold,' Courtney said quietly, voice sticking in his throat. 'I hope... I hope that I find you well.'

'Tolerable, sir,' Paterson had the bravery to reply.

'The *Lysander* has recently arrived in Gibraltar, awaiting your...' He stopped, not wanting to remind the men. 'I wished to pay you both a visit.'

'Thank you, sir,' they both echoed, though Courtney knew it was a paltry effort. But he could not simply watch Paterson and Arnold go to the trial, possibly to the hangman's noose, without speaking with them again.

'I shall do my utmost to ensure you have a fair trial,' he continued. 'You have been good hands on the *Lysander*. I hate to see men condemned.'

'Thank you, sir,' Paterson said, more meekly now.

The silence echoed – a silence of unspoken words and suspicions, of men facing their mortality and their guilt. Courtney did not know which one he felt; it seemed as though his own neck could be broken within the next day. Danger stalked his career from weather and tide and his convictions and what was in his heart. The balance of staying faithful to himself and of obeying those above him was an almost impossible task.

Finally, he said, 'Your tattoos. I meant to ask about them when I signed you onto the *Lysander*. I have seen many sailors with marks that reference a ship they served.'

Arnold looked down at his tattoo and laid a hand over it, as if ashamed that Courtney had noticed.

'They're marks of the *Crane*,' Paterson said. 'Our first ship. Many years ago.'

'I remember my first ship. It is good to have an ally on the lower decks.'

He allowed the implication to hang, the admission that he had once been of an identical rank to Paterson and Arnold. He knew, from their side, what a man thought of an officer, what they expected of him: untouchable, rigidly in their place in the hierarchy, able to maintain a firm visage when needed and able not to, also.

Now he had said such a thing, the temptation to continue flared in him. He had been trapped on the *Mallard*, unable to speak any truthful statements, unable to sit comfortably beside the decorated men. He still felt closer to Paterson and Arnold, to two prisoners from another world to the *Mallard*'s wardroom. And no one in the other cells was truly listening. The men before him, hearing of his past, might be dead by the next evening.

'I had an ally, a friend, amongst the lower decks too,' Courtney said, squeezing his hands together nervously. 'I would have defended him from anything. I did. Or, I tried. I—' He paused, and then made himself continue. 'I was once kept in irons as well, and perhaps I would have been brought to trial if the *Grampus* had not...'

If the fates had not spared him. Courtney sometimes felt it had been for a reason, if only to mock him and keep him tied to that one moment in time: no future, no hope, no place to speak the truth inside of him.

But he was an officer now. And Paterson and Arnold did not need to, should not, hear this.

He lowered his head and drew his hands behind his back, holding them firmly. When he looked up again, he knew that, in Paterson and Arnold's eyes, they understood. Men like him, like Nightingale, like these two sailors... They had ways of knowing, of acknowledging hidden meanings.

'I shall... I shall speak for your characters,' Courtney finally said. 'You both deserve a fair trial.'

'Sir,' Paterson suddenly uttered, and Courtney realised his heart was beating thickly in his throat. 'Will you write to my sister, Anne? She lives in Fareham and draws the money I send home to her from the Custom House there. Will you ensure she receives the pay?'

Courtney swallowed. He wanted to say that Paterson could do that himself, but he could not promise it. He nodded. 'I shall,' he said, the only thing he could vow.

'Thank you, sir.'

They both thanked him as he left. The visit had made Courtney feel even worse than he had before he set foot in the gaol, churning up his uncertainties. He had tried to ignore them, tried to press down his terror about Nightingale and the *Fantôme* but it threatened to crest. He could not give in to it now, not before the court martial.

He focused on the one remaining thing he had to do that night.

Sara's tavern was as crowded and boisterous as he had expected it. He pushed his way through the throng, finding a spare table. No one joined him, and nor did he expect them to. He was still dressed in his best uniform, gaudy and glittering. As much as he had felt out of place in Easton's great cabin, he sensed a wall here too. Truly, he was caught in the space between, too high for a regular sailor, too low for a decorated officer.

Sara's face eventually appeared through the mass. Her eyes widened at the sight of him. She hurried over, dropping into the seat opposite him. 'Artie,' she breathed. 'You came back. Did you... Did you find him?'

Courtney nodded. The letters the men had written in Palermo had obviously not found their way back yet. 'We found them.'

Her mouth moved wordlessly for a moment, obviously preparing herself for the answer. She wrung her hands and finally managed to say, 'Is he alive?'

'Yes. I saved him from the wreck.'

'The wreck?' Sara swallowed. 'The ship is gone?'

'Come to the harbour tomorrow and I shall make sure you see him.'

'Oh, Artie.' She released a long, shaking breath and reached across the table to grasp his hand. Tears brimmed in her eyes. 'I can't say how thankful I am. If there is anything that I can do to ever repay you...'

He smiled and gently patted her warm hands. For a moment, he wondered what would have happened if he had married her. Perhaps they could have found something in the way of Nightingale and his wife. The thought made Courtney pull away, ice gripping him. He did not want that; he only wanted Nightingale – wherever Mrs Nightingale stood in the tangled heart of their relationship.

'What is it?' Sara asked. 'You are dreadfully pale.'

Courtney shook his head. 'I've been suffering with a chill. Nothing more.'

'Let me fetch you a drink of something.'

'No. It is all right. I only came to tell you about Nathan. I would have had him send a letter ashore or come here himself, but we are chained to the ship for now. I must get back. We have…a trying day tomorrow.'

Sara nodded. 'Thank you, Artie. You have always been so kind to me. You shall make someone very happy one day.'

'I hope so.'

He hoped that he already made someone very happy. He wished that he and Nightingale, Paterson and Arnold, could wear their love as openly as Sara and Nathan could. But such a thing could not be, not now, and perhaps not in his and Nightingale's entire lifetimes.

Sara must have read his expression for she continued, 'Are you sure I cannot fetch you anything, Artie?'

'No,' he said again. 'No, I must leave for the ship.'

Feeling his heart brimming over with regret and pain, Courtney swept from the tavern and out into the cool night. He did not remember walking to the harbour, and only realised where he was when he stopped at the water's edge. The *Lysander* towered above him, surrounded by her fellow ships and the dominating force of the *Mallard*. Beyond her, the black waters rolled, further out into the Mediterranean. Courtney wanted to run, wanted to return to the familiar waves, but he had a duty here.

The *Lysander*, the *Scylla*, the *Grampus*… They had all given him fortune, and they had all given him grief. He had always tried to remain certain of himself, but every year, every ship, carved a new doubt within. He was not an able seaman anymore, yet nor did it feel that was he on firm ground as an officer. And now, without Nightingale, without Jane, he was alone with the past, the present, and the future.

All were clouded.

—

The sound of footsteps awakened Courtney. In the dingy, close gloom, he opened his eyes and squinted through the darkness. A shaft of pale moonlight dribbled through a hatch, throwing a square of illumination on the uneven timbers. Somewhere, a seaman snored and the sound rippled through the creak of the Grampus' hull, accompanied by the distant swish of the waves outside. He thought for a moment he had misheard the steps.

Then a shadow crossed the end of his hammock. A thin shoulder prodded against the cloth cocoon and Courtney had to stop himself from swinging into his neighbour, inches away from his head.

He recognised the tall form standing over him: the pale cheek and the tied red hair.

'Garrick,' Courtney hissed. 'Are you hurt?'

He hated that that was the first question that came to his lips. But the thought of it never left Courtney's head now. Each time he and Walker met, he found himself becoming more and more delicate with his body and his heart. The scars on his skin had not vanished. Sometimes, Courtney thought he could see new ones.

Walker hesitated, half-bent over Courtney's hammock. Courtney could not decipher his expression in the darkness.

'No,' Walker rasped. 'I'm just...'

Courtney waited. With every touch that became more hesitant on Walker's skin, his familiarity with him also waned. Courtney feared pushing him and breaking him.

'I was going to the head,' Walker finished.

'Want me to join you?' Courtney asked.

Another beat of doubt. 'No,' Walker finally said, decisively now. 'I'm not a child, Artie.'

The spite underlying his words caused Courtney's stomach to tighten. He did not know how to respond, so simply nodded and laid back against his pillow. Walker lingered for a moment more, then began to make his way carefully through the sleeping bodies of sailors. He had obviously wanted to alert Courtney, perhaps wanted to ask for his assistance, before changing his mind. Courtney hated the doubt and the chill that Walker's abuser had wedged between them.

With the confusion swirling inside of him, Courtney tried to catch a fragment of sleep. He had become accustomed to drifting off quickly; a seaman's rest was precious and sometimes hard to come by. But around him, the sailors kept snoring, the yards creaked high above, the sails fluttered...

...and Walker did not return.

Courtney could not lie there in ignorance, wondering what had happened to his friend. Perhaps he was yet making his way back to his berth. Perhaps he was loitering at the head for a moment's privacy and solitude. But darker suggestions surrounded the two of them, wherever they trod now.

As he rolled out of his hammock and eased his way through the maze of slumbering men, Courtney almost cursed the day he had befriended Garrick Walker. Every moment of warmth between them came with an equivalent moment of trouble, or threatened trouble. Walker had shared his body in the dimness of the hold but that was where it ended. That was where Courtney knew he should also leave it. But he could not. Not now. And so he could not bring himself to regret their alliance.

Only the external forces that menaced it.

The deck was cold beneath Courtney's bare feet but the last months of clambering through the rigging had hardened his soles, and he did not even wince as he made his way to the head. A night breeze ran through the open privy. To Courtney's worry, no one occupied it, or its twin to larboard.

He told himself he should leave now — return to his hammock and speak with Walker in the light of day.

But Courtney had not learnt to turn his cheek and ignore the swelling doubts inside.

Listening for the approach of footsteps, Courtney leant into the shadows and descended through the gun decks. All of the gun ports were shut, all lanterns doused. The further he dropped, the less the white moon penetrated through the hatches above. Courtney knew the Grampus *well; he knew her inner workings in darkness and in light. But the tension tightening in his throat made him cautious. Hoping he would not run across an officer, he felt with his hands and feet down the ladders, squinting into the gloom.*

He nearly jumped out of his skin at the first sound. He had reached the storerooms aft, that cluster of small spaces for the carpenter and the bosun — but no light indicated their presence. The doors were locked, tools downed. Courtney still pressed his back to the bulkheads as he groped his way forward, heading for the murky cable-tier. The ever-present smell of wet rope clung to the shadows.

A voice echoed towards him. After it, that sound he had heard before: a strike, impacting upon something soft and fragile. Then, a barely withheld shriek.

'Again!' ordered a boy.

Without thought, Courtney rushed from the darkness. He stopped as the shrewish, pale face of Mr Midshipman Lowe turned to him. For a moment, the lad's eyes widened. The two seamen at his side, ones Courtney had first seen teasing Walker, paused. A second, where all froze in their positions, clawed by like an age. Courtney noted everything: Lowe's unsheathed dirk, the starting canes in the sailors' hands, the scent of blood and urine permeating the damp hemp, a needle-sharp point sticking into Courtney's bare foot, the sound of pained sobs, and the taste of metallic fear.

Courtney's eyes lowered to the snivelling ball of limbs, curled like a dying spider, on the deck. Walker looked up from the meagre protection of his arms, face stained with red tears. His shirt was half-ripped from him and his breeches had been yanked to his thighs, revealing welts and bruises on his backside.

'God,' Courtney breathed, and the frozen silence broke. He rushed past Lowe and staggered to his knees, breaking whatever he had been stood upon. He realised it was a shard of a tooth. More were scattered about Lowe's shivering form. He grasped the boy by the shoulders but he writhed to get away, shoving Courtney with surprising force.

Lowe, above them, laughed. Courtney had known, known it was him who had hurt Walker. But he had been unable to act, not against the privileged and patronised Mr Midshipman Montgomery Lowe.

'You do not want him,' Lowe said. 'He is tainted. Dirty.'

'Come,' Courtney tried to urge Walker. He again attempted to move him by the arm, but Walker wailed and shied away.

'Do you know what he is, sailor? Do you know where he comes from?'

Courtney knew all he needed to about Walker, or at least he thought he did. And all he had to know now was that the boy was scared and in agony. At least hoping to save his dignity if nothing else, Courtney tried to pull the clothes back around his body.

Lowe's booted foot struck the timbers beside him. Courtney felt the sharp bite of his blade against his back. 'Out of my way, you bugger,' Lowe snarled.

Courtney whirled around. The dirk slashed his shirt but fortunately no further. He rose to his feet, towering above the midshipman. 'What did you call me?' he managed to rasp.

'You heard what I said. Get out of my way.'

Danger sparked between them. Courtney shook his head, staring at Lowe; they were around the same age, but the gulf of society and rank separated them. Courtney knew he would be punished for this: a flogging, a shackling, even a trial would not be out of the question. He still stood firm, in between Lowe and Walker.

'Little devil,' he heard himself curse.

Lowe's eyes flashed. They flicked to the two seamen, standing dumbly beside them. Courtney expected a blow from either one. But Lowe's arm shot up, blade in hand.

Courtney grabbed his wrist.

'How dare you,' Lowe hissed. 'I'll have you whipped!'

Courtney did not let go. Even as Lowe ordered his lackeys to strike him, he gripped the boy's bones tightly. The blows fell on his spine and back, but he yanked at Lowe, drawing him into the beatings. Lowe shouted. Walker wept. Courtney drove his elbows back into the other sailors, making them crumple and groan. Still, the hits came from somewhere, raining upon his skin and muscles. He gritted his teeth, snatched at the dirk which plunged out of the shadows, and refused to even cry aloud as the blade sliced at his palm. Blood and metal and timber and hemp mixed. Walker kept sobbing.

–

The last thing Courtney recalled was the red flash of the marines' coats.

He still saw them, hurrying down the companion-ladder, as he jerked awake, more than ten years later, on the *Lysander*. His heart hammered, sweat on his skin. Above him, the bell for the change of watch rang out. Courtney counted the knells, judging that it was midway through the middle watch. He had been asleep a mere hour and a half, but it felt as though he had slept through an entire epoch. The memories of the *Grampus* had a way of doing that, dragging him down, pulling him back into the troubled past.

Slowly, he willed himself away from the darkness. It was almost impossible, as he knew that darkness had never left him. It remained like the wounds he had gained under Lowe's orders, bleeding again and again. Paterson and Arnold's trial had been the thing to provoke it this time. On the *Grampus*, he had tried to save a boy he had cared for. Here, on the *Lysander*, he struggled again to find justice in an unjust situation.

Swinging his legs from his hammock, Courtney looked over at the empty cot nearby. If he stretched out his hand, he could almost pretend Nightingale was still there, sleeping soundly in the darkness. But those sheets had been vacant for too long. Nightingale might be in some dark cell, or languishing in chains, or even being sent ashore for some uglier purpose. Courtney could barely even begin to think of it. The frantic events of the past weeks had given him something to sink into. Yet the terror at Nightingale's fate simmered constantly, threatening to undo him.

Laying his palm on the cot, Courtney sighed, breath shaking. Shadows of Garrick Walker echoed through the years. After being found with Lowe in the cable-tier, Courtney had been clapped in irons. Walker, though, had been all he cared about. The boy, too broken to even give an account of the event, had been swiftly invalided onto the merchant vessel the *Grampus* had been protecting and shipped with her to the next port. Courtney had not even seen him depart. Courtney's final words to Walker remained a plea for him to rise to his feet and walk away from Lowe.

-

Perhaps that was what Courtney should have done too. As he festered in the bilge in chains, he knew his career and his life would suffer — but he could not bring himself to regret his actions. He readied his mind and defences for the trial which would surely come. Lowe would have him punished, beaten, condemned. He knew, above him, that the controversies and allegations of what had occurred in the cable-tier were being considered. He hoped deeply that Lowe would be investigated too. But within, he realised his prayers would be in vain.

-

On the *Lysander*, Courtney crossed his arms over himself, once again thinking of how close he had come to a possible execution, or at the least, ignominy and the loss of his career. The only thing that had saved him was the sea. A greater storm he was yet to see; even the tempest that destroyed the *Loyal* had not been as cruel as that which sank the *Grampus*. The green waves had swamped her as if she was a fishing skiff in the clutch of a hurricane. Timbers cracked, masts were sprung, and in their hundreds, men drowned. Courtney still wondered how, or why, he had been saved. It had been one of his messmates, loyal to the end, freeing him from his chains and pulling him to the defiled deck. They had jumped overboard, clung to the floating main topmast, and watched the horrible *Grampus* devoured by the waves. All record of Courtney's insolence, and of Lowe's barbarity, descended with her.

Courtney had hidden that past as much as he could, even to the panel who had examined him for his lieutenancy. He had lied about his behaviour; he had lied about his age; he had lied about his years served – because he knew he would not have a hope, otherwise.

Far away, Walker must have heard of the loss of the *Grampus*. Courtney tried to write to him, even once tried to find him in Plymouth. But the boy, who would have grown into a man as Courtney did, seemed to have vanished – until a note arrived for Courtney one day. It invited him to the marriage of Garrick Walker and Miss Lavinia Cartwright.

Courtney had torn it apart.

Even now, Courtney still wondered why Walker had sent him such a message. He remembered the pleasure and joy of their meetings, the only moments of light onboard the *Grampus*. But, at the end, Walker had shied away from him as much as he had quivered in the shadow of Lowe. Courtney simply tried to swallow the bitterness and wish the boy as well as he could. Perhaps Miss Cartwright had given him a balm to overcome the anguish of his youth.

Courtney knew, as he stared at the empty cot, that he had found such a thing in Hiram Nightingale. In Trinidad, he had realised what an honourable man Nightingale was. He came from such strife, as Courtney had, but he had not let it cloud his kindness. Despite their differences in rank and wealth, Courtney had found similarity in their backgrounds – and not only in that, but in the proclivity they shared. His youthful attraction to Walker did not match the affection Courtney had for Nightingale.

He knew that he loved Nightingale, adored him in every manner it was possible: as a friend, as a companion, as a lover. He wished he could this to Nightingale, and show him just how very much he wanted him. Although their physical needs did not always align, that did not matter. Courtney had been with other men beyond Walker and he knew that there were a thousand definitions of intimacy beyond consummation. Whether or not Nightingale shared Courtney's manner of attraction, it meant nothing more, nothing less. Courtney was content to follow Nightingale's guidance; he thought he would do anything in the world if Nightingale asked him to.

The trial of Paterson and Arnold, and his meeting with them, showed the perils of their connection. Courtney did not give a damn;

it was a scale he had weighed time and time again, and Nightingale always meant more than the fear. But Nightingale... Despite the time they had shared together, Courtney still fretted. He did not know how much Mrs Nightingale knew; he did not know Nightingale's long-term plans; he did not know if he could ever sit in the place of Lieutenant Sawyer, made a tragic love after his death at the Nile.

Courtney only wanted to be at Nightingale's side. He wished that the world and all its injustices did not have to be so complicated. He wished he could see a clear path. Instead, all still seemed lost. And, relentlessly, the *Grampus* and his past kept rising from the seabed, threatening to pull him down, as it had not been able to before.

Now, Courtney had to set aside his worries and prepare for the court martial.

He had to ready himself to condemn two men for the same love he felt within himself.

Chapter Twenty-Two: Condemnation

The boom of the *Mallard*'s great guns echoed across Gibraltar's harbour. Courtney had been sitting in the wardroom for what seemed like hours, Smythe beside him, but the report of the cannons told him it was six bells in the forenoon watch: eleven. He had only been there, stomach broiling and eyes swimming, for the last forty minutes. As if mocking him, his lingering chill had struck with a vengeance that morning, so his head pulsed and his throat seemed as if he had swallowed a razor. And yet that malaise was nothing compared to Arnold and Paterson's fate.

They had been rowed across the water earlier. Courtney had chosen not to watch, as so many others had done, ghoulishly gawping at the condemned. He had met with them in the gaol and he would see them in the cabin during the trial, and that would be enough.

Now the guns had fired, that time came sooner than he hoped.

'Lieutenant Courtney,' said a young clerk who appeared in the *Mallard*'s wardroom. 'The panel are ready for you.'

Grasping his shaking hands before him, Courtney followed the man up through the quiet decks. He had been in this same position two years before, about to testify about the *Ulysses* and her mutiny. Jane's life had been on the line then, and Nightingale's career. Now, he would speak against two more people who did not deserve to be where they were.

The door to the great cabin had been thrown open. Courtney fixed his eyes on a spot above Captain Easton's head as he walked in. The shimmering epaulettes and sparkling uniforms distracted him from the sorry sight in the corner. He tried not to look but could not avoid the curiosity: Paterson and Arnold, under guard from the *Mallard*'s marines, pale and wan in the cold winter light coming through the gallery windows.

'Lieutenant Courtney,' Captain Easton said. 'We thank you for delivering Captain Jerome Bryant's signed statement to us and the logbooks and journals of the *Lysander*. Although Captain Bryant is unfortunately not present due to his grievous injury, we have his account and his detailing of the event in question. I shall summarise for the court.'

Courtney looked along at the other captains who only the night before, he had been dining with in this same cabin. Nausea rose in him. He waited, realising he was yet to say a word.

'Captain Bryant writes in his log for the twelfth of September 1802 that Lieutenant Arthur Courtney and master of the *Lysander*, Gregory Pascoe, came to him with the complaint that Mr Felix Paterson and Mr Dudley Arnold had been found together in the hold, fornicating. Upon questioning the two men, they refused to speak, thus implicitly denying all accusations.

'Previous to this, on the ninth of September 1802, Mr Paterson had been confined to irons due to contempt to his captain and refusal to allow a search of his possessions following the theft of Dr Christopher Faulkner's scalpel. He acted hostilely and appeared to be about to strike his officers. Other acts of disturbance have been put to Mr Paterson and Mr Arnold's names: fighting before setting sail and upsetting a tacking drill.

'Aside from the logs, Captain Bryant has signed a statement saying he was fully aware of the accusations towards Mr Paterson and Mr Arnold and that he agreed to convene this court martial.'

Easton removed his spectacles and laid the paper down upon the table. His blue eyes bore into Courtney. 'Mr Arnold and Mr Paterson's testimony has already been taken. Lieutenant Courtney, Captain Bryant states you were the one to find the two men in the hold.'

Courtney swallowed. 'No, sir. I mean… I was not the first one to find them. I was awoken on the night of the twelfth by Mr Pascoe. He took me down to the hold, having already stirred the marines. The two men were down there.'

'Mr Paterson had recently been placed in irons?'

'Yes, sir. Captain Bryant ordered it when Mr Paterson refused to allow us to investigate his belongings, but at the time of Mr Pascoe's complaint, Mr Paterson had been freed. As for the previous accusation of theft, Dr Faulkner's scalpel had recently gone missing, as you say, and Captain Bryant suspected Mr Paterson of being involved, seeing as he accompanied Dr Faulkner and transported his medical supplies for him.'

'What was Mr Paterson doing aiding Dr Faulkner in such a manner?'

Courtney thought back. So much had happened that it seemed one avalanche of terrible event after terrible event. 'Madame Baptiste, who was aboard the *Fantôme*, our accompanying ship, came across to the *Lysander* and tripped down a ladder. She hit her head and seemed quite dazed.'

'Ah, yes.' Easton peered at the papers again. 'Captain Bryant makes mention of Madame Baptiste. He states she was in Capitaine Bonfils's charge as the wife of Hugo Baptiste.'

'Yes, sir.'

'Upon searching the possessions of Mr Paterson and Mr Arnold, did you find the missing scalpel?' Easton continued.

'No, sir. It was not found.'

'But Mr Paterson still took offence at the notion of being searched, yes? Was anything illicit found on his person or in his chest?'

'No, sir. And neither in Mr Arnold's. I believe that they are innocent of that crime.'

'Duly noted,' Easton said, and Courtney listened to the scratching of the clerk's pen. 'How was Mr Paterson's behaviour when you dealt with him during this inspection?'

'He was…aggravated, sir. But to say that he was on the verge of striking me or Captain Bryant… That I deny. He struggled but was quickly restrained by Sergeant Malcolm Dawes of the marines. Mr Paterson was kept in the hold in irons and his pay was docked and his grog stopped. As I say, he had been freed by the time of this…'

'Until this other incident,' Easton finished.

'Yes, sir.'

Another beat of silence passed and Courtney squeezed his hands behind his back. In the pauses, he kept running over his words again, praying he had not said anything too condemnatory.

'Lieutenant,' Easton continued, 'what precisely did you witness in the hold?'

The image of Paterson and Arnold in the hold, flanked by marines, as they were now, flashed into Courtney's mind. He had dissected it over and over, alongside what Nightingale had said to him afterwards. To speak up for them would shine a light upon himself, draw up questions about his own conduct. 'I did not see them together, sir,' he said. 'Mr Pascoe was the one who woke me with the accusations. When

I followed him to the hold, Mr Paterson and Mr Arnold were already under guard. But I saw no interactions between them.'

'What was their manner when you found them?'

'They were...nervous. As any man would be.'

'What of their behaviour before, Lieutenant? Captain Bryant mentions they fought in Portsmouth and then after the mistake during tacking.'

'They fought, yes, but many men, many sailors, fight. I separated them and put them in my division. They were punished for it and I saw no reason to pursue it any further. As for the mistake during tacking, Mr Paterson acted quickly to save Mr Arnold when he fell overboard. Dr Faulkner praised him for doing so. Mr Paterson spoke badly to Mr Arnold afterwards but I thought it must be to do with the excitement of the moment.'

'Do you know what they fought over, Lieutenant?'

'Our bosun, in Portsmouth, said it was over a family matter. Mr Paterson mentioned a woman. I didn't press for any detail. Fights have happened over women since men learnt to walk upright.'

Another of the captains – Courtney fought to recall his name – leant across to Easton and whispered something. The presiding captain nodded. 'Thank you, Lieutenant,' he said. 'I believe that shall be all for now. We shall call you back to the stand if you are required again.'

Courtney opened his mouth, feeling he should say something more. But he could think of nothing. He had no doubt that Pascoe's accusations towards Paterson and Arnold were correct. He simply did not agree with the vehemence behind them or the consequences they would lead to. And that, the court did not care about.

The Articles of War made that very clear.

'Yes, sir,' he heard himself say. Upon turning face and leaving, he cast another glance at Paterson and Arnold in the corner. Between this and his visit to them, he hoped they understood that he stood alongside them, but such a thing did not matter in sight of the noose.

All of the conflict that had brewed inside of him grew to a crescendo as he waited in the baited tension of the following testimony. Again and again, he thought of where he existed amongst the crew and officers. He was still the same man who had nearly struck a midshipman as a youth. He was still the same man who had defended Walker in the face of his own punishment. He was still the same man who had risen from the lower berth, clawing his way up to a senior lieutenant. He simply wore a different coat now.

And this was not a mere trial over insubordination or desertion. The crimes being laid out before the court were ones he harboured himself. If the ropes lashed around Paterson and Arnold's necks, he would feel the same choking sensation, the same censure. It would feel a betrayal not only to himself but the place he came from.

As he returned to the *Lysander*, he could not help thinking of Nightingale again. Courtney had not met many men he could admire or want to model his behaviour on. He had no one to rely on and no figures to guide him. Nightingale had sacrificed himself to do right by the *Ulysses* men and Jane. He had pushed through a mountain of grief and turmoil to carve a new life for himself, one under his own stars. Courtney wished he was here to talk to. But he was somewhere out there, lost while Courtney wrangled over this trial.

He sighed and looked across the harbour. There, he noticed a flash of blonde hair. Sara. He had almost forgotten about his promise to deliver Mr Waters, her husband, safely to her. Though he could not deny the flush of bitterness, he could not retract that deal. Under the eyes of two of Dawes's marines, he allowed Waters to go ashore. They reunited with the affection and love that Courtney wished Paterson and Arnold could show.

But they were condemned to be flogged, or worse. It felt so remorselessly unjust.

With Waters gone, Courtney visited Dr Faulkner, who was setting away his instruments. He had been nursing the last of the ailing *Loyal* crew, most of whom had recovered after their ordeal. Monsieur Baptiste had offered his services and now sat with the remaining patients, reading to them in perfect English. He had been a great help and comfort to them. Courtney wondered if his care had been to still his own troubled mind after the disaster of the *Loyal*. He nodded to Courtney as he entered.

'You should prepare yourself to go across to the *Mallard*,' Courtney said to Faulkner. 'They shall call you to the stand soon.'

Faulkner nodded. He spent far too long organising his tools, setting them down then changing their positions once more. Eventually, he looked up, squeezed his hands as if convincing himself not to fiddle with his medical chest again, and said, 'They shall not blame me, shall they?'

Courtney frowned. 'Blame you for what?'

Faulkner waved a shaking hand. 'This...' he began, but seemed to be unable to say more. 'I was not in my right mind during the storm or Captain Bryant's ailment. And when the scalpel went missing, I did not notice due to...'

His drunkenness. It was a nuisance but not something the court martial could condemn him for unless for a serious dereliction of his duty. Courtney could not see how Bryant's injury could have been improved, whether Faulkner was sober or not. 'They are not investigating Captain Bryant's misfortune, Doctor. Simply tell them the truth of what happened on the night you misplaced the instrument.'

'But I can barely recall. Between treating Madame Baptiste and falling asleep and Mr Pascoe waking me for supper...' Faulkner sighed. 'I have laid down my bottle, Lieutenant, or at least I have tried to. Monsieur Baptiste shall attest to that.'

Courtney glanced to Baptiste, who gave a small nod.

'I could not bear it if the captain was to... I did all that I could for him. I have never performed such an operation before, you understand.'

'Your behaviour is not under examination,' Courtney said. 'Not as Mr Paterson and Mr Arnold's is.'

'I understand.'

As frustrating as the man could be, Courtney could not help but feel sympathy for him. They were all caught in this wretched situation, without a captain, without a clear course, without knowing what awaited them. He saw Faulkner to the boats and then returned to the gunroom. The rest of the crew would go across soon, including Obi and other men from Paterson and Arnold's mess, but for now, it was the lot of the remaining officers. Pascoe would not be kind.

Pascoe. Dr Faulkner had remembered being awoken by Pascoe for supper. Doubt, sudden and disorienting, struck Courtney. He sat up, glancing towards Pascoe's cabin. The man was still on the *Mallard* and would be for a while longer. Smythe waited to be called forth by the panel, and Godfrey was on deck. Courtney waited, listening to the footsteps above and the remaining men on the ship, interspersed with the tide kissing against the hull outside.

His decision had been made as soon as the thought had appeared.

Rising, Courtney crossed to Pascoe's cabin. As the sailing-master, the man was entitled to privacy equivalent to the level of a commissioned officer. Courtney knew he overstepped that sacrosanct line by entering his space but with men's lives on the line, he did not care. Looking around the small area, he noted the bowl on the shelf, the books crammed next to it, the number of pen-and-ink drawings. Much of it must have been pulled from the larger great cabin upon the *Lysander's* conversion to a naval ship.

Courtney realised he was already sifting through motives as he dropped to his knees and fiddled with Pascoe's chest. The storm had battered it; Courtney remembered him saying how the lock had broken. Inside, it still smelt damp and rotten. Not much sat on its fouled bottom: a spare shirt and trousers, blank papers, a shaving brush and a razor. Courtney felt like a young boy again, rifling through things he should not for the sake of feeding Jane. He had always told himself it was for a greater good.

There was no contraband in the chest. Courtney made sure to set everything back where it had been, shutting the lid quietly. Disappointment, a flutter of shame, flickered in him. But, looking around, he could not shake the sensation that something was still wrong. Pascoe had woken Dr Faulkner for supper. That seemed far too kind for the man, or a task he would give to a lesser sailor.

Courtney stood and gently moved things off the shelf. A book tilted, pushing all of them over. Cursing, Courtney grabbed them before they could hit the floor. Heart skipping, he glanced back out the door. No one came.

He was the first lieutenant now, he told himself, not a boy sticking his nose where it should not be. God, Nightingale would reprimand him for this.

Too far into it to turn away, Courtney lifted the thin sheets from the cot and groped around. Nothing there, and nothing beneath the pillow either. He stripped the entire thing back and even lifted the mattress to look beneath. Desperation pulled at him. Perhaps it had been a fool's errand, a furious attempt to stay Paterson and Arnold's deaths. He slumped down, sighing. He despised feeling so helpless and here it was, laid out before him, mocking and cutting too close to the bone.

Why had he even suspected Pascoe? The man had been a cad, picking at him with his snide comments and general distaste for the refitted *Lysander* and his crew, but did he truly have reason to meddle? Not long before, the *Lysander* had been his. He had a duty to her, no matter her colours and commission.

The realisation struck Courtney like a blow. The *Lysander* had been Pascoe's, he thought again. Pascoe knew the ship; every commander was expected to be as familiar with their vessel as a husband to his wife. He knew her weak points, her secrets. And she had been a merchant ship previously, ripe for picking apart by press-gangs.

Courtney hurried up to the great cabin. Entering it in Bryant's absence seemed strange, and even stranger to be opening the door to his personal seat of ease. It was one of the luxuries of a captain: a private quarter gallery away from the heads shared by more than one hundred men. The trimmings were spartan, though, a simple hole positioned above a rudimentary tank and piping that led to the open sea. Hoping he would not be intruded on, Courtney levered the wooden bench up. He was greeted by an effluent smell, wafted on the breeze from far below.

Holding his breath, he leant in. There was enough room in the tank for one man, perhaps two if they were young or small. Other nooks and crannies of a vessel could be utilised: cavities in the 'tween decks, enclosed spaces in the hold... Courtney had seen the ruthless searching of a press-gang, had once had the distasteful job of it as a junior lieutenant. He knew the tricks of merchant captains, hiding their valuable sailors away.

And here, tucked away, he saw a glint of metal. Gritting his teeth against the smell, which he knew would cling to his clothes, he reached in and hooked it up. For a moment, he knelt against the wall, holding it in his palm. Anger boiled in his chest.

'Fucking bastard,' he hissed and stuffed the missing scalpel into his pocket.

Godfrey, on the main deck, jumped as he hurried across it. 'Lieutenant?' he managed, straightening up.

'I shan't be long, Lieutenant. I am needed again on the *Mallard*.'

The *Mallard* towered over him again. He sat in the cutter, looking up at the high flanks of the fourth-rate, past her closed gunports and yellow-and-black chequer to the rail. No one appeared so he cupped his hands about his mouth and hailed the ship. The perturbed face of a marine appeared, followed by a lieutenant.

'Lieutenant Courtney of the *Lysander*!' Courtney shouted. 'Is Captain Easton available?'

'You have not been called back to the stand, Lieutenant!' the officer responded.

'I have further evidence to give!' Courtney said, knowing he should probably not be exclaiming it aloud.

'The court has adjourned for the afternoon, Lieutenant. They shall not return for another hour.'

'Is Captain Easton aboard?'

'No, Lieutenant.'

If it was an attempt to throw Courtney off the scent, it did not work. He thanked the lieutenant and turned back to Harris. The poor man had rowed him back and forth so many times they could have circumnavigated the entire rock. But once more he went ashore, clambering onto the docks and following the streets towards the Convent. There were few places he could imagine Easton visiting; he could not imagine him entering Sara's tavern, for instance.

Yet Courtney didn't know if he would find him at the Convent, not until he turned the corner into the main street and saw the captain outside the building, smoking and talking with a handful of captains from the panel. He hurried his steps and then nearly froze as he saw the other man with them: tall, dressed in a tailored red uniform with golden band, royal-blue sash and glittering orders of merit: the Duke of Kent, who Bryant had wanted to keep Courtney away from. Courtney remembered Bryant warning him about the duke's severity.

'Lieutenant Courtney?' Easton had spotted him. 'Is there something the matter?'

The eyes of the duke and the captains raked over him. He saw their noses crinkle and remembered how he still must reek of the quarter gallery. He straightened his shoulders and joined them beneath the colonnade of the Convent. 'Sir,' he said, every bit as nervous as when he had stood in the *Mallard*'s great cabin. 'Your Grace,' he hurriedly added, lowering his head to the royal governor. 'I have further evidence for the court.'

'Speak freely, Lieutenant,' Easton prompted.

'I...' How to say that he had been rooting around the *Lysander*? There was only one way to announce it. 'I have found the missing scalpel, sirs.'

A frown crossed Easton's face. Courtney reached with a sweating hand into his pocket and extracted the object, holding it, glinting, in the sun. Easton took it. He considered it with interest, the duke's gaze hovering over them, and then nodded.

'We shall call you immediately to the stand once the court opens again, Lieutenant.'

'Yes, sir.'

And with fortune, Pascoe too.

Chapter Twenty-Three: Far Worse Men

Standing again before the panel in the late afternoon, Courtney no longer felt the frightened apprehension of the morning. Anger thrummed, almost thrilling, inside of him. Laid out before the panel, the scalpel glinted in the sunlight piercing the gallery windows. Such an inconsequential item, but one that could cut the noose from around Paterson and Arnold's necks if Courtney spoke his case correctly.

They still stood in the corner, guarded by marines. Courtney had heard one of them take a breath when the scalpel had been produced. He wanted to look at them, but the emotion throbbed too loudly in his chest.

'It has been brought to the panel's attention,' Captain Easton narrated, 'that a key piece of evidence has been found. Lieutenant Courtney has retrieved the scalpel which Mr Paterson had been accused of stealing from the *Lysander*'s stores. Lieutenant...' Courtney stood up straighter, if it was possible with his already rigid back and shoulders. 'Where, and how, did you come about this discovery?'

'I found it in the captain's seat of ease, sir,' he said, and saw the shock cross Easton's face. His eyebrows knitted together and each of the other captains echoed the reaction. Even the clerk paused. Courtney reddened.

'What was your purpose for searching in Captain Bryant's...quarter gallery, Lieutenant?'

'I became suspicious of the location of the scalpel, sir. I knew we had not been able to find it amongst Mr Paterson's possessions and so wondered if it was still on the ship somewhere. Dr Faulkner mentioned to me that on the day it went missing, Mr Pascoe awoke him for supper. I had not previously known Mr Pascoe had spoken to Dr Faulkner that evening.'

Easton waited for him to continue. Courtney would not shield Pascoe's name.

'I acted on a sudden intuition, sir. Perhaps it was not gentlemanly of me but with Mr Paterson being so accused, I searched Mr Pascoe's cabin. I found nothing there. And then I remembered that the *Lysander* had been Mr Pascoe's ship before she was bought and outfitted by the navy. I know that certain merchant captains have clandestine spaces where their hide their sailors when a press-gang comes searching.'

'How do you know this, Lieutenant?'

Courtney had thought that such knowledge was common – but then these post-captains had doubtlessly not been lieutenants for a long time. 'I led a number of press-gangs in Spithead when I was younger. And I was once a common sailor, sir. I know the stories of men from the lower berth and their origins.'

Paterson and Arnold already knew this, but Easton and the captains did not. The officers took the information with raised eyebrows. It was not entirely unheard for men to rise from their positions before the mast, but it was not common by any means. 'I know that the heads and seats of ease are frequent locations to hide men,' he continued. 'So I started with Captain Bryant's, a place that would not have been suspected. That is where I found it.'

Easton nodded. 'We are grateful for you for locating Dr Faulkner's possession, Lieutenant.'

'I believe Mr Pascoe hid it there,' Courtney rushed before he could be diverted.

Silence followed the swift accusation. Courtney swallowed, knowing he had to clarify.

'I think that...' he began, only to be interrupted by Easton.

'Why do you believe Mr Pascoe is the culprit here?'

'His behaviour has been of begrudging service since we sailed. Perhaps over the loss of the command of the *Lysander*. Aside from myself, he is the only one to know about the hiding places on the ship.'

'The scalpel was found in Captain Bryant's quarters, Lieutenant,' Easton said.

'I don't believe he always had it there, only after Captain Bryant's injury and vacation of his cabin. Mr Pascoe mentioned to me, after we were struck by the storm that wrecked the *Loyal*, that the lock on his sea-chest had been broken. I believe that he moved the scalpel at that point, and I propose that he was attempting to condemn Mr Paterson.

With that, I doubt the truth of his testimony about what he saw in the hold. It was very dark and he was the only witness.'

Easton considered this, allowing the clerk to scratch down Courtney's blatant conjecture: a conjecture he hoped would stick, even if only a trifle. 'Did Mr Pascoe quarrel at any time with Mr Paterson and Mr Arnold? Had he cause to accuse them or muddy their names with charges of theft?'

Courtney thought back, pulling apart all his experiences with Pascoe and the men. He had been incensed at the thought of their sodomy, yearning to bring them to so-called justice, but he could not pinpoint any particular incidents. Doubt, not in his allegations but in the court's assessment of it, simmered.

'He was eager to accuse and he more than once called them black-guards,' he said. 'But the prime event is the missing scalpel. If he was involved in that, and I believe he was, then I cannot say the truth of his other charges.'

'We shall discuss and analyse such things, Lieutenant,' Easton said firmly.

'Yes, sir.'

'Very well.' Easton nodded to the clerk. 'We shall recall Mr Gregory Pascoe to the stand and ask him to give further testimony. Thank you, Lieutenant. You may go.'

Courtney felt a weight shift from his shoulders. He had done all he could for Paterson and Arnold; the rest lay in the hands of the panel. He could only pray that the captains were merciful. Doubtless Pascoe would try and wriggle out of the accusations dumped upon him but Courtney hoped the doubt had been seeded.

The time was into the first dog watch when he left the *Mallard*. Nathan Waters would be in the town still, along with the men Courtney had allowed a short shore leave. With only time to wait, Courtney made his way through the streets to the Royal Oak. He opened the door of the tavern to see the Lysanders crowded around a table together, Waters and Sara in the midst of them. Courtney recognised Mr Lynde, sat with Obi, both men from Paterson and Arnold's mess. They drank and laughed as Waters's voice carried through them. He sang 'Leave Her Johnny' to the watching crowd.

Courtney lingered at the entrance, leaning against the open door. He smiled for the first time in days to hear the familiar tune, the same often sung on the forecastle during the men's leisure time. It reminded him of many things. He had once sung it to the gunroom on the *Scylla* and had looked into the shadows to see Nightingale watching him. That seemed so long ago now, but Courtney saw his bond with Nightingale in the way Waters cradled Sara's hand in his.

Although he had felt ashamedly envious of their open affection that morning, he could not begrudge them their love. With fortune, he had tipped the scales for Paterson and Arnold. Soon, he would do the same for himself and Nightingale. He would find him, wherever he was.

Waters's eyes swivelled to him. His words faded. Others stopped laughing and turned to where Waters looked. The Lysanders got to their feet in respect for Courtney's officer's authority.

'Do not stop on my account,' Courtney said, holding up his hands. 'You have a fine voice, Mr Waters.'

Waters put his knuckles to his forehead in a salute. 'Thank you, sir.'

Courtney took a seat at a table away from them, but he could still feel the difference in the air now he had entered. An officer carried the weight of the ship's and navy's law with him: a law which did not have much of a place in a tavern. Sara began to stand to serve him. He shook his head. 'Do you not know the next verse, Mr Waters?' he asked with a smile.

Waters's mouth opened and closed. 'I...' he began. 'Yes, sir.'

'The old man swears, and the mate swears too,' Sara prompted. Waters turned to her and she gave a beaming smile. 'Leave her Johnny, leave her.'

'The crew all swear and so would you,' Waters continued, and again the song rang through the tavern. Courtney sat back, half-tempted to join in. But he held back, knowing the lines he trod were already thin. He listened, tapping his foot idly, until Obi and Mr Lynde came to hover over his table.

'Mr Lynde? Obi?' Courtney asked. 'Is something wrong?'

'Oh, no, sir,' Lynde said. 'We only wondered... We wondered how Mr Paterson and Mr Arnold are.'

Some of the men, those closest to Mr Paterson and Mr Arnold's berths and within their mess, had already been called to the stand to give short testimony. Lynde and Obi had been two of them, having to speak about their close fellows. Courtney knew what a betrayal that would feel. 'I cannot say yet,' Courtney commented honestly. 'There are still questions to be asked before the panel will make their decision.'

'Will they die?'

A chill tripped through Courtney's stomach. 'I hope that won't be the case. I wouldn't want to see any man on the *Lysander* die.'

'Nor us, sir.'

Courtney smiled. The bond onboard a ship was unlike any other. A shipmate ranked above many other connections, as if the salt of the sea forged stronger links. Within the wooden walls, men formed their own brotherhoods and families. 'I am glad to hear that,' Courtney said.

Time rolled on to six. Courtney glanced at the clock mounted on the wall, knowing that the quartermaster would be ringing for the change into the second dog watch. Whether on land or sea, the routine continued. Rounding up the men, Courtney allowed Waters to bid a fond farewell to Sara. Courtney tipped his hat to her, gladly noted her ruddy cheeks and shining eyes, and led the men back through Gibraltar towards the *Lysander*.

Lieutenant Godfrey leant over the gunwale as they approached. The look on his face chased away any of Courtney's ease from the tavern. Tight-jawed, pallid, he watched Courtney climb up and onto the deck, and then was immediately at his side.

'Lieutenant,' he said. 'Mr Pascoe has returned. He is looking for you.'

Courtney ignored the sudden tightness in his chest and nodded. 'Thank you, Lieutenant. Where is he?'

'In the gunroom, sir. He...' But Godfrey did not finish the sentence. Courtney filled it in for him. *He is not happy.*

Steeling himself, he descended onto the gundeck and approached the gunroom. Pascoe stood by his cabin, hands clenched firmly behind his back. Courtney entered calmly, removing his hat and dress coat as if he did not know what awaited him. Pascoe's cabin door hung open, revealing the master searching through his belongings. Courtney knew he must have left something out of place.

'Good evening, Mr Pascoe,' Courtney said.

The master swung around. His face reddened, nostrils flaring. A vein popping in his forehead, he crossed the gunroom to stand before Courtney. Courtney did not move. 'You went to Captain Easton and accused me of theft?' he hissed, spitting each word.

'I did,' Courtney said plainly.

'On what… On what grounds do you dare give such an accusation?'

'I hardly believe it is an accusation, Mr Pascoe. I found the scalpel in one of the most obvious places that a merchant captain might hide a sailor from a press-gang.'

A flutter crossed Pascoe's face, a marker that Courtney had hit his target. 'You searched through my own possessions.'

'Two men's lives are in danger, Mr Pascoe. I acted for the best interests of the court martial and for them.'

'Their crime is more than stealing,' Pascoe said, his voice rising.

'If one accusation is unfounded then it throws doubt on other parts of the trial. It is unfair for them to be accused of theft when it is not true.'

'You will have my name blackened, while allowing sodomites on this ship?'

So that truly was the kernel of Pascoe's hatred. Courtney nearly said that such men had most likely existed when he skippered the *Lysander* too, but he knew it would light the fire beneath Pascoe. 'The court has not decided the outcome yet, Mr Pascoe,' he remarked instead.

Pascoe shook his head. 'I cannot tolerate the depths to which the *Lysander* has fallen. Her crew fighting and squandering her and allying her to Frogs while men couple like beasts in her. It is an abomination.'

Pascoe took a step towards Courtney. Courtney tilted his head. 'She is not your ship, Mr Pascoe.'

'And neither is she yours.'

'Then let us agree to treat her fairly.' He tried to move past Pascoe but the smaller, stockier master stood in his way. Courtney eyed him coolly. 'Mr Pascoe,' he said. 'Do not be foolish.'

'You have dishonoured me, Lieutenant. Dragged my name through a court martial and ensured I shall not skipper this ship again.'

'You hid the scalpel,' Courtney said. 'I did not force you to do that. And neither did I force you to accuse two men as you did. You are fortunate I don't have you clapped in irons myself.'

'How dare you,' Pascoe hissed, fury burning behind his tense expression. His hand twitched. Courtney's eyes fell to it.

'If you strike me,' Courtney warned, 'I will ensure you regret it.'

'Are you threatening me?'

'You do not frighten me, Mr Pascoe. I have faced far worse men than you.'

'I do not doubt it. It would be like you to go searching in a man's bed.'

A thousand interpretations of that barbed comment whirled through Courtney's head. The worst of them kept sticking, making his blood run cold. He tried not to let the reaction reach his face and said calmly, icily, 'Move out of my way, Mr Pascoe. This doesn't have to end with you joining Mr Paterson and Mr Arnold in front of a court martial.'

'Damn you,' Pascoe hissed. 'Damn you for taking my ship and filling it with blackguards. Damn you all.'

Pascoe had already done enough to seal his own fate but he cemented it by raising a fist and smashing it into Courtney's nose. Courtney staggered back, tasting blood. He spat it out, his face throbbing. Looking through the haze, he saw Pascoe advancing. In that second, Courtney knew he could not respond: an officer like himself would be damned for brawling, no matter the reasons. He held up his hands, anger raging, but Pascoe had come no further when the flash of red-coated marines interrupted him. Sergeant Dawes grabbed Pascoe's arms, wrestling him away even as he spat and cursed.

Holding his pulsing nose, Courtney straightened, feeling blood drip through his fingers. Voice muffled, he managed to say, 'Confine him to his cabin, Sergeant. I believe this is enough for the court martial to reconsider their verdicts.'

Dawes dragged Pascoe across the gunroom, yanking him into his ransacked cabin. Courtney leant back, gingerly feeling his injury. He had heard a crunch and prayed it was not broken. As he turned, about to search for Dr Faulkner, he saw the small crowd which had gathered outside. Obi and Lynde, from the tavern, stood at the front, next to Smythe. Courtney sniffed, tried to not to splutter on the blood, and nodded at them.

'As you were,' he said. 'There is nothing more to see here.'

He made his way through them, feeling each and every eye boring into him.

Chapter Twenty-Four: Unfinished Business

Dr Faulkner had set his nose as well as he could. After mopping the blood from Courtney's mouth and chin, he had taken a firm grasp of Courtney's face and shoved the bones back into place. Courtney had yelled but, looking vainly in his shaving mirror, had seen the effect was not too dismal. He would not spend the rest of his career appearing like a prize fighter.

Mostly, he was relieved he had removed his best dress coat before Pascoe had assaulted him. The blood only stained his shirt: something a scrub with lye and cold water would wash out. So it was in neater, clean clothes that he stood again before the court martial panel, spelling out Pascoe's actions. The bruise on his face said more than his words could. But with every accusation, he felt the rhythm of the trial shift once again: at first, it had been against Paterson and Arnold, then allegations against Pascoe, now a potential investigation into the master's conduct.

Courtney was well aware of Article Twenty-Two: if any mariner were to strike his superior officer, or even threaten to do so, a court martial could judge him worthy of death.

Courtney knew he had played a dangerous game in his bid to relieve Paterson and Arnold of the verdict. He had been injured, physically and perhaps professionally, in his efforts. The whole affair had turned into a quagmire, insubordination upon insubordination. But seeing the first shred of hope cross Paterson and Arnold's faces made him believe he had chosen the right pathway.

And, sitting with Smythe and Godfrey at the closing of a wretchedly long day, he knew he could do no more. His stomach rumbled with hunger but each mouthful of the salted pork sat heavily in Courtney's throat. He chewed it, gazing into the far distance, winding his fork through the thick gravy which Andrews, the cook, had stewed for too little time. At last, across the table, Smythe cleared his throat.

'Lieutenant Courtney,' he said, and Courtney blinked. A thousand thoughts had drained his energy and he suddenly realised how fatigued he was. Smythe peered at him, fair eyebrows furrowed.

'Yes, Mr Smythe?' Courtney asked.

'I only wondered... What will happen now? With...everything that has occurred?'

Courtney felt a spark of guilt. In serving Paterson and Arnold, he had been away from the *Lysander* for far longer than he would have liked – certainly now no captain manned her. The court martial only occupied one place in the long list of their problems. 'We will wait for the result of the trial,' he said. 'With Mr Pascoe accused, I don't know what the captains will decide.'

'Will Mr Pascoe be hanged?' Smythe had been there when the *Ulysses* mutineers had been strung from the yardarm. He had given testimony at their court martial, faced for the first time with the might of naval law. It was testament to his strength that he had done it again without wavering.

'The Articles of War say he will be,' Courtney remarked. 'Perhaps he deserves it. But I wouldn't wish to see it. Dismissed, possibly, but not hanged. Not for striking me. I have been struck before.'

Reason dictated that Courtney should want Pascoe to face harsh judgement for his actions. But it seemed a poor reason to die. The Articles were full of tenuous reasons to die, and perhaps it was treasonous to think so. Yet Pascoe had made his bed – and now he must lie in it.

'Will we sail,' Smythe continued, 'once it is over?'

'I hope so. The *Fantôme* is still out there, and the missing *Loyal* men. That was who we left England to find. All of this has been a turn in the road which we did not anticipate. But I will not stop until I find them. No matter what occurs.'

Yet their orders had not come. Courtney had not thought they would so quickly: messages and letters took weeks to travel over land and sea. At the Admiralty, a man might only just be opening the sealed documents, reading of the Tripolitan corsairs and Sicily and Captain Bryant's injury. They were stuck in an awful purgatory, with the danger of the pirates on one side and the twisted law of the court martial on the other. He could not promise Smythe that they would sail and find the missing men, though he had to keep up an appearance of confidence, if only not to worry the boy and the others of the crew. Courtney felt the weight of their expectations and their frets.

He tried to sleep that night, but the thoughts of the potential executions of the next day and of the *Fantôme*, somewhere out there, plagued him. He lay in his cot, delicately touching his bruised nose, and stared up at the low timbers above him. The *Lysander* rocked slowly at anchor. Silenced covered her decks for once, the calm in between the two storms – one already faced and one yet to conquer. Again and again, he wished Nightingale were there. When Courtney had been in the Caribbean after Nightingale's dismissal, he had been safe in the knowledge that Nightingale was secure at home. Now, he had no clue where he was.

Courtney turned over and wrapped the sheets about himself. He stared at the wall and tried to will his mind to calm. Nightingale had once told him what he did when his thoughts fluttered: naming the sails and yards of a full-rigged ship from skyscraper to spanker. Courtney found himself picturing the *Scylla*, not the *Lysander* which had trawled through such a mess. He remembered her well, the vessel on which he had learnt the most about his identity as a man and as an officer. All of this… It seemed to be muddying what he thought he knew about himself again. Courtney thought he understood who he was, until another event turned it on its head.

Tomorrow, he would walk into another test, and see how he emerged.

–

Courtney did not eat the next morning. He awoke, splashed water on his face, winced at the raw wound of his nose, and tried to dress with shaking hands. The boom of the *Mallard's* guns again echoed over the harbour and he drew in a trembling breath. Another few hours of testimony would be given and then the final verdict would come. Courtney spoke no more to the panel. He watched the Lysanders being rowed across again, the ones who knew Paterson and Arnold, the ones who had seen Pascoe strike him. A change had forced the trial in a different direction, and he wished he could predict the outcome.

When the time finally came, six bells in the forenoon watch, he made the crossing to the *Mallard*. Smythe and Godfrey sat in the cutter with him but none of them said a word.

Silence also covered the *Mallard*. Courtney remembered standing on the deck of the *Leviathan*, pushing to get as close as he could to the open cabin doors. He had not wanted to miss a single syllable of Jane's sentencing. And so too now did his heart beat sickly in his chest, his stomach in knots. How, he wondered, had it come to this again?

The court opened. In the great cabin, Pascoe sat at the starboard side, and Paterson and Arnold the larboard. Marines penned them in, red gleaming amongst the glittering medals and epaulettes of the officers' dress uniforms. Easton stood behind the table, looking out across the assemblage. Courtney almost held his breath to better hear his statements.

'It is of the court's decision,' he came to, after the short preamble, 'that in this, the year 1802, the tenth of October, Mr Gregory Pascoe, former skipper of the merchant ship, *Lysander*, now His Majesty's Ship, *Lysander*, for the crimes of seditious behaviour and raising a hand against a superior officer, shall be dismissed from the service of the Royal Navy, effective immediately.'

Pascoe's shoulders sank. Courtney could not tell if it was of relief or anger. No expression crossed his lined face. For himself, Courtney only felt a flash of consolation. He had not wished to witness a man hanged that day. The dismissal was enough: an exit not only from service, but also from the ship Pascoe had nurtured and once captained. He would find it hard work to step back into the merchant service with those charges. That would sit heavier on him than a noose.

'It is also of the court's decision,' Easton continued, 'that in this, the year 1802, the tenth of October, Mr Felix Paterson and Mr Dudley Arnold of His Majesty's Ship *Lysander*, for the crimes of disobedience and sodomy—'

Courtney felt men shift beside him at the word, so much that the noise almost muffled Easton's judgement.

'—shall be hanged by the neck until dead.'

The world lurched around Courtney. His gut dropped to the soles of his feet, so suddenly that his ears rang. He looked around, at the men gathered to watch the verdict, at the ships in the harbour, but saw no one make a single response. In the great cabin, Arnold crumpled like a ball of paper in a fist. Paterson's agonised groan reached Courtney. Suddenly, he found himself angling through the crowd to reach the great cabin. Even as the court was closed, the verdicts hammered down in final stone, he tried to enter.

Marines stepped away from the prisoners. Silent tears ran down Paterson's face. Pascoe still did not react.

'Captain Easton!' Courtney called without thought.

Easton's face was an impassive as Pascoe's. 'Let him through, Lieutenant Rowland,' he said to the marine commander.

Saluting, pulling off his hat in respect, anything to appease Easton, Courtney stepped into the cabin, knees shaking. 'The charges were invented, sir,' was the first thing that came to his mouth. 'These men are falsely accused.'

'I am sorry, Lieutenant Courtney,' Easton said coldly. 'Mr Pascoe's testimony was not the only given to us. He has been punished for his own actions.'

'This is...' Wrong, he had been about to say. Unfair. But he could not voice such treason to a post-captain. 'They are not at fault. I stand for their good character. The fabricated accusations of theft and...'

'Yes, Lieutenant, we have heard your voice and your vouches for these men. But testimony from other men of the *Lysander* and written evidence in Mr Paterson's possessions has confirmed Mr Pascoe's accusations.'

Courtney shook his head, then realised he must look like a petulant child there, screaming against the might of the navy.

'Your sense of justice is admirable, Lieutenant, if misplaced. The navy cannot be seen to be light on these crimes. We consulted the governor on such matters and he is in agreement with the verdict.'

The Duke of Kent, that man who ruled Gibraltar with iron will. What could Courtney do against him? Even the secrecy of the *Lysander*'s voyage had not saved the two men. They would still be killed, despite everything.

He shook his head again, every second reminding him how powerless he was. Once more, he felt all eyes on him, as he had when Pascoe fought with him in the gunroom. But now, it was not the men witnessing his behaviour, but officers and men with connections and power. There could be nothing more evocative of the crossroads he stood at, caught between two unforgiving rocks. Turning his back on one would mean he was flayed by the other.

Still, he looked at Paterson and Arnold. They wept silently together, one last moment of intimacy before their deaths.

He could not do anything. He could only watch them hang.

And that, he forced himself to enact. With Smythe and Godfrey at his side again, he observed the yellow flag of execution run up on the *Lysander*. Tradition dictated the punishment should be administered on the condemned man's ship, and now every single one of the *Lysander*'s company listened to Paterson and Arnold's crimes being read aloud. Courtney, hat clenched in a deathly grip beneath his arm, looked around at their faces. He bore them no ill will for their testimony. They were as helpless in the face of the law as he. But now, he saw heads bowed, tears in their eyes, pallor on their cheeks.

Obi bravely came forward, with Mr Lynde and other men who had known them and served with them, to man the ropes. It was some mercy that Paterson and Arnold would be killed together, without watching their own loved one die first. At last, the nooses were prepared. Beneath them, a gun fired.

Smoke swamped the *Lysander*'s deck. They had not yet fired the cannons at an enemy, only in salute and now in execution. Courtney waited for the haze to clear, gritting his jaw as he felt angry tears threaten. At last, the clouds pulled back and the whole awful spectacle was revealed: Paterson and Arnold, side by side, struggling for their last moments and eventually, stilling. Courtney thought how ironic it was that the law, and its enforcers, could feel more at ease killing two men rather than accepting their bond.

Finally, he allowed himself to look away. Furious sickness rolled over him.

And it was over. Without feeling, without thinking, Courtney dismissed the *Lysander*'s men by their divisions. Over them all, casting ghastly shadows across the scrubbed and cleaned deck, Paterson and Arnold swung. They would remain there for the next hour, a warning to all other sailors. Yet none of the Lysanders even glanced up at them again, not participating in the cruel pageant. Courtney caught Obi and Lynde's eyes and gave them a small nod. They had done a noble thing, even if it wrenched at their hearts.

Courtney felt the same as he approached Captain Easton. The man had come across from the *Mallard* to witness the punishment, rather than hiding on his own ship. The other captains had already dispersed; they were now free to return to their peacetime leave. Courtney's voyage, he knew, went on. Unfinished business sat heavily in his chest. It lay across the sea and also here, in the rotten aftermath of Paterson and Arnold's trial.

Easton caught his eye and gave a nod. 'Lieutenant Courtney,' he said. 'You conducted the ceremony well. Your Lysanders do you credit.'

If it was a compliment to soothe the burn of the executions, it did not work. 'Thank you, sir,' he said blandly.

'I wished to come across, Lieutenant,' Easton continued, 'because I wished to warn you of something. Shall we go below?'

Courtney was too drained to feel anything. 'Yes, sir,' he simply agreed and they descended to the empty gunroom. Easton did not sit but lingered awkwardly in the dim space with its cramped cabins and table.

'I hate to be indelicate and speak of such things, Lieutenant Courtney, but I feel you deserve to know some of Master Pascoe's statements when he was questioned. I believe it would be for your own safety.'

Courtney wondered if the man had threatened to murder him. He would not be surprised.

Easton glanced outside of the gunroom, but no one was nearby. 'Master Pascoe insinuated that you had committed a gross act onboard the *Lysander*, and that you were in breach of the same Article that Mr Paterson and Mr Arnold were condemned for.'

The numbness inside of Courtney raced away. He swallowed heavily and felt the gunroom sway about him. A thousand doubts struck him – whether he should act angry, indignant, confused... He had dreaded having to face this kind of situation, and now it had swept out of nowhere.

'I...' he began pathetically. The thought of Nightingale, of his name being blackened alongside Courtney's own, spurred him on. 'Mr Pascoe had already stolen from the Lysander's stores, sir. He had a history of untruths.'

Easton nodded. 'That is what we concluded also. They were the accusations of a desperate man who was already in a very precarious position by striking and insulting his superior officer. For that reason, we did not question the Lysanders about it and risk putting a dark mark upon your reputation. I apologise that I had to bring such an ugly subject up to you, Lieutenant.'

Courtney shook his head. 'I understand, sir.'

Easton made a move to leave but Courtney had not finished.

'Can I do anything for you, Lieutenant?' Easton asked.

Many things, but only one had a probability of being accepted. 'I was wondering, sir,' Courtney continued. 'What happened to Mr Paterson and Mr Arnold's possessions?'

Easton frowned. 'Their chests were seized from the *Lysander*, as you know, and investigated. I believe they are still below on the *Mallard*.'

'Would it be possible to have them returned to the *Lysander*, sir?'

'Of course, Lieutenant. My crews, over the years, have sold off dead men's possessions. A harsh business, but the way of the service.'

'Yes, sir.'

It was not the reason Courtney wished for the chests to be returned. Once they had arrived, hoisted up from the *Mallard*'s gig, he had them taken to the gunroom and, in solitude, he opened them for the first time since rooting through them under the eyes of Captain Bryant. Inside sat folded clothes, never more to be worn. Precious little more sat amongst the fabric, only a decorated scrimshaw and a small portrait of a girl in Arnold's chest. Nothing would sell for much when laid upon the capstan for the rest of the crew.

But Courtney wanted to know, before he put it all aside, what Paterson had been so incensed over when Bryant had ordered it searched. Not much lay within, and after lifting the spare shirt in Paterson's belongings, he found it.

Retreating to his cabin, Courtney closed the door and sat upon his cot. He laid the small piece of paper upon his knees and peered at the cramped handwriting. With every word, he felt his heart fall further.

My dear Anne,

Paterson had written.

I have been often thinking of you. Our arrangement has not left my mind. I know that we three agreed to it but I keep wondering if it would be bad for you. For me. For Dudley. I could not make you suffer just because of my selfishness. Dudley nearly died this last week. He fell overboard and I rescued him. I was angry with him and thought that his death would break your heart. It would not, I know. It would upset you but you would recover.

I do not think that I would.

When I come home, you do not have to wed him. If you wish to, then I will bear it. But to force it on you for my own benefit is wrong. We, Dudley and me, seem to have been tied since the Crane. We each were tattooed for it. That was our ring. A wedding between you and Dudley would be our excuse to meet. But you would be hurt by it.

I love each of you. But you are my sister.

I will see you soon.

Your loving brother, Felix

Courtney folded the letter and closed his eyes. It answered his questions and solidified why the court had condemned the two men. Pascoe's testimony had only been the final blow. Anne, Paterson's sister, had been due to wed Arnold, a shield for their own love. Paterson, by putting it in writing, had condemned himself. Courtney could not help thinking of his own love for Nightingale, with his wife amidst them. Events could so easily shift and put either one of them at the end of a rope. It had come frighteningly close today, and it was only with great fortune that Captain Easton had dismissed Pascoe's accusations.

But it did not make Courtney want to be with Nightingale any less. Nightingale had witnessed the death of his first love, a stable-boy named Tom who his father had caught with him. The threat of exhibition, the perils of condemnation, always hung over them. Courtney had known it since he was a young boy, solidified when he shared the time on the *Grampus* with Walker. He felt no shame for it, no guilt. He loved the idea of sharing his life with a man, with a woman, in the same capacity. But Nightingale… He transcended all of that. Nightingale was the sole person he wished to be with.

Courtney stood, tucking the letter inside his breast pocket. A thick lump sat in his throat that he had to swallow down. What was done was done. He could not save Paterson and Arnold, but he could treat their bodies with the respect they had not been given in life.

Courtney chose to be the man to pull them down from the yardarm. With further help from Obi, Lynde and their messmates, he sewed them into their hammocks with roundshot at their feet. Then, he pulled the letter from his pocket and slipped it into Paterson's shroud. Their written love would go with them to the bottom of the sea. Courtney only hoped somebody might afford him the same regard one day.

As he had done for Darius Wade, he performed the final rites for Paterson and Arnold, committing them to the water. The crew, who had watched them hang, observed their last ritual with the same silence. They were not simply men at the end of a court martial, criminals in the eyes of naval law. They had served with them and slept with them and eaten with them.

So it was to be expected in the service. A sailor's life and death could change on a knife edge. Wild seas, cannonball, pistol shot, fire and destruction could claim him. But for his own countrymen to condemn him, under the guise of the law, seemed so unjust, so futile. Courtney had questioned the decisions of his superiors since he sailed on the *Grampus*, but now, with more authority than he had had as an able seaman, he felt even more helpless. This, more than most orders, left a foul taste in his mouth.

Because, he knew, as he watched those white shrouds sink beneath the waves, it could so easily be him, or Nightingale.

Chapter Twenty-Five: Departure

Later that afternoon, the Lysanders auctioned off Paterson and Arnold's possessions. Courtney could have left them to it, but he stood upon the quarterdeck and watched as shirts and handkerchiefs and buckles were sold. He had no coins remaining to his name, otherwise he would have bought something of the executed men. Instead, he observed without comment or judgement. To others, it may have looked callous, but this was the way of the service. In some convoluted way, it kept the sailors' memories alive.

There was none of the riotous behaviour that sometimes occurred if the dead seamen had items the others coveted. A muted weight hung over the ship as Mr Lynde and Obi and Paterson and Arnold's messmates shared out what remained of their friends. Only once did voices raise, when a hand of the afterguard made a crass comment about the trial. Courtney did not have to step in, though he had been about to; Obi dressed the man down.

It was a stark reminder of the justice of the lower berths.

As the sun dipped below the masts in the harbour, Courtney descended below to struggle over the day's log entry. His words all sounded so callous, reducing the tragedy of the last hours to a mere sentence. He thought of when he had had to note down the deaths on the *Scylla*, yellow fever ripping through her decks. The demise of Captain Carlisle had rattled them all... And then Nightingale had arrived. Courtney would have never thought, from that first day meeting the new, timid captain to now, that his heart would be breaking quite this much over his absence.

He set down his pen and laid his head in his hands. Tears crept upon him. His grief fuelled his desire to run. He wanted to leave this harbour and escape to the open seas, delivering true justice to the pirates. But he was caged here.

If he acted wrongly, he would be the next victim before a court martial.

Footsteps hurrying to the gunroom made him quickly wipe his wet eyes. He looked up and took a breath, just as Godfrey entered. 'Lieutenant,' he said. 'There is a man approaching the *Lysander*. I do not recognise him.'

Courtney dreaded who he might see being rowed across to the ship. He reached the deck and peered over the gunwales, shielding his eyes from the final rays of the day. A small launch threaded its way between the moored vessels. In its stern sat a man in an old black coat and a straw hat. He did not appear to be a dignitary from the shore or a naval representative. Courtney hailed him as the boat neared the *Lysander's* hull. He ensured the marines were present, although he could not imagine an assault upon the ship in such a crowded bay.

'Ahoy there!' he cried. 'Please state your name and business!'

The man raised a peaceable hand. With it, he plucked the hat from his head. Courtney squinted and made out his face. Vague familiarity sparked: a middle-aged, stern-looking fellow who had been swamped by paperwork the last time he had seen him.

'My God,' he said. 'It is Sir Rodney Bryant.'

With hastily granted permission to come aboard, Sir Rodney scaled the *Lysander's* tumblehome side. Courtney greeted him by sweeping off his own hat but Sir Rodney waved to dismiss the formality. He looked in a sorry state with his dusty jacket and plain trousers, a loose neck-cloth tied about his throat.

'Sir Rodney,' Courtney managed to say. 'I did not expect to see you out here in Gibraltar.'

'That is for the best, Lieutenant,' Sir Rodney replied cryptically. 'May we speak? I should like to talk with you and Monsieur Baptiste.'

'I…Of course, sir. Lieutenant Godfrey…' The other officer stood there, appearing as dumbfounded as Courtney felt. 'Rouse Andrews and have him prepare some coffee for the gunroom. And pass the word for Monsieur Baptiste.'

'Yes, sir.'

Safely in the gunroom's relative privacy and with a pot of charred coffee to share, Courtney and Baptiste sat opposite Sir Rodney, unable to muster any words. The older man drank in silence, not even commenting on the acrid taste. His clothes smelt as if he had been on the road for some time. Baptiste glanced at Courtney but he was unsure what to do. Every possibility ran through his head: he was in trouble; the *Lysander* was being recalled; more information had been uncovered about the corsair or the *Fantôme*; Captain Bryant was no more... He barely knew where to begin.

'Are you... Are you well, Sir Rodney?' Courtney finally managed to say.

'Well?' Sir Rodney frowned and then glanced down at his attire. 'Ah,' he said, placing down his mug. 'I see. I must appear to be dressed as a hermit. That is necessary.'

'Necessary?' Courtney thought that the sun might have addled Sir Rodney's mind. He looked towards Baptiste but the Frenchman looked none the wiser.

'I know about everything, Lieutenant Courtney,' Sir Rodney continued. 'The *Fantôme*. The behaviour of Paterson and Arnold. Your meeting with the *Loyal* and her fate. The disappearance of the *Fantôme* and her brush with Tripolitan pirates. And this court martial.'

Courtney blinked. 'I don't understand, sir. I thought that... Do you not... You last spoke to us in the Admiralty Office at Whitehall.'

'Last spoke with you, yes. But my brother has been keeping me informed, and I have my own sources. I have been keenly following the progression of the *Lysander*.'

'How...' Courtney shook his head. Either the answer was staring him in the face or Sir Rodney was being intentionally, maddeningly, vague. He thought of Hargreaves and Fairholme and their shadow-shrouded ways, how infuriated he had been with their inability to speak plainly.

And knew precisely what Sir Rodney's business had been.

'Oh Christ,' he said without thinking. 'You're another spymaster, aren't you?'

Baptiste cleared his throat. The words echoed back to Courtney's ears and he tried not to wince. 'My apologies, Sir Rodney,' he said. 'I had bad experiences on the *Scylla* with...agents.'

'It is quite all right, Lieutenant,' Sir Rodney replied magnanimously. 'I know about the *Scylla* and Lord Fairholme. I assure you I am not like him. For one, I shall not manipulate any poor men into my service. I enjoy leaving the comforts of London. It is why I, myself, followed the *Lysander*'s progress. My brother, though he is a post-captain, is not always to be relied upon.'

Courtney did not think any more could shock him that day but that final statement made him raise his eyebrows. 'Your brother, Captain Bryant, he has been wounded dreadfully. It was during the tempest that wrecked the *Loyal*. A damaged mizzen cap...'

'I'm aware of what happened to my brother. I shall visit him in Sicily as soon as I am able. In fact, I planned to do so but had to follow your court martial. A nasty business, and one that has delayed you.'

Courtney wanted to ask if there was anything Sir Rodney could have done to save Paterson and Arnold. He bit his tongue, knowing that whatever answer came, he would feel guilty for it. 'Will there be an inquiry into Captain Bryant's injury?'

'Perhaps. But the *Lysander* was not lost. If Captain Myles survives, he shall go to a court martial for the loss of the *Loyal*.'

'There are still many men missing from the *Loyal*,' Courtney said. 'Including Sir William Haywood. Captain Kelly of the US Navy told me he had seen the *Fantôme* with the Tripolitan pirates. That is another crew who have been taken, perhaps into slavery. Hiram Nightingale, Capitaine Bonfils and Geneviève Baptiste...'

'My wife accompanied Capitaine Bonfils on his ship,' Baptiste interjected. 'I did not know she was going to leave France.'

Sir Rodney frowned. 'I do not know about this woman. I knew, of course, that the *Fantôme* would join you. That information was only imparted to my brother and Capitaine Bonfils.'

'I fear she is in grave danger,' Baptiste said.

'I fear they all are,' Courtney commented. With Sir Rodney Bryant before him, the man who had ordered the *Lysander* to be refitted for this very voyage, he had potential answers to the questions that had been plaguing him. 'What are we to do?' he asked. 'We know of the *Fantôme*'s last sighting from Captain Kelly. He identified that the pirates' ship was a polacre out of Tripoli. If she were sailing back to her port...'

Sir Rodney nodded. 'I shall accompany you to Tripoli. Monsieur Baptiste, you shall alight onto shore with me and we shall try to negotiate the release of the survivors.'

The abrupt transparency of his words struck Courtney. 'We are to depart from Gibraltar?'

'Yes. As soon as we have the tide.'

'I am not...' Although the relief of the departure flooded Courtney, he knew he had to at least acknowledge the awkward impracticality of his rank. 'I am not the captain of the *Lysander*. A lieutenant can only command an unrated ship.'

'You shall retain your position,' Sir Rodney said. 'This voyage shall still be undertaken with the utmost secrecy. I, and Monsieur Baptiste, shall negotiate. You concentrate upon the *Lysander*.'

'Yes, sir.'

A throb of hope pulsed within him. The return from Sicily had been a matter of routine, sailing from one point to another with no decisions to be made. This would be a voyage into the comparative unknown, one with shades of diplomacy and bureaucracy. Courtney disliked politics and its creeping influence upon ships. But here was Sir Rodney Bryant with a steadying hand. Courtney would not bear the blame if war threatened.

Hadn't he wished for the responsibility of command? He had only ever experienced shreds of it, just for it to be taken away and given to some other man.

Perhaps this, on the shadowy edges of authority and with some leeway, would suit him. This, he knew, was what he was good at, poor background or not. He had no other path.

Yet it did not allay the anxiety within him as the *Lysander* prepared to sail. Every sail and yard and mast had already been inspected after the tempest that had wrecked the *Loyal*, and Courtney, alongside Brooks, Godfrey and Macdonald, was satisfied she could easily weather another crossing of the Mediterranean. All stores were safely brought aboard and Courtney and Godfrey oversaw the fitting of the capstan bars. The messenger was attached to the anchor cable and slowly, ponderously, the men worked the capstan.

With Godfrey watching over the anchor's progress, Courtney felt the *Lysander* gradually awakening, ready for what might be the hardest leg of her journey. She had already traversed the Mediterranean, but this time the waters were unsure and even more perilous. He had to hold her steady for the sake of her crew, for himself, and for those still missing.

By the time Godfrey called, 'Anchors aweigh!', he had cycled through every conceivable stage of emotion: fear, grief, joy that they could finally move, and frustration that it had to be this way, with so many lives in danger. There was nothing more to do though – nothing more than to sail back into the unknown.

PART III

Chapter Twenty-Six: Rogue

24 October 1802, Ottoman Tripolitania

'They're not here.'

Courtney returned to the great cabin where Sir Rodney and Monsieur Baptiste sat around Bryant's table. He had not been utilising it, preferring the familiarity of the gunroom. Every remnant of the captain had been removed; his sea-chest was ashore in Palermo, all of his effects and possessions stripped from the ship. The only item that remained was the writing desk. Courtney could imagine Bryant there, penning the notes to his brother, informing him of the sad and dramatic tale of the *Lysander*.

There were still chapters left in her story, though. Part of Courtney had hoped for a grand resolution in Tripoli's harbour, locating the missing *Fantôme*.

But she was nowhere to be seen, and neither was the polacre Captain Kelly had described.

Sir Rodney barely looked up from the letter he wrote. He and Baptiste had been shut away together for long hours, discussing and re-discussing. 'This changes nothing,' Sir Rodney said. 'We did not expect to meet them here. That is why I am prepared.'

A small chest sat upon the desk, locked tightly. Courtney cast his eye over it and swiftly looked away as if it would suddenly catch ablaze just by sight. Inside obviously sat the ransom or bribery trinkets that Sir Rodney would go ashore with. He had spoken very privately with the governor in Gibraltar and seemingly dipped into their banks. Courtney was glad he was not accompanying Sir Rodney and Baptiste. He had had enough of gold and bribes on the *Scylla*. He did not enjoy the idea of paying for such a barbaric system to continue and thought of the *Ulysses*'s cargo, that gold which was to persuade Louverture not to foment any more slave rebellions. God, he thought, one day he would like to stand on a ship with a clear directive, clean from the dirty practices. Perhaps that was an impossible dream.

'Monsieur Baptiste and I shall go ashore,' Sir Rodney continued, finalising his note. 'I want to request Sergeant Dawes's presence and a marine guard.'

'Of course,' Courtney replied.

'These arrangements can last for hours or they can last for days. I shall know more once we have spoken to the consul-general and the dey's representatives.'

'Yes, sir.'

'Do not weigh anchor, and do not move,' Sir Rodney ordered.

'Do you anticipate trouble?'

'No, I should hope not. Before the current war, American negotiators frequently paid tribute to the dey and his representatives. Many prisoners, taken into captivity, were released. It was partially over tribute not being paid to the new dey that Tripoli declared war on America.'

'Yes,' Courtney said. There was no use in arguing with Sir Rodney; his was the guiding hand here. As Sir Rodney had said, Courtney's responsibility was the *Lysander*.

Letters written and the chest beneath Sir Rodney's arm, Courtney accompanied Sir Rodney and Baptiste onto deck. Ironically, despite the fraught situation, the late afternoon sun was warm and beautiful, lighting Tripoli with a rose-gold hue. The white stone walls rose around the harbour, broken by minarets and domes. All manner of vessels bobbed in the calm blue waters: feluccas rubbing shoulders with ketches and xebecs and simple fishing boats. Courtney trained his spyglass over them as the *Lysander*'s cutter weaved through the water.

He watched until it safely reached the shore and then turned to Smythe. He, along with most of the other men, had come to nose at the exotic harbour. The midshipman began to point things out to the others, explaining in excited bursts. Courtney had served from England to Trinidad and all in between, but he had never come to an African harbour before, though it was a short stretch across the Mediterranean. He wished he was of the mood to appreciate the architecture and the people but he could only think of the trials ahead, and the unknown world he was again dipping his toes in.

'I am going below, Mr Smythe,' he said. 'Fetch me if there is any news.'

'Yes, sir.'

But before Courtney could leave, Smythe piped up again, 'Oh, sir. If I may?'

'Speak freely, Mr Smythe.'

'Obi did not report this morning. He was not amongst his division or his station.'

That was unlike the man. Courtney had assigned him his position because of his dependability. Trying to ignore the disquiet, he nodded and said, 'Thank you, Mr Smythe. I shall deal with him.'

Courtney descended below, not returning to the great cabin or gunroom but to the gundeck. The hammocks had been stowed, mess tables winched up to the timbers, but Courtney knew where Obi's berth was located. Nothing indicated that he had deserted his post, so Courtney wandered the ship, inquiring amongst the men who had not gone above.

'I think he went to the sickbay, sir,' he finally heard from Mr Lynde.

That would explain his absence. But, entering Dr Faulkner's sickbay in the orlop, Courtney did not find the man laid up in a hammock or cot. Instead, he aided Faulkner himself, attending the remaining patients with their sprained ankles and crushed fingers. Fortunately, the journey from Gibraltar had been mostly free of injury, other than the mundane ones of working a ship.

'Obi,' Courtney said. 'Mr Smythe and I wondered where you were. You did not report on deck.'

'No, sir. Apologies, sir.'

'May I know the reason? It is not an easy matter.'

Obi had risen to talk to Courtney, but now his eyes lowered. 'I thought that, with Monsieur Baptiste's absence, Dr Faulkner might need an assistant.'

'Dr Faulkner's business is his own. And it is my responsibility, as acting captain, to assign duties. I do not believe that is your reason.'

He did not want to reprimand Obi, but, regardless of his background and previous reliability, he had to treat him with the same fairness as any other Lysander.

'You may be honest with me, Obi,' Courtney continued. 'In truth, I would advise you to do so.'

'Yes, sir,' Obi remarked, nodding. He was silent for a moment more; Courtney allowed him to be. Then, he continued, simply saying, 'I have not seen this continent for many years.'

Courtney opened his mouth to reply, but quickly shut it again. He was ashamed that he had not even considered such a thing. Many of the slaves in the Caribbean came from the western coast of Africa, but the slavery that also occurred in the Barbary States capitalised on the trade too. Courtney had been so focused on the horrors that lay ahead, that he had not fully seen those which had already occurred to his crew.

'I see,' he said, knowing how unsure he sounded.

'I left the Bight of Benin ten years ago,' Obi confessed. 'I did not expect to see African shores again. If I came on deck, I almost thought that I...'

'I will not allow you to be taken again, Obi,' Courtney said, finding his certainty in the face of Obi's pain. He could not reveal to the men what the purpose of the *Lysander* in Tripoli's harbour was, not as he had done for the officers, but he was positive that some of them had worked it out. They were not ignorant. 'This ship is not mine, just as the *Scylla* was not. But I will do my utmost to protect her and all who serve her.'

Just as he had tried to protect Walker, he thought. Just as he had tried to protect Paterson and Arnold. Just as he had tried to protect Nightingale. Guilt thrummed inside of him. But now was not the time for self-pity.

'You may stay below, Obi,' Courtney said. 'But I shall need you with your division as soon as we depart. You are a captain of the carronades, before anything else upon this ship.'

Obi nodded. 'Yes, sir. Of course, sir.'

Courtney smiled and left Obi with Dr Faulkner. He absorbed himself in updating the logs and even checking over Smythe's journals and navigation work. He knew he had to approach this voyage in its stages, leg by leg, yet it still dragged at him, making him itch with impatience and frustration.

He did not know what to expect but he did not foresee that, a mere two hours later, Smythe would appear in the gunroom, gushing, 'They are coming back, sir. Sir Rodney, Monsieur Baptiste and the marines.'

Courtney straightened, heart jumping. 'Already? They have barely had time to...'

Courtney did not know what precisely they had planned to do. How long did it truly take to ransom a mixed French and English crew, officers and men alike, alongside two civilians? Surely longer than this. He followed Smythe back on deck and looked over the harbour where, truly enough, Sergeant Dawes's marines glimmered in the dying sun's light. Sir Rodney and Monsieur Baptiste sat amidst them.

The ominous chest was still beneath Sir Rodney's arm.

Courtney glanced to Smythe, his stomach tightening.

Sir Rodney climbed the side of the *Lysander*, expressionless. With Baptiste at his side, he gestured for Courtney to follow them. Courtney did as commanded, shutting the great cabin door behind them. He could barely get the questions out of his mouth quickly enough, though he dreaded their answer.

'What happened, sir? Did they...not think the ransom sufficient?'

Sir Rodney glanced to Baptiste who lowered his gaze in a motion frighteningly like condolence. 'They thought it sufficient, yes,' Sir Rodney said. 'But they have no clue where the *Fantôme* is, nor the pirates who took her.'

A chill settled over Courtney's spine. He chewed on the inside of his mouth, trying to formulate the correct words. 'How is that possible? They operate from a Tripolitan corsair, yes?'

'This is what I said. I spoke of everything – the attempted capture of the *Loyal*, her wrecking, the *Fantôme*'s journey and how she is missing, Captain Kelly's testimony... I said that Britain and France,' as he gestured to Baptiste, 'are willing to pay for the release of these men. They do not know where the rogues are.'

'The rogue pirates.' Courtney did not know how to react. So many events had occurred over this last month alone that he could only accept that more things would go wrong before they could hope to be fixed.

'I wondered if perhaps they were not being entirely truthful. I went so far as to seek out the American consul. It appears that these pirates are indeed known to them, to the dey and his men. The US Navy has fought them in these waters. But they have been denied safe harbour in Tripoli. Their actions have threatened to upset not only the Americans but us and France and any other nation who they encounter. They have been profiteering off many of the slave trades, not only those along the Barbary Coast, but also the markets of West Africa. Nothing, no treaty or agreement, is sacred to them.'

'That is why they dared to attack a British frigate, and a French one.'

'Indeed.' Sir Rodney nodded and sat back in the chair. His eyes turned to the recently repaired gallery windows that looked out over the harbour and beyond. 'They do not know where the ship makes port or where it is. But they are as keen as we are to find it. Much more and the pirates will tip the uneasy balance in these seas. Tripoli already fights America.'

War lurked around every corner and seemed to dwell at the end of every pathway. Courtney had not known many a year where conflict had not raged. Sometimes, he imagined the natural state of men was war. The prospect of again spending years at sea, combating endless foes, never seemed far away.

'The American consul,' Sir Rodney continued, 'said that it was only a matter of time before these pirates attacked the wrong ship. It appears this is the wrong ship.'

'But we have no idea how to locate them. They could be anywhere along the Barbary Coast.' Courtney thought of the *Ulysses*. It had been by chance that they had located her after following a trail laid out by last sightings and information gleaned from agents in Trinidad and Salvador. This time, Nightingale was not beside him but out there, a pinprick in the wide blue.

'One positive aspect shone through, however,' Sir Rodney said. 'The men of the *Loyal* and the *Fantôme* have not been seen in the Tripolitan markets. It is not assumed that they have been sold yet.'

'Yet.' Courtney's heart thudded. He could not lose Nightingale – and certainly not in this way. What he would have to say to his wife when he returned home without her husband and her father... He gritted his teeth and swallowed the lump of emotion. 'What are we to do, then? This cannot be the end of our voyage.'

'Certainly not.' Sir Rodney crossed his arms and fixed Courtney with a stern look, staring through the pale helplessness Courtney thought must be on his face. 'You have charts and maps of the coastline, yes?'

'Yes, sir. Your brother... Captain Bryant has his own, and we officers do, also.'

'Fetch them. And have your officers join us.'

Courtney did as bid, laying the reams of charts out on the gunroom table. He was taken back to when he first came aboard the *Lysander*, listening to Bryant spelling out their journey for them. It felt so long ago, but had been a mere couple of months. Again, Smythe and Godfrey cast their eyes over the papers but this time, their focus fell upon Courtney. Sir Rodney searched through the charts until he found one of Tripoli and at its northern edge, Sicily. Another he laid alongside it – the blue swathes of the Ligurian and Tyrrhenian seas.

'Monsieur Baptiste,' he said. 'Tell me where the *Loyal* was attacked.'

Baptiste pinpointed the location, or its approximate one. Sir Rodney nodded.

'And Lieutenant, where did you come across her? Where was she wrecked?'

Courtney did not have to consult the logs he had written out that day. He would not forget it. A month before, south of Cagliari.

'Where did Captain Kelly encounter the pirates and make the final sighting of the *Fantôme*?' Sir Rodney continued.

'A month ago, around the same time we encountered the *Loyal*, but further south. Nearer to the North African coast, which is why I hoped...' Courtney cut himself off. There was no use in hoping now. 'This is old information now, though. Much has changed. If I could, I would talk with Captain Kelly again or to the other American officers who make port in Palermo. They might have a newer encounter to report.'

Sir Rodney nodded. 'I agree. They shall know what has occurred on the seas.'

'Then we shall make ready for Palermo? We cannot delay.'

'You are the *Lysander*'s caretaker, Lieutenant Courtney.'

'Yes, sir.'

The sudden command thrilled Courtney, but also filled him with uneasiness. The lives of these men, as well as the ones who were missing, were in his hands and he feared throwing them away. Desire to finish this awful voyage needed to weigh more.

'My brother,' Sir Rodney then said, 'told me about you, Lieutenant Courtney.'

Courtney smiled thinly. 'I suppose that he did, sir. We served together in the Caribbean.'

'That is what he said, amongst other things. He said that you did not always pursue the direction he would have done.'

'I'm sorry for anything that your brother said about me, sir. I did not mean to cause any offence.'

Sir Rodney, to his surprise, chuckled. 'No. No, that is not what I mean, Lieutenant. I believe that...in this situation, not pursuing my brother's direction may benefit us.' He paused and looked over the charts again, the wide blue peppered with islets and dangerous shores. This was a battleground Courtney recognised, even if he did not know the *Fantôme*'s precise location. 'Lieutenant,' Sir Rodney continued, 'you should do what it is you think is right. I am giving you permission to act in the way my brother condemned you for.'

'I don't understand, sir.'

'Yes, you do.' Sir Rodney smiled. 'These pirates will not obey naval law. Their very existence defies us and, indeed, the agreements we have with the Tripolitan state. We shall need cunning and we shall need invention. You, my brother said, sail very close to the wind.'

Courtney did not necessarily believe he did. Perhaps Bryant's own prejudice had biased him. But, shockingly, he thought there was a compliment in the statement. It had been a long time since he had heard praise, aside from Nightingale's comments – and Nightingale was biased for another reason.

'We shall need a plan, Lieutenant Courtney,' Sir Rodney said. 'A plan which will arouse the pirates' hunger. Do you believe you can face them?'

Courtney finally returned the smile. He drew himself up straighter and, for a moment, all of the anxiety faded away. He thought of Nightingale and the missing men, and said, 'I would face the devil, sir.'

Chapter Twenty-Seven: Cock-a-Bill

28 October 1802, Palermo, Sicily

Once more, Courtney saw the *Lysander* into the harbour at Palermo. Since the busy port and the heights of Monte Pellegrino had entered his spyglass, he had been scanning the masts and hulls, trying to identify Captain Kelly's *Franklin*. With Sir Rodney's blessing, he had a scheme: one that would be made easier by knowing everything that Captain Kelly or another American officer knew.

However, the brig was not amongst the vessels he scoured. Courtney drummed his fingers on the gunwale, frustration coalescing inside of him. 'I shall have to go ashore,' he said to the officers around him: the officers that now only counted Lieutenant Godfrey, Smythe and Dr Faulkner amongst their number. The rest had been cut down by injury and trial. 'There are other ships of the US Navy in the harbour. One of them must know about these Tripolitan pirates.'

'The American consul did not,' Smythe ventured.

'The American consul has not been sailing these waters for the past months.' Courtney knew it sounded desperate. It *was* desperate. But it was the best chance he had.

With Sir Rodney at his side, he left the *Lysander* and delved into Palermo's streets. A crowd had gathered near the harbour, fed by a steady stream of people stopping to mutter and stare. Courtney looked that way as curious voices rose. The growing noise was broken by the appearance of uniformed soldiers, hurrying through the mass and forcing men, women and children to stand aside.

'What is happening there?' Courtney asked Sir Rodney, who had stopped as well. Together, they followed the soldiers and eased their way back to the harbourside. A few men had turned their backs, expressions ashen. One woman had her face buried in her companion's shoulder, and another covered their child's eyes.

Sir Rodney spoke to one of the soldiers in Italian. But Courtney did not have to wait to hear a response.

Along the stony shore, humps of fabric bobbed in the waters like abandoned crab pots. He could see tangled masses of floating hair and amidst the scrappy material, flesh of many colours, but all mottled and bloated. The corpses beat against the harbour, both land and sea seeming to reject them. Courtney could not tell the sex of any of them. His stomach churned.

'My God,' Sir Rodney whispered. 'Who are these people?'

One of the soldiers said something to him. He nodded sombrely.

'They believe they have been heaved overboard by pirates,' Sir Rodney translated for Courtney. 'Many others have washed ashore here and elsewhere on the island.'

'God have mercy,' Courtney breathed. He had seen similar things in the Caribbean, slaves thrown into the waves from the ships that crossed the Atlantic from Africa. It was the ugliest of human suffering. 'Come. I can't look at this.'

Sir Rodney seemed equally glad to be away. They left the harbour and its wretched sights and walked up into the city. Away from the shore, market day had packed every available space with stalls and barrows. Courtney looked around at the crates of vegetables and fruit and fish and spices, breathing in the chaotic smells and trying to forget what he had seen. Men and women of every race and colour braved the crush to sell their wares. In his uniform of the King's Navy, Courtney knew he stood out and with every step, another hopeful trader would try and barter with him. He declined hats and potatoes and barrels and cloth, easing his way past all manner of human and animal obstacles. Even at its most heaving, Ryde's market had never been like this.

'There are sailors ahead,' Sir Rodney said. Courtney turned around to him as he pointed towards a group of men who Courtney immediately recognised as seafolk. It was a hard thing to disguise, no matter the nationality: weathered skin and long plaited hair, loose trousers and tattoos on their arms. Courtney squeezed his way through in their direction and immediately saw their heads snap up. They leant to whisper to each other and slowly started to back away through the crowd.

'Have we offended them?' Sir Rodney asked.

'No,' Courtney sighed. 'They're Americans and I'm a Royal Navy lieutenant. I'm the kind of officer who would press-gang them if the time demanded it. I've had trouble with press-ganged Americans before.'

Fortunately, the men could not seem to decide whether to run or not. In the throng, it would have been an impossibility anyway. Courtney managed to reach them with only a single distraction from a lad selling cod. All three of them eyed him suspiciously and the man behind the nearest stall made a visible wince, expecting trouble. Plastering a smile on his face, Courtney turned to him. An assortment of cloths and items of clothing decorated the bench.

'What took your eye, gentlemen?' he asked, knowing he was about to be robbed of his last pennies.

The Americans looked at each other and then him, perhaps sizing him and his motives up. At last, one cleared his throat. 'The stockings, sir,' a black-haired young man said. 'For my girl back in Boston.'

'These?' Courtney asked, signing to the worsted pair.

'Those, sir,' the sailor replied and waved to the embroidered set beside the simple ones. Courtney should have known. At least it was not the silken pair next to them.

Pointing to the stockings, he handed over five shillings to the elderly Italian stallholder. He nodded and, payment made, did not seem to anticipate trouble any longer.

'My name is Lieutenant Courtney of the King's Navy,' Courtney then said. 'I am searching for the *Franklin* of the US Navy, Captain Kelly. I know that she made berth here a matter of weeks ago.'

The black-haired sailor nodded. 'We know of her, sir. Saw her come into the harbour.'

Hope sparked in Courtney. 'Recently?'

'A few days past. Beaten to a pulp, she was.'

That hope fizzled out. 'Do you know what happened to her?'

'Masts all cock-a-bill, sails all dog-eared. There's only one enemy who'd take on the US Navy in these waters.'

Courtney glanced at Sir Rodney. He nodded, the same thoughts in his head too. 'Is she still in Palermo?'

'Brought in for some serious repairs, sir. She'll have to be careened right over and put back together something fierce.'

'And her captain? Do you know where he is? Or any of her officers?'

'In the hospital, sir. His arm was hanging off as much as the damned spars.'

Good God, Courtney thought. This one rogue pirate ship had left a trail of utter destruction in its wake, wrecked ships, dead sailors, drowned victims, captured crews…'Thank you,' he said to the men. 'You've been a great help. I hope your girl likes her present when you return home.'

The sailor smiled. 'Thank you for the gift, sir,' he said.

Sir Rodney hurried alongside Courtney as they made their way out of the marketplace. 'You have a way with the common sailor,' he said.

'I was a common sailor once.' Courtney did not wait for Sir Rodney's reaction. 'More bad news with the *Franklin*. We'll go to the hospital and try to find Captain Kelly.'

If he's still alive, he did not say.

'And I shall visit my brother,' Sir Rodney said.

If he's still alive, Courtney thought again.

The hospital did not sit far away from the harbour. It fared a little better than other such establishments Courtney had been to. Naval hospitals, outside of Haslar, could be places rife with more than just the diseases of the patients. He had had little faith in the wards in the Caribbean, where the surgeons accepted they could do nothing for their charges – before the sick were entirely condemned. Yellow fever had shaken every man, from ordinary seaman to post-captain.

Fortunately, no epidemic gutted the inhabitants of this hospital. Instead, the wounds came from visible sources; Courtney spied naval officers and seamen in the beds, some with their heads wrapped in linen, others sitting up and having their limbs examined. He wondered how many were from the *Franklin*. Looking between the aisles, Courtney finally saw the man who he had spoken to in the harbour weeks before, although this time stripped of the glittering finery of his captain's uniform. Kelly lounged against the thin pillow, eyes closed and cheeks a sickly pale colour. One arm rested on the sheets; the other stopped at the elbow, shirt dangling loosely over his chest.

Courtney removed his hat and thanked the doctor who had directed them to Kelly. He paused at his bedside, feeling regretful that he had to wake him. The poor man had been through hell – but so had many other people, out there in the pirates' clutches.

Carefully, he lowered himself into a chair and cleared his throat. Hesitating, he laid his hand on Kelly's uninjured arm and the captain slowly stirred. His eyes fluttered. His mouth twitched. Courtney waited as he awoke and groggily took in the sight before him.

'I know you,' Kelly croaked. 'You...'

'Yes, sir. I am Lieutenant Courtney of the *Lysander*. We met not long ago.'

Kelly tried to sit up. Courtney helped him and poured him a glass of water from the carafe at his bedside. The captain started to raise his amputated arm, realised, and used the other. Sipping delicately, he seemed to slowly regain his bearings. 'I remember,' he said through a clearer throat. 'We walked along the harbour and you asked me about a French ship. We spoke of...of pirates.'

'That's correct.'

'Those pirates,' Kelly moaned and winced.

'I hope you will recover, Captain,' Courtney said. 'That your injuries are not too...awful.'

'Aside from a missing arm?' But admirably, Kelly tried to smile. 'It could have been far worse. Fortunately, I am left-handed. But I fell and crushed this right side. Broken bones are not so easy to cut off.'

'I'm sorry, sir.'

Kelly shook his head. 'You did not come all this way to pity me, Lieutenant. You have not found your French ship yet.'

'No, sir.'

'I saw the *Fantôme*...again with the corsair. She still sails with the pirates, perhaps they want to use her start building a fleet of their own. It is why I went after them. I knew there were captured men there. And we had recently seen people in the waves, heaved overboard. They could have only been from that ship.'

Courtney's stomach swooped. By telling him of the *Fantôme* and her crew, he had signed the warrant for the destruction of the *Franklin* and for Kelly's pain. 'You did a very kind thing, Captain.'

'Kind?' Kelly chuckled and then winced again, holding his side. 'I would not have been kind if I had captured those bastards.'

Courtney smiled. 'That is what I intend to do, sir. If you have any further information about their whereabouts, I would be very grateful. We have been to Tripoli on a failed diplomatic mission. But I do not intend to leave the Mediterranean until those pirates hang.'

He was surprised at the venom which crept into his voice. But every word was true. He had watched two innocent men hang and waited around whilst his friends and other good people were kidnapped. If Nightingale had been harmed, he would personally tie the hangman's nooses himself.

Kelly nodded. 'I can do better than give you their whereabouts, Lieutenant. I can give you the name of the ship and the place I believe that they make berth.'

Courtney sat up straighter. Out of the corner of his eye, he saw Sir Rodney do the same. 'You know of it?' he asked.

'I do. The ship is the *Barbarossa*. And as for the berth site, I can make a very good guess, based on what I have seen of their movements and my knowledge of the Tyrrhenian Sea. As they have been denied safe harbour elsewhere, I believe they are desperate for supplies. That is why they have been killing their captives, throwing them overboard. Their only use now is about the ship or at the oars and those that cannot serve...'

Courtney filled in the details. 'Please,' he said. 'Tell us your thoughts.'

'I believe,' Kelly said, 'they make berth on one of the Aeolian Islands, just north of Sicily. Somewhere little populated, rugged and dangerous to approach. There are penal colonies on some of the islands and I have wondered if the pirates have supplemented their crew with them.'

The islands were but a half-day's journey, if the weather was favourable. 'We shall search there,' Courtney said. 'I have a plan to deal with them.'

Sir Rodney glanced at him. Courtney had not decided everything about his scheme yet, nor revealed any ideas to Sir Rodney, but the man had trusted his judgement. He would tell him the way they would act when reaching the islands, when he saw the lay of the land and the surrounding seas. For Courtney's ideas, he knew the isolated, craggy shores would fare well.

'I hope you do deal with them, Lieutenant,' Kelly said. 'Even if it will not make my arm sprout back, it would allow me to rest easier. They are a scourge to many people, not only our sailors but all races and all creeds. They make no discrimination.'

As they left poor Captain Kelly, Courtney thought about the strange winds of fate that had led to this moment. Peace still nominally covered Europe but he and the Lysanders fought in the cracks. They had united with a French ship and now travelled to help rescue her. They had encountered a vessel from America – another nation who Britain looked upon with unease. Familiar enemies were not familiar anymore, and the true foes were those Courtney could not see or understand.

Before returning to the *Lysander*, there was one other man to visit. Since their last time ashore in Palermo, Captain Bryant had been moved from the heart of the hospital. Sir Rodney had sent a message ahead and Parker, Bryant's steward, answered. He guided them through the ancient streets until arriving at a small garden in the shadow of a convent. Orange trees surrounded the shady area, throwing dappled light upon a number of patients who took the fresh air, far cleaner here than at the harbour's edge. Courtney caught sight of Bryant, sat in a wheeled chair, apart from the others. He wanted to wait but Sir Rodney urged him forward.

Bryant did not turn until his brother approached and laid a hand on the back of his chair. Then, slowly, he angled himself and revealed the extent of his physical injuries: the bandages still wrapped about his forehead, shielding a patchwork of scars, and his hair shaved to reveal a pink, mottled scalp. Courtney, looking him over, knew that would not be the fullness of it. His wounds would stretch deep, perhaps for the rest of his life.

'Hullo, Jerome,' Sir Rodney said. 'It is good to see you again.'

Bryant did not reply. His eyes roved to Courtney and Courtney noticed how one of them did not focus on him. Courtney, speechless, removed his hat.

'I did not think you would visit me,' Bryant said slowly. 'You have more important tasks.'

'Nonsense. I could not come to Palermo without checking that you were well. I received your notes.'

'My notes?' Bryant gave a strange, strangled chuckle and lifted a hand. It shook with a dreadful palsy. 'My dictated notes. I cannot write. I doubt I ever shall again.'

'You shall,' Courtney said suddenly, and wondered why he did. He could not bear the sight of Bryant, but not for the same reasons he might once have. He had wished the man had not captained this voyage, yet this was not the way he wanted his absence to be completed.

'I cannot walk or write or see out of this eye,' Bryant said. 'Parker has turned into my nursemaid.'

Parker, standing to the side, bowed his head.

'But you live, still,' Sir Rodney insisted. 'We must give thanks to that.'

Bryant turned away. 'The *Lysander*,' he intoned slowly. 'Where is she?'

'Your ship is in safe hands, brother. We have come from Gibraltar and are to take the fight to the fiends who have harassed her and her crew.'

'Good.'

Silence fell. Another sailor wandered past, leaning upon the stump of a crutch. Bryant's eyes followed him and to Courtney's surprise, he saw them fill with tears. He blinked, but they fell anyway. Sir Rodney laid a gentle hand on his brother's shoulder and Courtney wondered if he should step back. He made the move to, but Bryant stopped him with a curt, 'Lieutenant.'

Courtney swallowed. 'Yes, sir.'

'You,' he managed, and Courtney waited for the acerbic comment. It did not come. 'You saved the *Lysander* in the storm. You…discovered the truth about the *Loyal*.'

'I did, sir.'

'You chose to help those…men from the *Loyal* once you…knew the *Lysander* was safe. I have been thinking about it.'

Courtney looked to Sir Rodney who also did not seem to be following.

'You did the same with the *Meridian*,' Captain Bryant finished. 'When she grounded on the sandbar. I do not remember all now…but I remember that.'

'I…' Courtney did not know what to say. 'I did not want those men to drown, sir. Either time. I am sorry if I…'

'An apology? From your own lips, Lieutenant Courtney?' Another pained laugh emerged from Captain Bryant. He struggled to turn his head again and fixed Courtney with his moist eyes. Courtney looked down at him, barely breathing. 'You did well, Lieutenant. I shall not command soon, if ever. The *Lysander*… She is your ship now.'

Courtney felt a surge of emotion. He was not sure which one it was, but it bubbled up in him and threatened to overspill. He forced a small smile onto his mouth and nodded. 'Thank you, sir. I will look after her.'

When they left Bryant, Courtney could sense something different inside of himself. He did not know how to interpret it until they came within view of the *Lysander*. She, bobbing in the water with her sails furled, could not truly be his. She was a frigate and he was not a captain with his name posted in the Gazette. But Courtney had always performed in the margins, in the grey waters between tides. She, and all her men, depended upon him, and he depended upon her and them. For the first time, despite having had temporary command before, he felt the weight of it. It would be his plan which saved, or condemned, the lost men and this very ship.

And, looking upon her with Captain Bryant's blessing still fresh, he knew what he would do.

Chapter Twenty-Eight: Heeling Over

30 October 1802, off Stromboli

To windward, the forbidding island sat like an omen. Perilous, jagged cliffs, almost sheer in places, rose from the rolling waters. On one side, fragments of green scattered the land but as the *Lysander* rounded the rock, topsails furled in respect of the danger, the fertility was drowned by a black, flat slope. Tendrils of white smoke billowed down the incline, belched from a crater at the summit of the conical mound. For hours, Courtney had been able to smell the foul gases and here, in the shadow of the volcano, it grew difficult to draw a breath without wincing.

He must be mad to approach. But this was the place Captain Kelly had suggested the *Barbarossa* made berth. It made sense: the terrible face of Stromboli and its unforgiving shoreline would ward off any sensible seaman. And, as much as he realised it would make his men balk, Courtney knew it was the perfect location for his scheme.

'This is a wretched place,' Sir Rodney said, holding a handkerchief to his mouth. 'I shall be glad when this is over. I do hope you know what you are doing.'

Courtney could feel Sir Rodney's faith in him waning. But he put it to the test in the great cabin. With the *Franklin* laid up in Palermo's harbour for repairs, Kelly had graciously handed his charts of the Aeolian Islands to Courtney under the condition that he return them and make no mention of it to the US Navy. Now, Courtney silently thanked the man, looking over the new, detailed drawings. He pointed to Stromboli, the northernmost of the isles, and waited as Smythe and Godfrey leant closer.

'This,' he said, 'is where we shall halt.'

They stared from the inked northern coast of Stromboli and up to Courtney. Disbelief echoed in both of their faces.

'The small sea stack here,' Courtney continued, referring to the one they had seen while circumnavigating the island, 'is a short distance from the main island. It is there I propose we lay our trap.'

Sir Rodney had put the responsibility for this final plan in his lap. Courtney knew it hinged on no traditional tactics but on ruse and pretence. The *Barbarossa* obeyed no rules and so Courtney must meet fire with fire.

'You gentlemen remember the sorry state of the *Loyal* on the rocks. Dismasted, she veered onto them and sank. Do you also remember the *Meridian*?'

Smythe frowned, obviously thinking back to the Caribbean and their first encounter with Captain Bryant. Lieutenant Godfrey had been on the *Meridian* herself when she had grounded. He made the connection first and opened his mouth to argue, to question, Courtney did not know. He held up a hand to stop him.

'The *Barbarossa* has already wrecked two ships that we are aware of: the *Loyal* and the *Franklin*, almost. She has captured the *Fantôme* to possibly form a new fleet. She may very well desire another vessel. We shall make her think that she will have one.' Courtney tapped the small dot of the volcanic stack. 'I am suggesting we approach this. Put the islet to windward, near it, and heel the *Lysander* over as far as we dare. We shall move ballast, we shall shore her to the rocks or to the boats if we must, and we shall give her the appearance of being in grave danger. It will be a sight the *Barbarossa* could not resist.'

Beside Smythe and Godfrey, Sir Rodney shifted. Courtney wondered if he regretted giving him the duty of this task. 'A *ruse de guerre*,' he said. 'Though we are not at war.'

'You plan to heel her over in deep water,' Smythe said. 'A parliament heel. That is what the *Royal George* was attempting when she sank in Spithead.'

'Yes,' Courtney replied, knowing there was no use in denying it. 'It will be dangerous. But this ship is capable of it. She is not overloaded, as the *Royal George* was, and as soon as we are able, we shall right her.'

'How do you propose to do that, Lieutenant?' Sir Rodney asked.

Courtney smiled thinly. 'By quickly shifting her balance. We strike the shores, drop anchor from her raised side and when she finds her keel, throw her upright. Ideally, careening and refloating a vessel is a slow process. But ships that are grounded can be saved. We simply have to speed the procedure.'

'Simply,' Sir Rodney repeated incredulously.

'We will be a prime target for the *Barbarossa*,' Godfrey said. 'Sitting there for her to fire upon.'

'Yes,' Courtney agreed. 'I know that this will be dangerous. But if we are to save those left on the *Fantôme* and those who have been captured, we must think in the way of the pirates – draw the *Barbarossa* in close, and then unleash a full broadside across her decks.'

'Our sailors, and the French sailors, not to mention other captives, may be on there,' Smythe added.

Courtney's mind raced back to Captain Robinson, cut down by cannonfire from the *Cygne*. A full broadside at such close range would be devastating to the *Barbarossa* and would slash through the decks like a scythe. 'They may be, or they may still be on the *Fantôme*,' Courtney said. 'There is a possibility that they will be working the *Barbarossa*, certainly if she has oars, as Captain Kelly suggested. Our gun crews shall aim at the *Barbarossa*'s masts and spars to try and spare the prisoners. And, Mr Smythe, we have our signal flags, yes?'

'Yes, sir.' Smythe was still in the process of learning his signals, something Courtney had been trying to teach him since the beginning of the voyage.

'Do you think you remember the flag combination for "Disguise", Mr Smythe?'

Smythe was silent for a while, and then smiled and nodded. 'Yes, sir.'

'We shall run that up, and unless the pirates have an extensive knowledge of Howe and Popham's flag signals, we should be able to warn the English officers aboard while keeping our situation secret from the *Barbarossa*.'

The bulk of the plan laid out, Courtney entered into the detail with his officers and then his men. Although Sir Rodney had prevented him from telling them the entire truth, he knew some would have guessed. They had not begun this voyage as the strongest of crews, but throughout the journey from Palermo to the Aeolian Islands, Courtney had drilled them at the guns, over and over, never matter about wasted powder anymore. He had worked the cannons with them and, when directing them in the tops and amongst the sails, was able to reduce the number of orders given. They knew the *Lysander* now, having sailed back and forth over the Mediterranean in her, and his faith had grown and grown.

It was testament to their tenacity that they worked with him without complaint or comment. They were united by this scheme, no matter their background or their rank. A desire to save their fellow men spurred them on, from topman to waister to officer. For the first time, Courtney felt he truly belonged on the *Lysander*, performing in a way he knew and had confidence in. He worked alongside the hands – men from poor families, men from the streets, men running from home – as well as Smythe, the son of a distinguished officer, moving through the accepted hierarchy from midshipman to eventual lieutenant.

Here, amongst the ship, the sea, and this troubled task, they were as one.

The light of the sky dimmed, the watches changed and the list of tasks ran on and on. Courtney spent the last dog watch in the hold, shifting the *Lysander*'s ballast with Obi and the other strongest in the crew. Inch by inch, he had felt her soul protest. Already, her decks listed to starboard and he could feel the incline as he walked from one side of the ship to the other. It was a matter of balance: too far and she would truly careen onto the rocks, and it would be the devil to right her again.

Climbing to the gundeck, he walked along the line of the great guns and inspected each and every one. They had been run out, both in anticipation of battle and to keep them lashed to the ringbolts above each porthole. If one of them came loose, it could break through the hull and send the sea rushing in. Satisfied the cannons were ready, he examined the arms chests and had grapnels, pikes, boarding axes and hand grenades in positions ready to be grabbed when the battle began. A chance remained that they might have to board the *Barbarossa*.

Courtney had not yet ordered for the preparations that would come during the beat to quarters. There was no use in it until the *Barbarossa* was sighted. Then, it would have to be done in the deathliest of silences.

With luck, she would see what they wanted her to see: a ship, in danger of splitting herself on the rocks, signalling for aid.

Courtney glanced to the sky as he ascended onto the main deck. Night encroached and the sun teetered on the horizon. The masts, tilting to starboard, crossed the darkening heavens. Stars already glimmered, making some of the tension loosen in Courtney's chest.

There was little wind and the clear skies assured no heavy weather. That, he tried to convince himself, would work to their advantage.

Over the side, the *Lysander*'s boats bobbed in the calm waters, hidden from sight. Stays attached the sixth-rate to surreptitious moorings upon them and on the stack, acting as secondary standing rigging. The starboard bower anchor kept the ship further tethered. Courtney felt for the poor ship, dragged around and pushed into positions she should never have been. With luck, it would not be for long.

By the taffrail, Smythe knelt. The flag locker was opened and the canvas spread across the deck. Courtney joined him, making no comment as he sifted through the signal flags to find the correct ones. At last, he paused, the three required signal flags before him. He glanced up at Courtney for approval and Courtney smiled. 'Have them run up, Mr Smythe,' he said. 'There will be English officers who understand what we're about.'

By the time the signal flags were drooping from their lines, the lanterns at the *Lysander*'s stern had been lit. Courtney, for the first time, felt a pang of hunger, pressed down so far by the events of the day. He cast a look to the horizon, found it empty. Knowing that there was little more he could do than wait, he descended below.

—

'Lieutenant Courtney!'

The shout broke through the haze. Courtney jerked and opened his eyes to the empty gunroom. A plate of cold meat sat before him, the result of the galley fires long being doused. He had been resting on his hand, catching a few moments of sleep with the skill of a sailor who could nap anywhere. He had not anticipated being awoken so soon.

'Lieutenant Courtney!'

Smythe rushed into the gunroom, almost barrelling into the table. It must have still been his watch. Courtney blinked, glad he had not vanished for too long.

'What is it, Mr Smythe?' he asked, not daring to assume.

'Them, sir. Or, it may be them. Sails have been spotted from the masthead. Two ships.'

Courtney jumped to his feet. He grabbed for his sword, reconsidered, and left it to the side. Following Smythe up to the main deck, he immediately looked to the horizon. He could see no flash of white there so hurried to the shrouds, climbing them without a second thought. From there, the span of the sea opened up a little more, allowing him a view through the clear night. The stars and moon streamed down upon the water, illuminating a trail into the distance. Two dots interrupted that white path. Fumbling with his spyglass, he could make out three masts on one of them, two on the other. The three-master had a French design, that much he could tell. She was alarmingly familiar.

Courtney scrambled back down the rigging to the deck. Smythe waited, face pale in the moonlight.

'I would say it is her,' Courtney said, trying to hide his tension. 'Mr Smythe, I want you to spread the word to beat to quarters. Quietly, now.'

'Yes, sir.'

With a hasty salute, Smythe disappeared below. Partitions would be struck down, powder hurried to the guns, each man to his assigned station. Courtney would not join them. He would remain on deck, watching for the *Barbarossa* and how she would behave. Now, he walked to the stern and the bright lanterns. If the *Lysander* had seen the *Barbarossa* then the *Barbarossa* would have seen them, but to be certain, Courtney doused the lantern, relit it. It flickered across the dark waters, a flashing beacon the pirates would not ignore.

It was also a signal for the men still left on deck. They could not behave as sailors with all under control. Those upon the yards began to scamper through the rigging, as if preparing to reef or set the canvas. At the starboard side, lines were cast out into the sea, and in the chains, the log was thrown. No action was necessary; Courtney knew the depth of the water, the proximity to the rocks, the exact trim of the yards and sails – but the *Barbarossa* would not realise that.

Across the sea, he watched her approach. Behind, the *Fantôme* trailed her. There was no doubt now. He recognised the vessel which they had first seen off Brest, saluting the *Lysander*. The Fantômes would also recognise the *Lysander* and if they didn't, Courtney had presented the stern to the incoming vessels. Her lettering displayed proudly. God, he hoped the men were still there. For a moment, they would be discouraged, perhaps agonised by the *Lysander*'s situation, another potential victim of the *Barbarossa*. *Read the signal*, Courtney begged. *Read it and brace yourselves.*

Time stretched. Having lost his uniform coat on the *Loyal*, Courtney had taken to wearing his shirt without waistcoat or trimmings on deck. He waved his arms in the air, hoping the white material was vivid enough. He stood at the taffrail, climbing half onto the gunwale to ensure the *Barbarossa* and her men saw him. They neared to leeward of the *Lysander*: a bad position for a fight, but Courtney would not be obeying the rules and tactics of naval engagements he had studied his entire career. The *Barbarossa*, her canvas furled cautiously, sailed wide of the rocks. Courtney willed her to come closer.

Both of them, he knew, played a game of disguises. One, pretending she was approaching to rescue the stranded men. The other, pretending she was wounded to lure the predator.

At last, he could see the men on the deck. He could not see any uniforms of either the British or French navies. Perhaps they were below, hiding by the loaded guns, as Courtney's own men were. Or perhaps they still served on the *Fantôme*. The French frigate gave a wide berth to both the *Lysander* and the *Barbarossa*. Far from danger, but near enough to spring to action if bid.

He searched the helm and the quarterdeck for sight of the pirate captain. He did not know who he expected to see. Ransome, the mutinous *Ulysses* leader, had been, under the laws of the Royal Navy, a pirate, and so had Jane been at one point. Courtney could see no man who stood out amongst the crew.

His attention was lured away by the *Barbarossa* heaving-to two cables' lengths from the *Lysander*. Courtney observed her in the moonlight. She was a large polacre with two masts square-rigged and a lateen carried on the mizzen: big enough to be intimidating but nimble and weatherly with that mixed rig. Still, he could not see any reason for her success in that canvas; many other corsairs sailed similar vessels. As they stared at each other in silence, he ran his eyes over her decks. The portholes remained shut but he could make out swivel guns mounted in the bows and stern. They had been trained towards the *Lysander*, but no man stood by them, yet.

Courtney waited. Oars emerged from the *Barbarossa* and under one bank, she began to manoeuvre closer to the *Lysander*. The distance closed and Courtney calculated. He felt the moment she came within crippling range of the *Lysander*. If they decided, the *Barbarossa* could open fire on the *Lysander* as easily as the *Lysander* could fire upon them.

He hoped they would see her as a prize, an addition to their building fleet. Confirming it, he saw boats being lowered: two of them, manned by five sailors. Again, he recognised no uniform but a mix of European and African dress. A pirate crew, as with the Royal Navy, was a crew of few borders.

Upon the *Lysander's* rigging, his men cheered. Courtney had almost forgotten he had ordered that, a false joy of rescue. Men swept their hats in the air, bidding the Barbarossas closer. They must have thought the Lysanders were a stupid lot, willing a piratical horde on.

Courtney, stripped of any trappings of an officer, hurried to the side. In the starlight, he could see the glint of weaponry upon the pirates' belts. Closer up, he could not have distinguished them from many other crews he had served in and commanded. An uncanny feeling shivered through him.

'Sirs,' he said, ignoring the threatening thrum in the air and smiling. 'We feared we were doomed. Three nights and three days we have been impaled on the rocks. In sight of land but with nothing to do but bail out the ship and try and refloat on each kind tide. Yes, yes, come aboard.'

Courtney spoke loudly, ensuring the men in the gun deck below heard. They must have also heard the beat of the Barbarossas' boots upon the *Lysander's* flank. The first man reached the deck, a sailor wearing similar wear to his own men. Others followed until the ten of them were aboard. None of them made any efforts to hide their arms, pistols strapped across their chests and rapiers at their sides. In his shirt and breeches Courtney felt naked, but he reminded himself of the twenty-four nine-pounders underneath his feet.

'We have patched the hole in her side as best we can,' he said. 'But she still lists over. We have attempted to kedge and warp her but perhaps with the aid of another ship—'

The mouth of a flintlock appeared between Courtney's eyes. His heart jumped. For a second, he anticipated the blast. Not entirely acting, he held up his hands.

'I only ask for aid,' he forced himself to say, realising the madness of this scheme. 'The ship is still damaged.'

'Below,' the man said in English. Courtney recognised a Hull accent. He had not anticipated that. But it did not mean disaster; regular sailors were not expected to know signal flags, and not the updated ones

Courtney had used. These men might not even be Royal Navy; perhaps they were merchant sailors. But how were they here? He barely had time to think before the man continued, 'We will repair her.'

'Come now. She is my ship.'

'Below,' he repeated. 'We are taking her.'

Above the boarders, the *Lysander* men had descended from the yards and waited in the tops and shrouds. They too had armed themselves, hiding dirks and daggers that Courtney could see they now reached for. He kept his hands up, feeling them tremble. Knowing he had no choice, he nodded and began to walk towards the hatch down. The pirate with the flintlock guided him with the motions of his gun. One foot behind the other, Courtney stepped backwards. He dared to look out of the corner of his eye to the waiting *Barbarossa*. Had she approached closer during their talk? He thought she had, only a few yards perhaps, but near enough to threaten.

Near enough to broadside.

Courtney reached the hatch. The pirate waved the flintlock at him, urging him to descend. 'I am going,' Courtney insisted. 'I am going.'

He took one more step. The next, he knew, could result in a hole being blown in his head. But he thought of Nightingale, thought of the imprisoned men, thought of Captain Kelly, thought of the victims who had been washed ashore, and with all his might, screamed:

'Hands to stations! Loose her! And, fire all!'

Chapter Twenty-Nine: Fire with Fire

Ropes lashed the air as the stays heeling the *Lysander* over were struck. The starboard anchor cables were slipped whilst the larboard bower anchor dropped. Courtney heard the cables running out amid the sudden clamour. Upon the deck, men rushed to the braces, yanking the *Lysander's* yards around so the wind eased her way up. She lurched back onto her keel with a violence that threw nearly every standing man off his feet.

Courtney expected it. He used the pirate's shock and dashed into him, shoving him away and wrenching the flintlock from his hand. His Lysanders leapt from aloft and onto the stricken boarders, pummelling them with axes and hammers. Feeling the balance of the *Lysander* return and then teeter again as she listed to lee, he cried, 'Fire all!' once more.

The shudder of twelve guns firing simultaneously ripped through the night. Courtney saw the flash of fire erupt from the *Lysander's* side and then a haze of smoke obscured the deck. His ears rang but even through that, he heard the shots smashing into timber. He struggled to his feet and beat away the pirates who had swarmed him and the men. They tried to break off to race for the gundeck before another salvo could be fired, but Courtney and the Lysanders held them back.

He stared across to the *Barbarossa*, willing the smoke to clear. He tasted the gunpowder and the iron tang of his own fear. Slowly, the shadow of the polacre reappeared. Chunks had been taken out of her gunwales. Her mizzen hung dangerously. Rigging cascaded in tangles. Their trajectory had avoided the mass of the hull – and now, the *Barbarossa's* guns appeared: swivels, long nines and upon the squat quarterdeck...

'Carronades!' Courtney shouted. 'They have carronades!'

The *Barbarossa* could smash a ship apart if she approached close enough. A blinding crash echoed from her flank and almost one hundred pounds of metal flew across the water. Courtney threw himself to the deck and felt the barrage sear above his head, crunching through the yards. The *Lysander* still lurched and bobbed in her dramatic manoeuvre; it was that which saved her hull from a terrible beating. He looked up as soon as he was able. The fore topmast veered to the side but held in the standing rigging.

'Fire!' he cried down to Smythe. 'Lay aloft, men!'

With orders to loose all available canvas, from mizzen t'gallant to fore course, the *Lysander* slipped her larboard anchor cables and strained against the dull wind to move from the rocks. Her guns roared again, trajectories lowered to aim for the *Barbarossa*'s hull. Courtney feared getting too close to her. Those carronades could easily sweep hell across her decks. But he could not stay still and allow the *Barbarossa* to pummel the *Lysander* against the stack. This would be a running battle.

The *Lysander*'s bows aimed for the open sea. Courtney watched the *Barbarossa* follow. Her part-lateen rig allowed her to manipulate the wind far closer than the *Lysander* could and she easily rounded the rocks, bow guns trained upon the *Lysander*'s stern. With a heave on the braces, the little frigate avoided the risk of a raking fire. She could not turn enough for a full broadside but the aftmost cannons spat violently, raining balls about the *Barbarossa*'s head.

The pirates had doused their lanterns and it was only by starlight that Courtney saw her predatory form. He could no longer find the *Fantôme*, somewhere on the dark horizon. Calculations ran through his head. If she was to engage, the *Lysander* could not match her firepower or weight. He could only pray that the *Barbarossa*'s captain wanted her unscarred and unharmed for the sake of his fleet.

Even with all sails set, the *Lysander* struggled to outrun the *Barbarossa*. The waters between them narrowed, illuminated by garish slashes of cannonfire. Courtney heard the boom and whistle of them a fraction of a second before he felt the impact: blasting water up the *Lysander*'s timbers, making her tremble with the near-misses. Her carronades would have a range of a few hundred yards; as soon as she could use them, she would. But she was not the only ship to house carronades. The *Lysander* carried them too. How the devil had these pirates obtained carronades?

Courtney had no time to muse on that. The *Lysander*, splitting through the night-time sea, still sailed within plain sight of Stromboli.

The dark form of the volcano loomed over the ships, wreathed in white smoke, as if in mimicry of the battle. As Courtney glanced to it, judging their distance, he noticed a flash of fire upon her conical peak. Spitting flames fizzled out of her crater.

A crash below tore him back to the *Lysander*. The shatter of broken glass told him that the recently patched windows had smashed again. Cries resounded from the gun deck, the shout of Smythe and Godfrey at both batteries. Courtney, with a look behind to the *Barbarossa*, hurried to the hatchway. In the gloom, lanterns guttered, their light shining off the bare skin of the sweat-soaked crew. A ball had split one of the trusses, leaving a carpet of splinters. Gunmetal and smoke invaded Courtney's lungs as he called for Smythe. The boy ran to him, streaked with powder.

'It won't be long until she overhauls us,' Courtney said, lowering his voice. The preparation of guns and shot muffled him anyway. 'They are armed with carronades. But once they are within range, I shall utilise ours also. It'll be hot work, but our first broadside did some damage.'

Less than he would have liked, but Courtney would not say that to Smythe. His eyes had already widened at the prospect of carronades.

'Where is the *Fantôme*, sir?' the midshipman asked.

'Not present,' Courtney replied, only hoping she was safe as she could be.

In the time it had taken him to speak to Smythe, the *Barbarossa* had gained on their stern, sailing two points on the starboard quarter. Courtney could see the men aloft in her yards and the ripped snarl of her shrouds. Glints of her bow guns shone in the rippling moonlight, interspersed with an array of weaponry and grapnels brought to the deck. There was no doubt: the pirates planned to board the *Lysander* and take her as a prize. Courtney would die before he allowed this English frigate to turn pirate, and terrorise the Mediterranean to take slaves and hostages.

Damn it, Courtney thought, there was only one thing for it.

'Lieutenant Godfrey!' he shouted again through the hatchway. The lieutenant hurried to him, bleeding from a wound on his scalp. 'You're wounded,' Courtney said, shocked at the sudden sight of blood under his command.

'It is nothing, sir.'

'Assemble a party of men,' Courtney urged, no time for more. 'I want Obi, the gunner's crew and men from the afterguard. I am going to board the *Barbarossa*. She must be taken. Incapacitated. We will not fall to her.'

Fetching his sword, flintlock pistol and two hand grenades, he then gathered Sergeant Dawes and the marines who had been helping at the guns. Godfrey arrived within minutes, leading a band of Lysanders including Obi. By the time he appeared, Courtney had gathered men to work the carronades, which, across on the *Barbarossa*, were also gaping at the *Lysander*. Remembering their drills, they laboured like devils to ram the charge and hefty shot home, run the squat guns out, and prime them. Courtney toiled with them, grasping the ropes to heave the carronade forward and finding its elevation. It was all achieved in a matter of minutes, a furious race against the Barbarossas.

Heart thudding, Courtney looked to the other gun crew, saw they were prepared, and shouted, 'Fire!'

The savage guns roared into life. Courtney felt the impact from the *Barbarossa* as if into his own abdomen. His legs wobbled and he groped for the belaying pins to stop his fall. The *Lysander*'s hull groaned brokenly but across the water, the *Barbarossa* teetered too. Their fire from the carronades and the great guns had struck true, gouging cavities above the polacre's waterline and turning over two of her gun carriages. One hung out of the porthole and through the gap, Courtney finally saw what he had been waiting for: there were men imprisoned below, pressed together in the slaughterhouse. He prayed his own fire had not harmed them. He could have sworn he saw a French uniform, an officer of the *Fantôme*.

It fuelled his desire to take the *Barbarossa*.

'Grapnels and boarding pikes!' he shouted to the Lysanders. 'Prepare to board!'

The two ships sailed on a course destined for collision. Now, the *Barbarossa*'s sails had been drawn in and oars sprouted from her sides. Yards swayed, each roll of the waves moving them closer and closer. It was madness to brave those guns but each vessel played a game of balance. The first throw of the *Lysander*'s grapnels echoed the *Barbarossa*'s. Simultaneously, tethers to lash the ships together flew over the water. Men on either one fought to cut the ropes but their boarding was unavoidable now; one side simply had to win the race.

Courtney looked at the crew awaiting them. He clutched his sword until the whorls of the handle dug into his palm. Sailors across from him had climbed into the tops, balancing out on the yards to make the leap between the lurching ships. Dawes and his marines shot them down. Bodies splashed into the water below.

And then, before a breath could be taken, the hulls bumped together. 'Boarders!' Courtney shouted. 'Away!'

As one, the two crews crowded onto the gunwales. A wave of pirates surged forward, met by the Lysanders. Courtney, still only in his shirt-sleeves, slashed with his blade but the quarters were already too close. He shoved forward, blocking the *Barbarossa*'s boarders with his body. Back and forth, they raged between the ships, rigging tangling above them, timbers scraping. The oars had almost been shipped but a few still sprouted from the *Barbarossa* and, out of the *Lysander*'s portholes, gun crews yanked at them, breaking them in the crush.

The congested mass meant sailors were pressed upon each other, balanced dangerously. One unexpected wave was all they needed. The *Barbarossa* lifted, rolled back and then forward again, enough to destabilise her men. Some fell, bouncing off the blades of the oars.

'Boarders!' Courtney screamed again, but they already pressed forward.

A red haze of marines passed him as he clambered from the *Lysander* and onto the *Barbarossa*. He struck down heavily on the main deck, avoiding a fallen gun carriage. Scrambling up again, the roar of his men engulfed him, streaming at both sides. He shouted with them and ploughed into the pirates at one of the carronades. As his sword opened the man's chest, blood rained down upon the metal. These were British guns, Courtney thought. Few ships other than British vessels carried such armaments.

A blast pulled Courtney's thoughts away. Men on the poop deck had turned the swivel guns inward, cutting into Lysanders and Barbarossas alike. Courtney staggered away from the deafening shot. His ears rang but he still fought, deaf and half-blind in the smoke. In the chaos he found Obi, who was fighting alongside Smythe, shielding the midshipman he had joined the *Lysander* with.

'Below,' he croaked. 'Get below.'

Courtney and Obi struggled their way through to a hatchway where Obi charged into one of the men, armed with a whip, coming up the ladder. He slipped back down, smacking his head on every rung. Courtney glanced at his crumpled body and rushed into the gloom.

The stench immediately hit him. Festering through the smoke and powder and charred wood, cramped, crushed bodies oozed sweat and effluents. His throat tightened. Amidst the cloud of battle, he made out unclothed figures, hunched at the oar banks. White, black and brown skin bled and shimmered. Manacles glinted around their ankles. The only air came from the small gaps for the oars, one of which had been blown open by the *Lysander's* barrage. Splinters covered the deck but miraculously, no one had been hurt other than gashes across limbs and chests.

Courtney thought of Obi beside him. He thought of all that Obi had said, and not said, about his past. He thought of the suffering of these men before him.

'Obi,' Courtney croaked. 'Strike those damn chains off.'

'Yes, sir,' Obi said determinedly and began to squeeze through the tight aisles of slaves. The bloody din still raged above as he and Courtney freed them. They did not thank them, barely spoke at all, but Courtney did not expect it. He encouraged them up on weak limbs, urging the fit ones to arm themselves and join the fight. One bearded man, dressed in a torn and dirty shirt and trousers, grasped his arm as he rose. Courtney tugged at him, thinking he needed support, until he looked into his haggard face.

'Sir William,' he gasped. Nightingale's father-in-law, the very man the *Lysander* and *Fantôme* had been tasked with finding, stared back at him. Courtney did not know who was more shocked.

'Lieutenant Courtney,' he said. 'Hiram said you would find us.'

Courtney braced himself. 'He's well?'

'He is on the *Fantôme*. I have not seen him for days.'

Courtney felt a wave of emotion crest over him. His legs weakened and his heart throbbed, confused between relief and turmoil for Nightingale's ongoing agony. 'I shall find him and the rest of the Fantômes. Arm yourself and get across to the *Lysander*. My crew are going to take this ship.'

'Your crew?'

Courtney gave a strained smile. 'It is a long story to tell.'

With his hand upon Sir William's back, Courtney ascended back to the deck where half of the Lysanders had now swarmed. No pirates remained on the deck of the English frigate. Courtney could see his own men at the swivel guns and the long nines, spiking them and rendering them useless. He ferried Sir William through the crush and directed him across to the relative safety of the *Lysander*. Sir Rodney stood by the helm, flintlock in hand. Courtney waved to him and he came running to support Sir William.

'Sir! Lieutenant Courtney!'

Courtney whirled around at the sound of his name. Amidst the previously manacled men staggering up from below, he caught sight of Godfrey, blackened with smoke and blood, pointing astern. Courtney turned aft and his heart leapt into his throat. Across the sea, lanterns burnt. They trailed a stream of light that reflected off the billowing sails of the *Fantôme*. The ship raced to the engagement. Courtney did not know what side she would fight on.

'Lysanders, to the guns! Obi, the carronades!' he called, aware that it would be an almost impossible task amongst the pirates. He struggled his way through and reached one of the carronades. The metal was searing hot. A pile of shot awaited by the carriage, alongside a powder horn. Like on the *Lysander*, this was an eighteen-pounder. Obi and the same men who had fired the gun on the *Lysander* raced to work it here. They rammed the shot home, ran her out, and waited, barely breathing as the *Fantôme* approached. She came within range but no fire erupted from her flank. He did not want to shoot upon her, not upon a French frigate in a time of peace. Even Sir Rodney could not save him from condemnation then.

And then, at her bows, a man leapt into the air. He frantically waved a handkerchief above the blazing lantern, flashing white in the darkness. Courtney recognised Proulx, the *Fantôme*'s aspirant. Relief flooded him.

A relief that lasted a mere two seconds before Proulx staggered and collapsed against the gunwales. Blood sprayed on the timbers as he plummeted into the sea.

Unknown men hurried upon the *Fantôme*'s deck. Courtney could only stare whilst they grappled with the Fantômes who trailed them. He turned to Godfrey. 'The *Fantôme* is not safe yet,' he said, as if the man needed telling. 'We have to secure her too.'

Godfrey nodded.

'Grapnels and boarding pikes,' Courtney ordered again. 'You and I must have boarded a dozen French frigates, yes?'

'Yes, sir.'

The ways of battle and war returned to Courtney as easily as opening up a book and finding the page he had once read. But never before had he boarded a ship from another captured one. Vaguely, he recalled Lord Nelson doing such a thing at Cape St Vincent. It was a shame, he thought, that people would not know of this battle, for the *Fantôme* settled beautifully against the *Barbarossa*, her sides rising above her. Like fiends, Courtney and the Lysanders swarmed upon her and clambered up her high flanks. The energy pulsing around him made the climb a blur. He hauled himself over the rail and vaulted onto the French deck. Separate battles raged and rolled apart between individual sailors and pirates. It was impossible to tell who had the upper hand.

'Where is Bonfils?!' Courtney shouted to Godfrey, but the lieutenant had already disappeared in the crush. Courtney followed, lashing out with cutlass and pistol, clubbing men about the head with it, carving a path for himself towards the helm. He could not sight Bonfils's uniform or his tall figure. He whirled around, trying to locate any familiar faces – only to stumble straight into the mouth of a flintlock. His heart jumped, he groped for his own, but not in time to avoid the deafening shot. His ears rang, echoes of gunfire and screams echoing in a hail of buzzing. He waited for the pain.

The pirate dropped to the deck, dead. And behind him, gun in hand, finally a man he knew.

'Hiram!' Courtney choked. He jumped over the fallen sailor and snatched Nightingale's arm. Nightingale, shaking, streaked with sweat and blood, touched his cheek and for a moment, seemed about to pull him into his arms. Courtney grasped his hand against him, weak with the tears which suddenly raced to his eyes. 'Are you hurt? Tell me you're not hurt.'

'No. No. Are you?'

'No. God, I thought that I... I thought that you...' Courtney swallowed the surging emotion. The battle still raged. 'Where is Bonfils?'

'Dead. He has been for these last three days.'

Courtney did not know how to feel. 'Who is in command?'

Nightingale smiled. 'Now? I am. And the *Lysander*?'

'Now?' Courtney repeated, almost wanting to laugh wildly. 'I am.'

'There are still Fantômes and Loyals locked below,' Nightingale rushed. 'A small number of us rose up after we saw the *Lysander* fighting.'

'We'll release them.'

Side by side with Nightingale, he fought through to the hatch below. The gundeck was eerily quiet, or perhaps Courtney's ears had deadened. The fight had condensed on the main deck, drawing all the men. Nightingale led Courtney down, explaining hurriedly as he went.

'They captured us only a short way off the coast of Algiers. Capitaine Bonfils decided to adhere to the shore, thinking perhaps the *Loyal* had been wrecked. We did not imagine piracy but we found out the truth from the captured Loyals. Many of them and the Fantômes were forced to man the *Barbarossa*. None of us knew what was happening. The *Fantôme* was commanded on a skeleton crew, always under the eyes of the pirates. The rest were locked up, or sometimes drawn across to the *Barbarossa*. My father-in-law went with them.'

'We found the *Loyal*,' Courtney said, barely knowing where to begin. 'She was wrecked. And then I spoke with an American frigate captain in Palermo who knew about the Tripolitan pirates, but these are not Tripolitan pirates, not in the words of the dey. Who are they?'

'They are from all over,' Nightingale replied. 'They bicker and fight and I'm not sure who has the upper hand or command. But...'

'What is it?'

'Many of them sound like Englishmen.'

Courtney tried to process that. He had heard English accents and seen English dress, but could not fathom how it came to be. He did not have time to think much more for they had reached the orlop deck. In amongst all its compartments and rooms for stores and supplies, men had been imprisoned. The doors were jammed and locked.

'Where is the key?' Courtney asked.

'I have it,' Nightingale responded, reaching into the pocket of his breeches. 'A handful of us were freed with the expectation of going across to the *Barbarossa* and helping ashore to bring on water. We've had a devilish time, no water and no food, after being denied safe harbour anywhere. The pirates... They started to heave people overboard, the sick and the wounded and the vulnerable.'

Courtney's stomach tightened as he again thought of the bodies at Palermo. 'I saw some washed ashore,' he said.

Nightingale nodded. 'They threw Bonfils overboard not long ago. When we were gathered up to be sent across to the *Barbarossa*, I thought the same would happen to us. But then we saw the *Lysander* and how she fought. We overpowered some of the pirates and I took the key.'

'Are all the men here?'

'Some joined the pirates. Bonfils's cook, Gabriel, he helped them. He was the one to strike the killing blow on his captain.'

Courtney remembered Gabriel, the man that Bonfils had plucked from his former master's château and pressed into service. He was not shocked.

Now, Courtney took the key from Nightingale and with shaking hands, used it on the locked rooms. In each, many men had been stuffed as if they were as inanimate and senseless as the tools that had been pulled out to make space for them. He recognised men he had seen on the deck of the *Fantôme*. English and French accents thanked him as he urged them up and out.

'Arm yourselves, men,' Courtney rushed, directing them to the deck. 'Quickly now. The *Lysander* battles the *Barbarossa*.'

He knew it would be easier said than done for these men. They appeared to have been imprisoned for some time, looking haggard and thin and with untamed beards. This wasn't only the *Fantôme* crew; this was the remains of the Loyal too. Near the back of the sorry crowd, a man in a post-captain's garb staggered. Nightingale hurried to help him.

'Captain Myles is wounded,' he said. 'He needs a surgeon. I tried to tell that to the men on the *Barbarossa* but...'

'My surgeon will tend to him,' Courtney assured. 'Captain Myles, sir, I am glad to see you well. Hiram, can you assist him across to the *Lysander*?'

'Of course.'

Courtney looked around Myles into the dim space but he could not see the person he looked for. A pit in his throat, he asked, 'Where is Madame Baptiste?'

Nightingale looked at him, mouth drawn. 'She, other women and some children were taken across to the *Barbarossa*.'

'I did not see them.'

'They may be in the captain's cabin.'

Courtney remembered the *Ulysses*, and the terrible fate of Olivia, the purser's wife. She had been violated and raped by the mutineers, until she had turned a knife upon herself. Courtney had already made his decision on what to do before Nightingale had even confirmed Geneviève's absence. And to know there were other women and children suffering...

'Up to deck,' he said. 'I must go back across to the *Barbarossa*.'

With Nightingale helping Myles, they ascended back on deck where, bolstered by the released prisoners, the fight on the *Fantôme* was turning in favour of her own crew and the Loyals. Barbarossas fled the French frigate, swinging back across to their polacre. The Lysanders met them with fire and blade. Two wedges cut the pirates' advance and retreat.

And above the battle, the smoke of the volcano had grown, swathing the mountain. Red tongues of fire split through the white haze and an occasional rumbling provided a deep bass-note to the fight.

'I think it is best for you to stay here, Hiram,' Courtney said. 'I shall send for Dr Faulkner as soon as I am able to. I am going back across to the *Barbarossa* and I shall try and find the other prisoners. She must not disengage from the fight.'

Nightingale opened his mouth, perhaps to disagree with his plan. But the naval officer still lived within him; he understood that the place to be was usually the place of danger. Courtney still had the pistol he had wrenched from the pirate who had boarded the *Lysander*; he now pressed it into Nightingale's hand. 'Look after yourself, Hiram. I shall be back soon.'

Still, it pained him to leave Nightingale, pained him to shout, 'Lysanders! To the *Barbarossa*!' and hurry back towards the polacre.

The *Barbarossa*'s deck was choked with bodies, some dead, some living. Courtney landed awkwardly, catching himself before he could fall entirely. The fight had raged for twenty minutes, but the pirates showed no sign of surrender. It was all a seething mass, pushing and shoving, ebbing and flowing, men still falling all around Courtney, some toppling off the sides. The moonlight bounced off blades and smashed pulleys and blocks. Above, the lateen rig hung to starboard, yanking with it a cat's cradle of cordage. Split spars rolled underfoot every time Courtney moved, before jamming into the red-rimmed scuppers. As he fought his way towards a choked hatchway, he nearly tripped on a swivel gun which had been blown entirely from its mount.

Now the prisoners at the oars had been rescued, Courtney felt more confident in reaching into his belt and extracting one of the *Lysander's* hand grenades. Lighting the fuse, he rolled it along the timbers and down to the deck below.

The explosion jerked the pirates back from the hatchway. Courtney beat a path through them and into the smoke-clogged gloom. Blood smeared the companion-ladder, glistening on each rung as he descended. Coughing and waving an arm through the haze, he strained to see before him. The oar banks were empty, chains lying beside the shackles.

With the fight still roiling above him, Courtney stepped through the cramped aisle and, sweeping his flintlock ahead, he reached the captain's cabin. The door was bolted fast.

Glancing behind him, Courtney rapped upon it.

'My name is Lieutenant Courtney!' he called. 'I am from His Majesty's frigate *Lysander*! Is there anyone there?'

A tumble of voices immediately answered. Courtney heard female and children's tones and his stomach squeezed.

'Stand back from the door!' he ordered. He had not yet discharged his pistol so delivered his one shot into the crude lock. Splinters flew off and mercifully, the door shivered. With a firm kick, it wrenched back on its hinges.

Geneviève stood on the other side. Her arms cradled two children, one brown and one white, and at her side, a girl with skin as black as ebony gently rocked a newborn. The infant began to sob as Courtney ploughed his way into the room but was quickly shushed.

'What…' he began. 'Are any of you harmed? Madame Baptiste…'

'I am fine, Lieutenant,' Geneviève said calmly, though Courtney could see her trembling. 'We are fine. We are fine. Awa, she is a new mother, she has only just given birth, she…'

'You shall be safe now, all of you,' Courtney said. 'You must get out of here. Come, quickly now. The *Lysander* and the *Fantôme* are battling the *Barbarossa*.'

He knew he could not take them up to the deck where the fight was still too hot. Hitching one of the children into his arms, he guided the women amidst the oar banks where their fellow prisoners had suffered.

The port he had seen earlier, the one that had been blown open, let in paltry gasps of air. Through it, he could see the ravaged hull of the *Lysander* still almost beating the flank of the *Barbarossa*, her gun ports so near.

Courtney returned the child to Geneviève's grasp and urged them all to stand back. Another grenade he plucked from his belt and hastily lit. Shielding the frightened group, he listened to it erupt with a deafening crack and felt the children quiver at the noise. Men would soon be down to investigate the sound and to fight. Courtney had been lucky they had not yet.

Across the water, Lysanders had also been drawn to the din. Courtney shouted to them in as loud a voice as he could muster. Through the smoke, peering through the gun port, he recognised Mr Lynde and the rest of his gun crew. Unbelievably, Monsieur Baptiste had joined them in his shirt-sleeves, muddied with powder.

'Mr Lynde, Monsieur, there are female and young prisoners!' Courtney shouted. 'I am going to pass them through to you!'

'Yes, sir!' Lynde cried.

Immediately, the men worked to unclasp their cannon from its ringbolts. Heaving between them, they wheeled it away, leaving the port empty. It would be a tight fit for the women, but the children could easily squeeze through.

'Miss Awa,' Courtney said, beckoning her forward. 'You and your babe first.'

The girl nodded bravely. She did not flinch as she clambered up to the port. Across on the *Lysander*, Mr Lynde extended his arms as far as he could, reaching for the babe. Courtney held his breath, looking between the ship and the companion-ladder up to deck, expecting at any moment for them to be attacked.

The Lysanders safely pulled Awa and her child across, but still Courtney barely breathed. The two other children followed and then Geneviève ducked into the gap. For the first time, Baptiste's eyes fell upon her.

'Geneviève!' Courtney heard him shout.

'Hugo!' she cried, the sound of her husband's voice drawing her forward.

'Come across quickly, my love!'

But no sooner had Geneviève started to clamber across did footsteps echo above, heading for the ladder. Courtney yanked his sword from its sheath, protecting her with his body. Geneviève whirled around.

'No, keep going, Madame,' Courtney urged. 'Do not look back.'

'Are you coming, Lieutenant?'

'No. Not yet. Go, go.'

She obeyed, manoeuvring across the gap to her husband. Seeing she was safe, Courtney hurried away. In the darkness of the deck and the fallen night, he could just about discern the figure descending the ladder. Courtney prepared to climb up and meet him. As the shadowy form came into sight, he lashed out with his sword. It met the steel of a blade.

And Courtney froze. A tall, familiar man looked down upon him.

'What,' Courtney rasped, 'are you doing here?'

Chapter Thirty: Infernal

Garrick Walker wore the same expression that Courtney knew must be across his own face. They stared at each other in silence, balanced upon the companion-ladder, the battle above slowly fading into the distance. Courtney looked at the wounds marring Walker's skin: wounds that he had stopped from turning into death blows on the *Grampus*. The scars still told their shared story, of their trysts on the *Grampus*, of Midshipman Lowe's cruelty.

'What are you doing here?' Courtney managed to say. again. 'Are you... Were you on the *Loyal*?'

Walker glanced down at their crossed blades. As Courtney waited, heart thumping, he suddenly gave a shove and forced Courtney to the bottom of the ladder. Courtney caught himself awkwardly against one of the banks of oars, staggering onto the bench. The chains clanked below his feet.

'Garrick,' he tried to utter, but the man approached him with his dagger still glinting.

'Why are you here?' Walker rasped: the first time Courtney had heard that voice since his removal from the *Grampus*. All his memories of Walker and that ship came rushing back, but did not match with what he saw before him. Walker brandished the blade at him, grip wobbling. 'You cannot be here,' Walker spat.

'What are you doing?' Courtney muttered. He looked at the weapon and how it aimed at his throat. Instinct told him to back away – and also brought a terrible realisation. 'You were not on the *Loyal*,' he breathed. 'You are part of this ship.'

Courtney scrambled up again. He stepped over the oars as Walker neared. Bewilderment surged in him, but ideas were starting to stick. The English dress amongst the *Barbarossa* crew, the familiar accents, what Nightingale had said about them...

'There are Englishmen amongst these pirates,' he said aloud, still barely able to believe it.

'They gave us no choice,' Walker replied, chest heaving. The blade danced in front of Courtney's eyes. He could not make himself raise his own sword against his former friend. 'They attacked our merchant ship. They stole our carronades and our cargo. Some resisted, many were thrown overboard or killed where they stood. I couldn't be a slave again. I have been a slave before.'

The face of Midshipman Lowe rose to Courtney, his cruel beatings and his dreadful ways. Courtney had been obsessed with protecting Walker from him; the boy had been so defenceless and vulnerable against the might of the navy. They had been allies in the densely packed lower decks – more than allies; they had been friends, lovers. But in the darkness of the *Barbarossa*, Walker looked unfamiliar. Something had snapped inside of him, something that Courtney had seen once when Walker had said he desired to punish Lowe and his other abusers.

'These men are pirates,' Courtney said. 'They are slavers. There were men chained to the oars, women and children locked below. I saw bodies washed up on the shore of Palermo, thrown overboard, and the markets in Tripoli... They don't care for colour, or sex. It is barbaric.'

'Slavers,' Walker repeated. 'Like the commanders of the merchant ships I sailed in, the ships the Admiralty commissions. The damned navy! The *Grampus* made a slave of me. I had no choice but to join her and when I was there, they did not care how I was hurt. Are you telling me, telling me—' Walker's voice strained and shook, as if he were near tears, '—telling me you would have not done the same if you had the choice?'

'To join these pirates? Garrick. I was never that desperate, that blinded. I made my choice.'

'And you chose to abuse me as much as Lowe did! *You* pressed me into service. *You* violated me.'

Courtney searched his face and saw that he was perfectly serious. Notes lay in his voice that had had only surfaced briefly as a boy: bitterness, mania, hatred. During their last times together, Courtney had tried to ignore the wedge between them. Walker had said they would grow out of their attraction as they aged, but Courtney had believed it came from fear of their unveiling and from Lowe's attacks, not this, whatever it truly was.

'We were friends, Garrick. You had no issue with me then. We were shipmates, for God's sake. What happened to you?'

'I tried to run away from it. I tried to marry and escape.' The blade wavered before Courtney and for a moment, it did not threaten him any longer. Courtney stopped moving away and stood rigidly beside the blown gun port, the *Lysander* on one side and Walker on the other. Above, the fight grew dimmer. 'I wed Lavinia Cartwright and I loved her, I did, I did. I am sure I did. I had to. But she grew to abhor me, she started to become disgusted with me. Because she saw the darkness inside of me, the evil that you put within me on the *Grampus*.'

Courtney could feel the blood draining from him. Coldness seeped into his bones, despite the heat of the battle and the energy that still thrummed. He knew what Walker meant: the sin that so many called detestable. But Walker had been willing, had enjoyed Courtney's company and his love. Courtney had never hurt him; it seemed the world had done that – only Courtney was an easier target. He did not know what to say.

'I went to sea again,' Walker continued. 'I joined a merchant ship but fate hated me for escaping the wreck of the *Grampus*. She was attacked by Tripolitan corsairs and pulled apart. I and many others were taken prisoner. It was then that I made my choice. No one had ever been good to me. So why did anyone else deserve any of my kindness or my mercy?'

'Tripoli have renounced these pirates,' Courtney said. 'They hate what they have been doing. The *Loyal* was an English ship, one bound for Malta with important crew members onboard.'

'You speak like the people we once hated, Artie,' Walker spat. 'Why are their lives worth more than anyone else's?'

'That is not what I mean, and you know it. Please, surrender. Have all these men surrender. We have already rescued your prisoners.'

'The only path for all of us is the noose. There is no way that I can turn back now.'

'Yes, there is!' Courtney cried. 'You—'

A deep rumble interrupted him. Above, shouts rippled along the deck. It did not sound like any gun or shipboard sound. Walker stared up and Courtney clearly heard the words, 'the volcano!' cried through the night.

Taking his chance, Courtney leapt over an oar bank and groped for the dagger in Walker's hand. He tried to cling on but Courtney grabbed the blade and ignored the pain as it sliced open his palm. The knife clattered onto the deck and he snatched it up.

Leaving Walker behind, he hurried up the ladder. On deck, to his horror, he could not see any other Lysanders, no sign of Obi or Godfrey or Smythe. Unknown pirates filled the polacre, suddenly more connected to him that he had thought possible. Orders for men to set the sails and throw the attackers back onto their ships echoed.

But above that, looming in the black night, the volcano of Stromboli groaned and seethed. A distant fiery eruption blazed into the sky, spitting and gushing. Gouts of smoke billowed around the crater, before drifting down the mountainside.

Grapnels and lines to the *Fantôme* and *Lysander* snapped from their tethers. With a sharp yank of the braces and the helm, the *Barbarossa* lurched and slammed into the *Fantôme's* bows. Courtney fell against the rail, staring at the two ships' retreat. He wanted to vault onto the gunwale and take a mad leap across to the *Lysander* but someone grabbed his arm, yanking him back.

Walker had returned. Courtney stared into the wild face of the first boy who had understood him – or so he had thought.

'This ship must tack!' Courtney shouted. With the damage to her masts and spars, the *Barbarossa's* course had been set too close to the deathly island and the jagged, unforgiving shore loomed. 'Her course must be changed or she'll be wrecked!'

Walker looked behind, towards the black reaches of the mountain. A geyser of flame vomited into the air, the sea seeming to tremble with its violence. As they both stared, a deafening thunderclap nearly split Courtney's eardrums. The very timbers of the *Barbarossa* shook. Beneath her keel, the waves churned, rising about her low draught.

'Get her away from this island!' Courtney shouted, but the masts already tilted. He lost his footing and nearly dragged Walker overboard with him. A remaining carronade broke their fall. Agony raked through him as he accidentally staggered onto the sharp point of the blade still in Walker's hand. He frantically felt his side, hand coming away wet with blood. His shirt stuck to it. Shock pulsed with the pain.

Above, shadowy forms of men plummeted from the tops into the angry waters. The sails, peppered with shot, some torn from head to foot, became backlit with a furious glow. Through the rips, Courtney watched arcing, blazing spurts of fire spout into the air like the death throes of a harpooned whale. Orange showers glittered amongst the stars before beginning to topple. They splattered and burst, only broken by another terrible fountain of lava streaming into the night. The volcano roared, turning the mountainside into a seething cradle of flame and smoke.

Courtney fought to rise to his feet. His knees wobbled and his side throbbed. He felt tiny, wounded and shaking at the bottom of the fearsome volcano. A black halo engulfed the crescent moon, eating away the stars. Pitch-dark vapour bloomed and spread.

And the *Barbarossa*, shedding her crew, drifted towards the jagged teeth of the island. Relentlessly, Courtney tried to stagger towards the helm. Walker followed.

'We must move!' Courtney insisted. 'We are too close!'

Walker did not reply, struck mute by the awe of the volcano. Courtney could smell the acrid fumes and feel their heat. Men continued to throw themselves overboard. Some were jerked from the spars as another eruption reverberated through the hull. The *Barbarossa* was tossed like a child's toy, listing to starboard and then back as another wave lashed her.

The spokes of the helm slipped beneath Courtney's blood-covered hands. It would not respond, not with the wreckage of the masts and with no men to guide the ship. He looked frantically astern but the *Fantôme* and the *Lysander* had vanished. They could not approach, anyway, not this close.

'Surrender this ship and all her men!' Courtney tried to order, knowing no one listened. 'Garrick, surrender!'

'And return home to be hanged?!' Walker shouted, his voice returning. 'The navy will not show me any mercy!'

'Do you think you deserve mercy?'

Courtney could not believe he was asking it of a man, a boy, he had once loved, perhaps. He had once thought Walker deserving of all the mercy in the world, and had tried to find justice for him. But the world had not given him that, and nor had Courtney; Walker's pain had birthed more pain. And now, Walker stared at him, a shadow of his former self. His face had been turned into a mosaic of flashing light and shadow as the volcano continued to belch. Courtney could no longer see the boy he had defended. He saw the youth he himself had once been: running from home, alone in the world, not knowing he would ever claw his way out of the dirt. And then the instant had passed. He knew, for certain, that he stood on the right side.

The *Barbarossa* drifted out of control. Panic littered her deck, her men abandoning her to float, unbridled, towards the island. High above, further down the mountainside, black ash rained, mixed with hails of fire and stone. With every moment, smoke covered the land, only broken by lava. An infernal spout sent pinwheeling debris through the night sky.

Destruction loomed. Ahead, there was nothing but death.

Courtney only had one choice. He turned and ran, hearing the cloud of ash and dust and vapour racing down the mountain. Mustering his last strength, ignoring the hurt in his side, he climbed onto the gunwale. Without looking back, he leapt for his life. The hot night soared by him and then the frigid sea knocked out all of his breath. He plunged beneath the dark surface, kicking to maintain control. Staring up, he saw the surface fracture as the *Barbarossa* pitched and careened in the churning sea.

Pain raking through him, Courtney swam, pushing against the pain of his wound. When he could no longer hold his breath, he resurfaced, gasping for air and tasting the smoke. Half-blind, he struggled towards the nearest thing: a piece of the *Barbarossa's* foremast, fallen overboard in the destruction. Along the shore, a great black cloud rose from the sea, towering into the night sky. The infernal pillar swallowed the moon and stars, rumbling, growling, spewing ash and fire over the waters. The entire mountainside had been swamped, lit only by the streams of burning lava, a beacon of fire in the night. Courtney stared, clinging to the bobbing mast.

The last he recalled was the *Barbarossa*, floating uncontrollably into that dark mass.

Chapter Thirty-One: Resolution

In slow, hazy rhythms, the world stirred. One by one, Courtney's senses drained back to him. His vision was distorted, his eyes awash with specks of dust. His throat hurt with its sandpaper-like dryness, so much it pained even to move his tongue. He could smell nothing, hear nothing. All felt curiously soft as he gently, hesitantly, shifted his arm.

A soft pressure immediately eased him back down. He blinked and managed to focus on a blurred form close by his head. 'Don't move,' it said, and Courtney could only obey. He groggily opened his mouth and tried to ask for water. A cup appeared and he drank from it gratefully. The motion of swallowing made his head and side ache.

In that pain, shades of the recent events arose. Courtney remembered the helpless form of the *Barbarossa* as she vanished into the black ash. He tasted the salt of the heated sea and the destruction of the volcano's eruption. Walker had been in front of him in the midst of a pirate crew, insulting their shared past.

Courtney could hardly believe he had survived that. Perhaps he hadn't, and this was a figment of his dying imagination.

'I shall send for Dr Faulkner,' the voice said again. Courtney reached out and touched the hand upon his shoulder.

'Hiram,' he managed. The misty aura around his companion started to fade and he looked upon Nightingale, keeping vigil at his side. Relief coursed through him. 'Are you well?'

Nightingale smiled. 'I am. Better now that I see you awake.'

'How long… How long have I been sleeping for?' Time had stagnated between Courtney's memories of the *Barbarossa* and now, laying in his cot on the *Lysander*. He recognised the small cabin off the gunroom, its soft lulling motion as the ship sailed.

'A little over twelve hours. You woke briefly when we brought you back onboard. It is fortunate we rescued you from the sea when we did.'

'We?' Courtney could not recall being plucked from the dark ocean around Stromboli.

'I made Obi, Mr Smythe and some of the Lysanders accompany me in your cutter. Some of the Fantômes even came. They said they owed you a debt after you saved Capitaine Bonfils on the *Cygne*, God rest his soul.'

'That was not safe.'

'Perhaps not.' The look on Nightingale's face told Courtney that he would have done it again without hesitation. 'But you were wounded and would have drowned or been engulfed with the ash. The *Lysander* and the *Fantôme* avoided the worst of the blast and the aftermath. But the *Barbarossa*...'

'She was destroyed?'

Nightingale nodded.

'Were there any survivors other than me?'

Nightingale was silent for a moment. 'I don't know. Perhaps some got away, but we did not pull anyone else from the sea.'

Hollowness rang inside of Courtney. He did not know why; mere hours before, he had been intent on capturing the *Barbarossa* and allowing all her men to hang as pirates, or at least face justice in the face of the *Lysander*'s guns. But knowing Walker had been onboard gave it a bitter note. He was ashamed at his regret.

'You spoke with one of them,' Nightingale said. 'I saw you before they disengaged from us.'

Courtney nodded. 'I knew him,' he admitted. 'I knew him from very long ago.'

'He was...'

'English, yes. From Plymouth. We were friends, once, on the *Grampus*, my first ship as an able seaman. We served together, just as you and Lieutenant Sawyer did, only we weren't mids or even officers.'

Courtney had not spoken to Nightingale about Walker. He barely even spoke of his life before he had become a lieutenant or before he had entered the navy. Perhaps he had been embarrassed about it, feeling himself unworthy of someone like Nightingale who came from such privilege and honour. For so long, he had doubted Nightingale would be able to find strength in their connection, that he would find their differences too great. He wanted to be able to speak of it freely to him but necessity put them both in the shadows. Their friendship, their attraction, had to be so secret as to barely put words to it.

'I did some foolish things when I was young,' Courtney continued. 'I was not the most obedient sailor. With Jane, I'd run away from my father and my mother, even from Mr and Mrs Woods. I did not always respect the hierarchy of the navy or the officers who represented it. Garrick Walker was my first friend.' Courtney hoped Nightingale understood the implication. 'But there was a midshipman, Lowe, on the *Grampus* who was a petty little tyrant, as some of them are when they have a mite of authority. He had personal dealings with Garrick from before the *Grampus*. Garrick had... He was a runaway as I was, but not the same. He had come from privilege, but his family had lost a great deal of money. He saw himself as having been forced into the navy. Lowe singled him out for attack, along with other boys who were very cruel to him. One night, I stepped in and was going to strike Mr Lowe.'

He heard Nightingale draw breath, the exact reaction he had expected.

'I was fortunate not to be whipped for it, but I spent time in irons. Garrick was invalided out, so terrible were his injuries. Mr Lowe never faced any justice for it. I would have been condemned for almost striking Lowe, for being cruel to him, if the *Grampus* hadn't been wrecked soon after.'

'You have not told me about this before.'

Courtney shook his head. 'I didn't know what on earth you would think of me if you knew the truth. I lied to...everyone, back then. I lied to the panel who conducted my lieutenant's examination, about how long I had been in the navy, about my age. I didn't even know my age or much about myself. But I knew they would not look kindly on me.'

'Many in naval authority lie. The muster books have been misrepresented since they were instituted.'

'I thought that I had laid it all to rest,' Courtney continued, not wanting to dwell on Nightingale's feelings about his past. 'These last months have shown me that I haven't.'

'How did Mr Walker come to be a pirate?' Nightingale asked. 'In the employ of Tripoli?'

'Those pirates were not under Tripoli, just in the way of Ransome not acting for the Royal Navy when he mutinied.' Courtney paused, forming the words. 'Garrick left his wife not long ago. He blames me for it.'

'You?'

'I…' Courtney shook his head. 'We were on the *Grampus* together. He and I… Well, you understand. Apparently he hated himself for it, though he gave me no real indication of it. He never refused me, and when he was unsure, I thought it was about his fear of being found out, or what Lowe had done to him. Garrick's wife found out or he feared she had. He said he joined the merchant navy and his ship was attacked. The crew were tormented and rather than becoming a slave, he chose to join the pirates themselves. He once talked about wanting to punish the people who had hurt him, but this…' Courtney could still not believe it, could still not believe such hatred and bitterness could exist. But he had seen plenty of the world and its ugliness. 'I cannot bear to think I had a hand in it.'

'Arthur.' Nightingale leant forward again and laid his palm over Courtney's. 'That was not your fault. You saved him as a child. You are not to blame for this world's hatred for… men like us. It has forced men to make awful decisions.'

'I don't blame myself,' Courtney said, half-surprising himself. 'I made my choice. I have done all that I can with the hand that was dealt me. I do not come from much. No, I do not come from anything. Perhaps I still do some foolish things but I am not the same boy I was on the *Grampus*.'

'Of course not. Your success has been in your own right, not because of some relative who has patronised you or some deal amongst the hierarchy of the navy. Your behaviour worries me sometimes but… I am proud of you, Arthur. You saved the men of the *Loyal* and a French frigate, and all of the other prisoners. And you have stopped the *Barbarossa* from threatening war and enslaving others.'

'I doubt that the Admiralty will see it that way. I doubt they shall say anything about this voyage. Sir Rodney emphasised how secret it is.' But Courtney could not deny the flush of pleasure to hear Nightingale's pride in him. He admired Hiram Nightingale more than any other man, for standing up to the people who had hurt him and for doing what he thought was right. Perhaps they were not so different, after everything.

'I won't say the Admiralty doesn't matter. I was in the navy for almost three decades and I know how fickle it is. But there are countless families who will have their sons and husbands and fathers home. You know more than most officers what it is like for a regular seaman, how important their survival is for loved ones in England.'

Courtney nodded, but the reminder of such a thing twisted his heart. Nightingale did not know about Paterson and Arnold's fates. He could not speak of that yet. 'Are they well?' he asked instead. 'The prisoners? Monsieur Baptiste told us about how the *Barbarossa* captured the *Loyal*. It did not sound pleasant.'

'They will be, now that we are en route to Gibraltar and they will receive the proper attention. Auclair is commanding the *Fantôme* in the absence of Bonfils.'

'And you?' he asked again. 'Did they hurt you?'

'I have been hurt many times before.'

'But not this time?'

Nightingale shook his head. 'No. My father-in-law was not hurt either, though he will be frail for the coming weeks, perhaps months. He wanted to convey his thanks to you.'

By the next day, Courtney was able to hear that gratitude himself. He limped out of his cabin as the bell rang for the afternoon watch and, supported by Nightingale, ascended to the deck of the *Lysander*. The fresh air of the Mediterranean helped to scour away some of his pain, although his side still throbbed where he had fallen onto the knife. Dr Faulkner had stitched it up with a thankfully steady hand and given him willow bark and laudanum for the lingering ache. The sight of the crew, working in the tops and at the braces, was a further remedy. They were his men, even in a temporary capacity, and they had followed him into battle, even fighting alongside their former enemies.

Nightingale reassured Courtney that the captives were recovering well under Faulkner's care and the assistance of the *Fantôme*'s surgeon. Courtney, with Nightingale beside him, toured the sickbays of both ships and spoke to as many as he could, telling the Loyals that they would soon be united with their brothers in Gibraltar. Faulkner, who had pulled himself away from his bottle as much as possible, worked tirelessly, sometimes aided by Obi, who was on the path to becoming a dependable loblolly boy, as well as his duties at the carronades.

Following in Courtney's footsteps and also keeping an eye on the sick was Smythe. Courtney was pleased to see him taking such an active involvement; he told him so as they crossed ways. Smythe blushed and ducked his head.

'Thank you, sir,' he said. 'And, sir, if I may—'

'You may speak freely, Mr Smythe.'

'Thank you for all your aid during this voyage. Allowing me onboard, helping me with my navigation and signals, showing me how an officer should behave.'

Courtney had not thought he had behaved as an officer should; certainly Captain Bryant had not thought so, and Courtney had frequently had his doubts. But to hear it from Smythe warmed his heart. He found himself almost lost for words.

'You are most welcome, Mr Smythe. You have been a good student.'

Smythe smiled like a boy, before trying to school his face into something more serious. 'Thank you, sir. Thank you.'

Nightingale squeezed Courtney's arm as they walked away. 'Do you see your impact?' he asked softly.

Courtney was just as glad to discover that the *Lysander* had not been too badly mauled during the battle. The main gripe, in fact, was the broken windows in the great cabin, something Courtney apologised to Brooks for, after his beautiful repair work in Palermo.

During Smythe's watch that day, Sir William joined him and Nightingale as they sat at the taffrail. He had shaved and cut his shaggy hair, and now wore fine clothes that Monsieur Baptiste had lent him after buying them for himself in Gibraltar. Courtney stood in respect, as if Sir William was his own father-in-law, but Sir William waved him down.

'You have been through quite an eventful month, Lieutenant,' he said as he lowered himself gingerly next to Nightingale. 'I needed to thank you personally for your efforts.'

Courtney reddened. He still did not know how to speak to Sir William. 'I do not need your thanks, sir. It was my duty.'

'I believe that you went above your duty, Lieutenant. If you and the Lysanders had not come, I do not know what would have happened to us. I have spent many years campaigning against the trade of human beings. I did not ever expect to experience it myself.'

'It is a barbaric practice, sir,' Courtney said honestly, and knew he could in front of such a staunch abolitionist as Sir William.

'I agree.'

'Speaking of which, sir,' Courtney continued. 'I wished to ask you about one of the Lysanders. He served on the *Scylla* in the Caribbean. I signed him on myself, turning a blind eye to the fact he had escaped from a plantation. Obi, sir. Mr Nightingale can vouch for his conduct and skill also.'

'I can indeed,' Nightingale said.

'I wanted to ensure his protection, sir. He and Mr Midshipman Smythe have quite an alliance and he has served very well upon the *Lysander*, manning the guns and aiding Dr Faulkner. If it could be promised that Obi would not end up in barbaric hands again, I would be very grateful.'

Sir William nodded. 'I know of Obi. Hiram has spoken to me often about him. I have referred to the loyalty and aid of the black sailors in the Royal Navy when speaking against the trade in Parliament. And I know of Mr Smythe's father and his uncle. They also share my opinions. I shall do what I can to ensure Obi's protection.'

'Thank you, sir. We also rescued a woman from the *Barbarossa*, Miss Awa. She has been helping…'

'I know of her also, Lieutenant. She has been aiding Monsieur Baptiste's wife in caring for the injured sailors. She and her babe will be looked after by the Baptistes, I am certain.'

Sir William handled the conversation with poise and confidence; it was difficult to believe he had been so mistreated and harmed recently. Courtney was glad he had found him when he did – for Sir William's sake, for Nightingale's and for Mrs Nightingale's. And he hoped, almost selfishly, that it would engrain him more firmly into Mrs Nightingale's trust.

That evening, Auclair invited him across to the *Fantôme*. It felt strange to sit in the great cabin without Bonfils; his absence cast a heavy pall over the French officers and sailors. But Auclair and Maître Carré and the sub-lieutenant Maistral spoke politely and genuinely, helped by Geneviève's translations. At the end of their dinner, Auclair pulled Courtney aside and offered him the picture of the château on the wall, something he and Bonfils had talked about in the previous dinner. Touched, Courtney felt his throat tighten, but he accepted it gladly, knowing that one day, he might have to once again battle these men.

The greater gift was seeing Geneviève at the table with them, side by side with her husband. She had barely left him since being rescued, and they both had been caring for the young children and Miss Awa. All of them been frequent visitors to the rest of the wounded, and Courtney made sure to check on them. Geneviève and Baptiste had resolved to take the children and Miss Awa to France and provide for them. Courtney took comfort in that, as well as what Nightingale had said: families brought together after months apart, the promise of security.

Yet despite the safety of the crews and the thanks he had received, a hollow note would not stop ringing inside of Courtney. He felt a part of him had been suffocated on the deck of the *Barbarossa* and he could not find the words to explain it.

When the time came to speak to Sir Rodney about the truth of the *Barbarossa*, Courtney debated what he would say. He debated what he would not say. He revisited the battle with the *Barbarossa* and what had occurred on her decks in the shadow of Stromboli. But when he asked about the pirates, Courtney made his choice and shook his head.

'I did not know them,' he said. 'They seemed to be men desperate to make a living and desperate to make an impact, but they achieved that through awful means. They are gone now.'

Gone now, with the rest of Courtney's memories of the *Grampus*.

—

Gibraltar had become familiar over the last month as they had sailed in and out of its harbour. Now, Courtney and the *Lysander* arrived with better tidings, able to set the former captives down on dry land for the first time in weeks. Messages were ferried up to the governor and his council, Sir Rodney, Monsieur Baptiste and Sir William personally traipsing back and forth with news and papers. Courtney had scribbled a hasty report during the eleven-day journey from Sicily, but Dr Faulkner's draughts of medicine made his head and pen swim. He would wait a little while before composing a full missive to the Admiralty. If he was fortunate, Sir Rodney would quell any damning questions about how Captain Bryant had come to be gravely wounded and smooth over any snags in the tale.

Courtney tried to take heart in seeing the beaten, enslaved men and women walking freely once more. The weakest received attention at the naval hospital where Dr Faulkner had taken a leading hand. Geneviève Baptiste accompanied her husband to the governor's house and then, unflinchingly, she and her new bosom companion, Miss Awa, helped to care for the ill men they had been imprisoned with. Courtney walked with them through the wards and saw the sailors' eyes brighten. French and English shared the sickbays, just as they had shared the fight against the *Barbarossa*. Regardless of nations, some of the men helped at each other's bedsides or took the air together.

Now the journey was over, there was little more to do but look after the wounded and deal with the thorny administration that came after any action. Courtney granted as much shore leave as was sensible to the Lysanders, hoping that was enough to express his gratitude to them. He knew from both positions, the regular seaman and the officer, that thanks were unnecessary; this was the service they tied themselves to, occasionally gave their lives to, but his first taste of command upon the waves made his mind stray in harsh directions. He thought of the dead and the wounded and the still-living and could not form his emotions into sensible shapes. Walker's interpretation of their shared past had made him fret over all else that he had thought was certain. He doubted his actions throughout the voyage; he doubted what waited for him at home; he doubted the path ahead of him; and more than all, he doubted his strength to speak with Nightingale about their future.

And returning to Gibraltar brought back images of Paterson and Arnold. Courtney still saw them, shivering and afraid, at their trial, and then, choking at the end of the noose. More than anything, he could not rid himself of that guilt. Sitting around, with little other action to distract him, he kept going over the court martial again and again, wondering if he could have said any different.

With the *Lysander* safely moored under the care of Lieutenant Godfrey, he and Nightingale left the confines of the ship and visited Sara at her tavern. Nathan Waters sat with her at the bar and, as they entered, he sprang to his feet to greet Courtney.

'Sir,' he stammered, saluting hastily, 'they have been speaking of it all along the harbour. Men I didn't think I'd ever see again from the *Loyal*... They're freed?'

Courtney blushed at the appreciation. 'They are,' he said.

'Thank you, sir. Thank you for finding them. May I shake your hand, sir?'

Courtney smiled thinly. He allowed it, but the curious hollowness still fluttered inside of him. Even Sara's beaming face and her offer for them to eat and stay at the tavern did not ease the feeling. He and Nightingale sat before the fire, drinking coffee and dining on a simple beef pie, and Courtney thought of the last time they had done this: back in the Fisherman's Catch in Ryde, avoiding a subject that now reared its head again. When they left the parlour, going up the stairs and into a room with two neatly dressed beds, he knew he did not want to avoid it any longer.

'You seem tired,' Nightingale said as he drew shut the drapes. Courtney sat at the edge of one of the beds and felt the truth of Nightingale's words. His shoulders slumped, his side twinged.

'I am tired,' Courtney admitted. 'I don't think I've slept more than a few hours for…days? Weeks? Other than that stint after Stromboli, but I don't think that counts as a good night's rest.'

'I should have had Rylance help you,' Nightingale said with a smile, sitting beside Courtney.

'I couldn't have asked for that. He was a saviour to you on the *Fantôme*. Madame Baptiste told me how he refused to leave you.'

'Rylance is too good for all of us.'

Courtney nodded, trying to smile. 'Would you help me?' he asked.

Nightingale paused. Then said, softly, 'Of course.'

Courtney remained still as Nightingale unlooped his neckcloth and helped him to shuffle out of his uniform coat. Courtney remembered doing this for Nightingale in Trinidad, a night that he had been in knots about until he had laid his mouth against Nightingale's for the first time. He knew, in that moment, that it was right, that it was honest, that it was what he desired.

As Nightingale undid his waistcoat's buttons, he took a shivering breath and said, 'Paterson and Arnold were killed.'

Nightingale stopped for a second, then continued without looking at him. 'I thought that might be the case when I did not see them onboard. Although I did hope… Well, that they may have been spared.'

'I tried all that I could. Mr Pascoe had been the one to hide the scalpel that they were accused of stealing. But, in the end, their effects were searched and there was damning evidence in their letters. Mr Paterson had written to his sister, Anne, about her upcoming marriage to Mr Arnold. He made his feelings about Mr Arnold quite clear, or…clear enough to be suspicious. I thought that I might have done enough to save them, but they…' Courtney suddenly felt tears race into his eyes, the emotions of the previous months flooding over him. His throat constricted. 'I had to preside over their execution. They were hanged from the *Lysander*'s yardarm.'

Nightingale glanced up at him and saw his sorrow. He left his buttons and reached out to touch his face, hesitating at the last moment. Courtney gripped his hand and laid it against his cheek, nuzzling against it and feeling his tears drip onto Nightingale's skin.

'Arthur,' Nightingale soothed. 'What is it?'

'I have seen men hanged before,' Courtney continued. 'I saw nearly the entire *Ulysses* crew swing from the yards, but this… Knowing that I shared the thing that they were being killed for. I could see myself, I could see you, and afterwards, Captain Easton said that Mr Pascoe had tried to condemn me for the same thing…'

'Hush.' Nightingale stroked his thumb over Courtney's cheekbone, trying to soothe him. 'I know how it feels. I have witnessed the same thing. My Tom, and other men afterwards.'

'They were my men.'

'I know.'

'How did you… How did you bear it?'

Nightingale was silent for a while, gently caressing Courtney's face, breathing softly. Courtney knew what he had been through, what he had suffered, not only these last weeks, but for nearly his entire life, at the hands of his father, at the hands of others, at the hands of himself. He felt guilty putting his own frets upon him, weeping tears Nightingale had most likely wept a thousand times. The shade of Tom, of Leroy Sawyer, Nightingale's first love, hovered over them. In his blackest moments, Courtney wondered how he could ever live up to that. He'd thought he had been a force of good for Walker; he'd thought he had been a fair leader; he'd thought he had acted well, but every action had a dark side. He felt as if he still stood at those crossroads, but every path, before him and behind him, had been cast into shadow. The sacrifices he had made weighed so heavily upon him.

'I bore it,' Nightingale eventually whispered, 'by thinking of the living.'

'I thought of you,' Courtney said haltingly. 'I thought of you so often. I wondered things. I wondered if you could bear being around me with the threat of Paterson and Arnold's fate. And seeing your house when I came to visit you, seeing your wife, I worried how I could fit into your life. I come from nothing, I have nothing and...'

'Arthur,' Nightingale said again. 'Stop this. Stop. I know where this ends. I do not want you travelling the path I have before. I should have said it before I left on the *Fantôme*, because there were moments I was not sure I would be back. I love you, Arthur. I could not love you any more than I do.'

'You do?'

'Of course. I know that we are different, in many ways. And do not think I have not thought of the risks of what we have. I am forty-two, Arthur, I have had every thought under the sun about it. You are probably more than aware that I do not take many risks, but this...' He lowered his hand, caressing Courtney's neck and down to his chest where his heart beat. 'I would not change a thing. I would take this risk one hundred times over.'

And, as if Courtney still did not believe it, he leant in and pressed a soft kiss to his lips. It was the first time Nightingale had initiated any form of intimacy; more than a year apart and then these awful weeks of purgatory had not allowed more. Courtney revered it, sinking into the closeness, the comfort. When Nightingale pulled away, he let his forehead rest against his, their breaths mingling.

'I am not like Lieutenant Sawyer,' Courtney said, brave enough to utter it in this quiet moment. 'I thought there might not be room for him, for Mrs Nightingale, for me.'

'I do not want you to be like Leroy,' Nightingale said. 'I never had the courage to admit how I felt to Leroy, even to myself. And do not fret about my wife. I told you of her outlook and her acceptance. She is too intelligent for me to hide you from her, and nor would I want to do so. I adore you, and I wish I could do more for you.'

'You do not have to do anything for me, Hiram. I told you.'

'But I wish to. If it means attesting for you, if it means helping you with your house...' Nightingale stroked his hand through Courtney's curls and cupped his face again. 'That is what I was trying to tell you with those offers. I enjoy being a part of your life, my dear, in every capacity.'

Courtney flushed with warmth. 'You said that when I visited your house. I thought that you were talking to me for a moment.'

'What did I say?'

'"My dear". You said it to Mrs Nightingale, but I like hearing it too.'

'Then I shall say it more often.' Nightingale smiled.

'Can I kiss you?'

'You do not have to ask.'

Courtney did not. But this connection he and Nightingale shared, it seemed too precious, too true for a man like himself; he could not bear the thought of ruining it in any way. He laid his mouth against Nightingale's, kissing him with the love he felt thudding inside his breast. He treasured being able to wrap him in his arms and pull him close, knowing that he was finally safe and here alongside him.

Nightingale did not retire to the other bed. Courtney laid him down upon the quilt and brushed a lock of auburn hair from his eyes, tracing the old scars from the Nile. They both had wounds – some sustained together, some sustained apart – and both understood the trials they represented. No barrier of society could hinder that bond, forged in fire, and now kindled in more than just war and violence. Courtney wished Nightingale to be beside him in the worst times and the best times, and all in between.

Placing kisses over his cheek and down to his jaw, his throat, up again to his mouth, Courtney whispered, 'I want to be everything to you, Hiram. I want to be your friend, your companion, your lover... Anything you want of me, only allow me to be in your life.'

'My dear,' Nightingale whispered, cupping Courtney's face and rubbing his thumb over his bottom lip. Heat flickered in Courtney. 'I do not ever want you out of my life. You are the other half of my soul.'

Smiling, Courtney pressed his forehead to Nightingale's, letting their breath mingle, half-covering him with his body and ignoring the twinge in his side. For a moment, all else seemed far away: the ship, the voyage, the ugliness of the world. They had to exist in the shadows, but they could create their own life in the cracks of society. Although he wished he could say it aloud beyond Nightingale's confidence, Courtney's love was no less real for being whispered.

As they embraced in the falling night, that was what he took comfort in.

Chapter Thirty-Two: The Crossroads

2 December 1802, Fareham, England

Courtney closed the door to the small cottage and laid his hat back on his head. For the first time, he allowed himself to breathe easier. Everything he had wanted to say had been uttered, unburdening him of the awful weight. Seeing the shift of that sorrow to another person had not been easy; he wished he had not had to do so. But Paterson and Arnold's trial had not finished with the tying of the noose. Their families still existed, far away from the scene of their deaths.

Walking up the small garden path, Courtney thought of Anne Paterson's face as she learnt of her brother's demise alongside her betrothed. Two people had been carved from her life in one blow. She had not wept, not in front of Courtney, but she had sighed a long, trembling exhale and closed her gleaming eyes. She listened to Courtney without looking at him, nodding and clutching the hand of her father beside her. She must have only been a few years older than Jane.

With the loss of Paterson and Arnold heavy between them, Courtney had offered the remains of Paterson's family ten pounds. It was not his money, but Nightingale's, a token Courtney knew was bare recompense for Anne. Still, she had thanked him, again and again saying that he did not have to give such a thing. But he did, if only to know that someone else would not suffer for the injustice given Paterson and Arnold.

Nightingale waited him for down the lane towards Fareham. Courtney had told him he did not have to come, the December weather biting through the cold day, but, just as Courtney had dismissed Miss Paterson's bashful thanks, Nightingale had insisted. He rose from the tree stump he had been sitting on and Courtney felt lighter again for seeing him.

'How were they?' Nightingale asked as he fell into step beside Courtney. Courtney offered him his arm and Nightingale took it with a grateful smile, letting Courtney enjoy the comfort of being close to him.

'I think that Miss Paterson knew,' he said. 'Her brother's letter implied it but seeing her and her reactions... When I said they had fallen together – I didn't say how, but that silence... She knew.'

'You did a good thing by visiting her. Better that than her having to live with the unknown.'

'The money will help them a little, along with their pension and the pay Mr Paterson set aside for his sister. Mr Arnold did not seem to have much family. It appears Mr Paterson and his kin were all he had.' Courtney fought the swell of sadness. 'Thank you for helping.'

'The gift was from us, Arthur.'

Us. The word filled Courtney with warmth. He hoped, somehow, that this gift, from two men who understood Paterson and Arnold, helped to alleviate the unfairness. For a moment, he raised his hand and set it upon Nightingale's where it rested against his elbow. Nightingale squeezed it, saying what they could not aloud.

'Let us think about Jane's wedding now,' Courtney continued. 'I am so very glad we reached England in time for it.'

The matter of the *Loyal* felt as though it was finally coming to rest. Courtney had attended Captain Myles's court martial and given testimony in addition to his official reports. It had been a purely procedural trial and had not been a surprise that the captain had been acquitted: a far fairer outcome than for Paterson and Arnold. He hoped that was the end of it.

'Are you still going to accompany me to Norfolk?' Courtney asked.

'Of course,' Nightingale said. 'I would not miss the ceremony.'

'Your wife is very welcome also.'

'She is tending to her father now. He's recovering well. It won't be too much longer until he returns to his work. You shall have to manage with my company alone.'

Courtney smiled for the first time that day. Nightingale joined him and they continued through the fields towards Fareham where they had ridden from Portsmouth earlier that morning. They had crossed only a few roads before Rylance appeared, hurrying down the bridleway.

He waved a note in his hand, huffing and gasping. Nightingale released Courtney's arm and hurried to meet him.

'Sir,' he puffed. 'Mr Nightingale, sir, Lieutenant Courtney, sir. A letter came for you. I ran all the way to find you.'

Another unexpected note. Courtney felt his stomach twist. He took the paper and saw the neat writing addressed to him, and inside – the seal of the Admiralty. Reading quickly, then going back to read again, he held his breath. 'I have been called up to London,' he finally managed to say to Nightingale. 'I have to report to the Admiralty Office.'

'I am sure it is nothing terrible,' Nightingale tried to assure, but the entire voyage of the *Lysander* suddenly raced through Courtney's head. It plagued him for the whole journey northward, bundled in a carriage which he shared with four others in the short time he had to arrange the route. He tried to swear Nightingale did not have to come but once more, he insisted – and when they arrived in London hours later, under the falling evening, he was grateful for the company.

At the inn, he hastily changed into his best uniform, cleaned and brushed by Rylance's fastidious hand, and hurried to the Admiralty Office, hoping that he would not be sent away at this late hour.

A few months before, he had entered this building to receive the news of the vanished *Loyal*. It simultaneously felt like an age and a matter of minutes ago. He had faced storms, pirates, bitter actions and shades of his past since then, and taken his first major wound in many years. Looking up at the impressive façade of the Admiralty Office, Courtney hoped another injury would not be forthcoming. He could stand the pinch in his side, where Dr Faulkner had stitched him up, but a blow to his career… He was not sure he could weather another.

Instead of being shepherded through the servants' corridor, he was allowed to walk through the public halls and shown into a waiting room. The parlour, adorned with gargantuan oil paintings of British victories, was eerily empty, a world away from the usual hopeful crush of officers wanting an interview. The only visitor sat in a wheeled chair by the window, looking out over the square Courtney had just crossed.

'Captain Bryant,' Courtney said in shock.

The sight of the wounded man twisted Courtney's stomach even more. He had not expected to see him, not after he had looked in such a sorry state in Palermo. Bryant had not attended Captain Myles's court martial, again giving his statements in writing. Relief that he had survived clashed with Courtney's hesitation around him. Their last meeting had been strange. For a while, Courtney stood haplessly in the middle of the waiting room, unsure whether to approach any closer.

Bryant turned to him. His skin looked healthier than before, his eyes and mouth less gaunt. The bandages were gone from around his head and as Courtney stared at him, he started to stand.

'Don't trouble yourself, sir,' Courtney rushed to say, fearing he would topple over.

'I am fine, Lieutenant,' Bryant responded curtly.

'You… You returned from Sicily, sir.'

'I did. My brother informed me what happened to the *Lysander* and her prey.'

Courtney nodded, unsure what else to utter. He could not read Bryant's tone.

'You found the missing men, and rid the world of those fiends.'

'I did,' Courtney said, though he would not have phrased it in that way. He certainly had not in his official report, which he was now certain Captain Bryant had supplemented with his own. All manner of condemnations and questions about his conduct floated before him. Although Bryant had had an air of politeness in Palermo, Courtney had thought that may have been the result of his dire injury. Now he had had more than enough time to dwell over their shared voyage. 'I have been called to a meeting here,' Courtney continued.

'I am aware.' Bryant nodded. 'My brother wished to speak with you. I wish you fortune.'

His words did not comfort Courtney. He agonised over them as a clerk collected him from the waiting area and led him towards Sir Rodney Bryant's office. Inside, the man had shed the façade of a pauper that he had donned in Gibraltar and sat again amidst the impressive splendour of his role. It was with some effort that Courtney kept his mouth shut as he stood before him. He felt he walked a thin line already and did not want to stumble off the edge of it.

'I suppose, Lieutenant, that you spoke with my brother in the parlour,' Sir Rodney suddenly said.

'Yes, sir.'

'He shan't go to sea again, not for many a year, at the least. He will chafe at that but he should be thankful that he survived such a blow.'

'I…hope he will be well, sir.'

'I have read both of your reports, and that of Midshipman Smythe and Lieutenant Godfrey. We can rest easier knowing that the *Barbarossa* will not threaten our trade and standing.'

Or take away the lives of innocent men and women, Courtney thought, but knew, for the Admiralty, that took a secondary position to the prospect of war and squandered finance.

'My brother had much to say about you, Lieutenant,' Sir Rodney said, finally fixing Courtney with a severe look. 'I have heard many things.'

'We did not always see eye to eye, sir,' Courtney could not help blurting. 'I do not know what he has said, but I am willing to defend myself. You have read my report, sir. I always tried to conduct myself in a way I saw fit. Perhaps I made some errors in my judgement but I believe that the ends justified the means. I found the *Barbarossa* and the *Fantôme* and the Loyals have been safely returned. If I could have prevented Captain Bryant's injury, I would have. I certainly did not wish for it or try to...'

'Lieutenant, please.' Sir Rodney held up a hand. Courtney closed his mouth like a trap. He had said too much. 'I am aware of all of this. Your report explained every event. Your justifications and defences are not what I need to hear.'

Courtney nodded, twisting his hands behind his back. Once again, he felt nailed down to those crossroads, unable to see to the next path. The decision rested in the hands of people he had no power over.

'Please sit down, Lieutenant. You look ready to collapse.'

Gratefully, Courtney did as asked, perching on the edge of the chair opposite Sir Rodney. The man looked at him, that stern coldness still in his eyes.

'I wished to speak to you personally, Lieutenant Courtney, rather than converse over paper. I saw for myself your actions onboard the *Lysander* and the risks you took for your country and your men.'

'I apologise, sir.'

Sir Rodney answered by picking up a packet and handing it to Courtney. He took it hesitatingly.

'Stop defending yourself, Lieutenant,' Sir Rodney said. 'You are being promoted to commander.'

Courtney nearly dropped the papers in his hand. He reiterated the words in his head, turning them over and over as if there were hidden meanings. Commander. After so long waiting, almost relenting to the idea he would never hear that title, it did not feel real.

'I am being promoted to commander,' he repeated. And finally, it struck true. 'Thank you, sir, I… I do not know what to say, I…'

'Do not become too excited. We have more commanders than we have ships. But following your conduct on the *Lysander*, certainly after the difficult situation of Captain Bryant's injury, it was thought apt. You have been a dedicated officer for many years.'

A dedicated officer, drawn from the lower berths and with no helping hand up the ladder. Pride swelled through Courtney and he had to stop himself from grinning like a lunatic. The practicalities would not dawn on him for a while; he wanted to simply savour this feeling of relief, of elation.

'I will not keep you much longer, Commander. I am aware that the hour is late and you shall want a bed. I believe your sister is being wed in a few days?'

'Yes, sir, she is.' Courtney had briefly mentioned it on the *Lysander*, but had not expected Sir Rodney to remember.

'I wish her well, after what she has been through. And to you, Commander Courtney.'

Once he was outside of Sir Rodney's office, Courtney allowed the encroaching smile to spread across his face. He grasped the official notice in his hand and felt the ecstasy of it flood through him. Almost a decade and a half of serving onboard Britain's ships and he was finally in sight of that hallowed success every officer craved: his name being posted in the Gazette, cementing his rise to captaincy.

As he hurried back through the corridors, thinking only of telling Nightingale, he passed the waiting room where Bryant still sat. Courtney paused at the door, clutching the packet close to his chest as if Bryant would take it away from him. He had thought, coming here and seeing the captain, that he would stifle any chance he had of promotion. But now Bryant looked up at him and gave a polite nod. Courtney entered and determinedly held out his hand. Bryant looked at it for a moment and then grasped it. Courtney felt his shoulders relax as they shook hands like allies.

'I was not always friendly towards you, sir,' Courtney said.

'We are two very different men, Commander,' Bryant agreed.

'You knew of my promotion?'

'I did. Did you expect me not to be honest in my report?' A flicker of a smile crossed Bryant's mouth.

'I am not sure what I expected, sir. Thank you, sir.'

'Having one's head almost split open does throw into illumination the pettiness of grudges. You were not to blame for the tension in the Caribbean or for pursuing the *Cygne*. You acted like an officer, if not a gentleman.'

'I have never claimed to be a gentleman, sir.'

'And for that, I wish you fortune, Commander.'

With the consolation of that meeting sitting in him, Courtney left the Admiralty Office building and hastened down Whitehall. Night had fallen, the moon hanging pale in the sky, and lights blazed from the buildings of the wealthy and the noble. Courtney brushed past crowds awaiting entry into social functions, catching sight of military and naval uniforms amongst the throngs. He received nods from some of the men as he hurried by, but their stoic approval meant nothing compared to the person waiting for him at the inn.

Nightingale almost leapt from the armchair as he burst into the apartment. The newspaper he had been reading fell to the floor. At the look on Courtney's face, he managed to splutter, 'What is it? What has happened?'

Courtney dashed forward, pressing the packet into Nightingale's hands. 'I am a commander,' he gasped, uncaring about the restrained façade he had to wear at the Admiralty. 'They have made me a commander!'

'Oh, Arthur.' Nightingale's eyes raced over the words on the paper, reading them again and again as he smiled. 'I am so glad for you, so proud. You are so deserving of it.'

He pulled Courtney into a tight embrace, squeezing him in his arms. Courtney clutched him, burying his face in Nightingale's hair. Affection and relief flowed through his veins that he had the chance to share this with him, with someone who understood and who accepted every part of him. Drawing back, he cupped Nightingale's cheeks and ran his thumb over his beaming mouth. He pressed a kiss there, long and lingering. Nightingale eased against him.

'May I be the first to call you Captain Courtney,' Nightingale murmured.

The sound of it brightened Courtney even more. He was only called 'captain' out of courtesy, but hearing it on Nightingale's tongue made him flush with joy. 'You may,' he said softly.

'Captain Courtney,' Nightingale repeated.

Nightingale had been there for the forging of that title, the baptisms of fire in the Caribbean and on the *Scylla*. He had known him as a lieutenant, as a man, and now as a commander of sailors and other officers. They shared the journey, one that Courtney prayed would continue for many years. He wrapped his arms again around Nightingale and sank gratefully into the sensation. At last, he felt at peace.

Chapter Thirty-Three: Union

Waiting outside the parish church of Great Yarmouth, Courtney did not think he had ever been more nervous. No battle or Admiralty meeting or captain's conference had tangled him like this. In his full dress uniform, complete with a finely stitched satin-lined cloak that Nightingale had bought, he could barely feel the December chill, but he still fiddled with his tight stock and adjusted his warm gloves. For the past day, Lieutenant Wainwright's seven sisters had fussed over him, having him rehearse his steps and his posture as if he had not spent most of his life on unstable decks. Nightingale had watched, amused at the display in the garden of Wainwright's family cottage.

Now, Courtney could hardly remember a thing. He found himself pacing, looking at the closed church doors and imagining the congregation waiting inside. This, he imagined, would be the closest event to his own wedding. He would not be doing anything other than walking with Jane along the aisle, but the desire for it to be perfect for her made him fret.

He had thought that, with the voyage of the *Lysander*, he would have to miss this prodigious event. Sea journeys had already dictated Jane's marriage. She and Lieutenant Wainwright had met upon the doomed *Ulysses*, suffering the tyranny of Lieutenant Davidson and then, after he had led a mutiny, the American sailor, Ransome. Wainwright had escaped with a number of men in a cutter, emerging scurvy-ridden and beaten on the shores of Antigua. Jane had weathered Ransome and his lackeys until she had been forced to take a gun and murder him to stop his reign. She had briefly led the ring of *Ulysses* survivors, to be brought back to Trinidad where she faced trial for her deeds.

She had been pardoned, but one simple royal acknowledgement did not erase the months of pain she had endured. In Wainwright, she had found someone who understood her torment, who had faced it himself. Their marriage was a symbol of a love that Courtney hoped would ease their mutual grief, a chance to form better memories in each other's presence.

He wanted to be the one to help her into this new life.

'Arthur?'

Courtney turned. Across from him, Jane stood on the path. She was dressed in blue, her gown shining in the cold winter light with the embroidery lovingly stitched by her new family. Flowers framed her long dark curls, bound up stylishly. As children, they had barely been able to afford the clothes on their backs. Now, she could comfortably manage some frivolity – and that levity was echoed on her face. She smiled, her cheeks healthy and red. When she extended her hand, it shook, but with the laughter which bubbled up in her.

Courtney realised she was giggling at his tears. He wiped them, though made no attempt to hide his joy.

'You look beautiful, my girl,' he said, taking her arm. The scent of the freshly picked flowers in her grasp washed over them. She leant her head briefly on his shoulder and for a moment, they stood in the church's entrance, united.

'I am so pleased that you are here,' Jane said.

'As am I.'

'You, a commander and me, a wife again. It does not seem so long ago that I walked down the aisle to Bill.'

It had been almost three years, a match that had begun and ended in the Caribbean. Wainwright had promised Bill Howard that he would care for Jane, and Courtney had no doubt he would have approved of this match. Just as the royal pardon had not cured all of Jane's aches, this wedding did not efface his memory, but carved a place beside it. Such a thing could be said for both of them; they each came from heartache and tragedy, as did their loved ones. Both tried to move beyond it, whilst knowing they could never trample it entirely.

'I am nervous,' Jane admitted as they looked at the church doors. 'This seems to be a much bigger step for me than before.'

'Lieutenant Wainwright shall look after you. And you shall look after him. Not that I truly believe you need looking after.'

Jane smiled. 'I think every one of us does, at some stage.'

'Perhaps.'

'Are we the only members of the Courtney family left now?'

'I believe so.'

Even if they were somehow still alive, Courtney barely considered his mother and father members of his family anymore. Mr and Mrs Woods had done more to raise him and Jane. Only their aunt and uncle still survived, though they did not have the Courtney name.

'Thank you, Arthur,' Jane said.

'For what?'

'For taking us away from where we started. We could so easily have never moved.'

Courtney smiled. For so long, he had thought he had not been able to shed the skin of his youth, the way it still clung to him. He realised now that he could not truly escape it, but he and Jane had travelled a long journey. One that had not ended yet.

'Are you ready to go in?' he asked.

Jane drew a deep breath, blew it out, and nodded. 'I am.'

The doors opened and Courtney waited for Jane to step forward. When she did, he matched her pace and entered into the chapel of guests looking their way. He caught sight of Wainwright's impressively large family, each of them smiling at their new sister and daughter. Men who had survived the *Ulysses* attended, dressed in their best clothes and with no sign of what had happened to them before. Sailors and officers from the old *Scylla* had joined them. Mr Smythe was there, soon to enter his lieutenant's examination, next to Obi, who was to join his next ship in the capacity of surgeon's assistant. Rylance, Dr Archer, even Mr Richmond in his wheeled chair, had joined them. They held their hats to their chests in respect and bowed their heads as Jane passed.

Suddenly, Courtney knew that he did not mind being the final bearer of the Courtney name. He had his family here – Jane, Lieutenant Wainwright and his seven sisters, the alliances he had made on the sea, and of course, Nightingale. On the pew at the front, he sat. His eyes swept from Jane across to Courtney and they shared an affectionate look, one that made Courtney's stomach flutter.

Lieutenant Wainwright beamed as his bride took her place beside him. Courtney released her arm and pressed her hand between his in one last loving squeeze. He did not feel he was giving her to Wainwright; she had proved that she was her own mistress, a woman who had come from poverty to now, just as he had. It was for this that

Courtney had fought and striven all his life: safety, a place amongst friends and family, the security of the future.

As the minister began, addressing the bride and groom and their congregation, Courtney sat down next to Nightingale. He felt the man's gloved hand brush against his for a second. In his best uniform, beside the man he loved and amidst his closest and dearest, he felt that this moment had been worth all the pain.

The December sun shone into the chapel and Courtney allowed himself the time to enjoy its warmth.

Acknowledgements

Thank you to everyone who has been with me on this writing journey. *Leeward*'s release was beyond incredible, and I have been so fortunate with the response, both from editorial reviews and from the readers. It means the world that people are reading my work and connecting with it!

Thank you again to Canelo and their wonderful team, especially Kit, Kate, Thanhmai and Miranda, and thank you to my agent, Francesca Riccardi at Kate Nash Literary Agency. All of them have done so much to support me and my writing, and I would not be on this journey without them.

Writing *The Devil to Pay* was a lot lonelier than *Leeward*, which I initially had posted all online until I was picked up by Canelo. This sequel was the first real time I've written offline with no real idea of what landed and what didn't until sending off the manuscripts. So thank you to all my family and friends who listened to my doubts and my break-throughs. My mum and dad have been so encouraging and supportive, especially, and I know that I can always message my friend, George, with any obscure naval question and get equally excited about maritime history with him.

I want to also thank the amazing people I've met online. Larry has been there from nearly the start of my writing adventure, and Emmarey has been such a champion. I am grateful, as well, to the brilliant Discord communities I'm a part of. The Flirties and the Rainbows have been absolutely fab, and are such a lovely collection of writers and readers. I also have had warm support on X (Twitter) and Instagram. Although social media is quite bewildering at times, I have found some wonderful people through it.

Very warm thanks also go out to the bookshops that have supported *Leeward*. The people at Medina Bookshop on the Isle of Wight, especially Paul Armfield, have been beyond incredible. The Isle of Wight Waterstones are also so amazing at uplifting local authors.

The Times also deserve an especial thanks, especially Antonia Senior who championed *Leeward*. Being chosen as one of *The Times*'s Best Historical Fiction Novels of 2023 is something which will always stay with me.

Multiple sources helped me with this book and its historical research. I particularly found Roy and Lesley Adkins's *Jack Tar and The War for All the Oceans* beneficial, as well as Stephen Taylor's *Sons of the Waves*. For more technical detail, John Harland's *Seamanship in the Age of Sail* was a fantastic resource, as well as *The Oxford Companion to Ships and the Sea*, and the videos of the *Star of India* on YouTube for some great visual indicators of tacking and sailing manoeuvres.